SEDUCED BY THE ENEMY

ABBY GREEN

EMMY GRAYSON

MILLS & BOON

First published in Great Britain 2025
by Mills & Boon, an imprint of HarperCollins*Publishers* Ltd,
1 London Bridge Street, London, SE1 9GF

www.harpercollins.co.uk

HarperCollins*Publishers*, Macken House, 39/40 Mayor Street Upper,
Dublin 1, D01 C9W8, Ireland

ISBN: 978-0-263-34489-9

11/25

MIX
Paper | Supporting
responsible forestry
FSC™ C007454

This book contains FSC™ certified paper
and other controlled sources to ensure responsible forest management.

For more information visit www.harpercollins.co.uk/green.

Printed and Bound in the UK using 100% Renewable Electricity
at CPI Group (UK) Ltd, Croydon, CR0 4YY

BRIDE OF
BETRAYAL

ABBY GREEN

MILLS & BOON

PROLOGUE

Rome

LEONARDO FALZONE STOOD against the car, the folded arms and nonchalance of his stance giving no indication as to the thrumming tension in his tall, powerful body. The other drivers looked sideways at him, as if sensing there wasn't something quite right about this particular chauffeur. Even though he wore a uniform and a hat, the clothes looked somehow...*wrong*.

And they'd be right, because Leo Falzone was no mere chauffeur, even if he had been hired—under a different name—to help ferry the guests away from the funeral of the man who had betrayed him heinously, taking advantage of a friendship that had been forged in the foster-care system.

A friendship Leo had believed to be as solid as a rock, until his friend and business partner had betrayed him not only professionally but also personally.

Except, Leo couldn't exactly blame Aldo Bianchi for the personal betrayal. After all, Leo's lover had chosen to turn her affections to Aldo, no doubt seduced by his promises to make her a rich woman. Rich from the years that Leo had spent sweating and toiling to create Falzone Industries.

You rejected her first. His conscience pricked. Yes, he

had sent her away because she'd been saying nonsense, about loving him. He hadn't asked for her love. He wasn't in the market for that. So he'd told her to leave. And then she'd gone straight into his best friend's bed.

Aldo had been his business partner, but they'd both known that Leo was the brains behind the company. Leo had thought Aldo was happy playing to his skills, utilising his social charm to bring in business and create financial partnerships, but Leo had underestimated just how jealous and bitter his friend had really been.

Aldo's sense of injustice had grown along with his drug addiction, something Leo had failed to notice, much to his regret. Leo had only realised the full extent of the disaster that had unfolded when he'd had time to figure it all out in jail, where he'd spent the last three years. Accused of embezzlement and insider trading, by his closest ally. Set up and arrested before he'd had time to even get his wits together.

Aldo had demonstrated all too well that, in spite of his laissez-faire attitude to working, he had somehow managed to frame Leo so comprehensively that it had taken three years to prove his innocence. And in the meantime, Aldo had been at the helm of Falzone Industries—renamed Bianchi Industries.

Not only that, he'd married Leo's ex-lover, a mere month after they'd split, demonstrating how little Leo had really known her. And her real agenda all along—to feather her nest.

Leo's sentencing and incarceration had coincided with the news that Aldo Bianchi and his stunning wife had just bought a sumptuous holiday home in Sicily.

On his recent release from jail, Leo's desire to seek

revenge on his ex-friend had been thwarted when Aldo Bianchi had been found dead a week ago. He'd died of an overdose, in an alleyway behind one of Rome's most famous nightclubs.

Leo's mouth firmed. Maybe it had been Aldo's guilty conscience that had pushed his drug-taking to dangerous levels, but more likely not. It had been the success of the company, which had thrived in the last three years—purely because of the way Leo had set things up. It couldn't have failed to succeed. No doubt another consideration by his friend when timing Leo's fall from grace.

But now Aldo was dead, depriving Leo of any sense of catharsis or revenge. But there was someone else in this equation. Someone who had arguably betrayed Leo even more heinously. Because she'd been the one who had lain in his bed and whispered lies into his ear. Had she been scheming with Aldo while she was with Leo? He couldn't rule it out. In any case, she'd gone straight to Aldo and destroyed Leo's life's work and reputation by helping to put him in jail for a fraud he'd never committed.

Three years he'd spent in that stinking place, until his legal team had finally managed to prove his innocence.

Now, he wanted to regain full control of his company again, put it back into his name, and all that stood in his way of achieving that goal was the woman who had inherited Aldo's share of the business. His duplicitous grieving widow.

The woman standing alone by the grave was a tall, still figure. Dressed in black, in a dress that on the surface looked demure—lace overlaid silk covered her from neck to wrist to knee, but it clung to her figure showcasing a classic womanly shape. High full breasts, narrow waist flaring out to her hips, and endlessly long legs. Feet encased in high, sharp heels. Thick, dark hair pulled back into a low bun.

A short veil hid her beautiful, treacherous face. A face that had haunted Leo for years. Three years to be precise. Green/golden eyes. Finely etched brows. Straight nose. High cheekbones, a delicate but defined jaw. A wide, lush mouth made for—*Basta!* Leo shut down his rapidly unravelling thoughts.

She did not affect him. Not any more. He had plans to regain control of his business and at the same time rehabilitate his damaged image. And for that, he needed not only the other half of his business, but also a wife.

And not just any wife. A wife who would understand that he had no desire for a *real* wife. A wife who would perform her duties in public but keep her distance in private. A wife who would hand over what he was owed.

After watching his entire family be gunned down by a Mafia thug in front of him as a young boy, Leo had never harboured any desire to risk inflicting such a horror on a child. He didn't want a family. He'd *had* a happy family, parents, brothers, and it had all been wiped out in a few hellish minutes, instilling within him a deep primal fear of ever having that and losing that again. He'd only survived because his mother had shoved him behind a cabinet.

No, all he needed was a temporary wife and there was only one woman in the world who could perfom this duty for him.

His blood roared. The woman standing by the graveside was about to pay for her sins…by becoming Angelica Falzone.

CHAPTER ONE

FREE. AT LAST. Angelica wanted to rip off the net veil that covered her face, and throw it aside, tip her head back and let the rays of the sun blast all the way through her, incinerating the last three years of purgatory, cleansing her of the toxicity she'd had to endure.

Cleansing her of the cynical shell she'd had to build around herself to survive. Not just the sham marriage she'd never wanted, but also the pain of the earlier rejection she'd suffered at the hands of her first lover. And love. Who she'd thought had loved her. When she'd told him she loved him he'd turned arctic and told her to leave. Now she cursed the day they'd ever met.

She'd felt like such a naive fool. She'd fallen for the first man she'd slept with. She'd been mortified. She'd grown up on the edges of the systemic Mafia violence and crime in Sicily and she'd considered herself tough and street smart, yet out in the big world, she'd realised that she was as vulnerable as the next woman.

She'd been twenty-one and now she was twenty-four but sometimes she felt much, much older.

But three years ago, her lover had shown her that she'd still retained innocence and hope, even after seeing so much and losing her father to a violent murder by the criminal gangs who'd embroiled him reluctantly in their criminal activities.

That had made her lover's rejection even worse, the fact that he'd not only taken her innocence, literally, but also destroyed her nascent hope for a life not blighted by violence. A life that could contain the ordinary, yet extraordinary pleasures of normality like having a family and not living in fear for their lives.

In a way she was glad she'd learnt that lesson, harsh as it had been, because she could move on with her life, and know what to expect. And being free was enough for now. She didn't need anything more.

She only had to walk away from this grave and get to the car, instruct the driver where to take her and then... she could finally rip it all off. The veil hiding her lack of grief. The custom-made Dolce & Gabbana dress. The outward display of wealth that had hidden so much.

'Signora Bianchi, your car is over here.'

She nodded at one of the funeral directors and said *grazie*, turning from the grave to follow him. She felt like telling him not to call her *Bianchi*, she was free of that hated name now. But she held her tongue. He led her over to where a driver was standing by a car. He opened the back door.

Angelica lifted her face slightly from where she'd been looking at the ground, as much to watch her step in the vertiginous heels as to avoid eye contact with anyone.

The driver was tall, tall enough to send a tiny frisson of *something* down her spine. She lifted her head a little more but the sun was in her face and she couldn't make out much more than his height and broad shoulders. His cap was pulled low.

She told herself she was being ridiculous. For the first year of her marriage she'd thought she'd seen her ex-lover everywhere but of course she hadn't because he was in jail. Incarcerated because of his business partner Aldo's greed and jealousy. As much as she'd known he hadn't deserved it, she'd been in a jail of her own, albeit a gilded one, so they'd both been punished for their ill-fated association with each other, and Aldo. Did that make them even? She wasn't sure. But what she was sure of was that she never wanted to see him again, and she was pretty certain he wouldn't want to see her either. Not after that brutal break-up and everything that had ensued.

Leonardo Falzone undoubtedly wouldn't understand why on earth she would have gone from him to his best friend. He'd see it as a betrayal even if he had been the one to dump her. Aldo hadn't missed the opportunity to stick the knife in even deeper. It hadn't been enough to steal his friend's business and get him locked up on false charges, he'd had to steal his lover. But even when Angelica had tried to tell Aldo that it would mean nothing because Leonardo hadn't felt anything for her, Aldo hadn't listened.

She knew that Leonardo had been released from prison because the press had been full of it, but there had been no sign of him coming to collect his dues. Angelica was sure that it was the news of his nemesis's release that had pushed Aldo over the edge, making him even more volatile than usual. Hence his overdose. A sad, pitiful end to a sad, pitiful human being.

Time to move on, finally. She stopped just before stepping into the car and lifted her face slightly and said, 'Straight to the airport, please.'

She was aware of the driver dipping his head to indicate he'd heard her and then she was in the back of the car, in the dark cool interior. The privacy division between her and the driver was up, so she couldn't see him walk around the car. She breathed a sigh of relief and finally yanked off the veil. She wasn't even taking a suitcase with her. All she needed was her passport. She was leaving everything behind.

She pulled the pins out of her hair and loosened it, wincing a little with relief. She also kicked off the shoes, stretching out her pinched toes.

She put her head back against the seat and felt tension slowly draining out of her body as the car moved away from the graveyard in central Rome and out into the city.

She was exhausted. She wanted to sleep for a month. At least. And then—she lifted her head when she saw a sign indicating a turn for the airport. A turn the driver didn't take.

Another turn-off for the airport approached and again the driver sailed past. Angelica sat up straight. Tension flooded her body and something that had been familiar for three years now, and constant. Fear.

She leaned forward and knocked on the privacy window. No response. She knocked again. No response. The fear churned and turned to panic. She tried the door of the car. Locked. It wasn't as if she could hurl herself from a car that was speeding into the outskirts of Rome. She hadn't survived the last three years to fall at the final hurdle.

And then anger started to rise, eclipsing the panic, and she welcomed it. She *knew* she was safe from harm now. Aldo was gone and anyone in league with him had scuttled back under whatever rock they'd come from, and good riddance. If she'd had any doubt otherwise she would have been much more circumspect today.

So there was no one who could possibly want to harm her—her blood ran cold. The driver. Tall, broad shoulders. Angelica shook her head as if that might clear it of the ridiculous notion that perhaps it could be— At that precise moment the privacy division slid down a few inches.

The driver had taken off the cap and Angelica could see the top half of his face. It took a second for her mind to compute what she was seeing. A broad forehead. Thick dark hair. Messy. But it was those eyes, under dark slashing brows. *His eyes.* Indelibly burnt onto her brain, and into her memory.

Dark. Dark as the night. It was only when you got really close that it was possible to make out lighter hints of gold. And she'd been as close as one could get. She'd drowned in those golden lights.

She breathed out his name as if she had to say it out loud to be sure. 'Leonardo Falzone.'

Those eyes flicked to the road and then back. 'Ciao, *Angel.*'

Angelica went cold. If she'd been in any doubt that this man was who she thought he was, it was removed. *Angel.* He was the only one who used to call her that.

'Don't call me that.'

His eyes were on the road now. Hard, obsidian. 'You used to like it.'

A memory flash of two bodies, sweat-slicked, joined as one, straining to reach the pinnacle, hearts pounding, ecstasy just out of reach, and him, this man, reaching his hand down between their bodies to touch her, saying, *'Come for me, Angel, I need you to—'*

Angelica snapped, 'I used to like a lot of things. What are you doing here? Where are we going?'

Her heart was pounding now. Not out of fear. Even in this situation, Angelica wasn't scared. She knew that no matter what had happened between them, this man wouldn't hurt her. Physically. It suddenly struck her that she'd just spent three years with a man where the threat of violence hung in the air like a noxious perfume, but who could never have really harmed her because he never had access to that deepest most secret part of her.

The ways he'd had to harm her had been external. Through the people she loved.

But this man who was now driving her to some unknown location, he'd had the power to decimate her. And he already had. But she'd survived. He no longer had that power and never would again.

He asked mockingly, 'You're not going to congratulate me on my exoneration of a crime I didn't commit? On my freedom?'

A guilt that wasn't hers made her insides cramp a little. 'I know you didn't deserve what Aldo did to you.'

His eyes met hers through the mirror and she shivered. No gold in those eyes today. Just endless dark depths. 'And yet you did nothing to stop it, or defend me. You were in on it with him, obviously.'

He did believe she'd betrayed him, as she'd feared.

No, she hadn't done anything, because she couldn't. She'd had nothing to do with it but Aldo had made sure she was implicated by forcing her into a relationship. Not that this man would listen to her. Not that she could tell him. She still had too much at stake. Too much to protect. If there had ever been a time when she would have confided in this man, it had long gone.

She asked, 'Where are you taking me?'

He just said enigmatically, 'You'll soon see,' and the privacy window slid back up. Angelica sat back, folding her arms tight across her chest. She was reeling. She hadn't expected this. She'd never expected to see Leonardo Falzone again. *Really?* asked a small voice. *Didn't you dream of him? Dream of him telling you, 'I love you too' after you'd blurted out how you felt?*

Angelica's lips pressed together, as if that could help block out the memory of the horror-struck look on his face when she'd told him she loved him three years ago. She'd been so wrong. She'd read emotion into his desire for her but it had just been physical. And, to give him his due, he'd never promised anything other than that. There'd been no talk of a future, or feelings. Just a mutual fascination, bonding over a shared background, both growing up in different parts of Sicily. Both blighted by the violence endemic in that society. Both of their lives ripped asunder because of it. And then there had been the mutual combustible chemistry. Like nothing she'd ever experienced. *Or ever would again,* whispered a voice. She ignored it. It still mortified her to think she'd fallen for her first lover. More fool her.

Leonardo had lost his entire family right in front of his eyes. A horror he'd told her about one night in bed, in a suspiciously dispassionate voice. She'd told him about losing her father, who'd been on the periphery of the Mafia violence but not peripheral enough. She'd told him about being scouted by a modelling agency and how that had helped her to get away from Sicily.

And not just her, her mother and younger brother. Her brother had already been in danger of aggravating the local Mafia gangs by the time she'd had enough money to set them up in a new place, far away from Sicily to protect them from any chance that the same people who'd killed her father might consider them to be too risky to stay alive. Her brother had been angry and disillusioned after the death of his father. Angelica had seen too many young people fall foul of the gangs and her brother had had good reason to antagonise them, which would have only put them in the crosshairs of danger.

It had taken all of Angelica's and her mother's fortitude to make him see that he would have to let it go and move on with his own life.

She'd been advised not to tell anyone about their new whereabouts, to almost treat them as if they were in a witness protection programme, for fear that anyone from their past would try to contact them or expose their location, and so Angelica had remained vigilant, telling no one, not even her lover. Even though she'd wanted to.

And, after growing up in a society where silence about criminal activity was ingrained in your blood, it had been terrifying to think of trusting another with their safety. It had led her to keeping herself to herself, while working, avoiding close friendships or relationships. Leonardo had been the first person to sneak under her guard and he'd done it before she could pull the drawbridge back up.

She'd almost told him about them so many times, but she'd always held back at the last moment. Their affair had been so whirlwind, literally just a few weeks. She was going to tell him on the day that she'd told him she loved him, feeling as if she could trust him with her most precious secret, but he'd rejected her and it had been one consolation at least that she hadn't spilled everything to him.

Not that that had kept her family safe, because Aldo Bianchi, Leonardo's business partner, had somehow found out about her mother and brother and their whereabouts, even though she didn't live with them, and had taken huge care to always protect their new lives.

He'd then used that information to blackmail her into marriage, demonstrating the terrifying reach of the Sicilian gangs. By then her brother had been about to do his final year school exams. They'd been happy, settled. He'd been talking about university courses he wanted to do. He no longer talked about seeking justice or vengeance for their father, but Aldo had threatened all of that, telling Angelica it would only take one phone call for her father's killers to come and finish the job.

Aldo had grown up in a foster home with Leonardo. He too had been a part of that toxic violence, but where Leonardo had cut all ties with anyone from his past, Aldo had assured her that he still had contacts. He'd shown her a video of her brother, going to school. Laughing. Messing. Being a carefree young man. And her mother—shopping. Doing mundane tasks. Also happy.

The terrifying knowledge that he had someone close enough to put her mother and brother under surveillance had meant she had no choice but to comply. This wasn't a situation where she could go to the police. This was a threat that operated on a far more dangerous and insidious level.

Angelica dragged her mind back from things she couldn't change. So what did Leonardo want now? Revenge was the most obvious thing. And now that Aldo was gone, clearly all the blame was to be lain at her feet.

She'd been wrong to believe Leonardo when he'd told her that he had no interest in living under the yoke of the cycle of violence and retribution of their forbears. Clearly, he was no different, seeking his vengeance. And yet… could she really blame him? She couldn't even begin to imagine what he might have been through while in prison.

She pushed aside any hint of remorse or sympathy. It was because of her association with this man that she too had suffered, and her family had been in danger.

She cultivated the rising tide of anger, anything to distract her from the far more disturbing emotions making her chest tight.

Leo had to try and control the tumult in his gut, but Angelica's scent lingered, even now with a privacy window between them. That distinctive scent of gardenia mixed with something much earthier. It had instantly evoked a slew of images in his head—seeing her for the first time at that function in Rome. Reeling at her beauty.

The first kiss. The first touch. The first time he'd seen her naked, and put his hand to her flesh, feeling as if he were tainting her. He'd been her first lover…or had he? That had tortured him in recent years, the idea that she'd feigned her innocence while laughing at him behind his back for his romantic gullibility.

Leo shut out the memories. She *was* tainted now, by her relationship with his ex-business partner, but he had no intention of ever touching her again. He just needed her presence.

Before sitting into the car, when she'd lifted her face briefly and he'd seen the familiar lush outline of her mouth, it had taken all of his strength not to haul her into him and crush it beneath his. Driven by anger, *not* desire, he told himself now. But his hands clasped the steering wheel tightly betraying that inner turmoil.

He shouldn't have come here. He'd had no choice. She'd haunted him for three years of torturous incarceration.

There was unfinished business between him and Angelica Malgeri. Angelica Bianchi. Soon to be Angelica Falzone. Leo's mouth tipped up into a mirthless smile as he saw the steeple of the chapel appear in the distance. After all, wasn't this what ran in his blood, in spite of everything, handed down from generations? The need for vengeance?

This woman had proven to him that he was no better than his ancestors, in spite of his attempts to pretend otherwise, and all he could do now was lean into that need and exorcise her from his system for good. He would have no peace until she'd paid her dues.

Angelica was tense as the car slowed and came to a stop outside a small church. Ornate. Old. Forbidding with its time-mottled walls and crumbling religious statues. She could see a small cluster of men in suits near the entrance. Her heart beat loudly. What was going on?

Leonardo got out of the car and came around to open her door. Sunlight blazed into the dark, making her squint. Now that she knew who he was, she couldn't *un*see that formidable build. Tall and powerful. Every muscle taut and honed. And yet even now she could sense something that hadn't been there before. An edge. As if he'd cultivated another layer of steel since she'd seen him last.

Well, so had she. She pushed down the tumult inside her and determined not to let him see how much he'd surprised her. He put out a hand to help her out but she ignored it, taking her time to put back on her shoes before stepping out with as much grace as she could muster.

She regretted undoing her hair and taking off the veil now. Clearly she'd celebrated her freedom too soon. But when she stood up straight she was much closer to Leonardo than she'd anticipated, because he hadn't moved back.

They were practically touching. Even in the heels, her head only came to his shoulder. His scent wrapped around her, mocking her for not noticing it before. Musky and woodsy. Sandalwood. His scent had always made her feel safe and that reminder made her jerk back so suddenly that she would have fallen if he hadn't reached out to take her upper arm in his hand.

His touch was like a bomb detonating inside her, blasting apart the ice that she'd cultivated over three years. The ice was melting and becoming molten faster than she could stop it. She looked up, stunned and dismayed that he could still have this effect on her.

His eyes were golden now, blazing down into hers. Nostrils flaring. Jaw taut. He was the one to let her go and she took a jerky step back, thankfully not falling down.

'What's going on, Leonardo?'

He closed the door of the car and leaned back against

it, folding his arms across his chest as if they had all the time in the world. 'No chit-chat? I think after three years where you've lived handsomely off the proceeds of my work you owe me a civil conversation.'

Angelica felt the sun on her head, beating down. Merciless. Like this man. He had definitely changed. Gone was the kindness she'd seen in his eyes and face when they'd first met. It was one of the first things that had attracted her to him—the fact that he didn't appear to have the same air of jaded, brittle ennui as everyone else around them. He'd still had an almost childlike enthusiasm.

Not any more. He was as hardened as everyone else. And no wonder. He'd been in jail. She swallowed. 'What do you want?'

He tipped his head on one side as if considering. 'Well, for a start, it would have been satisfying to look Aldo in the eye and make him tell me why he set me up.'

She'd known why. Aldo's jealousy for Leonardo's success had turned into something toxic and bitter.

Leonardo went on, 'But he denied me that by dying.'

'You've been fully exonerated,' she pointed out, as if that could make up for what had happened.

'The least that I'm due. I've lost three years of my life.'

So have I, Angelica responded silently.

'You've been busy.'

Angelica blinked. Her work was the only thing that Aldo hadn't sought to control because he'd liked the kudos of being married to one of the world's top models too much. It had probably saved her life.

'Yes, I have.' This year alone she'd traversed the globe more times than she could count. And she was weary. Weary of the travelling and the work. She'd used it as a shield for the last three years but the truth was that she wanted out. And she wanted so much more. To spend time with her family. To see them with her own eyes. Touch them. Talk to them. Aldo hadn't allowed her to visit them, threatening them if she did.

She hadn't seen them now for four years. Her brother had almost finished his university course. Angelica was so proud of him. And in a few hours she would finally have her longed-for reunion.

She lifted her wrist and looked at her watch, panic solidifying in the pit of her belly. She looked at Leonardo. 'I have to be at the airport now or I'll miss my flight.'

He arched a brow. 'Going somewhere nice?'

'It's none of your business.'

'I think it is actually.'

Angelica's heart palpitated. 'Why is that?'

He straightened up from the car and unfolded his arms. 'Because you've got something far more important to attend to.'

Tension spiralled inside her, making her voice sharp, and she spoke without thinking using the shortened version of his name. 'Stop these riddles, Leo, and tell me what's going on.'

His eyes flashed. Angelica cursed her lapse of judgment. *Leo* had been a term of endearment.

But now he was speaking. 'I'll tell you what's going on. There's a local legal official inside that church, vested with the power to marry us. You, Angelica Malgeri, are going to marry me and become my wife until such time as I feel like I've got all the retribution and rehabilitation I need out of our relationship.'

CHAPTER TWO

ANGELICA HAD GONE very still. She looked up at Leo, unblinking, her face pale and set in an expression of… utter disbelief. He might have enjoyed it if the effect of her calling him *Leo* didn't still run through his blood like an electric current. No one else had ever called him that. Not even Aldo.

And then she blinked, long dark luxurious lashes screening those world-famous almond-shaped eyes for a second. Her mouth opened and she said, 'Have you gone quite mad?'

'I've never been more sane.'

'This is the day of my husband's funeral.'

Leo let his mouth quirk up on one side even though he wasn't feeling remotely humorous. 'I can't deny that I do find that quite satisfying.'

'It's not possible.'

There were two spots of colour high in her cheeks now.

'Oh, trust me, it's possible. Once you have the right connections and the funds with which to pay. As you were on your way to the airport you have your passport. That's all the documentation you need. And your hand, to sign the registrar's form.'

Leo knew on a rational level that what he was doing

was unorthodox. And ill-advised even. But he was acting on an instinct too strong to ignore. Bring this woman to justice. *His* justice. Make her pay for what she had done. He'd been tortured by nightmares for three years where this woman and a faceless man stood on the other side of the bars and taunted him, before kissing and starting to make love. He always woke up, his body rigid with rejection, pumping with adrenalin, nausea in his gut and a renewed vow that she would pay.

Yet now, she stood before him and he was enacting his revenge and she looked somehow less robust than she had in his nightmares. There was a fragility to her that he didn't remember from before. Dark shadows under her eyes. She looked…somehow older, even though she was still luminously beautiful. As if she carried another layer of…something he couldn't quite define.

Maybe they'd both been shaped by the previous three years except she'd had her freedom and he hadn't.

Angelica took a step back. 'This is crazy. OK, you've had your fun, Leo, I need to get to the airport so can we please leave?' She turned as if to open the car door again but Leo reached out and wrapped his hand around her arm. It felt slim and fragile under his hand, reinforcing a sense of vulnerability. She turned back to face him and he took his arm away and pushed down any such notions.

This woman had gone from his bed to his business partner's and had watched him be hauled off to jail for a crime he didn't commit. She was about as vulnerable as a rhinoceros.

He shook his head, 'You're not going anywhere until you've paid your dues.'

* * *

The touch of Leo's hand to her arm lingered, like a brand. She wondered if she was hallucinating. The fact that she was free must have gone to her head and she'd fallen asleep in the back of the car and she would wake up at the airport at any moment...

But no, the sun was still beating down and Leo Falzone was looking at her. Feeling a level of emotion that surprised her, she said, 'I wish we'd never met.'

Leo made a *tsk*'ing sound. 'And lose all those happy memories? We had some good moments, Angel. Unless, of course, you were playacting the whole time, setting the ground for your lover, Aldo.'

Angelica's emotion turned to nausea. 'It wasn't like that.' And much as she hated to admit it now, because everything felt tainted, she and Leo had had good times. The best. Enough to make her believe he was falling in love with her. The anger spiked again and she welcomed it. 'Why on earth would I marry you?'

'You told me you loved me once.'

Angelica's face got hot but before she could respond to that Leo was adding, 'Tell me, were you in league with Aldo for long before we broke up? Or was it the fact that you knew you weren't going to get a commitment from me that drove you into his arms?'

Angelica shuddered inwardly at that image. She'd never been in that man's arms. One saving grace of the last three years.

'I was not in league with anyone.'

'Yet you were married within a month of our break-up.'

Angelica lifted her chin. 'A break-up *you* insisted upon.'

Leo's voice was mocking, 'Are you trying to tell me now that you meant it when you said you loved me?'

Angelica's insides twisted. She had. Not that she'd ever admit that now. 'Don't be ridiculous.'

'So why say it, then? We could have continued as we were, but obviously you were gambling for more.'

She'd said it because it had burst out of her like an unstoppable force. And she'd learnt her lesson. Her heart was cold and hard now. It wouldn't melt again until she saw her family.

'Leo, we have nothing to say to each other, it's all over. Aldo is gone, you're out of jail.'

'And you're still here. Do you really think it'll be so easy to walk away and not face the consequences?'

Angelica went cold inside. 'I've done nothing.'

'Except warm the bed of the man who put me in jail, not to mention colluding with him.'

She got colder. 'There was no collusion.'

'You were married. You inherited his share of *my* company.'

Something eased inside her. Now she knew what the stakes were.

'You can have it. I have no interest in owning any part of your company.'

But he dashed her hope that she could see an end in sight when he said, 'It's not that simple. It would be a long and legally laborious process to transfer your inheritance of his estate to me, but if we were married…it would be a lot simpler.'

'I've had my fill of marriage, I've no intention of getting married again.'

'Sorry to hear that. It wasn't the idyll it appeared to be?'

He didn't sound sorry at all. Angelica clamped her lips together. She'd fallen so hard and so fast for this man that it had taken her totally unawares and she'd almost lost herself entirely, but not before he'd shown her how he really felt. She could never trust him again. They'd spent a heady few weeks together, indulging mostly in the insane chemistry that had sparked between them, she needed to remind herself of that, and that there hadn't been much time for getting to really know one another. It had all been surface level—which she'd subsequently found out was all he had wanted.

'Come to think of it,' he ruminated now, 'you did seem to spend a lot of time apart, so maybe all really wasn't well. Did Aldo's sheen wear off once you realised what a snake he really was?'

Angelica hid behind attack to disguise any hint of just how flimsy the marriage had been. She raised a brow. 'Reading the gossip columns in jail, were you?'

Now his face flushed but Angelica was too agitated to enjoy it. Her flight would have gone by now. She had to contact her family.

'Look—'

'No, you look.' He cut her off. 'We are not leaving this place until we are man and wife. I want my rightful share of the company back and I need a wife to rehabilitate my image.'

Angelica had heard that steely tone before. She'd heard him speak to adversaries in that tone when they'd been together. And he'd used that tone the day he'd told her to leave, because the relationship was over. Because he had no intention of embarking on a long-term commitment. He hadn't elaborated on that, but Angelica had surmised at the time that the trauma of watching his family be slaughtered had marked him for life. Not that that knowledge had helped her broken heart. It had only made it ache for him and that reminder was like a thorn now.

Worse had been the prospect that it wasn't even trauma holding him back from loving her, but that it was because he just hadn't been that into her.

This man didn't deserve her sympathy. 'You told me the day you kicked me out that you weren't into long-term commitment. What's changed?'

His mouth thinned. 'Unsurprisingly spending time in a prison affords one time to think. But nothing has changed in that regard. This will not be a long-term thing. It'll be marriage in name only—to take back what's mine and to show people that I am settling down, to promote an image of stability and respectability. I can see the merit in that. The business thrived under the image of Aldo's supposed respectability.'

Angelica felt like snorting. Her husband had been any-thing but respectable. It occurred to her that perhaps this was all a bluster to demonstrate that Leo was serious about getting his due—and Angelica had meant what she'd said, she had no desire to keep Aldo's half of the business. She'd happily sign it over to Leo.

He didn't want to marry her. He couldn't wait to see the back of her three years ago. Maybe if she called his bluff he'd realise how ridiculous this all was. And she couldn't deny the appeal to shake him up a bit—after all, he'd hurt her badly in the past. But that was gone. He didn't affect her any more.

Angelica angled her face up. 'You're right, you know. You didn't deserve what Aldo did and you do deserve to have your life and business back. I have no desire to stand in your way. If that means getting married, then let's do it.'

He tensed visibly and inwardly Angelica breathed a sigh of relief. He had been bluffing. But then his demeanor changed and he took her arm and led her over to where the men were standing outside the church building.

'Let's get going.'

Angelica's blood went cold. She resisted Leo's attempt to urge her into the dark interior of the chapel. 'No, wait.'

The other men had gone in ahead of them. Leo looked down at her. For a second, Angelica felt dizzy. Was she really standing here with Aldo just buried, still in her funeral clothes, and with Leo expecting her to walk down an aisle? In spite of how he'd rejected her before, she couldn't deny that she'd still had dreams... She shook her head to dislodge the humiliating reminder of the pull he'd had over her.

'Wait...'

He arched a dark brow. 'You thought I didn't mean it? Don't you remember that I don't bluff?'

A memory flashed back of this man taking off his shoes and socks by the Trevi fountain in central Rome, with Angelica looking on in horror saying, 'You wouldn't dare...' only to watch as he'd calmly rolled up his trousers to his knees and climbed over the fence around the fountain and stepped down into the blue/green water, beneath which shimmered all the coins thrown in by tourists making their wishes.

A cheer had gone up and he'd smiled at her and turned around, arms in the air, a moment that had gone viral. She couldn't even remember what they'd been talking about but clearly he'd called her bluff. He'd had to pay a fine for that act but the authorities had let him off any other charges, as charmed by him as she had been…

So, no, he didn't bluff. He obviously meant to go through with this outrageous act. And suddenly Angelica was somewhere between past and present, her body humming to be close to this man again, humming in a way that told her she hadn't got over him at all. *Physically,* she told herself desperately. Emotionally, he could never hurt her again.

She pulled her arm free of his loose grip. 'Are you kidnapping me all the way to the altar, Leo?'

He took a step back. 'You're free to go. But I can assure you that marrying me will be so much easier and efficient in the long term.'

'Because if I don't you'll drag me through the courts to get what's yours?'

'Something like that. Even if you were to sign over Aldo's shares to me, it wouldn't be that simple. It's your inheritance from him and it's bound up by all those legalities. Probate et cetera. But through marrying me, it will become my property too.'

She frowned. 'Won't probate still take time?'

He said, 'Yes, but marriage to you will expedite the process, helped by the fact that I've been proved innocent and have a right back to my company. It was your choice to marry Aldo, and to collude with him and to let me rot in jail. Now you face the consequences.'

Angelica's brain was racing. Leo had a point but he didn't know the truth of it. She'd had no choice. She couldn't tell Leo about the blackmail without revealing the truth about her family, and she couldn't trust what he would do with that information. He'd probably use it as Aldo had, to make her comply. She couldn't go through that again. They were safe now and she wasn't going to jeopardise their safety.

He'd also just assured her that if she walked away, he'd come after her and he'd end up finding out about them anyway.

'How long?' she blurted out.

'How long what?'

'How long would you want to be married?' She wasn't going to even contemplate this without a get-out date.

'Six months minimum.'

'One month.'

He shook his head. 'Not long enough.'

'Two months.'

He cocked his head on one side. 'Four months. That's about enough time to work out the legalities and establish myself on the scene.'

'Three months. That's the most I'll agree to.' Three months she could do. There was an end in sight. It wasn't insurmountable. And then she'd be free of this debt owed to Leo and she could *finally* move on with her life.

'OK.'

She blinked. 'OK?'

'Yes. But we get married right now and you're mine for the next three months.'

Angelica shivered delicately. He'd said those words, *you're mine*, to her before, sounding desperate. It was why she'd hoped that when she told him she loved him, he would feel the same. Surely he'd had to have felt it too…the intensity between them.

But he hadn't. And now she was in a bind with the

man who had crushed her heart to pieces. But that was OK because she had no illusions any more. She was as cynical as he was. Probably even more.

'I will marry you, Leo, but I belong to no one, not now, not ever. I also have work commitments that I'm not prepared to renege on. I have a professional reputation to consider.' She wasn't going to tell him about her jadedness with her job, and how she wanted to move on and do something more meaningful with her life.

'As long as you're available when I need you we won't have a problem. If there are conflicting interests we'll discuss it.'

How could he sound so reasonable when he'd just kidnapped her from her husband's funeral and was now about to march her down the aisle? Because he had been reasonable once. Kind, even. Part of what had made her fall in love with him was how he'd treated others and how he'd always had an air of being able to handle anything.

Any veneer of civility was well and truly gone though, and in that moment she said with feeling, 'I truly wish we'd never met.'

His jaw tightened and then he said, 'Too late for regrets.'

'You'll wish you never married me. Do you really think I'll make this easy for you?' She'd locked herself away mentally and emotionally from Aldo and she would utilise those skills again. Three months. She could do it.

He huffed an unamused laugh as he took her arm again. 'Believe me, after what I've been through, marriage to you will be a cakewalk. Time to start paying your dues, *cara*.'

He urged her in through the door into the gloomy interior and when her eyes adjusted to the light, Angelica could see the men waiting for them near the altar. There was a priest, presumably to bless this non-wedding of a wedding. It was a farce, and yet, as Leo walked her down the aisle, it galled her to acknowledge that anger at the fact that her life was being derailed *again* wasn't her uppermost emotion, it was a mixture of far more conflicting things that she'd never expected to be feeling again.

And actually, it was fear she was feeling, fear that she might forget just how badly this man had hurt her, because seeing him again was reviving far too much and she was fast being hurtled into a future she'd never expected before she had time to catch up with herself. Or, worse, protect herself.

The hum of the aeroplane was the only sound. They were on their way to New York where Leo had a life and business to reclaim, with the help of his new wife. Angelica hadn't reacted when she'd been told of their destination.

Why didn't he feel more triumphant? Leo brooded as he sat in a sprawl across the aisle from his new wife. He'd achieved exactly what he'd set out to achieve. A swift and comprehensive lesson delivered to the woman who had betrayed him with her lover/husband, *his* ex-business partner. But instead of triumph all he felt was a certain level of frustration.

She'd barely looked at him during the short and businesslike marriage ceremony. The most emotion she'd shown had been when they'd had to exchange rings and Leo had held up a gold band only for her to lift her hand where Aldo's ring had still sat. She'd said, 'I already have one. It seems a waste to use another one.'

A red tide of emotion had made Leo bite out, 'Take it off.'

She'd just looked at him, face pale and set. Eventually she'd removed it and handed it to him, and he'd slipped the ring he'd bought onto her finger, very aware of the distaste deep inside him in that moment for what he was doing and yet he couldn't *not*.

The urge to cleave her to him even like this was too strong. He told himself he welcomed her hatred and resentment. Her reluctance. The more she hated this whole situation, the more it would salve his bruised soul. But... it *wasn't*.

She was sitting on the cream leather couch opposite him, shoes off, legs pulled up and to the side. Hair down and over her shoulders, in waves of dark brown silk. She was on her phone, intensely absorbed, fingers moving fast as she communicated with someone.

An unsavoury thought occurred to him. 'Do you have a lover?'

She looked up and those unusual green eyes caught him right in the gut, much as they had when he'd first seen her.

'That's none of your business.'

His insides tightened at the thought that she was communicating with someone. 'I won't tolerate infidelity.'

She put her phone down on the seat beside her. Face down, Leo noticed. He had to curb the urge to reach across and pick it up. He'd never been jealous over a woman. *Until this one.*

She sighed. 'No, I don't have a lover.'

Leo didn't believe her. He knew who she was now. A liar and a cheat.

'Do you?' She looked at him.

Leo felt like laughing, but didn't. He shook his head. 'No, I don't.'

A slightly panicked expression crossed her face. 'We aren't sharing a bed.'

Leo's blood spiked as if rejecting that assertion, every cell humming with awareness, his body telling him that as much as he wanted to deny it, he still wanted her. But he said, 'Don't worry, I have no intention of sleeping with Aldo's leftovers. This will be purely an exercise in appearances.'

Everything within Angelica demanded that she defend herself against Leo's low opinion—*leftovers*—but she bit her tongue. He had no right to know the truth of her existence. He'd got her where he wanted her for the next three months and then she would walk away.

She told herself it was a good thing that he no longer wanted her. *You still want him.* Even now her skin felt sensitive and the blood too close to the surface. She couldn't stop her gaze from getting caught on his jaw, his shoulders, his chest and down...that lean waist, those formidable thighs.

She resolutely fixed her gaze on his face, not that that was any better. She'd traced those hard-cut planes with her fingers and mouth too many times to count. 'Good,' she bit out. 'We're on the same page.'

Appearances. She could do appearances. After all, she was a model, it was her job to *appear* and put a mask on. She would just approach this as a three-month gig. Something audacious occurred to her and for the first time since she'd seen Leo again she felt a smidgeon of control. He might have compelled her to be his wife but he couldn't control any other aspect of her. She certainly didn't have to give him an easy ride.

'What is that look?'

Angelica felt a jolt in her gut. She'd forgotten how easily he could read her. And she'd spent the last three years hiding behind a serene mask. She couldn't let it drop now. She thought of something to divert his attention, 'Actually…if you're so concerned with appearances, won't it attract the wrong sort of attention when people realise you've married the widow of your ex-partner, the man who put you in jail?'

He shrugged. 'It's not ideal, no, but in the circumstances I don't think I could have found a more convenient wife. It's common knowledge we were together before. People will just assume you're the fickle one, following whoever has the money. I'm sure something or someone else will come along to divert their attention away from speculation.'

At that moment Angelica vowed to do everything in her power to ensure that people's attention wasn't diverted. And if it helped to hurry up the demise of this marriage, then all the better.

She forced a sweet smile, 'I'm sure you're right.'

Leo finally looked away from her face and down at the tablet in his hand. Angelica sucked in a breath. He still affected her. After three years encasing herself in ice, it was disconcerting to *feel* things again. Even if it was just physical sensations. Not emotional, just physical.

Her phone buzzed silently on the seat beside her and she turned it over to see a message from her mother with a sad crying-face emoji. Her heart felt sore. She'd told them she wouldn't be able to see them just yet, but, for her, knowing that they were safe and getting on with their lives was enough to sustain her. It had to be, because she had nothing else.

As if hearing her thoughts, Leo asked abruptly, 'Why do you have no luggage?'

She looked at him again as she pulled her legs out from under her. They were getting crampy. She saw how his gaze dropped to her thighs before coming back up. The slight flare of colour in his cheeks. Maybe he wasn't as immune to Aldo's *leftovers* as he made out to be. Damn it but that shouldn't be making her feel a spurt of adrenalin. Her heart rate increasing. Blood flowing to parts of her body that had lain dormant since...*him*. She pushed that uncomfortable revelation to one side.

'Because there was nothing I wanted to take with me.' It was true. She'd wanted nothing of what her husband had bought her. He'd had all of her own personal items taken and destroyed.

A swooping sense of panic gripped her as she realised that she had kept one personal item. A necklace that Leo had given her when they'd been together. Not an expensive item...but sentimental.

She could feel it almost burning against the skin of her upper chest now like a brand. She sent up silent thanks she was wearing a high-neck dress so he couldn't see it. She'd put it on, almost without thinking, as soon as she'd heard the news that Aldo was dead.

Not that Leo would remember the moment when they'd been walking hand in hand along a small Venetian street and they'd passed by a tourist shop full of Murano glass trinkets. One had caught her eye, a heart-shaped piece of glass on a gold chain. Green and gold and orange. Like a beating heart.

Leo had stopped and seen where her gaze had fallen and as soon as she'd realised she'd blushed and tried to pull away but before she'd known what was happening, he'd been urging her into the shop and had asked the proprietor to take the necklace out of the window before paying for it.

Angelica had objected but secretly she'd been touched. Her father had never exhibited such thoughtful gestures to her mother. Leo had tied the necklace around her neck and it had been the following day that Angelica had told him she loved him, high in a beautiful frescoed room in his apartment in a palazzo on the Grand Canal.

She'd never considered herself a sentimental person, given to romantic whims, and yet she'd fallen hard for this man and she'd taken out her heart and presented him with it.

Only for him to crush it.

And then when Aldo had put her in an impossible situation, he'd only hammered home the realisation that she'd been beyond weak and naive. Never again.

Leo cut through the unwelcome memories, 'When we get to New York, I'll arrange for someone to meet with you and you can give them a list of whatever you need. I'll also arrange for a stylist to come and discuss what you'll need for social events.'

'I have my own money and I know how to dress myself,' Angelica pointed out.

'While you're married to me you won't spend your own money.'

Another reminder, as if Angelica needed it, that Leo

had always been incredibly generous. The opposite to Aldo, who'd been mean and tight. The only reason he hadn't got his hands on her earnings was because she'd questioned why he would need them, wasn't he rich enough? His colossal pride had stopped him from pursuing her money ever again. So at least she'd had that—her financial independence.

It chafed to have a man pay for her but Angelica told herself now that Leo owed her as much as she owed him—if she'd never met him she wouldn't have been humiliated and she wouldn't have met his business partner—so she just shrugged minutely and said carelessly, 'Whatever.'

She picked up a magazine from a pile on the coffee table near the seat and idly flicked through it, no more interested in the glossy photos than the fact that it was *her* face staring out at her in many of the pictures.

She willed the plane to get to New York as soon as possible because the sooner they got on with this charade, the sooner it would be over and she could finally reunite with her family.

CHAPTER THREE

'I NEVER ASKED you where you were planning on going after the funeral.'

Angelica didn't turn around from the window where she was looking out at the view, which spanned from where they were in midtown Manhattan, all the way down to the One World Trade Center.

The Hudson River sparkled under the low autumnal sun. Flashes of gold and brown were visible here and there.

She didn't respond to Leo's remark, saying, 'I assumed you'd be going to the apartment on the Upper East Side.' It was where she'd spent a lot of time over the last three years and if Aldo said he was coming to New York she'd invariably find a reason to leave before he arrived.

'I believe Aldo had it redecorated.'

Angelica shuddered delicately. He had, and it hadn't been good. 'You could say that.'

Leo's tone was dry. 'I can imagine exactly how he did it. Lots of gold and bling. It'll be up for sale as soon as I can get it back into my name and on the market.'

Angelica glanced at him where he'd come to stand beside her at the window. This apartment was in a futuristically designed building, gleaming and soaring into the sky. She found she liked it better than the slightly stuffy atmosphere around Central Park. Even though she loved that park.

Curious, she asked, 'How can you afford this now...? Isn't everything still tied up in the company in Aldo's name?'

He looked at her. 'Your name.'

A reminder of her worth to him now. 'Believe me, the sooner I can disentangle myself from what you rightfully own, the better.'

'I'll believe that when you have a piece of paper in front of you with your signature on it. You did warn me you wouldn't make this easy.'

Yes, she had, but she hadn't meant it like that. Angelica turned towards him, feeling injured, 'You know I was never interested in anything like that.'

He raised a brow. 'Do I? After you ran straight from me into Aldo's bed?'

Angelica stifled her response. How could she deny how it looked? It killed her that she couldn't just blurt out the truth but she daredn't. There was too much at stake. Her mother and brother. Awful things had happened to family members of people who'd ever had the misfortune of getting entangled with the Mafia in Sicily. They were safe now but that could all change if Leo chose to use them as leverage as Aldo had.

The only reason she'd been relatively safe was because she'd got out early and had become an internationally recognisable face. They didn't need the kind of PR that would come from harming someone like her. But her mother and brother were still at some level of risk. As Aldo had proven only too effectively.

Leo continued, 'My personal wealth and assets were

frozen while I was in prison, which inadvertently helped me because all Aldo had access to was the business finances and any assets in the company name. Something to be grateful for. Needless to say I won't be going into business with anyone else, ever again.'

'Not everyone is Aldo,' Angelica pointed out.

'I don't care, I won't take that risk.'

'You knew him since you were kids, how did you not see that he was harbouring such resentment against you?'

Leo had told her of how, when he'd gone to the mainland to an orphanage run by a charity that specifically helped to remove children from the tentacles of Mafia gangs, he'd bonded with Aldo, who'd also come there in similar circumstances.

Leo looked away, out of the window. 'It was the biggest mistake of my life, trusting that man.'

'You loved him. He was like a brother.'

Leo looked at her again and she could see the bleakness in his expression. 'My brothers were killed in front of me. Aldo was a leech who played the long game.'

Again Angelica had to curb her tongue. She'd heard Aldo drunkenly rant over and over again about how he and Leo had been equal until it had become clear that Leo was on a level that Aldo could never hope to achieve. Jealousy and bitterness had eaten away at him until he'd masterminded Leo's downfall, which had ultimately led to Aldo's downfall too.

'You haven't answered me—where were you going after the funeral?'

Angelica said as carelessly as she could, 'Spain.'

'Why Spain?'

To reunite with her family. She shrugged one shoulder. 'I'd booked a holiday for myself.'

He made a whistling sound. 'Straight after your husband's funeral? With no luggage? I don't think so.'

Angelica looked at Leo and his eyes were dark, bottomless. He said, 'Whoever your lover is, you cut off all contact now, understand? He'll have you back soon enough, if he wants to wait around.'

She shouldn't be surprised that he didn't believe that she was telling the truth on the plane. The thought of a lover was laughable. It had taken all of her energy to deal with a petulant, immature, vengeful husband and try to keep her professional life afloat.

'Believe what you want, Leo, I'm not going to waste my breath again.'

She was suddenly overcome with a wave of weariness. It had been a tumultuous day and she still wasn't entirely sure if she was dreaming. 'If you don't mind, I'd like to get out of these clothes and wash and rest. It's been a long day.'

Leo felt a trickle of discomfort when he had to acknowledge the air of fragility around Angelica that he'd noticed earlier, compounded now by shadows under her eyes.

He still couldn't quite believe she was here, in front of him, wearing his ring. *And still wearing the clothes she'd buried her husband in.* Suddenly he wanted any association with Aldo Bianchi gone.

'Fine, absolutely, make yourself at home.'

A glint of something like humour came into her eye. 'Why, thank you, so considerate.'

It mocked Leo for letting his guard drop for a moment.

This woman wasn't fragile, she was just human. Aldo had died of an overdose, Leo had to assume that Angelica had partaken of that lifestyle too, even though when he'd known her, she'd been vehemently against drugs, and hadn't even drunk that much.

She was turning away from him to leave the room but he caught her arm in his hand, relishing the feel of her toned muscles. She looked up at him and he could see how she held herself tightly. Tense. Which automatically made him want to move that hand from her arm to her waist, and put his other hand there and pull her into him until he could feel those womanly curves pressed against his body.

Angry with his wayward libido, he said more harshly than he intended, 'If you've changed your habits to include taking recreational drugs like your husband, I won't tolerate it.'

A flash of disgust came over her face before it was gone. She pulled her arm free and said with a mocking smile, 'What a shame. If I'd known a coke habit would turn you off the marriage, I would have mentioned it a lot sooner.'

But then her smile faded and she was deadly serious. 'I've never done drugs and I still don't do drugs.'

She turned and walked out of the room, back straight, legs long. Hair like silk down her back. Regal, stunning.

Leo turned to face the view, tugging at his tie, staring out unseeingly. Once again he questioned his sanity but then he told himself again that he never would have found a woman willing to be his convenient wife with no strings attached. And Angelica owed him. Even she acknowledged that.

But the reality of following through on his plans, the

reality of looking at her, smelling her scent, talking to her—convenience was the last thing on his mind. It was a tangle of emotions and desires and the anger that had kept him going for the last three years. He smiled mirthlessly. Yes, his anger at, and hatred for, Angelica Malgeri had actually helped him survive the last three years, because he'd pictured this very scenario. Having her at his mercy. Aldo too, but Aldo had not afforded him that opportunity.

He cursed his introspection. He had to stop ruminating on the past and get on with rebuilding his future. With his new wife at his side.

Even though Angelica was exhausted, she couldn't rest. She'd found what she assumed to be a guest suite, decorated in muted elegant tones with a luxurious cream carpet. She'd taken off the funeral clothes and had a blissful shower, scrubbing every bit of the last three years from her body. And now she was in a robe with her hair piled up turban-style on her head. She'd come out onto the small terrace outside the bedroom and was taking in the view as dusk stole over the iconic skyline of Manhattan.

In spite of everything that had happened and the fact that within hours of burying her husband she was now married to her ex-lover, she couldn't deny that she felt a measure of peace. The kind of peace that had been elusive for three years. *Since Leo rejected you.*

Even though she knew she couldn't trust Leo, she knew he wouldn't hurt her. Life with Aldo and his moods and mercurial nature had kept her in a constant adrenalised state. At least she'd been able to use her work as an excuse to stay away from him as much as possible and he'd never really objected because his ego had loved having a supermodel for a wife. They were only seen together for public events, and as few of those as Angelica could get away with.

She'd had to fly back at short notice on a private jet from Bangkok to Rome in order to placate him when he'd had a tantrum that she wouldn't be with him for an event. But thankfully those incidents hadn't been too common. Aldo had never mentioned specifically what he'd do if he went after her mother and brother, the threat of any kind of harm to them had been enough. She'd never been able to push things too far.

But at least with Leo, it would just be about getting through the charade of the next three months, less if she could manage it. She was counting on being able to encourage Leo to change his mind about this marriage. After being Aldo's wife, and after fake smiling her way through social engagement after social engagement, doing everything not to stand out, she now knew exactly what to do, to stand out.

The following morning Angelica woke up and it took her a couple of minutes to figure out where she was. On another continent. Married to a different man. Her ex-lover. *Leo.* She sat up in bed. She was still wearing the robe she'd put on after the shower.

She couldn't hear any sounds and, after freshening up, she belted the robe tighter around her—because it was either that or what she'd been wearing yesterday—and went out into the apartment.

All was quiet and then she heard noises from the kitchen area. She went to investigate and found an older man dressed in smart black trousers and a black top. He smiled and introduced himself as Michael. 'I'm Mr Fal-zone's apartment manager. He told me to let you know that he's gone to meetings but he's arranged for the glam squad to come at four to help you get ready.'

Ready for what? Angelica didn't ask. 'I… OK.' Obviously there was an event this evening and Leo expected her to go with him.

'What would you like for brunch?'

She gulped. 'What time is it?'

'Midday.'

She'd slept for hours. 'I'm so sorry, I didn't realise.'

Michael waved a hand, 'Mr Falzone said you weren't to be disturbed. I can prepare something for you now?'

Angelica wanted to get out onto the streets and breathe some fresh air and orientate herself but— 'I'd like to go out actually, but I have a small problem, I didn't bring any luggage with me and I only have what I was wearing while travelling.'

Michael walked out of the kitchen and said, 'Come with me.'

Bemused, Angelica followed him to a room adjacent to her bedroom suite. He opened a door and she looked inside. It was a dressing room, full of clothes. She walked in. They were all in her size. An array of casual clothes and evening-wear. Sports clothes. Underwear. She turned to Michael. 'How long has this been here?'

'Mr Falzone had a stylist deliver the clothes this morning. I have her number if you need to contact her for anything but she'll be back later with the glam squad.'

The fact that this hadn't already been here before her arrival settled something inside Angelica. Leo obviously hadn't taken it for granted that she would comply.

A flash of gold caught her eye and she reached out and touched a dress. It was like a liquid waterfall of silken folds. She recognised the iconic designer label.

'If there's anything else?'

Angelica forced a smile at the man. 'No, thank you, this is very helpful.'

He left and Angelica pulled out some jeans and a long-sleeved top. Fresh underwear. It didn't surprise her that Leo had done this, although the speed with which he'd managed to do it was impressive, but he'd always been generous when they'd been together before.

She found a soft, light leather jacket and grabbed her bag and left the apartment, taking the elevator all the way down to the ground floor and then stepping outside.

The air was cool, but hadn't yet got to that frigidly cold state. It reminded her of a snowbound Christmas she'd spent here. She'd actually been happy to be here alone because Aldo had been in Europe and the adverse weather had meant she couldn't travel. He hadn't been happy of course because there had been several high-profile winter social events to attend, but there hadn't been much he could do about it.

Angelica had called her mother and brother and they'd video called for hours. She hadn't revealed the extent of the threat she, or they, were under, not wanting them to worry. She'd had to let them believe that she was still under advice to avoid physical contact in order to shore up their safety. She'd also used work as an excuse. She'd despised Aldo for that, because it would have been safe enough after a year of no contact to visit them. But he'd ruined that chance.

And, thanks to Leo, she was still being held back from

seeing them, but now at least she knew they were safe. And she might not be free, yet, but she was a lot freer than she had been.

She sucked in a deep breath of Manhattan's finest air and went to find a diner. Clinging onto her independence as much as possible had helped her survive marriage to Aldo, and she was sure it would do the same with Leo.

Except, you don't mind spending time with him, pointed out a small voice. Angelica scowled and slipped a pair of shades on against the late autumn sun. She'd merely lost one gaoler, who had been replaced by another. Leo Falzone meant nothing to her and any notion that he still affected her was just down to shock and memories.

It was early evening and the stylist and glam squad had left the apartment. Angelica hadn't seen Leo all day but he had returned to the apartment and there was a knock on the dressing-room door now. Her silly heart kicked up a notch. 'Yes?'

'We'll be leaving in five minutes.'

Angelica felt like childishly sticking her tongue out at the door but refrained and said, 'OK.' He hadn't checked in with her all day, had merely married her, brought her across the globe, dumped her at his apartment and now expected her to perform like a puppet on a string for his benefit.

Not so different from Aldo after all. She checked her reflection in the mirror. She looked the epitome of classic elegance. Hair up in a smooth chignon. A strapless black sheath of a dress. High heels. Discreet jewellery. Understated make-up.

Aldo would have approved. And she was sure that Leo

would take one look, and also approve. Something about that now chafed. She could walk out of the door now, a picture of acceptable perfection. She *could*. But she wouldn't.

With an efficiency born of changing clothes a million times a day for work, Angelica took off the dress and hung it back up before choosing an entirely different outfit.

Leo paced back and forth in the main living area. He was wearing a classic black tuxedo and he'd never noticed before that it felt constrictive, but it did, around his neck.

He'd found it hard to concentrate today, distracted by Angelica. Even when he wasn't with her. He knew she'd left the apartment and for a couple of hours, until he'd been notified of her return, he hadn't been entirely sure she wouldn't just disappear. As much as an internationally renowned model could disappear.

She'd always been independent. It was something he'd forgotten about her. It was one of the qualities that had attracted him to her. She'd been so much more grounded and self-sufficient than other women he'd met.

But he'd also felt uncomfortable about just leaving her at the apartment, and he'd intended calling to let her know about the event tonight but the meeting with his legal team to get the process under way of putting the business back in his name had been intricate and intense.

But things were under way and soon Leo would have everything back in his name. Never again would he be caught out and now, with his wife by his side, there was no reason why— There was a sound from behind him and he turned around to see Angelica in the doorway.

He frowned. She was wearing jeans that clung like a

second skin to every inch of her long legs and shapely hips, and a plain black T-shirt. High heels. Her hair was up though, in a smooth and elegant chignon. She wore chunky diamond jewellery around her neck and wrist.

He said, 'You're not ready.'

'I am ready. I didn't feel especially like wearing a dress.'

'It's a black-tie event.'

She indicated the T-shirt. 'I'm wearing black.'

Leo assessed the situation in an instant. So this was how she was going to play it. Something kicked to life inside him, a spurt of excitement, even though he wanted to deny it. He walked towards her and saw her eyes widen, a little flush come into her cheeks. He stopped just in front of her. 'You know I don't respond to bluffs, Angel.'

There was a spark in her eyes at *Angel*. She tipped up her chin. *Dio*. She was stunning. And treacherous. He couldn't afford to forget that. And three years with Aldo had clearly encouraged a penchant for games.

She said, 'I'm not bluffing, *Leo*.'

He hid his reaction to *Leo*. 'Ready to go, then?'

He saw the chink of uncertainty and then it was gone. 'Ready.'

He put his hand lightly around her arm, the touch of skin on skin igniting his blood. He gritted his jaw against her effect. She was a siren and he'd chosen to marry her so he would just have to control himself.

They were almost at the door when she stopped in front of the mirror to check herself. He let her arm go. She said, 'Coco Chanel's advice was to always remove one thing before you walked out the door.'

Leo said, 'I can help with that.' From her head, he

plucked the diamanté comb holding her chignon in place. Her hair fell down under its own weight, tumbling around her shoulders in silken waves.

He had to curb the urge to bury his hands in her hair and left the comb on the table. 'There, perfect. Let's go.'

There was some sense of satisfaction in the surprised expression on her face but by the time they stepped outside and into the back of the car, her face was a cool mask again.

In the car, Leo was acutely aware of Angelica's long legs provocatively encased in that soft denim. The T-shirt that did little to hide the swell of her perfect breasts.

But it wasn't just her physical perfection that had first caught his eye, it had been something in her manner. Unguarded. Genuine. At odds with the people around them at the exclusive event in Rome.

They'd bumped into each other when he'd been jostled by someone moving through the crowd. She'd ended up with a glass of champagne down the front of her pristine pale-pink evening gown. Leo had braced himself for an explosion of feminine outrage but she'd looked up at him and smiled and he'd almost collapsed under the impact of her beauty. Thick brown hair, caught up and exposing a long neck, high cheekbones and defined jaw. The greenest eyes he'd ever seen, under black brows. Long lashes. And her mouth, wide and generous.

She'd smiled and held up the empty glass, saying, 'Thank you, I was just looking for a reason to give my excuses to leave.'

Leo had shaken his head, trying to get out something coherent, an apology for knocking her drink, but she'd already been moving backwards, away, and instead of apologising he'd croaked out, 'Who are you?' Even though he'd realised that there *was* something familiar about her.

She'd answered, 'I'm no one. Thanks again.' And she'd turned and left, slipping through the crowd and disappearing so quickly that he'd wondered if he'd just dreamt up that little exchange with the most beautiful woman he'd ever seen.

The next day Leo had seen her face high on a billboard advertising a very luxe brand of jewellery. *I'm no one.* She was 'Angelica', one of the few models whose first name was enough to identify them. He hadn't stopped until he'd contacted her and until she'd agreed to meet him for a date.

In the years since then, he'd wondered if that first *meeting* had been as innocently spontaneous as it had seemed. Had she in fact contrived to bump into him and pique his interest? Only to then run into the arms of his business partner once he'd told her he wouldn't commit?

It was a theory he'd found himself clinging to because it was easier to believe that, and that she'd been playing him from the very first moment they'd met, than to live with the fact that she'd been as innocent as he'd believed her to be. And that he'd let a woman get too close, after years of keeping them at a distance for fear of an emotional connection that could lead to loss and pain.

She'd captivated him and that was a weakness he'd never forgive himself for. But he'd learnt his lesson. Now he was in control. She wouldn't play him again.

A car horn sounded nearby in the traffic jerking Leo back into the present moment.

He felt something in his pocket and he remembered. He took a box out and said, 'Actually, I'm afraid we're going to have to add something again.'

She looked at him and then down at the small velvet box. He opened it and her eyes widened fractionally.

Angelica looked at what was obviously meant to be an engagement ring. And it caught her right in the gut. Because she would have chosen it for herself. It was a square emerald stone, flanked by two smaller sapphires, in a platinum setting.

A vast contrast to the ostentatious and totally over-the-top massive pear-drop diamond that Aldo had made her wear. She'd had to remember to put it on when around him. After he'd died she'd gone straight out and found the nearest homeless shelter and had handed it over as a donation, telling them they could do what they liked with it.

But this was…lovely. Before she could stop him, Leo was taking it out of the box and reaching for her hand, sliding it onto her finger where the wedding band sat.

She looked at him and said almost accusingly, 'It fits.'

He drawled, 'The perks of having a wife who is one of the most well-known models in the world. Your sizes are a matter of public information.'

Angelica pulled her hand away and made a choked sound and looked out of the window. He'd just articulated another reason why she wanted to leave the industry—the fact that she was a public commodity. A public clothes horse. Yet, she felt churlish because the business had been very good to her and it had saved her sanity when married to Aldo. She did appreciate it but she was ready to move on. She wasn't even sure where to exactly, but she knew she hungered for something more meaningful.

The car pulled to a smooth stop outside one of Manhattan's most iconic buildings, wide steps leading up to a massive entrance garlanded with foliage and flaming lanterns. The steps were covered in a red carpet and thronged with people in a glittering array of colours, and with jewellery sparkling at ears, throats, wrists and fingers.

Leo got out of the car and came around to help Angelica out. When she would have pulled her hand back, he held it. She looked up at him. They were at the bottom of the steps and he lifted her hand and pressed a kiss to her palm. It was unexpected and felt shockingly intimate. An arrow of pure lust shot straight to the core of her body.

He was urging her with him, up the steps before she had time to absorb all the sensations of that one relatively chaste touch. She wanted to pull her hand away but the bank of paparazzi on one side had already noticed her and were calling out her name, and Leo's. Acting on autopilot, she stopped and posed for the photographers, Leo by her side.

Voices rang out, *'Angelica, over here, please! Who are you wearing? Are you and Falzone really married?'*

She ignored the questions and forced a smile. They moved up the steps and got closer to the door. By the time they had reached the entrance, Angelica realised she was holding onto Leo's hand for support as much as to put forward a display of unity. Paparazzi had never bothered her too much before but now she felt exposed. Self-conscious. Even more so when they stepped into the magnificent ballroom space and Angelica knew she stood out like a sore thumb in her jeans and T-shirt, even if they were designer label.

She tried not to let the prickle of regret or her conscience bother her. After all, she was trying to encourage

Leo to realise that marrying her had been a mistake. But, as they entered the room and moved through the crowd, her choice of attire seemed to be making waves but for all the wrong reasons. When Leo was accosted by someone, the other man's partner said to Angelica, 'You're making the rest of us look overdressed and fussy.'

Angelica smiled weakly, 'That really wasn't my intention.' She'd just wanted to irritate Leo.

The woman winked at her, 'Believe me, if I thought I could get away with jeans and a T-shirt I'd be joining you. These dress codes are so outdated.'

The couple moved away and Leo bent his head towards Angelica saying with a definite hint of humour in his voice, 'It looks like your stunt isn't going as well as you planned it.'

Angelica smiled sweetly and looked up at Leo, trying not to be distracted by the growth of stubble along his jaw, stubble he hadn't attempted to shave away to look more...presentable. 'Oh, believe me, I could engineer any number of situations to draw adverse attention.' She snagged a glass of champagne from a passing waiter's tray and took a healthy sip, and said, 'I never was good at holding my drink.'

Leo neatly took the glass out of Angelica's hand and placed it on another passing waiter's tray. 'Don't even think about it. Let's have a dance, *darling*. After all, our wedding was so rushed we didn't have time for the festivities.'

Angelica scowled at Leo. 'Hardly my fault.' But he was already tucking her hand into his and bringing her with him through the crowd to where people had started to dance in front of a band playing smooth tunes.

He pulled her close to his body and Angelica tensed against the inevitable way she wanted to cleave to him. She suddenly appreciated that at least while married to Aldo, she hadn't had to battle her own rogue hormones. She'd been quite happy to let him pursue his extra-marital affairs with women. And men.

Leo noted, 'You've lost weight.'

Angelica tensed. The result of living on her nerves for the last few years. 'Not really your business.'

'I'm your husband.'

Angelica snorted softly. 'And as such you care for my welfare?'

Leo tipped up her chin with his finger. She had no choice but to look at him. 'As my wife, of course I care about your welfare.'

Her heart twisted. She'd once thought that he really had cared about her welfare. And he had. In bed. Not out of it. Not long-term. After all, through her association with him, he'd practically handed Aldo the invitation to use her for his nefarious ends. The fact that he'd also tried to ruin Leo wasn't much comfort.

'If I'm too thin for you—'

He pulled her closer and another couple swept past. 'I didn't say that.'

Angelica felt spiky and exposed. Defensive. Leo's chest rumbled against hers when he spoke. 'You don't need me to tell you that you're easily the most beautiful woman here.'

She wanted to duck her head. She knew that she was lucky to have been blessed with a face and body that photographed well, but she knew that there was so much

more to her and at one time, she thought Leo had seen
it too.

'I've been working hard the last few years.'

As they spoke, Angelica was aware that Leo was effortlessly moving them around the floor. She didn't even
have to think, he was so easy to follow.

'Are you saying you didn't want to spend time with
your beloved husband?'

Angelica's skin prickled. He was very close to the bone
there. And she felt tired of keeping up a facade. 'My marriage with Aldo wasn't exactly…all that it seemed.'

Leo tugged her closer again to avoid another couple.
Angelica's breasts were crushed to his chest and her nipples drew into hard points, helplessly reacting to his proximity. She was drowning in his scent.

'Are you saying you made a mistake?'

Angelica felt like laughing out loud but stifled it. 'I'm
just saying that things weren't perfect.'

Leo's tone was dry. 'You're hardly the picture of a
widow in grief so I think that's the most honest thing
you've said since we met again.'

And then, 'Why did you do it? What was Aldo offering you? What did you want?'

Angelica stopped as the song came to an end and
pulled back in Leo's arms. How did she begin to frame
an answer to that without putting her family in danger
again?

She said, 'You lost the right to know anything about
me when you told me to leave, three years ago.' She
pulled free completely and walked off the dance floor.

CHAPTER FOUR

LEO WATCHED ANGELICA weave through the crowd, and noticed how everyone she passed turned to look at her. He could commiserate. She was captivating. He also noticed, now that he was alone, a creeping sense of claustrophobia as people brushed past him, making a faint sense of nausea swirl in his gut.

He'd noticed this since leaving prison, the way he was acutely aware of crowds and quickly felt a need to move, find space. He'd spent three years in cramped conditions, fighting for his own space. It was only natural. But it was only now that he realised that Angelica had successfully distracted him enough to not be aware of it here.

But now he was. He gritted his jaw and focused on her again to drive out the rising sense of panic, plunging after her into the crowd. Mercifully the crowd thinned out and Leo was free again. He saw Angelica at the entrance, her back to him.

He could still feel the fragility in her body, held against him, reinforcing his impression of vulnerability. He shook his head. An erroneous impression.

As was the notion that her marriage to Aldo was a regret. She'd amassed a fortune through her marriage to that man—Leo's fortune—and he didn't expect for one second that she was going to just sign away her rights to it.

But, the following day in a sleek office high above Manhattan, Leo watched Angelica do exactly that. Every piece of paper that was put in front of her with an asterix beside where she had to sign, she signed, without even looking at the rest of the document. She'd refused the offer of having her own legal representation present.

Leo watched her from a corner of the room. She was surrounded by legal assistants, unfazed, her dark hair shining, pulled over one shoulder carelessly, exposing her neck.

She was wearing a loose silk top and jeans. Flat shoes. The luxe/louche uniform of the top model. The papers were full of them today. A front-page splash. Breathless speculation about what it could possibly mean for Angelica to turn up at an event with her new husband...*in jeans*!

Nothing about the fact that she had been widowed and remarried within an indecently short amount of time. Nothing about Leo's bid to reclaim what was his. And, he was recognising now, that wasn't necessarily a bad thing. As much as he needed to rehabilitate his image, he didn't necessarily need the scrutiny on his business affairs, the speculation as to how Aldo could have wreaked so much havoc because, with Leo in jail and disgraced, he'd had full control of everything. That was a weakness Leo would never forgive himself for and he didn't want people speculating that it could happen again. *Which it wouldn't. Ever.* So perhaps it was not such a bad thing that Angelica was drawing attention, even if for her controversial sartorial choices.

One of the assistants looked up at Leo. 'All signed.'

Leo pushed off the window he'd been leaning against and walked over to the table where another assistant was gathering up the documents. His chief legal advisor said, 'The only other documents to sign are the ones in Rome.'

Ah, yes. The most important legal documents; they hadn't been ready to sign before they'd left Italy. The documents that related to the fact that it had been Leo who had set up the business. Aldo had tried to change history while in control, naming himself as the brainchild behind Falzone Industries, and changing its name. They would have to return to Rome for that, as Aldo's legal team was based there.

Perhaps Leo was being complacent in assuming Angelica's amenability here would be the same in Rome. Maybe that was her plan, to lull him into a false sense of security before hitting him with terms and conditions, which he had fully expected.

But now, she put down the pen and stood up, turning to face him. Nothing in her expression to indicate any nefarious plans. But then she'd always been good at projecting innocence.

'If you don't mind, I told a designer friend I'd do a photo shoot for her new collection while I'm in town.'

Leo felt slightly wrong-footed. She wasn't heading out to lunch. Or to go back and lounge in the apartment. Or going shopping. She was going to work.

'Of course. We have an event to attend this evening, leaving the apartment at six p.m.'

'I'll be back by then.'

'The driver will take you wherever you need to go and wait for you.'

'It's OK, they've arranged transport for me. It's waiting outside.'

Leo was reminded that she'd always valued her independence. Clearly Aldo hadn't changed that. Something about that heartened him even in the midst of her throwing up contradictions he didn't like to consider.

'See you back at the apartment.'

She nodded and left the office, appearing totally unconcerned that she'd just signed away her right to a majority share in Leo's business. But the real test would be in Rome when she signed the paperwork there because up until that point she could still cause major problems for Leo. So he wasn't taking anything for granted.

It was shortly after Angelica had left the office that they received word that the rest of the paperwork in Rome was now ready. Leo had his assistant cancel all upcoming plans so they could return to Rome as soon as possible.

Angelica felt that prickle of her conscience again later that evening as she regarded herself in the mirror. What she was wearing now would make what she'd worn the previous night look positively elegant and refined.

She refused to let nerves assail her. She'd already started the process of untangling herself from Aldo's toxic legacy today by signing away most of what she'd inherited over to Leo. She had no desire for anything that man had touched, or corrupted. Even if she didn't have her own money, she wouldn't take a cent. It wasn't hers.

The rest would happen in Rome—Leo had sent her a text today alerting her that they'd be travelling there the following day, to meet with Aldo's lawyers. He clearly didn't fully trust that she wasn't going to turn around at the eleventh hour tomorrow and lay down demands. He would soon see though. And hopefully that would then be enough to convince him to let her go. To end this farcical marriage. To let her get back to her life. And her family. Once she'd proved that she had no designs on anything of his.

But for now, all she could do was test Leo's patience again. She tweaked her hair, pulled back into a high ponytail, and stepped into sky-high bright red stilettos. She took a deep breath and went into the main living area where Leo was ready and waiting, in a tuxedo, this time with a white coat and bow tie. He looked so devastatingly gorgeous that it took a second for Angelica to notice that his face had gone red and his eyes were bugging out of his head.

Sounding choked, he said, 'What is that?'

'It's a dress.' Even Angelica winced at that. It *was* technically a dress but she could appreciate that it might defy such a banal description.

Leo felt as if his eyeballs were burning. Certainly Angelica's image would be forever branded onto his brain. A dress, she'd said? He would have laughed if he'd been capable. But right now he was in the eye of a storm that gripped him on so many levels he couldn't think straight.

He had impressions. Red. Lace. Defying gravity. *Naked.* Outrageous. He tried to be rational, to formulate his thoughts. Piece together what he was looking at. He knew he wasn't exactly sartorially experimental, so maybe he was being too hasty.

The...*dress*...did obey some conventions. Material clung to Angelica's breasts—how? Leo didn't even want to know because it looked as if the lace was spray-painted onto those perfectly shaped orbs of flesh. He could see the thrust of her nipples and blood went straight to his groin.

There was a vee in the material that went to her midriff, then the see-through lace clung to her hips and thighs and stopped, around mid-thigh. There were sleeves on her arms, but not up as far as her shoulders. A small red flower was tied to her neck in a choker.

His gaze travelled down over her endless legs to where her feet were encased in red. Towering, spindly heels.

All in all, he could definitely say that the quota of flesh to material was vastly in favour of flesh. Bare flesh. Plump, succulent flesh. Honed. Olive-skinned. Soft like satin. Because he could think of nothing else now except how she'd felt under his hands, soft and yielding and hot and moist and—

'You cannot wear that.' Mercifully he'd found his voice. Just in time. Before he went up in flames and disgraced himself.

'I promised my friend I'd wear it to help promote her work. She's just won Emerging Designer of the Year.'

'So evidently she doesn't need your help.'

'She does—she's known among her peers but not by the public.'

Leo had to curb the urge to retort that maybe they weren't missing much.

Clearly Angelica was intent on pushing the boundaries again. It wasn't even the fact that she'd cause such a stir that bothered him—after all, as he'd realised earlier, it did have its merits, her scene-stealing stunts diverting attention away from how he'd come to let everything implode so spectacularly—no, it was far more personal and prosaic. How the hell was he supposed to keep his hands off her when she was all but naked?

Angelica wondered if she'd pushed Leo too far. He had always been on the conservative side of behaviour and how he appeared in public. The opposite to Aldo. And so had she. But she had to admit that pushing her own boundaries in this situation was more thrilling than she had expected.

That's because Leo's eyes are on you. She scowled inwardly. She knew that it wasn't for the thrill of shocking the public. It was this thrill, the way he was looking at her, as if he were about to blow a gasket.

'I can assure you that, while daring, this dress is entirely acceptable.'

Leo sounded grim. 'At least you know better than to say respectable.'

Angelica's cheeks got warm. 'Yes, well, Idrina is known for pushing the boundaries.'

Leo waved a hand in her direction. 'Pushing the boundaries, is that the name for it, then?'

Angelica rolled her eyes. 'You sound like an outdated outraged father.'

Leo's eyes met hers in a snap movement that almost felt like the sting of a whip. 'Believe me, there's nothing *fatherlike* about how I feel right now. Except perhaps for the urge to tell you to go to your room and change into something more appropriate.'

'I'm not changing. Take me, or leave me. I'd be quite happy to stay in, order takeout and watch the latest series on cable TV.'

Angelica held her breath. The tension in the air was like a live crackling force. Leo's jaw was gritted so hard, she could see a muscle bulging and had an urge to go over and put her hand on him, smoothing away the tension. That she had put there.

'Fine. Let's go, we're already late, which will ensure your entrance will be as headline-grabbing as possible.'

Angelica barely had time to grab her bag and register that he wasn't caving as he took her arm and led her out of the apartment, into the elevator and down to the lobby area, and out, to the waiting car.

She hardly noticed the chill in the air because the chill emanating from Leo on the other side of the car was more frigid. As they made their way through traffic uptown she felt him glancing at her periodically. She was very aware of her bare legs and the material barely covering the strategic middle of her body from mid-thigh, which had become upper-thigh sitting down, up to where the dress sat over her breasts.

In spite of its skimpyness, Angelica felt relatively secure. What Leo couldn't obviously see was the flesh-coloured lace that held everything in place.

'What'll be next? Just a thong?'

Angelica turned to look at Leo. His face was all harsh lines and dark brows. More stubble on his jaw. She pointed out, 'You're obviously not overly concerned with your appearance.'

He frowned. 'What's that supposed to mean?'

Before she realised what she was doing, Angelica reached out and touched a finger to his jaw, tracing the short spiky hair along his jaw-line. Too late, as her blood surged at that touch, she tried to pull her hand back but it was caught in his.

And somehow she seemed to have gravitated closer. So close that their thighs were almost touching. The air between them now felt hot and volatile. Angelica couldn't take her eyes off Leo's mouth.

His gaze was locked on her mouth too, and then it dipped down to her chest and back up again. She could see those golden depths in his eyes now. Fires burning. She wanted him to kiss her, to root her in some kind of reality even if it was an inferno. Everything had been upside down for so long…

She didn't even notice the car coming to a halt. And neither did Leo. The driver cleared his throat in the front and Leo tensed. He dropped her hand so fast it fell uselessly into her lap. She realised she was leaning towards him, her body betraying her spectacularly.

She pulled back too but Leo was already out of the car and coming around to let her out. Door opening, reaching for her hand. She'd prefer not to touch him again but it was impossible to get out of the vehicle gracefully so she had no option but to slide her hand into his, sparking a million nerve endings to life again.

They were walking up another set of steps now. Angelica was only vaguely aware of the location but it was a suitably formidable building and there was a steady stream of New York's glittering crowd entering the main door.

Paparazzi spotted them and went predictably wild, but Leo didn't want to stop. He tugged her with him until Angelica dug her heels in and he had to stop. He looked at her, his expression stormy, and bit out, 'While the news coverage isn't entirely unwelcome, I think I'd like to avoid hitting the front pages of every paper two days running.'

Angelica didn't have time to ask him what he meant by that. She said, 'I promised my friend I'd get the maximum coverage for her dress.'

Leo snorted. 'Your altruism is to be commended. I'm sure it's nothing to do with the fact that getting photographed in little more than a lace napkin is the main aim here.'

Angelica pulled her hand free with a forced smile and made a motion to shoo Leo aside so she could be photographed on her own. To anyone else it would look like the kind of exchange that happened between celebrities on the red carpet all the time.

Angelica took her time, making sure they got all the angles and made sure they knew who the designer was. When she finally gave a wave and turned to walk up the steps, Leo practically had steam coming out of his ears.

Angelica slid her arm through his, even though that brought her uncomfortably close to his body. But she steeled herself against her reaction and said, 'If this is all too much for you, there's a very quick solution.'

'What's that?'

'A divorce.'

'Not before everything is back in my name.'

Angelica pounced. 'So you will divorce me, then, when I sign everything back to you?'

They were at the top of the steps now. Leo stopped and looked at her. 'Not a chance, not even if you decide to attend an event in nothing but body paint. We agreed to three months, and that's the minimum I'll accept to rehabilitate my image.'

Angelica swallowed down her frustration and smiled sweetly. 'It just so happens that I know a very talented body-paint artist who I've worked with on several campaigns. I must drop him an email.'

Leo urged them forward and into the event, where thousands of lights lit everyone and everything in a golden glow. Ominously he said, 'Do your worst, Angel, it won't change a thing.'

They were at the top of a set of grand marble steps that led down into a vast ballroom. Almost as one entity the crowd seemed to stop and turn to face them. A hush fell. Once again Angelica was pricklingly aware of herself. She would wear clothes like this for a shoot, no problem, but out in public was another matter. But she couldn't regret it now. He'd just confirmed she was doing the right thing. A couple of events drawing all the wrong sort of attention and he would be begging for a divorce once she'd signed everything back over to him.

Leo started walking down the stairs and she could feel his tension. She gritted her jaw against the urge to turn and flee and return in something more suitable. Did he really mean it when he said he'd make her wait out the three months? She had the sinking feeling that if she did appear in just body paint, he would call her bluff and parade her in front of everyone, rendering her little sartorial rebellions futile.

The hush became a chatter of voices that stopped and grew loud again as they passed through the crowd. People seemed to be crowding around them and in the middle of the room, Leo stopped. Angelica felt his hand tighten on hers, almost painfully, and looked up at his face and her belly swooped. He was pale and there was visible perspiration on his brow.

She squeezed his hand. 'Leo, what is it?'

His voice sounded thick. 'Need to move, get some space.'

Angelica spied an opening and moved forward, tugging Leo behind her until they'd got to the side of the ballroom, where the crowd dissipated and there was space. She turned to face him. 'Are you OK?' Theatrics with her outfits and everything was forgotten. She felt a real stab of concern. She'd never seen Leo like this.

She saw his throat swallow. A waiter passed nearby with a tray of glasses. She snagged one. Luckily it was water. She handed it to Leo. 'Drink this.'

He clasped the glass and she could see the knuckles of his fingers, white. The concern got more pronounced. He took a gulp of water and Angelica took the glass back.

'Leo?'

He shook his head. 'I'm sorry... I felt something like this at the last event but it wasn't as bad.'

'Felt what?'

'Claustrophobic. The crowd, around me...nowhere to go. Trapped.'

A chill went down Angelica's spine. 'You experienced this in prison, didn't you?'

The deathly pallor was finally lifting from his face. The faintest colour coming back. He nodded slowly. 'Something like that.'

Until now Angelica hadn't truly appreciated what he must have gone through in prison but this was giving her a glimpse.

Leo put an arm across his body as if to hold himself.

Angelica instinctively moved closer and put a hand on his back. He looked at her and she saw a bleakness in his gaze for a moment that shocked her. But then it was gone. He seemed to straighten up. He took his arm down. 'I'm OK now.'

Angelica was sure he wasn't but she could read the determination in his demeanor. 'We don't have to stay, you know that. It's just a social event.'

He shook his head. 'No, we're staying.'

We. Angelica tried not to let that impact her, a sense that they were in this together, when it was anything but, but she couldn't shake it.

Leo took her hand and they skirted around the edges of the room, before she felt him literally steel himself and they moved back into the crowd. She looked at him as he conversed with a steady stream of people who came to talk to him and marvelled that unless she'd seen what had just happened—a near panic attack—he looked as vital and powerful as ever. As if it hadn't happened.

It humbled her a little. She'd endured a sort of torturous prison with Aldo but she'd managed to minimise their time together as much as possible, leaving her relatively free. Leo had been sequestered in an actual prison, where she shuddered now to think of what had happened to him to give him that reaction to being in a crowd.

Soon they were ushered into a large banquet room where an eye-wateringly long table was laid out with sparkling crockery and crystal glasses. Silver and gold cutlery. Angelica couldn't risk eating much with her outfit but in any case the food wasn't exactly meant to be eaten. It looked more like an art display. Luckily she was used to this and had eaten something earlier. She glanced at Leo, who showed no signs of his earlier stress and who was tucking into the food with enthusiasm, reminding her that he had a healthy appetite. Her cheeks got hot. For *everything*.

'You're not meant to really eat the food,' she said.

He wiped his mouth with a napkin and looked at her. 'It's delicious, you should try it.'

'I ate earlier at the shoot.' She waved her hand at herself. 'I can't really afford to dribble food down my front.'

That was a mistake. It gave licence to Leo to drop his gaze to her chest and the acreage of bare skin on display. He took his time moving his gaze back up and drawled, 'I don't think it would be all that bad.'

Instantly an image from their past came into her head. Leo spooning little blobs of ice cream onto her breasts. Specifically her nipples. She could still feel the delicious shock of the cold, followed by the even more delicious sensation of his hot mouth. Her cheeks flamed. She glared at him. He just smiled and when the person on the other side of him sought his attention, he turned away.

A couple of hours later, the dinner over and people mingling in the main ballroom again, Angelica was heartily sorry she'd ever thought of provoking Leo with her choice of clothes. People were tripping over themselves, tongues out, eyes glued to her breasts. She had to keep resisting the urge to pull the dress down over her thighs, knowing there was no give in the fabric.

She'd been in the bathroom earlier and had overheard two women tittering about her, saying, 'She's obviously in her *exposure era*.'

The other woman had sighed then and replied, 'Well, if I had a body like that, I'd come naked.'

They'd left and Angelica had sat on the lid of the toi-

let for another ten minutes, hoist by her own petard and
feeling increasingly uncomfortable. Especially when she
thought of the fact that how she was dressed was con-
tributing to the people crowding around them and freak-
ing Leo out. She wanted him to see her as a liability. She
didn't want to cause him stress.

You still care about him, whispered a voice. She told
herself it was natural to still have feelings for someone,
even if they'd rejected you. Even if they hated you for
what they believed you had done to them.

Angelica was standing a little to the side near the entrance. A man had stopped Leo on their way out. He
broke away now and came towards her, apologising. So
different from Aldo, whose default had been total lack
of consideration of anything but him.

A chill breeze made Angelica shiver lightly and Leo
spotted it. He took off his jacket and draped it over her
shoulders. His warmth seeped into her skin and bones,
along with his scent, and Angelica had to fight not to
close her eyes.

'Thank you.'

'You couldn't even bring a coat. You had to go for
maximum effect.' He sounded so disapproving. And yet
once again he was proving that he couldn't not be considerate.

'I forgot to think about a coat and it's been unseason-
ably mild,' Angelica said defensively. Until today. There
was definitely a bite of winter in the air.

Leo's car pulled up and he leant forward to open the
back door. Angelica got in, instinctively burrowing
deeper into Leo's jacket, pulling it around her.

The journey back to the apartment was quick and uneventful. But Angelica couldn't relax. Seeing Leo so affected by being in the crowd had melted something inside her. A wall of defence. Dangerous.

Back at the apartment, Leo was still a little shaken by how quickly the sense of claustrophobia had come over him earlier and not even Angelica in her red lace excuse for a dress could have distracted him out of it. For someone who had seen some of the worst things and then experienced the foster system, Leo had always considered himself robust, but he had to admit that prison had got to him on levels he hadn't really fully acknowledged.

The lack of privacy and space. The constant danger. The sheer…hopelessness of it all. The anger and frustration. The impotency. It was all churning inside him as he opened the apartment door and let Angelica walk through.

Her scent tantalised him. She'd tantalised him all evening, once he'd got over his momentary lapse. He'd found that having her near had definitely calmed something inside him, even if her choice of outfit had ensured that they'd been the center of attention all evening.

He was certainly back on the map. That was for sure. He watched her now as she gracefully lifted one foot behind her to slip off a shoe and then the other, lowering her height by several inches. His jacket was far too big on her. It made her look somewhat younger and fragile. It came down lower on her thighs than the dress did. He should have made her wear it all evening.

The glimpses of her curves underneath sent Leo's blood roaring through his veins.

She looked at him and her eyes had never looked so

green. Bright and vibrant. But in spite of that he noticed the slight shadows underneath. Hinting that perhaps this provocative game of hers was not as straightforward as she made it seem.

She slipped the jacket off and held it out to him. 'Thanks.'

Leo stepped forward and put a hand on it, inadvertently trapping her hand. Electricity sparked between them. Neither moved to take their hands away. The moment became charged.

The control he'd had to wield all evening—to not let the crowd overwhelm him and to not let his wife send him hurtling into a volcano of need—was fraying badly.

Right now, all he could see was her and that body that had haunted his dreams and nightmares for years, covered in not much at all. In fact, she'd be less dangerous if she were naked. The fact that the red lace drew the eye to dips and hollows and plump flesh was far more provocative. The lace was strategically placed on her breasts to draw the eye—he could see the press of her nipples against the thin fabric and that made his mind blank with the need to cup that flesh and explore her with his tongue, feel the sharp tip hardening against his tongue as he drove her wild—

'Leo.'

Leo looked at her, disorientated.

'Stop looking at me like that.' Her eyes were bright. Two spots of colour in her cheeks. Mouth very red. He knew it was lipstick and he wanted to kiss it off her. Reveal their natural pink colour.

It was hard to form a coherent thought but he tried. 'Looking at you like what?'

CHAPTER FIVE

LIKE THE WAY the Big Bad Wolf would look at Little Red Riding Hood, thought Angelica. Her heart was beating so fast she could barely breathe. They were caught in a strange tableau, both still holding the jacket between them, Leo's hand on hers. Something shifted.

A longing, a yearning, rose from deep inside her. Unstoppable. It went deeper than desire, although that was there too, sharp and insistent.

She tried to pull her hand away but he tightened his hold. His gaze was on her mouth. Hungry.

'Leo…' Her voice came out low and husky, not how she'd intended at all.

'*Dio*, Angel, how you haunted me.'

'I did?'

He nodded and moved closer, tugging her to him. She went. 'How?'

'Dreams…nightmares.' His mouth tightened. 'Mainly nightmares.'

'I'm sorry,' she said helplessly. She'd had dreams and nightmares too.

'The past is gone. We're here now.'

Angelica swallowed. 'What does that mean?'

'That the present is all that matters. Moving on. And for that to happen... I can see only one way forward.'

Angelica could feel his intention as he moved closer because it echoed within her. A beating drum of desire, flames licking up and out to every extremity, making her tremble. She knew that this was a really, really bad idea but she couldn't seem to stop herself even when she knew the jacket had fallen to the floor and Leo was wrapping his hands around her waist, pulling her even closer.

'Did you really think I could see you dressed like that and maintain some kind of illusion that I was in control?'

'I didn't dress like this for that...'

His mouth twisted a little, 'No, you did it to irritate the hell out of me and make me look like a fool.'

Angelica thought of his pale face and the fear in his eyes earlier. It had thrown her, made her heart squeeze with concern, but she couldn't deny that irritating him *had* been her intention. But now her reasoning for it all felt a bit hazy. 'Yes,' she agreed simply. And then, before he could say anything else, she said, 'But I'm sorry that it brought more attention... I didn't know that you...' She trailed off.

'Neither did I,' he said. 'But I don't want to talk about that now. I don't want to talk at all.'

Neither did she. When Leo lowered his head to hers, she tipped her face up, telling him that she wanted him. His mouth hovered over hers for a long moment and Angelica's hands went to his shirt, fingers clutching at the material. She was about to pull him closer in a bid to close the gap when those firm contours that she remembered so well settled over hers.

Her legs instantly felt weak and she had to lock her

knees to stay standing. Apart from the shock of being kissed by Leo again, the yearning emotion caught at her gut. It felt as if she was coming home. And that was so disturbing and disconcerting that she opened her mouth to him, so the kiss could deepen and become much more explicit. Leo wasted no time in matching her, showing her so effortlessly who was the master here.

She was drowning in sensations and needs and when Leo pulled back after long drugging minutes, it was hard for Angelica to open her eyes and when she did he was out of focus.

He was looking at her, her face caught in his hands. He wiped his thumbs across her tender mouth and said, 'That's better.'

She wasn't even sure what he was referring to, only that she wanted his hands on her bare flesh. She'd felt cold for so long and, finally, heat was reaching all the way into the deepest part of her and spreading out.

'Leo, please…'

'Do you want me?'

She nodded. 'Yes.' There was no hesitation. She'd never thought she'd be here again with him, like this. With him looking at her like this. The last time she'd seen him…there had been such coldness in his eyes. Voice. In a bid to banish the memories, Angelica reached up and pressed her mouth to his, showing him.

It was like setting a match to dry kindling that was already burning. His arms and hands were wrapped so tight around her, he was lifting her off the floor and Angelica was not a small woman.

Her breasts were crushed to his chest, thighs pressing together. She felt his erection against the juncture of her legs and she moved against him as a sense of desperation mounted.

He dragged his mouth away and she heard him curse. She let out a small laugh. For the first time in three years, something light and effervescent bubbled up inside her.

Leo dipped slightly and caught her under her legs and carried her through the apartment to his bedroom. She hadn't been in here. It was vast with windows taking in the night view—Manhattan lit up like a bauble under a clear night sky. They were floating above it all as if in some kind of a cocoon. He put her down by the bed and looked at her. Impatient, she reached for his bow tie and undid it, pulling it off, fingers finding and undoing his buttons.

He stood there and let her open his shirt, push it back and let it slide off his body. She looked at his chest, eyes greedy to see him again. The perfect musculature, the golden skin. She reached out a hand but just as she did something caught her eye and she stopped breathing.

A nasty scar, just under his ribs. Jagged. It hadn't been there before. Instinctively, she moved her hand down and touched it lightly with her fingers. She heard Leo's indrawn breath and looked up. 'What happened?'

He put his hand over hers and lifted it away gently. 'Let's just say it was an early lesson in where I came in the pecking order in prison. They don't think much of white collar crime.'

Angelica felt her eyes prickle at the thought of such violence being meted out to this man, who hadn't deserved it for a second. All while Aldo had been creating havoc. She couldn't look at him, for fear he'd see the emotion in her eyes. 'I'm sorry.'

'You didn't stab me.'

Maybe not, but he still thought she was complicit with Aldo and therefore responsible on some level. The urge to make him understand how sorry she was and that she'd had nothing to do with it all made her open her mouth but Leo put a finger to her lips, stopping her words before they'd even formulated.

'No more talking, it's not important now.'

Angelica swallowed her words. Leo put his hands to his trousers and undid the belt and top button.

'Let me,' she said, replacing his hands with hers and pulling the zip down over the hard bulge. Her blood was boiling in her veins. His trousers fell to the ground. He stepped out of them. Angelica hooked her fingers into the sides of his underwear and pulled it down. His erection sprang free and her legs almost buckled again. He was as magnificent as she remembered. A potent, virile male in his prime.

She only noticed her hand was shaking when she reached out to touch him, fingers tracing the veins that ran along the shaft. She heard another indrawn breath, more like a hiss. He caught her hand again and said thickly, 'I won't last if you keep touching me like that.'

Angelica let her hand drop and looked up at him, then she turned around. 'There's a zip in the material at the back.' In the flesh-coloured fine mesh that held the dress in place.

But Leo didn't put his fingers on the zip, she felt him undoing her hair, pulling out the tie and then letting it fall before furrowing his fingers into her hair and onto her scalp, massaging it. She groaned softly. It was bliss.

He said from behind her, 'I never forgot how your hair

feels like silk.' Then, he swept it over one shoulder and found the cleverly hidden zip, although at this point Angelica wouldn't have objected if he'd ripped the fabric asunder. But he took his time, pulling the zip down to just above her buttocks. She pulled free of the arms of the dress—designed to make it look as if it were sleeveless—and pulled down the body, over her hips and down all the way. She wore no bra, only a thong. The dress had precluded wearing anything underneath.

She hadn't been naked in front of anyone since Leo. Not even Aldo had managed to get that far. Thank God. Angelica shuddered a little just at the thought.

'You're cold.'

She turned around and shook her head. 'No.' But what she was, was nervous. It made her bring her arms up to cover her breasts. Leo had said she'd lost weight, maybe he wouldn't find her attractive any more.

But he caught her arms and pulled them apart gently. She could feel his eyes on her and her heart stuttered.

He said reverently, 'I thought… I'd dreamt you up. That maybe you'd never really existed…that such beauty couldn't be possible.'

Angelica looked up. 'I'm just flesh and blood…there's a million women out there who are infinitely more alluring than I am.'

Leo shook his head. 'I don't think so. Come here.'

He pulled her towards him until their bodies were touching. Every part of Angelica's skin prickled with anticipation. Need.

He kissed her again and she fell into it, twining her arms around his neck and bringing their bodies even closer. His hands were smoothing up and down her back, her waist, hips, fingers tugging her underwear down and off.

Now, cupping one breast and squeezing the firm flesh. Angelica pulled back, breathing heavily. 'I need you, Leo…now.'

She could only read the stark need she felt mirrored on his face and it buoyed something inside her. In this… they were equal. No messy past, no tense present, no uncertain future. Just *now*.

Somehow, he manoeuvred them to the bed and Angelica tumbled back, looking up at Leo. He was so tall and proud and powerful, and yet she could imagine that even he hadn't been a match for a gang in the prison, intent on showing him who was master of that domain. Certainly not him.

The lurid scar hovered on the edge of her vision and made her feel emotional again. She reached out her arms. 'Leo…'

He made a move towards her and then stopped, cursing softly. 'I need to get protection…'

He'd turned and was walking towards the en suite before Angelica could get a word out to tell him she was protected. Still protected. She'd gone on the pill during their brief affair and she'd stayed on it through the marriage to Aldo, terrified that if things changed and he hadn't been inhibited sexually by her, that he might force her into his bed…and the thought of that, and possibly a baby… Angelica couldn't countenance such a thing, so she'd made sure she was protected.

Leo was still in the bathroom. Angelica felt a slight draught from somewhere skate over her skin. She came up on one elbow. 'Leo?'

* * *

'Leo?'

He heard her asking for him and every single cell in his body was straining to return, wanting to obey the drumbeat of need in his blood. But Leo had just caught sight of his reflection in the mirror and couldn't move.

His expression was stark. He looked almost fevered. Eyes glittering with hunger. Jaw tight with need. Muscles bunching, taut. His head was filled with the image of *her*, as she'd lain on the bed just now. Long limbs, soft curves. Dark hair spread out on white sheets. Dark, sharp nipples, asking for his tongue to surround them and make them even sharper.

Curls at the juncture of her legs where he could remember how she'd felt when he'd entered her, how she'd moulded around him so tightly, sending his mind into orbit.

It struck him like a slap across the face. He was about to dive back into the fire that had almost consumed him three years ago, leading him down a path where he'd almost forgotten who he was and where he'd come from. What he'd witnessed, the senseless brutal murder of his entire family at the hands of a rogue Mafia goon, high on drugs and calling in a debt. Trying to impress his peers. That's when Leo had vowed to himself—to never be in a position where he had to watch everyone he loved be destroyed again.

Angelica had told him she loved him. But it had been a lie. When he'd rejected her, she'd gone from him straight into his best friend's bed. Together they'd betrayed him. And yet here he was about to forget the three years of purgatory they—she—had inflicted on him? The knife scar itched, as if her touch had brought those awful moments back to life, when he'd been surrounded, unable to move and then he'd felt a sharp, inexplicable pain, followed by intense heat and shock. Blood everywhere. Men backing away laughing. 'Now you have real blood on your hands.'

But their faces morphed into hers. She must be laughing at him, at how easily he was forgetting his outrage. How quickly he was opening his arms to her again. How weak he was. He went cold inside, the flames of desire doused by a reality check.

Leo stood up straight and grabbed a towel, lashing it around his waist and tying it. He went to the door and opened it. Angelica was on the other side, wearing his shirt, holding it together with one hand. She looked concerned. 'Are you OK?'

Leo forced down the heat he could already feel pooling deep down, just at the sight of her in his shirt, knowing she had nothing underneath, hair tumbled around her shoulders. That beautiful sexy mouth plump from his kisses.

Dio. Before he could change his mind, he said, 'I think you should go back to your room. This was a mistake.'

It took a second for Leo's words to register but when they did, Angelica felt them in her gut, like a physical blow. She was winded. Almost felt like doubling over. *Of course*, rang in her head. Of course he had planned this. How to humiliate her with maximum effect. Get her on her back, naked, begging him…and then…slap her aside.

She took a step back, clutching the shirt to her chest, glad she'd put it on at the last minute. She'd been concerned. Leo had been in the bathroom for long minutes. Her concern mocked her now. Had she learnt nothing?

She heard herself say, 'Why?' Even though she knew the answer.

Leo's face was tight. Eyes dark. 'It's just… I wasn't thinking. This isn't a good idea.'

A little harsh laugh came out of Angelica's mouth before she could stop it. 'Oh, you were thinking all right. You knew exactly what you were doing, but you've done us both a favour. You're right, this isn't a good idea.'

She turned before he could see the emotion rising to choke her and went to the door of the bedroom, pulling it open. From behind her he said, 'Angel, wait… I didn't intend to do this…like this.'

Angelica didn't turn around. She said, 'You didn't used to be a bastard, Leo, but maybe you've changed, like I have.'

She walked out.

Leo had slept badly. Angel's words reverberated in his head all night. *You didn't used to be a bastard.* His conscience pricked. He could see how it might look to her, but he hadn't set out to seduce her and then reject her.

But he couldn't have trusted that she was sleeping with him with no agenda. Especially after what had happened.

Except she hadn't looked as if she had an agenda. She'd looked as if he'd punched her. The colour leaching from her face. Eyes wide. *Hurt.* They'd reminded him of her expression that morning in Venice, when he'd told her to leave. After she'd declared she loved him.

But that had been an act, in league with Aldo, he asserted, even though it suddenly felt a lot less easy to believe.

Maybe subconsciously he had wanted to expose her,

humiliate her, but he knew the bigger motivation had been the speed at which he'd forgotten everything and just wanted her. Needed her.

Dio. Where was she? They had to leave for Rome shortly. If she didn't appear in the dining room in the next five— There was a noise at the door and Leo looked up from his paper that he hadn't been reading.

She stood in the doorway, dressed in dark trousers and a dark long-sleeved top. Flat shoes. Hair pulled back into a knot. A million miles from the sorceress in the barely there red lace dress that had almost tempted him over the edge. A voice mocked him now. *Would it have been so bad? Even if she had laughed at you?*

He stood up. 'There's a few minutes for breakfast. Do you want something hot?'

She didn't meet his eye as she came in and took a seat at the other end of the table. Michael appeared with a coffee pot and cup and put them down. She looked at him and smiled. 'Thank you, Michael.'

'No problem.'

When Michael had left Leo watched her pour herself some coffee. His insides were tight. She looked pale, a little drawn.

'Angel, I—'

She looked at him and her face was a smooth expressionless mask. 'Please, don't call me that. And if you're going to say anything in reference to what happened last night, please don't, there's nothing to discuss.'

The tension throbbing between them begged otherwise but Leo took her cue. For now. 'Fine, we leave in five minutes, OK?'

She just nodded and took another sip of coffee.

* * *

Angelica was aware of Leo across the aisle of the plane but she was doing her damndest not to be. To her mortification last night, she'd gone straight into her shower, turned it on to hot and had cried like a baby.

It hadn't just been the humiliation of Leo's rejection, it had been three years of pent-up stress and emotion. The grief she'd never really expressed for the end of their relationship.

She'd meant what she'd said. The Leo she'd known would never have done something so cruel. But then, when she'd known him he'd been an idealistic young man, revelling in his success without being arrogant or complacent, eager to make a good mark on the world. Half of his ambitions had had to do with philanthropy as much as achieving personal success.

No wonder she'd fallen so hard for him.

Now, he *was* different, and that scar marking where he'd been stabbed was just the tip of the iceberg. Maybe prison had also taught him to be cruel. Vindictive. Vengeful.

And yet, he hadn't looked triumphant last night, as if he'd got her where he wanted her, rejected and humiliated. He'd looked a little…shaken. As if maybe he'd looked in the mirror and seen something. Or, remembered that he hated her and shouldn't debase himself by touching her.

In any case, he'd done them a favour. He'd reminded her of what was at stake. Her family's safety. After last night, she knew she had even less reason to trust him. And to think that she'd almost wanted to blurt out a defence—to tell him that she hadn't been complicit with

Aldo. By revealing everything. That made any sense of humiliation fade into insignificance.

Since she'd met Leo again—since he'd ambushed her, kidnapped her—she'd been running to catch up, get her breath. Revealing too much. Reacting. Provoking. When what she really needed to do was retreat into the space she'd inhabited when she'd been with Aldo, where nothing could touch her, or harm her. Where she was numb.

She'd done it for three years, to survive. She could do it for another few months.

The journey from the private airfield just outside Rome into the city was silent. As silent as the plane journey had been. All eight hours twenty minutes of it. Leo knew, he'd felt every minute. Admittedly, Angelica had slept for almost half of it, curled up on the seat across from him, refusing his suggestion to use the bedroom with a curt shake of her head.

Once again she hadn't met his eye. It was disconcerting because he knew she wasn't sulking. Or being petulant. It was literally as if he weren't there. Or consequential.

He'd put a cashmere throw over her as she'd slept, and had had to sit down again before his fingers had traced the smooth curve of her cheek, lashes long and dark.

You could have touched her all over last night, but you didn't. He didn't have a right to touch her. *You didn't used to be a bastard.*

Leo spoke now to break the silence as much as anything else. 'We're going straight to my legal team's offices. They're working late especially for us.'

'OK.'

The first time Leo had heard her voice since this morning. He gritted his jaw and looked out of the window. It was as if she had retreated behind some invisible wall.

When they arrived at the offices, she was out of the car by the time Leo reached her door. Sending a strong signal to keep back. He put out a hand to indicate for her to precede him into the sleek building, gritting his jaw even harder.

Maybe this froideur was all a precursor to this moment when she would reveal that she wasn't so sanguine about letting Aldo's wealth go, after all. Right now, Leo almost welcomed that scenario, as if it would salve his conscience. But somehow, he had a feeling that Angelica would confound him again, as she'd been doing from the very start.

Angelica signed the last piece of paper. There was a hush in the office. She could sense Leo behind her, eyes boring into her upper back. His surprise was palpable.

'Can I get some water, please?' she asked.

About three assistants scrambled to get her water. She almost smiled when she heard a soft curse behind her and then a familiar scent washed over her and a strong masculine hand was putting down a glass of water on the table by her elbow.

'I'm sorry, you shouldn't have had to ask.'

Angelica took a sip and saw one assistant's face go pale, clearly under Leo's fierce look of censure.

She figured he might not be so accommodating if she'd kicked up a fuss over signing away any last links to Aldo's money. But of course she hadn't. Now she really was free of his toxic tentacles.

She stood up and the solicitors, lawyers and assistants

melted away. She turned around to face Leo, who was looking at her a little warily. She'd been avoiding looking at him for most of the day and now he filled her vision.

Tall and broad, light blue shirt, dark trousers. Top button open. Sleeves rolled up. Hair messy. Jaw stubbled.

She wished she hadn't looked at him because now she couldn't look away and the humiliation of the previous night came flooding back. She clung onto her impassive shell, loath to let Leo see how he affected her.

Eventually he said almost accusingly, 'I don't get it. Why did you marry him if it wasn't for his money or power?'

Angelica went over to one of the windows. Night had fallen outside. The city was lit up. She could see the outline of the Colosseum in the distance. She could also see Leo reflected in the window behind her. She felt brittle and exposed. 'You're so cynical. Maybe we were in love.' She nearly choked on the words.

He made a snorting sound. 'Yes, your grief is admirable.'

Angelica turned around, arms folded across her chest. 'It's none of your business. You dumped me, remember? You don't get to know about my life after that.'

Leo frowned. 'Did you go with him to get back at me?'

Angelica almost laughed at the quaint notion. But then she just felt incredibly weary. 'No, I did not marry that man to punish you for rejecting me.'

Leo opened his mouth again but Angelica put up a hand, 'I'm quite tired now. It's been a long day. Where are we staying?'

'I'm renting an apartment in a hotel not far from here.

Aldo sold the apartment I had here under the company name. I'm looking at properties to buy.'

Angelica's insides twisted. She'd loved Leo's Rome apartment, high in one of the oldest buildings with an outdoor terrace that gave 360-degree views of the ancient city. She'd known that Aldo had sold it and when he'd crowed about it she'd just looked right through him and pretended she couldn't care less.

Leo said, 'I'm going to stay here and do a little bit of work. We have a charity function to attend tomorrow evening at the art museum. This is our first appearance in Rome. I'm sure you'll make it as memorable as our appearances in New York.'

That weariness washed over Angelica again. The thought of seeking out the most outrageous outfit to wear was no longer remotely appealing. She was eternally grateful when Leo said, 'The driver is downstairs. He'll take you to the hotel. I'll see you in the morning.'

She didn't respond, she just walked out, feeling both lighter for having signed away any right to Aldo's tainted legacy and heavy, to be back here in Rome with the man who had made her both happier than she'd ever thought she could be, and more devastated.

When she got to the sumptuous apartment at the top of one of Rome's most exclusive hotels, she blindly went into the first empty bedroom she found, pulled off her clothes and tried not to think of Leo undoing her zip on that dress last night. She took a shower and crawled into the bed with the robe still on and fell into a deep sleep.

Even though he'd told Angelica that he wanted to work, Leo couldn't settle after she'd left. Things just weren't adding up. *Why* hadn't she demanded some of Aldo's fortune? Which, admittedly, was all Leo's. She could have named her price and Leo would have given it to her in order to own his own business outright again. But she'd just signed every piece of paper handed to her. Much as she had in New York.

Of course it had occurred to him over the years that, in a fit of pique at his rejection, she'd flitted into the arms of his best friend, but not really until now, until it had become clear she had no designs on taking anything for herself. Which she was entitled to.

She'd even point-blank refused a percentage of what she had inherited on Aldo's death. She'd almost looked ill at the suggestion.

Leo stood at the window in the same spot where she'd stood. No, things were not clear at all, and now that she had effectively signed everything back over to him... could he really insist that they remain married?

He thought of the press coverage, especially after *that* dress last night. The dress that had pushed him over the edge of his reason. The dress that had appeared splashed over every tabloid from New York to London.

No, he still needed her. If she wasn't providing such a distraction, the press would be all over his current situation and asking questions and speculating as to how he could have possibly been weak enough as to almost lose everything. And, could it happen again? He knew not, but he needed to be in a strong position of power when eyes turned to him again. He didn't want there to be any doubt that he would ever risk his company again.

As of this evening, it was returned to his name and with a new title: Falzone Global Management. He was back on track, a bit bruised and scarred but otherwise intact.

He should just accept the fact that she had chosen not to contest her inheritance and move on. Maybe she was that proud and independent. Far more than he'd even given her credit for. She still owed him for her betrayal and, as she'd pointed out, maybe it was none of his business what her motives were. She'd given him what he wanted and he would make use of her until he was ready to let her go.

Last night he'd almost forgotten everything. He wouldn't make that mistake again. Even if Angelica turned up naked to the next event.

CHAPTER SIX

ANGELICA WOKE THE next morning to a low buzzing sound. She kept her eyes closed, relishing the soft cocoon of the bed. She felt disorientated and images came back—signing legal papers, *Leo*, maintaining a cool and icy distance that had taken more out of her than she had admitted to herself.

Somehow it was much harder to do around Leo than it had been with Aldo. *Because you never wanted Aldo.* She eventually opened her eyes with a scowl on her face and blinked, looking around.

Sounds from the street far below trickled up through an open window. Curtains fluttering gently in the breeze. *Rome.* Then that humming noise again coming from a doorway on the other side of the room.

Angelica pushed back the covers and got out of the bed, pulling the robe around her tightly. She approached the door and opened it and her eyes widened on the sight of Leo—bare-chested, with nothing but a small towel slung around his waist.

He was shaving and he stopped and looked at her. She asked, 'What are you doing here?'

'You slept in my bed last night. All my things are in this bathroom. It was just easier to come here.'

Angelica looked behind her into the room and saw things she hadn't noticed last night. A man's watch on the nightstand. Books. A clock. A suit-bag hanging from a wardrobe door. This robe that she was wearing, which was too big.

Her face got hot. 'I'm sorry, I just came in and had a shower and went straight to bed. I didn't think...'

'It's fine, I took the guest room.'

'I'll move there this morning.'

'You can stay if you like, I don't mind.'

That just brought up images of her and Leo in the same bed, waking up...as they'd used to, entwined.

'I'll go and get some coffee.' She needed to wake up.

'Breakfast should have been delivered by now.'

Angelica fled, without looking at Leo again. When she emerged into the dining area there were some hotel staff who greeted her deferentially and then left.

They'd left a breakfast spread of hot food, and pastries. Fruit and granola. And coffee. Angelica poured a cup and took a sip, hoping that would restore some sense of equilibrium.

For a moment there, finding Leo in the bathroom had felt far too much like déjà vu.

'Have you any plans for the day?'

Angelica jolted slightly. She must have been lost in a daydream for long minutes. Leo was there, clean-shaven, wearing a three-piece suit. Every inch the successful financier. His business restored. She couldn't deny that he deserved that.

But she strove to maintain that cool front. 'I have some personal admin to do.'

Leo sat down and helped himself to coffee and a big

portion of hot food. That reminder of his healthy appetite. Not welcome. She wondered if he'd been with anyone since being released from prison. She hadn't been with anyone since him. And now she was glad he'd come to his senses last night because the thought of him realising that he was still her one and only lover…made her squirm with a sense of exposure.

'I also have to go to my agent's office. They have some upcoming jobs they want to discuss.'

Leo said, 'I can drop you on my way to my office if you like.'

Angelica shook her head. 'No, it's fine, I'd like the walk.'

'Did Aldo like your independence?'

It took a second for Angelica to register Leo's question. She looked at him and said coolly, 'He had no choice.'

'I'm glad he didn't diminish that.'

Angelica felt a surge of emotion to hear Leo say that. To acknowledge that he remembered how important her independence was to her. Ever since she'd left Sicily she'd been conscious of providing for her mother and brother, and then, taking on the bigger responsibility of getting them out of harm's way. She was proud of how she'd been able to do all of that off the back of her earnings. A mere trifle compared to Leo's fortune, but no less significant for that. After losing her father, and with her leaving Sicily, she'd always felt as if she'd abandoned them so to be able to do something for them had been amazing. And that had been her whole focus, until Leo had come along and sent her world into a spin. And now he was sending it into a spin all over again.

Terrified he'd notice the chink in her armour, Angelica

stood up and grabbed a pastry, along with her coffee. 'I have to get ready, I'll see you later.'

Just before she got to the door, Leo said from behind her, 'I'll arrange for a team to be here to help you get ready for the event.'

'OK, fine.' And she slipped out of the room and made sure she used the guest suite this time. Although, it didn't help that she noticed the crumpled bed sheets and felt an almost overwhelming urge to press her face into the pillow to smell his scent.

That evening Leo waited in the living area. He was dressed in his tuxedo. The glam team had left shortly before. He hated to admit it but he felt an illicit frisson at the thought of what Angelica might wear for this evening.

When she did appear, he almost felt a spurt of disappointment. She was covered from neck to toe. A black dress, very elegant and classic. Her hair was slicked back and left loose down her back. Discreet diamond jewellery. Positively demure.

'I'm ready.'

Leo looked at her face. That cool impenetrable mask she'd been wearing since the previous night was still in place. It made him want to go over and take her face in his hands and kiss her, or do something to bring back the spark. *No.*

'OK, let's go.'

It was only when they were walking through the lobby to his car outside and Leo noticed heads swivelling in their direction that he looked down and noticed that Angelica's dress had a slit on one side, giving an eyeful of one long, sleek, toned leg as she walked. Almost all the way up to her underwear. And that the dress was made of some kind of semi-sheer clinging material.

Not so demure after all. The ever-kindling spark inside him burst into flame. It was going to be a long evening.

Angelica's face was sore from fake smiling as people came up to greet her and Leo. She'd been aware of his tension in the crowd and hated that she was. Hated that she cared. But he didn't seem to be exhibiting the same signs of stress as before.

No one mentioned Aldo. It was as if he'd never existed. He hadn't ever really been welcome among Rome's high society in any case. He'd used Angelica in a bid to make himself seem less...connected to a dubious past. Something Leo had never had to worry about. He'd never hid where he came from but he'd also taken great pains to distance himself from any association with Sicily's darker side.

Aldo hadn't. Maybe if Leo had taken more notice of that he might not have trusted Aldo so much. Angelica had never much taken to him, while she'd been with Leo. She'd never liked the way his eyes moved over her, as if she were a piece of meat. And he would invade her space, as if to provoke a reaction. But she'd always stood her ground with him, staring him down until he was the one to break.

And when they'd married, she'd discovered that that had all been bluster. When it came to it, the man had been a coward.

But, she didn't want to think about him now because she had something potentially very exciting happening, which could lead to her arranging a secret meeting with her family. A job in Madrid, where they lived, on the outskirts of the city. Surely she could arrange a trip on her own without causing Leo to suspect anything?

When the next person came up to talk to Leo, Angelica smiled for real this time, at the thought that within the next twenty-four hours she might see and hug her mother and brother. Even if it was just a short meeting, it would sustain her, because clearly, even though she'd proven that she wanted nothing of Leo's business or fortune, he was determined to have his pound of flesh. His three months of revenge.

'That's better.'

Angelica looked up as Leo's arm snaked around her waist, pulling her into him and emptying her mind of anything rational. Damn him. Her smile faded.

'No, don't go back into robot mode. You were looking human again for a second.'

'I don't know what you're talking about.'

Leo sighed audibly and took her hand, expertly moving them to the side of the vast ballroom. He stopped and stood in front of her. She couldn't help but notice that he made sure he was still facing the crowd, that no one was at his back. Angelica pulled her hand away. It felt too nice. Too disturbing. This man had humilated her in the worst way and she'd never forgive him for that.

'Angel...'

She looked up at him, 'Don't call me that.'

He scowled, but then said, 'Angelica. I want to say something about last night—'

She went to turn to walk back into the crowd. 'Well, I don't.'

He caught her arm, stopping her. 'Please.'

She eventually turned back to face him, focusing on his bow tie.

'Look, last night… I didn't intend to do that, to stop. I wanted you, I *want* you. We both know it'd be a lie to deny that.'

Angelica swallowed and did her best to ignore the ominous prickling at the back of her eyes. 'You don't have to say anything.'

'I do. You know I'm not like that. I wouldn't lead someone on only to reject them, out of some sense of spite or cruelty.'

She lifted her eyes to his, feeling very vulnerable. 'So, why?'

He sighed again. 'Because I felt exposed.'

'I was exposed too.'

He nodded. 'I know. I'm sorry. You didn't deserve that.'

Angelica hadn't expected that. It broke something apart inside her. Another piece of the wall she'd built to survive.

He said now, 'I don't trust you…not after everything that happened. But I still want you.'

'I don't trust you either.' Except, Angelica had to admit that her lack of trust was probably a lot shakier than his. He had more reason not to trust her.

'We don't need to trust each other to want each other.'

The thought of putting herself out there again, after last night, made her go cold. 'We might want each other, Leo, but you were right, last night was a mistake.'

'I think it was a mistake…to stop.'

Angelica's heart beat faster. The noise of the crowd around them faded. All she could see were his eyes and the golden flames in the dark depths.

Then he said, 'I haven't been with anyone, since you.'

Another piece of the wall crumbled. Angelica shook her head, even as she could feel her body subtly moving closer to Leo. 'I won't let you humiliate me again.' That was twice now. When he'd dumped her on that fateful day three years ago, and last night.

'I won't.'

'No, you won't, because you won't get that chance.'

'Never say never, Angel.'

'I told you not to—'

'*There* you are, Leo. We've been looking all over for you…'

The voice came from behind her. The interruption stalled Angelica's words in her throat. Leo looked at her and all but smirked. He took her hand and slid his fingers through hers. It felt shockingly intimate. He wouldn't let her pull away but the worst of it was that she didn't want to.

She hadn't seen this side of him since they'd met again and it was seductive. And she knew that if he really turned on the charm, he'd be nigh on impossible to resist.

It was how he'd persuaded her to go out with him the first time. She'd been focused solely on her career, no interest in a romantic relationship, too invested in making enough money to support herself and her mother and brother—plus, she'd never met anyone who'd remotely interested her—and then Leonardo Falzone had appeared at her agent's office asking them to send her a message on his behalf.

She'd been there for a meeting and had recognised him as soon as she'd seen him across the room. The man she'd bumped into a few evenings before at the function, when her drink had spilled all over her dress. She hadn't been able to get his beautiful face out of her head. Or, the way something about him had piqued her interest.

She'd told her agent to go ahead and give him her number. He'd called almost straight away...

'Let's dance.'

Angelica blinked and looked up, past and present merging for a second, making her feel a little dizzy. The person talking to Leo had left and now he was tugging her around the edge of the room to the dance floor.

She asked, 'How are you...in the crowd?'

He seemed OK but she did notice little lines of tension around his mouth. He nodded. 'Much better.' He looked down at her as he swung her into his arms, and her body collided gently with his, all of her softness pressing against his much harder form. He said again with emphasis, '*Much* better.'

Angelica wanted to groan softly but she held it back and tried to remain rigid in Leo's arms but it was next to impossible. She'd been holding herself rigid for so long that her body longed to just...flow and relax. And as if he could sense that, Leo seemed hell-bent on accommodating her body's wishes.

Feeling angry now that Leo seemed intent on dismantling all of her defences, Angelica looked up at him, gaze skipping off the danger of his mouth and up to his eyes. 'How can you want me when you hate me?'

He stopped dancing for a moment and looked down at her. A fleeting expression crossed his face, unguarded, but too fast for her to decipher it.

'I don't...hate you.'

And, Angelica realised, she didn't hate Leo. Not even after he couldn't love her, because he'd never promised that. Not even after he wanted to punish her. What she did feel was tangled and complicated and too much to think about right now.

But as if a little devil had taken control, she heard herself blurting out, 'Why did you dump me?'

He tensed. She felt it. He said after a long moment, 'Because I never promised you anything more than what we had. I didn't want a long-term commitment.'

She stayed silent. As if the words were being dragged out of him, he said, 'You know my background, so similar to yours. I never wanted a relationship, family. When you said...what you said, I knew things had gone too far.'

Too far. Meaning she'd lost the run of herself and had been building happy-ever-after castles in the air. It was small comfort that she knew Leo didn't believe she'd meant it when she'd told him she loved him, and the last thing she needed now was him reflecting on that. But before she could say anything to deflect him, he was saying, 'No, I don't hate you, Angelica, but I do want you.'

They'd started dancing again, which was causing a far too distracting friction between their bodies. Especially considering that Angelica's dress was gossamer thin. She could hardly deny she wanted him—it was out in the open now, like an electric current that couldn't be switched off. Any attempt to maintain a cool facade was fast melting like snow on a hot stone.

Almost as if musing aloud, Leo looked down at her and said, 'You say it's not my business but I think it is.'

Angelica was having trouble thinking straight. 'Your business about what?'

'Why you went to Aldo if it wasn't to get back at me or get your hands on his, that is, *my*, money.'

Angelica's brain was suddenly crystal clear again. She could feel herself tensing. She really didn't want Leo going down this route of looking at her motives because she had no defence except the truth about her family and now that she was so close to seeing them she really didn't want to jeopardise anything.

Instead of an answer she couldn't give, she said, 'Now that you have everything back in your name, are you sure you don't want to divorce and be rid of me?'

Leo pulled her closer as a couple nearly collided with them, and when they'd passed by he didn't loosen his hold. Angelica was sure she could feel every ridge of every muscle, and one in particular, hardening against her. She flushed.

Leo seemed oblivious to what was happening below their necks but she could see the heated look in his eyes. He shook his head. 'Three months minimum. You've proved to be very valuable at diverting attention away from the danger of speculation as to my ability to protect myself from future attack.'

Angelica couldn't begrudge Leo this. Even if it did mean her little plan to attract the wrong sort of attention had backfired spectacularly. And thankfully he wasn't insisting she tell him the truth of her reasons for marrying Aldo.

'I'll start dressing like a nun.'

'No doubt that'll only send them into further paroxysms of delight. There's nothing you could wear that would dim your beauty or sensuality.'

Angelica's insides flipped. This man was the one who had opened her eyes to her own sensuality. She'd never considered herself a very sexual person until she'd slept with him. He'd awoken something primal inside her and she could feel it now, clawing for release. It had been so long.

Feeling a little exposed all over again, she said, 'Careful, that almost sounds like a compliment.'

'You don't need me to tell you how beautiful you are.'

Angelica shook her head. 'I'm well aware that I'm lucky enough to photograph well and fit into the current beauty parameters but there are far more beautiful than me.' She looked to her side and said, 'See that woman there?'

Leo looked. 'The older woman, with the grey hair?'

Angelica nodded. 'She's stunning. You can tell she's had no work done. All of those beautiful lines on her face tell the story of a life lived. She looks happy.'

'Were you always such a romantic?'

Angelica's face got hot. She was losing it. Proximity to Leo was scrambling her brain cells. This time when she pulled back he let her go. 'I need the bathroom.'

She walked off the dance floor, aware of looks and whispers as she went. She felt a little unsteady, as if she were on a ship. When she got to the bathroom she sat in a stall and got her breath back.

She had been a romantic. Right up until he'd told her their relationship was over. And then Aldo and his toxic cruelty had further eroded any belief in romance. But it hadn't been fully decimated in spite of everything that had happened and now Leo was seeing right inside her to where she was still vulnerable. And that was a shock, to fully acknowledge how much she still hoped, and wanted for *more*. How she wanted to imagine a life with someone again, having a family full of love and security. Longevity. Growing old together. Not cut short by violence. A life full of meaning and satisfaction, in the small everyday things. Nothing outrageous.

Perhaps it was the prospect of finally getting to see her mother and brother, exposing her vulnerabilities. But she knew it wasn't. It was him.

Something had shifted between her and Leo. She hadn't been expecting him to apologise for last night. To admit that he'd felt exposed. She couldn't arm herself against him when he was like this.

But she had to. If she slept with him, she'd never be able to protect herself and emerge from this marriage arrangement intact.

He'd broken her heart into a million pieces once already. She wouldn't survive if he did it again.

Steeling herself to go back to Leo and try to ignore the pull between them, she wasn't expecting to see him waiting outside the bathroom. He was leaning against a wall and stood up as she approached. He said, 'I'm ready to go, do you mind?'

Angelica felt relieved. She shook her head. 'Not at all.' She didn't miss the way Leo still had that heated look in his eyes. She would ignore it. Go straight to bed when they returned. In the guest suite. Which had been cleaned by staff earlier. So she wouldn't have to worry about his scent on the sheets.

When they went outside, Leo took his jacket off and gave it to her, settling it over her shoulders. His warmth seeped under her skin. She gritted her jaw and she said *thank you*. He knew exactly what he was doing.

When they got back to the apartment in the hotel, Angelica avoided looking at Leo as she slipped off his jacket and handed it back to him, very careful in case he tried anything. But he just took it without touching her hand.

She looked at him, suddenly feeling foolish, as if perhaps she'd just imagined the crackling chemistry between them, but as soon as she took one look at his face and eyes she knew she hadn't imagined it.

He wanted her. Exactly as he'd told her.

He said, 'There's no reason why this can't be a marriage in the bedroom too. We want each other…clearly there's unfinished business.'

Angelica straightened up. 'If you don't mind, I think I'd prefer to take my chances and let unfinished business remain unfinished. There were plenty of women at that event who I'm sure would be only too happy to accommodate your…needs. After all, it never stopped Aldo.' Her husband might not have been able to perform with her—thank God—but he'd been perfectly capable with others.

And she only realised the impact and meaning of what she'd just said when Leo frowned. 'Is that what happened? He was unfaithful?' He issued a curse word.

If Leo thought she'd been unhappy in her marriage with Aldo because of infidelity then she'd have to leave it at that. She couldn't explain the truth. *You could try.* Her heart beat fast at the thought of telling him everything but then the fear returned. She couldn't yet trust that he wouldn't use her family to get back at her. And she was so close to seeing them.

'That was it,' Angelica said tonelessly.

'And you?'

She looked at him, outraged. '*No.* I would never be unfaithful.' Even while married to Aldo, the thought of another man…other than Leo…had been anathema. Angelica had frozen over inside. Until now.

'Aldo didn't corrupt you completely, then.'

Angelica clamped her mouth shut, afraid of what might come out.

Leo said, 'I would never be unfaithful within a marriage, even this one. Why would I? When all I want is standing right in front of me. There's not one woman back at that event who I would look at twice.'

Angelica had a flashback to Leo appearing in the doorway of the bathroom and telling her it was a mistake. 'It's not happening. I won't be some plaything for your cruel amusement.'

'I wasn't trying to be cruel.'

Angelica forced herself to meet his eye. 'It didn't feel that way.'

'I'm sorry.'

Angelica shook her head. 'There's too much history between us.'

'I agree. And maybe the only way to deal with it is to acknowledge it. Acknowledge that it's still in our present.'

'Because you engineered this whole situation.'

'I would have come for you,' Leo said in a low fervent voice, making Angelica's skin tighten. 'I never stopped thinking about you.'

She swallowed. 'You mean, wanting me to be punished.'

He shrugged minutely. 'Yes, I can't deny that…but since we've been together again, it's becoming less about that and more about…*this*.'

Angelica couldn't even formulate a word in response because Leo had moved closer and snaked a hand around the back of her neck, under her hair, and was tugging her towards him with no force. She was moving towards him willingly in spite of everything she'd just said and as soon as she realised that she dug her heels in.

'Leo…' Her voice sounded thready and weak.

'Yes, Angel…'

'I thought I told you—'

'Not to call you that, yes…'

But clearly he was unrepentant. He said, 'What will it take?'

Angelica's head felt fuzzy. 'Take for what?'

'To show you that you can trust me.'

'I…' She trailed off. Angelica knew in her heart of hearts that she did trust Leo. With this at least. He wouldn't do to her again what he'd done last night. And, in a way, she could see that if she had come to her senses, she might have had a similar reaction.

Then Leo said, 'How about if I…let you tie me up?'

CHAPTER SEVEN

A FLASH OF heat went straight to Angelica's core at the audacious suggestion. To have Leo at her mercy, begging and pleading. She could walk away and leave him there… get her own back. But of course she wouldn't have the nerve to do such a thing. Wouldn't want to.

'You'd let me do that?'

A flicker of uncertainty crossed his face and then it was gone. He nodded. A little devil inside Angelica made her say, 'OK, then.'

She stepped back and dislodged his hand and put out her hand. He looked at it for a moment and then put his hand in hers. As Angelica led him to the bedroom, her insides swooping and fizzing, she felt some measure of control for the first time in a long time.

In the bedroom Angelica let go of Leo's hand and turned to face him. Feeling bold, she said, 'Take your clothes off.'

He arched a brow. 'Please?'

'Please.'

Angelica wasn't sure if Leo would even comply. Maybe he'd come to his senses again and tell her to get out. But no, his fingers went to his bow tie and undid it, pulling it free and letting it drop to the ground.

Then he was undoing his shirt, button by button. Had time slowed down? Stopped even? It felt like that to Angelica. She couldn't take her eyes off his long fingers, the chest he was revealing, inch by muscled inch. The smattering of hair. The defined pectorals and then down, to the ridged abdominals.

His shirt was open and he pulled it off completely. It fell to the floor. Then his hands were on his belt. He opened it and then the top button. The zip. Angelica could see the bulge pressing against the material. *Good.* He wasn't as cool as he looked.

Her breaths were coming short and shallow. She had to focus and suck more air in. His hands were on the sides of his trousers now and with one graceful movement he pushed them down, taking his underwear with them.

He stepped out of the pile of clothes at his feet. He was naked. Gloriously, unashamedly, naked. Tall, proud. Virile. Angelica's gaze travelled over his form, relearning his body. Taking in that scar. The narrow hips. The hair at his groin, his erection. Long and heavy. Potent.

Muscled thighs. He was more ripped than she remembered him being. More densely muscled.

'Where do you want me?'

Angelica looked up, her mouth dry. He was really just letting her order him around? It was heady, this feeling of power. Although she knew if he touched her any illusion of power would be gone in an instant.

'On the bed, on your back.'

Leo went over to the bed, skin gleaming, muscles bunching and moving. He lay down on his back, one arm above his head. He said, 'You should probably get protection from the bathroom now.'

Angelica kicked off the shoes and went into the bath-room, finding the box of protective sheaths. She avoided looking at herself in the mirror. She could feel the heat in her cheeks. She took two foil packages out of the box and got even hotter.

She went back into the bedroom and saw the bow tie on the ground. She picked it up, not thinking too much about what she was doing because if she did she'd lose her nerve. She put the protection down on the bedside table, noting that Leo glanced at it but without looking at his expression. She knelt on the bed beside him and said, 'Give me one hand.'

He lifted the hand above his head and held it out. He was even more intimidating up close, and definitely far more muscled than he had been. *Prison.* Her heart spasmed. She ignored it and took his hand, wrapping the bow tie around his wrist and tying a knot, then she said, 'Your other hand.'

He dutifully held the other one out and in seconds she'd tied his wrists together securely. There was nothing else to tie them to, the headboard was solid wood.

He asked, 'Where did you learn to do that?'

'My father taught me. It's a sailor's knot.' She didn't want to think of her father now and the chain of violence that had ripped her family apart.

'I'm feeling a little undressed.'

Angelica looked at Leo. Her slicked-back hair was no longer slicked back, it was falling around her face. She got off the bed and in one fluid move—because the dress was made of jersey material—she pulled it up and off.

Now she wore only underwear. She reached behind her and undid the bra. She'd always had bigger proportions than the other models—breasts, hips—and had made something of a name for herself as *sexy*, which had come at a time when she was still figuring herself out.

It was only when she'd met this man that the moniker had made any kind of sense and she'd felt it. And the way he was looking at her now, she could see his eyes burning and his hands in fists, tied together.

She tucked her fingers into her lacy underpants and pulled them down, stepping out. She was naked. She could feel her nipples pulling into hard, tight points. Her breasts felt heavy.

'Come here, Angel, I need to touch you.'

She didn't have the wherewithal to tell him not to use that name. The truth was she liked it. She'd missed it. She walked to the bed and climbed on, and knelt before Leo.

He came up before her, on his knees too, and they faced each other for a moment. It felt, absurdly, almost spiritual. Then he lifted his bound hands and cupped her face and leant towards her and put his mouth on hers and then they were tumbling down onto the bed and all Angelica was aware of was the drugging, drowning sensation of losing herself in Leo's kiss.

Their bodies were pressed togther, her softness against his harder planes. He put a thigh between her legs and the centre of her body hummed in response.

Leo was on his back and Angelica was draped over him. The fact that his hands were bound meant his movements were curtailed, but as much as she wanted his hands everywhere, she was also enjoying his obvious frustration, eyes glittering hotly.

He said roughly, 'Come on top of me, Angel. I won't last long… I need you now.'

She needed him too. Her body was aching to know him again. First, she reached for the protection and then, with barely steady hands, she took it out of the package and knelt before him again. Carefully, slowly, she rolled the protective sheath onto Leo's body, aware of his hitched breathing, the hiss between his teeth. The way his hips jerked.

And then, she came over him, legs either side of his hips. She lifted herself, and, reaching behind her, she took him in her hand and guided him to where she was on fire. He breached her entrance and Angelica closed her eyes for a moment, hovering in that place between being full, and not.

And then, when she was ready, she slowly sank down, taking Leo's body inside hers. It was all at once exquisitely familiar and new.

'*Dio*, Angel…'

She looked down and, through her own hazy vision, she could see the perspiration on Leo's brow and the almost fevered look in his eyes. She couldn't speak, could hardly breathe at the sensation. It had been so long.

Slowly, she started to move. She put her hands on his chest and she could feel his heart pumping, in time with hers. Getting faster.

'Yes, like that.'

It was a primal dance, and Angelica was swept along, at Leo's urgings. He lifted his bound hands and squeezed the flesh of her breasts, one after the other, pinching the peaks. She leant over him, so he could put his mouth around her and suck the pebbled flesh. Her hair fell around them in a curtain, and then, when she needed more, she sat back up again and Leo spanned his hands across her midriff, to her waist, holding her as best he could.

Their movements got more frantic as the climax approached and it took Angelica by surprise, mocking her belief that she had any kind of control, as she felt her body hover on the edge for a second before falling down and down into a pulsating, clasping ocean of pleasure.

Leo wasn't far behind her, hips thrusting up, his body tight and taut as he too went over the edge and she could feel the release run through his muscles. She thought she'd have his finger marks in her flesh like a brand as he sought to hold her still. And then, with a hoarse cry, he sank back and all that could be heard was their ragged breathing. Their skin was damp.

Angelica couldn't do anything else but slump over Leo and she felt him bring his bound hands and arms over her head and body to hold her against him.

She closed her eyes and fell into a dreamless place of peace and satisfaction, so profound, she knew even then that it was far too dangerous for her to analyse, so she didn't.

At some point, Angelica woke again and found she was on her side, facing Leo. His eyes were open. Their bodies were close together, close enough for her to feel him stir against her. And then she realised that his hands were no longer bound because one hand was rubbing up and down her back and the other was between them.

'How did you untie the knot?'

'I never told you but my grandfather was a fisherman and taught me how to undo all the sailor's knots.'

'You knew the whole time.'

He nodded, a smile ghosting across his mouth. Like this, Angelica could almost fool herself into believing the past three years hadn't happened. That they hadn't broken up. That maybe, outside that window was Venice and the Grand Canal and if they could go back in time and she didn't tell him she loved him then maybe—

He put a finger over her mouth. It still felt tender after his kisses.

'Stop.'

She scowled. He'd always been able to see her brain whirring. She put her tongue out and tasted his finger before putting her mouth around it and biting gently.

His body hardened against her belly and the air between them became thick with desire and urgency. This time, with no restraints and no need to fear that he would stop and reject her, Angelica gave herself over to the lavish attentions of Leo, his hands running all over body as if he needed to relearn every dip and hollow.

When he came over her, she widened her legs and as he entered her she sucked in a breath, her body still a little sensitive after the first time.

He stopped. 'OK?'

She nodded. 'Fine, keep going.' She put her hands on his buttocks and squeezed and Leo pushed all the way in, before moving out again, and taking them on a slow and sensual dance, building to a climax that ripped through their bodies simultaneously, wringing pleasure out of every nerve ending and cell in their bodies, leaving them clinging to one another as if they'd both been buffeted by a massive storm.

* * *

The next morning, Leo felt disorientated. It was light outside. He was used to waking at dawn. He was on his own in the bed and the only signs that he hadn't hallucinated the previous hours were the discarded foil packets of protection they'd used, and the bow tie, lying on the pillow beside him.

His body felt…replete in a way it hadn't for a long time. Sated. At ease. The constant state of adrenalin that had stayed with him even since his release from prison had also diminished.

He closed his eyes for a moment and his brain was filled with images. Angelica above him, astride him, her sleek body taking him in with such exquisite slowness that he'd almost spilled then and there.

Her perfect breasts, and those pebbled nipples. Dark. Sweet and sharp against his tongue. The silky hot clasp of her body around his. He frowned and opened his eyes. She'd felt…almost like she had the first time he'd slept with her. *She'd been a virgin.*

But she'd been married since then. With Aldo for three years. *No.* He didn't want to go there. Anyway, she'd revealed that Aldo had been unfaithful so maybe she'd shut him out of the bedroom. Maybe that had been the cause of the discontent, but the thought of Angelica being so humiliated and badly treated—possibly emotionally upset because of Aldo's infidelity—drove Leo up and out of bed and into the shower.

Where was she? Before, when they'd been together, she'd always surprised Leo by not wanting to wake up together. He'd been used to her leaving early or, if they'd been in her small apartment, she'd be up and making breakfast, busy.

It had only been after a couple of weeks that she'd confided that she'd been aware that his relationships never lasted longer than a night or two, so she hadn't wanted to seem clingy.

It was Leo who had encouraged her to stay in bed… when he'd never done that before, with a woman. While in prison, that had tortured him, the idea that she'd played him so well, but now…

After washing, he pulled on clothes and went out into the main part of the apartment suite. Angelica was having breakfast, dressed, in jeans and a long-sleeved cashmere top. Hair damp and tied up loosely. Face fresh. No make-up. She looked at him and a little flush came into her cheeks. Leo felt slightly off-centre, as if she was ahead of him on something. Knew something he didn't.

'Hi, sorry, I forgot that I have to go to Madrid today for work, for a couple of days. I meant to tell you last night but then…' She trailed off, her cheeks going pinker.

'You could have told me at the party, or before.'

She looked down at the croissant she was cutting open, and shrugged minutely. 'To be honest, it went out of my head.'

Leo went over and sat down opposite her and helped himself to some coffee. She was still avoiding his eye. Something about that…some sense that something else was going on here made him say, 'I'll come with you.'

Now her head came up and she looked at him, the colour fading from her cheeks. 'Why would you do that? You have work here.'

She was up to something. He felt exposed. Had last

night just been a diversionary tactic? 'It's no problem,' he said easily. 'I have some contacts in Madrid that I could use meeting again, face to face, to asssure them that all is well. We can use my plane.'

'My agent has organised transport.'

Leo smiled but he felt grim. 'I'm sure it can be cancelled.'

Angelica picked up her coffee cup and Leo noticed the slightest tremor in her hand. She said, 'OK, if you're sure you don't mind changing your plans.'

'Oh, I don't mind at all,' he said, calling himself all sorts of a fool for not suspecting that she had been up to something all along. *You seduced her,* pointed out a little voice. Perhaps, he had to concede, but after living with Aldo for three years maybe she'd become as adept as he had been in the art of making you believe you were the one in control and making decisions. If he'd learned one thing in the last three years it was not to let himself ever be taken for a fool again.

As the plane descended into Madrid, Angelica tried to keep her expression neutral. She couldn't believe that she'd let Leo distract her so much that she'd almost forgotten that she was coming here. And that she might have a chance to see her mother and brother.

Surely, she could carve out an hour somewhere to meet them, before or after the job she'd agreed to do. If Leo was having meetings it should be easy. And she would finally, *finally*, see them again and be able to hug them and touch them and tell them everything.

She'd had to be so careful, and she hadn't been able to go into the full details of her marriage with Leo, saying only that she was OK and that she'd explain when she could.

'Penny for them?'

Angelica looked at Leo and realised she was smiling to herself. She composed herself and mentally crossed her fingers, saying, 'The photographer I'm working with, she's one of my best friends, we started out together in the business, I'm looking forward to seeing her...' That wasn't a lie. It just wasn't the reason why she'd engineered to come here.

'What's her name?' Leo asked sharply. Angelica's insides sank. He sensed something was up.

'Natalja Jordan Segal. She's just returned to work from maternity leave. She had her third baby over a year ago.'

The thought that, even after last night, Leo still didn't trust her made something inside her shrivel up. And made her more determined than ever to connect with her family. She was glad now that she'd woken before him this morning and had managed to get her bearings. She needed them.

She said, 'A car is meeting me at the airport to take me straight to the shoot. I'll be back at the hotel early this evening.'

'I've lined up a dinner with some business associates. I'd like it if you were there too.'

Angelica looked at Leo. 'OK, sure.'

When the plane landed, Angelica was directed to the sleek SUV waiting for her, and she tried not to let Leo see how excited and also trepidatious she felt to be in the same city as her family. She'd never have dared to come anywhere near them while married to Aldo.

'See you this evening, Angel.'

She glanced back at Leo just before she got into the car. He was wearing a dark blue suit and shades. Every inch the powerful titan. All at once achingly familiar, and almost like a stranger that she was still getting to know. *To trust.*

He hadn't been a stranger last night. In a bid to avoid thinking about the significance of what had happened and wondering if it would happen again, Angelica said, 'See you later,' and got into the car.

That evening, Leo's car pulled to a stop outside a warehouse on the outskirts of the city. He'd got a text from Angelica during the afternoon, Hi, I'm really sorry but we're going to have to go late here, I won't make the dinner.

After finishing the business dinner Leo had decided to come and pick Angelica up from the shoot. He went into the cavernous space where there seemed to be hundreds of people milling about.

Something eased inside him to see she'd been telling the truth. Maybe he was just being paranoid?

And then he saw her and stopped. She was standing against a black backdrop in a gold dress made of some shimmery material that looked as if it had been poured directly onto her body, lovingly outlining every curve, dip and hollow.

For a second, Leo had to battle with a blast of pure lust so strong that he wanted to stride in there, yell at everyone to stop looking at her and pick her up and take her away.

He took a breath. She looked smaller and somehow more fragile against the massive backdrop and with everyone scurrying around her. He noticed that she looked faintly weary and thought of how little sleep they'd got the previous night. His body tightened at the memory. And in anticipation of re-enacting it. It was just lust. Physical desire. Unfinished business.

Suddenly everyone seemed to snap to attention. A couple of people were touching up Angelica's make-up and hair, and the dress. A slim woman with blonde hair tied up in a messy bun had a camera in her hands and was directing proceedings. That had to be Angelica's friend.

And then, after about another half an hour, someone called out, 'OK, guys, thanks for a great day, that's a wrap.'

There was a smattering of clapping and laughter. Angelica was smiling and hugging the photographer. And then over the woman's shoulder she saw Leo and her eyes widened and the smile faded. He felt it like a punch to the gut. She wasn't happy to see him.

When she'd extricated herself from her friend's embrace, she came towards him, holding the dress up with one hand. Her hair was styled in glossy Hollywood waves. She stood before him. 'You didn't have to come all the way here.'

'It was no problem. Dinner finished early.'

'How did it go?'

'Fine. Constructive.'

'I'll just get changed and get my things.'

Leo nodded, and watched her walk away. Someone came up to her with what looked like her handbag and Angelica smiled at them in a way that he remembered from before. She'd smiled easily a lot, and she'd been sweet. Or, she'd certainly faked it well.

Leo ignored the voice calling him churlish. What else was he supposed to think when she'd gone and betrayed him so heinously?

But then another memory came back—he'd gone to one of her shoots while they'd been together and when a photographer had bawled out a young assistant, Angelica had gone over and had words, forcing the photographer to apologise to the tearful assistant.

Afterwards he'd told her what he'd seen and she'd said, 'I don't like people treating others badly. There's no need for it.'

He'd been impressed by her kindness. It was a rarity in the circles he moved in.

He lost Angelica momentarily in the crowd of people and searched her out, finding her eventually in that gold dress. She was standing on the other side of the space, head bent, looking at her phone. Fingers flying over the screen. Texting someone.

A dark weight slid into his gut. His instinct had been right all along.

Almost without thinking, Leo found that he was moving towards her. Until he was standing right beside her. She was oblivious. There was a small smile playing around her mouth, a secret smile. Like on the plane earlier. He went cold inside.

Acting on an impulse driven by something hot and red, Leo reached out and plucked the phone from Angelica's hands. Her head jerked up and she saw him and her phone in his hand and went white.

Leo looked down and scanned the text quickly, reading: I know, mi amor, I can't wait to see you too, if I can get away I will, I'll be in touch…

Like lightning, she had snatched the phone back and clutched it to her chest. There were two spots of pink high in her cheeks. 'How dare you?'

The thing uppermost in Leo's head was the familiar acrid sense of betrayal. Even more acute after last night. *You can tie me up.* The exposure was excoriating.

He bit out, 'You can tell your lover that you'll be free to meet him after all.'

But she was shaking her head. 'It's not like that…like you think.' She had a stricken look on her face, reminding him of that morning when she'd told him she loved him and he'd sent her away, out of his sight, before she could annihilate him.

She'd annihilated him anyway. He was done. He'd been weak to pursue revenge like this. She'd all but made him a laughing stock over the past week—had it only been a week? It felt longer. He was a fool.

He turned away but she put a hand on his arm. 'Leo. Stop. Wait.'

Against every self-preserving instinct inside him, urging him to keep walking all the way out of this studio, until she was far behind him, he stopped. She came around him to stand in front of him and even in the midst of his recrimination she was exquisite. He knew in that moment that if he never looked at another woman again, he wouldn't care. Damn her.

'Angelica—'

She put up a hand. 'I'm not texting a lover.'

'Then who are you texting?' How was she going to weasel her way out of this? And also, why wasn't she just standing aside with a triumphant smile on her face, watching him walk away? Asking for a divorce? *Because she wants more. She's up to something.*

He saw her swallow. She looked nervous. Looking at him as if she wanted to look all the way into the deepest part of him. Losing patience, Leo was about to look away when she said, 'It's my brother. I'm texting my brother, Paolo.'

The words hung between them. Leo couldn't fully compute them. A brother. 'You never mentioned a brother before.'

'I couldn't. It wasn't safe.'

What on earth was she up to now? As if hearing his thoughts she shook her head. 'Just…please give me a chance to explain. I need to change out of this dress. Security are waiting for it because it's haute couture. Will you wait for me?'

Leo didn't know which way was up right now. She'd blindsided him. Much as she had when he'd seen pictures in the paper of her and Aldo.

'Please, just wait, OK?'

Angelica was changed back into her own clothes, jeans and the cashmere top. Make-up scrubbed off. Hair pulled back. She looked pale in the mirror. She hesitated before leaving the dressing room. She wasn't even sure if Leo was still outside. He might be gone. He might feel that whatever she was about to tell him was just one more provocation too far.

The intimacy of last night felt like aeons ago. Two steps forward and ten steps back.

Was she really going to reveal her family to him? *You just have,* pointed out a voice.

Yes. She had to tell him. She owed him this. The past week had worn away at her defences as she'd seen a man who had been betrayed heinously pick up the pieces of his life and start to rebuild it, brick by brick, with a cool, determined pragmatism.

She had to trust that he wouldn't use the information to threaten them, or her. *He wouldn't.* Somehow she knew that now. He had integrity. He wasn't Aldo. He hadn't changed in that respect.

She collected her bag and went outside where crew were packing up. At first she couldn't see him but then she did, and felt a spurt of relief. His tall, broad-shouldered figure was silhouetted in the opening to the studio. Back to her, hands in his pockets.

Her heart tripped and her pulse quickened. Damn him. As if sensing her, he turned around. She walked over, aware of her skin prickling.

His face was expressionless but he put out a hand for her bag, and just that small courtesy made her feel as though she was doing the right thing.

His car was waiting and he opened the back door to let her get in, before getting in on the other side. No words were exchanged. Angelica could feel the tension thrumming between them.

When they pulled up outside a Madrid hotel they got out. The concierge greeted Leo effusively. Angelica barely took in the sumptuous furnishings and hushed exclusivity. She just followed Leo. The elevator journey up to the suite was made in silence.

Their suite was at the end of a plushly carpeted hall and Leo opened the door, allowing Angelica to precede him. The suite was gorgeously lavish and luxurious. French doors led out to a terrace and she opened them, needing air.

The sun had set and Madrid glittered like a bauble spread out below. The air was mild. Still. An almost full moon hung in the sky. She hoped it wasn't a bad sign.

'Angelica.'

Angelica. Less than twenty-four hours ago it had been *Angel*. She forced herself to turn away from the view to face Leo. He was standing with hands on his hips. His face was no longer expressionless, it was grim. He'd taken off his tie and jacket.

Without preamble she said simply, 'I don't have a lover. I have a mother and brother who I helped get out of Italy to protect them and give them new lives.'

CHAPTER EIGHT

LEO MUST HAVE just been looking at her stupidly for a long moment because as he watched she went and fished her phone out of her bag and then she was holding it out to him. He looked down and saw an elegant middle-aged woman with dark hair going a little grey, and a young man, tall and skinny.

They were unmistakably related to Angelica. They all shared the dark hair, amazing bone structure and unusual eyes. They were smiling and the young man had his arm around his mother.

'I haven't seen them in four years.'

Leo looked at Angelica, still reeling. He handed back her phone. 'Why did you never tell me about them?'

'I couldn't. I was told to tell no one.'

'By who?'

'The charity who helped me get them out.' She put down her phone and paced away from Leo. He wanted to grab her arm and pull her back. There was a tightness building inside him.

She turned around. 'After my father was killed—'

'I just assumed you had no other family.'

She nodded. 'I know, and I didn't correct you.' She went on, 'After he was killed, Paolo was young, vulnerable, angry with the Mafia. And there was always a chance they could come and kill him and my mother too even though my father had been very peripheral to the gangs. It hadn't stopped them killing him. I was afraid Paolo would do something reckless to demonstrate his anger.'

'Where were you?'

'I was already gone, modelling. I was eighteen. I was terrified that Paolo would get caught up in the violence. Mama was, too. Then I read about the charity that does work getting people out…most people don't have the money to leave Italy and so they're still in danger, but I had enough to send them further. Mama changed their name to her grandmother's maiden name. Paolo found it difficult to adapt at first, understandably…but now he's graduating from university with a degree in law and they've both built new lives for themselves, away from the grief and violence.'

Leo could hear the pride and emotion in her voice. But this was…huge. Acting on instinct and needing a moment to get his wits together, he went over to the drinks cabinet and poured himself a slug of whiskey.

Remembering himself at the last moment, he looked back at Angelica. She was pale, eyes huge, and it caught at him deep inside. He tensed against it. 'Would you like anything?'

She shook her head. 'No, thank you… Leo… I—'

He held up the glass, stopping her. 'Just give me a second…'

He put the glass down and ran a hand through his hair. He felt as if he were coming undone. He also felt…a kind of gut-punch sensation to acknowledge that she hadn't told him before.

'Why didn't you tell me? Before?'

Her throat moved as she swallowed. 'Because I was told to trust no one for at least the first year of their re-location. I wasn't allowed to see them. You know the world we came from. You know how anyone affiliated with people they've killed are at risk. It was dangerous. Paolo was just starting to settle down… I couldn't jeopardise their safety…'

'You didn't trust me.'

'I was going to tell you. The day…the day that we broke up.'

The day she'd said: *I love you, Leo.* He recalled all too easily the terror that had entered his veins at the thought of what those words meant. Destruction. Devastation. He'd wondered how had he let it get that far?

But, if he was being entirely honest, those words hadn't just evoked terror, they'd evoked something even worse. *Hope.* The very tiny fledgling seed of something he hadn't ever dared to imagine because it could never happen. In case it was taken away from him again.

But *she hadn't meant it.* Or, had she? Leo didn't know any more. He couldn't think of that now.

'Did Aldo know?'

She nodded slowly. Leo's jaw tightened and fire filled his veins. He hadn't known but that snake had. Of course, just more evidence of her collusion.

'But not like you think.'

Leo almost didn't hear her through the roaring in his head. He frowned. 'What do you mean?'

'I never told him. He found out…he must have done some digging… Not long after you and I broke up, he came to my apartment in Rome.'

Now Angelica looked green. She said, 'Actually, maybe I will have a small drink.'

Leo poured her a measure of whiskey and brought it over. She took it and threw it back, wincing. It took some of the green from her expression though. She handed it back to him and he put the glass down, and took a step back, folding his arms. 'Go on.'

She started to pace again and Leo had to force his gaze up and not let it move down over her body. Even now she had the power to distract him.

'He came and I couldn't understand why he was there because I barely knew him…only through meeting him at events with you.' She stopped and looked at Leo and her eyes were very green. 'You have to believe me, there was nothing going on.'

Leo said nothing. She went on, 'He told me that he had information about me, and he showed me pictures of my mother and brother going about their business. I couldn't believe it…' She was shaking her head, and Leo could see the memory of that terror on her face.

If she was acting then she deserved an Oscar, and, uncomfortably, he had to admit that he didn't think she was acting. After everything that had happened, he could fully accept Aldo was capable of such a thing.

'Aldo told me that unless I did as he asked, he would instruct people to hurt…and do possibly worse, to my mother and brother.'

Leo had always known that Aldo had kept ties with some of the people from his past connected with the Mafia but he'd never appreciated how much until everything had blown up.

'What did he ask?' But he knew. And now Leo felt sick. Because if what Angelica was about to say—

'He told me I had to marry him.'

Just as *he'd* told her she had to marry him. For a moment Leo thought he would be sick but it passed. He felt clammy. Made her say it again. 'He, what?'

'Told me I had to marry him, or he would go after my mother and brother.'

'So you…him…'

She shook her head and he saw her eyes burn. 'I despised that man. He was odious.'

An awful image sprang into Leo's head. 'Did he force you—?'

Angelica put up a hand. 'No.' She stopped, swallowed. 'He wanted to…he tried—' She shuddered visibly before continuing, 'But he couldn't…do it. I think it was the guilt at what he was doing to you, and me. He obviously looked at me and saw you. Then because I'd witnessed him not being able to…perform, he didn't come near me again in any kind of intimate way. He got angry, blamed you. He blamed you for everything. He hated you so much. He was so envious of your success because he knew it wasn't really down to him. Throughout the marriage he slept with multitudes of women, and some men. He wasn't above paying for their services.'

Leo obeyed an instinct too strong to ignore—he closed the distance between him and Angelica and put his hands on her arms. 'But he didn't touch you… Did he ever strike you? Take his anger out on you?'

She shook her head. Her hair had been tied back but it was loose now, falling over her shoulders. 'No,' she whispered. 'I think once he couldn't…perform, every time he looked at me I was like a symbol of his guilty conscience or something. He just used me for public appearances and I made sure to work as much as possible. But he didn't mind that because he loved being married to a model, someone in the public eye.'

The relief rushing through Leo to know that Aldo hadn't touched her made him almost feel weak. He took his hands down. Angelica wrapped her arms around herself. Leo went and closed the French doors, and pulled a throw from the back of a chair and put it around Angelica's shoulders. 'You're cold.'

'I'm OK, really.' But she sat down. Leo got another small slug of whiskey and brought one over for her and one for him. She held it in her hands. This was huge… what she was telling him. Almost too huge for him to interpret because, frankly, it was horrific.

But one thing was clear and he had to address it. He put down his glass and sat down on a chair opposite her. 'Angelica…'

She looked at him and suddenly he could see the toll of the last four, three, years on her face. In a weariness. He saw it because he felt it too.

I love you, Leo. He pushed the memory down because if everything she was saying now was true…then that also…had been true.

'If you had never met me, you wouldn't have met Aldo and he wouldn't have come into your life like a poison, threatening your family, forcing you into an impossible situation.'

She looked at him. 'You believe me.'

'Yes,' he said simply. It was all too awfully believable. But he couldn't untangle everything now. There were more important concerns. 'Where are your mother and brother now?'

Angelica's eyes shimmered. 'They're here, in Madrid, that's why I jumped at the opportunity to come here for work. They're in a suburb just outside the city. Now that Aldo is dead, they're finally safe.'

Anger surged inside Leo. 'They should have always been safe.'

'That wasn't your fault. Aldo was toxic, more toxic than you ever could have imagined. There's no point looking back.'

Leo felt cold inside. 'We were both in a prison of Aldo's making. I'm so sorry.'

He thought back to the day of the funeral, all but dragging her to a church to force her to marry him. He shook his head, 'How could you let me treat you the way I did?'

She shrugged a little. 'I didn't know who you were any more, who you'd become. The Leo I knew would never have threatened another person but you'd been in prison. I had no idea how that might have affected you. I knew you must believe I'd betrayed you. And after Aldo using my family to blackmail me, I was hardly going to trust someone who clearly hated me.'

He shook his head. 'I never hated you, Angel... I was angry, betrayed...but what I feel for you is not hate.'

It certainly isn't love, either. Not that she wanted love, she told herself hastily. Been there, got the heartbreak T-shirt. What they had now was the remnants of the chemistry that had first brought them together. And maybe now that was gone too...not for her, she could still feel every part of her humming just to be near Leo, but maybe this would have pushed him too far.

Even so, Angelica felt as if a weight had been lifted from her entire body. This was the first time she'd ever willingly told anyone about her family.

There was something very fragile between them now. As if scaffolding had been ripped away, leaving them exposed, with nothing to hide behind. She felt vulnerable. Now he knew…and she had to be sure.

'You won't use this information to…threaten them or hurt them, will you?'

Leo looked at her and numerous expressions crossed his face, disbelief, horror, disgust and then anger. He stood up. '*No*, how could you think such a thing?'

'Because I've lived with that fear for the last three years.'

Leo paced back and forth. He stopped and looked at her and his face was stark. He said in a slightly more modulated tone, 'Of course I wouldn't do anything to harm them, or use them against you.'

Angelica sucked in a breath. 'Thank you.'

Leo said, 'If Aldo had touched you…'

Angelica stood up. 'But he didn't. He couldn't. He was a coward.' But she understood what Leo meant. If Aldo had really wanted to violate her, she wouldn't have been able to stop him.

'That's where you were going to the day of the funeral? To see your mother and brother?'

Angelica nodded. 'Yes, I was coming here.'

Leo looked at his watch. 'You're here now, you shouldn't have to wait any longer.'

Angelica's heart beat fast, her eyes widened. 'You mean it? Now?'

Leo nodded. 'I'll get my driver ready.'

Angelica put a hand to her mouth, afraid the emotion would tumble out, and then she acted on impulse, crossing the space to Leo and throwing her arms around his neck. For a moment he did nothing, as if stunned, and then his arms came around her and they were welded together, torso to torso, hip to hip. 'Thank you,' Angelica said brokenly and pressed a kiss to his neck. His scent flooded her nostrils and by the time she pulled away she was shaking.

'I'll just...freshen up and let them know.'

She left the room before she threw herself back into Leo's arms and got ready in a daze, not even sure if she wasn't dreaming. She was afraid to pinch herself and wake up.

She pulled on some fresh clothes, trousers and a shirt, and got a soft leather jacket out of the wardrobe. She pulled on flat boots. She did her best with some make-up to try and look less...emotionally wrung out.

When she went back into the main part of the suite, Leo was on the phone. He terminated his conversation, eyes raking over her. He said, 'My driver is waiting downstairs. He'll take you wherever you need to go.'

Angelica felt as if she were on a precipice. What happened now? After this? Where did this leave them?

He said, 'Maybe we can talk after you've spent some time with them.'

Angelica nodded. 'Of course.' She went to make her way to the door but Leo didn't move. She looked back. 'Aren't you coming?' It hadn't even occurred to her that he might not be with her and she didn't want to analyse the significance of that now.

'You want me to come?'

'I'd like you to meet them.'

'But you haven't seen them in years.'

'I know…it's OK.' She felt exposed now. 'That is unless you have something else to do, it's—'

But he was grabbing his jacket and saying, 'No, let's go.'

The journey to the suburbs seemed both endless and quicker than a nanosecond. They pulled into a quiet street with very ordinary apartment blocks. Leo could feel Angelica almost vibrating beside him. He had to to curb the urge to take her hand in his.

Everything had changed with this revelation. But they would discuss that. He could see a woman and a tall young man under a streetlight. Waiting outside a building. Angelica let out a sound and he looked over to see her hand over her mouth and tears falling freely from her eyes.

He instructed the driver to stop. The car had barely pulled in before she was out of the car and running straight into the arms of the woman and young man.

For a second, Leo stayed in the car, feeling a tightness in his chest, and expanding outwards. For years after his family had been killed in front of him, whenever he'd seen any kind of family unit, he'd experienced panic attacks. He hadn't had to see a psychologist to understand that he most likely had PTSD and saw danger and horror in a scenario that anyone else would see as totally benign.

But over time he'd learned to control his reaction. Except now, with Angelica lost in a tangle of arms and heads, he felt close to one again, for the first time in a long time.

He forced himself out of the car and the young man looked at him over Angelica's shoulder. He said something to her and she extricated herself from the tangle of arms. Leo saw the tears on her mother's face.

Angelica beckoned him to come over and he forced himself forward even though an instinct was telling him to run. She introduced them to him and he shook hands, aware of their curious looks, especially Angelica's younger brother, who stood beside her protectively.

'Can I have a word?' Leo asked pointedly.

She nodded and moved away from her mother and brother. Leo said, 'You need some time with them. Take as long as you need. I'll be in Madrid for two more days. We should talk before I leave.'

She looked at him, eyes wide, glistening, full of emotion. 'I… OK, yes, I'll be in touch. Thank you, Leo, for letting me come to them.'

He shook his head. He owed her. So much. This was the start. They'd both been victims of Aldo's perverse toxic jealousy. Perhaps her, even more so.

Leo gave a little salute to her mother and brother and then went back to the car, instructing the driver to take him back to the hotel. He didn't look behind him to see the family unit again. He didn't need to. It was ingrained on his brain, and it tugged far too dangerously on the tiny little seed of hope he'd felt when Angelica had told him she loved him, before he'd crushed it three years ago.

If anything, this only reinforced his determination to never put himself in that danger again. It was time to let Angelica go. For good this time.

Two days later

Angelica returned to the hotel in the centre of Madrid. For the first time in years, she finally felt at peace. Whole again. The past forty-eight hours with her mother and brother had healed her. And the fact that she could see them any time…still felt like a dream.

Her brother was doing so well, getting an internship with a big legal firm and moving in with a girlfriend. Her mother was embarking on a very slow and tentative relationship with a retired widowed man who she'd met at a local bookclub.

They were happy. Thriving. And so now it was just Angelica who needed to get on with *her* life. But she couldn't see past Leo. As she ascended in the elevator to the suite, she truly had no idea what to expect.

She stepped into the suite and heard Leo's deep voice before she saw him. Her skin prickled with awareness. The cacophony of voices and questions in her head stopped when she saw him standing at the open French doors with a phone lifted to his ear. Wearing a white shirt tucked into dark trousers. The plain clothes did nothing to disguise his powerful body. She could imagine him in a boxing ring. Maybe that was what he'd done in prison. Imagining her and Aldo as he'd taken lumps out of someone.

He'd told her he didn't hate her but she had a feeling that whatever he did feel for her most likely wasn't enough to sustain a marriage built on a need for revenge and rehabilitation. The need for revenge was gone and Angelica hadn't really done much to help Leo's image in public, apart from, as he'd said, diverting attention away from his rebuilding and rebranding of his business.

And then he turned around and saw her and her heart palpitated. *She still loved him.* No. *No!* She couldn't still love him. He'd crushed her love for him three years ago, ground it into dust. All she felt now was desire but that assertion stuck in her chest like a boulder, constricting and tight.

After he terminated his phone conversation he said, 'I wasn't sure if I would see you again.'

And he didn't seem to be too devastated by that prospect. Angelica pushed the vulnerability down. She lifted a hand where her rings sat. 'We're still married, in case you forgot.'

'We don't have to be. We can initiate divorce proceedings as soon as you like.'

Angelica spoke slowly. 'As soon as *I* like.'

He nodded. 'I forced you into this marriage, Angelica, seeking revenge. I did you a great disservice.'

Angelica. Her insides clutched. He looked so distant. Sounded so formal. 'You didn't know—you didn't have all the information.'

His mouth twisted. 'Because you were terrified I would threaten your family's safety if you told me.'

She swallowed. 'I think I knew, even then, that you wouldn't ever do anything like Aldo had…but it all happened so fast…and I did feel guilty. I knew you were innocent but I couldn't do anything to help you.'

'Because you were in a prison too.'

'Not like you.' Angelica shuddered when she thought of the scar on Leo's body. What he'd had to endure in that place.

'How are your family?'

Her tension dissipated. She couldn't help smiling. 'They're amazing. Thank you for letting me be with them.'

'You're free now to do whatever you want.'

'What does that mean?'

'I'm letting you go, Angel. I should never have come for you. I needed to punish someone…and Aldo was gone.'

Angel. There was the spark of something…she could cling onto. All she knew was that the thought of turning around and walking back out of the door and out of Leo's life was impossible. Even if he was actively trying to get rid of her.

Bluntly she asked, 'You said we had unfinished business. Do you still want me?'

Leo's cheeks flushed. 'Looking at you right now, I don't know if I can imagine a time when I won't want you.'

Angelica nearly sagged against the chair near her. She couldn't believe she'd had the nerve to ask that. He still wanted her. The relief was sharp and sweet.

She slipped off her jacket and let it and her bag drop into a chair. She walked towards Leo. His gaze narrowed. 'What are you doing?'

She stopped in front of him. 'We made an agreement, to marry and rehabilitate your image.'

'It was hardly an agreement. That's why I can't ask you to stay.'

'Do you want me to, though?'

His eyes flared golden. But he said, 'It's not about what I want.'

'Well, what about what *I* want?'

'What do you want?'

'You.' She couldn't believe she was being so forward but since she'd unburdened herself and seen her family again, she felt liberated.

'This isn't a good idea, Angel. We have too much history.'

'Precisely why we need to exorcise it. Aldo took three years of our lives and almost ruined your reputation and everything you built up. You deserve to have it all back.'

'And what about you?'

She felt emotional. 'I have my family and for now that's enough. I've used my work for the last three years as a buffer between me and a sadist, but I don't even know if I want to do that any more. I want something more meaningful.' *A family.* The words popped into her head and she had to push them away. That was not something Leo could give her, she'd known it subconsciously three years ago and he'd only confirmed it since then, but she knew she'd never be able to move on with someone else while this electric charge existed between them.

As if he couldn't help himself, Leo reached out and touched her jaw. 'So, what are you proposing?'

She moved a tiny bit closer. 'I can act the part of a dutiful, socially acceptable wife. Let me do that for you.'

'No more Lady Godiva moments?'

She shook her head and felt her face heat up. 'Not unless you specifically request it.'

'And?'

Her throat suddenly felt dry. This was the most forward she'd ever been in her life. 'And…while we both still want each other, why not let it burn itself out?'

He took a step back and said, 'Three years ago, you told me you loved me. Nothing has changed… I can't offer anything more.'

Angelica strove to look as nonchalant as possible. 'Three years ago I was naive. You were my first lover. I was infatuated.'

'I'm still your first and only lover,' Leo pointed out.

She flushed. She wasn't in love with him. She wasn't. 'And you won't be my last. I know that. I do want a family some day, Leo, and I know you don't want that, but that day is a long way off.'

He went a little pale. 'We both come from a past where family puts you and them in jeopardy. How can you risk that? You've seen it first hand—your own family have been used against you.'

'And they're the only thing that kept me going and sane through the past three years. If we lose hope in the future, then what's the point in anything?'

Angelica held her breath, waiting for Leo's answer. Eventually he said, 'Nothing has changed for me in that regard. If anything the last three years have only made me more determined not to subject loved ones to what you went through with your mother and brother.'

'I'm not asking you to change.' *Liar.*

The distance between them suddenly seemed like a chasm. Feeling a sense of defeat, Angelica said, 'Look, Leo, if you want to end this marriage now, then we go our separate ways for good. Maybe that's for the best...' She looked around for where she'd dropped her bag and jacket when her upper arm was taken in a firm grip.

She looked up and into Leo's face and the stark intent and hunger in his expression told her all she needed to know about what he thought of that idea. Her heart leapt.

'Why would I want to end this marriage when we haven't even had a honeymoon yet?'

Angelica blinked at him. She hadn't expected that. 'A honeymoon?'

He nodded and tugged her closer, until their bodies were touching. He cupped her jaw and his thumb rubbed her bottom lip. She wanted to flick out her tongue and taste him. Her knees felt weak.

'I can't think of two people who deserve a honeymoon break more, can you? After everything we've been through?'

A slow unfurling of heat made Angelica's insides tighten with anticipation. She shook her head. 'No.'

'Good, then how ready are you to leave right now?'

Angelica smiled and it felt good. She pushed aside the voices telling her she was playing with danger, courting Leo like this. He'd already hurt her once, he couldn't do it again. 'I'm ready.'

CHAPTER NINE

ANGELICA WAS IN HEAVEN. She'd never been so relaxed. The sun beat down but she was under the shade of an umbrella so it wasn't too intense. The lapping of waves against the shore came from nearby. The only other sounds were birds, circling high in the air. And insects in the lush vegetation that bordered the small, private beach.

The entire island, a little jewel in the Caribbean, was private. The only thing on the island was a luxurious and very exclusive resort, with dwellings so spread out that, since they'd arrived, Angelica had only caught glimpses of other people in the distance.

They had a beach villa. A vast open-plan space, with a private pool and this private section of beach. When they'd arrived the day before, Angelica had had a massage in the villa's spa room and her bones still felt like putty.

She'd lain down on the bed after her massage, while Leo had his massage, and had woken up this morning, still in the robe, after sleeping straight through.

She'd found Leo, bare-chested, wearing shorts, on the terrace having breakfast, which had been set up for them by staff. She'd felt shy, still not believing that he'd really spirited them away to this paradise for a honeymoon, even if it wasn't a real honeymon. It had suddenly felt like it.

She'd said, 'Sorry, I had no idea how tired I was.'

He'd smiled, and admitted, 'I fell into a coma too.' Then he'd held out an arm and said, 'Come here.'

Angelica had gone over and he'd pulled her into his lap. He'd looked at her for a long moment and then just said, 'Hi.'

Angelica had felt absurdly emotional. 'Hi.'

'How hungry are you?'

Sitting on his lap, his hard body under hers, all around her, she'd only been hungry for one thing. 'Not very.'

Needing no further encouragement, he'd lifted her effortlessly and brought her back inside to the bedroom. Within seconds they'd been naked and on the bed in a tangle of limbs, urgency in the air. When Leo had reached for protection, Angelica had stopped him, saying, 'I'm still on the pill… I didn't come off it during…the marriage. I was afraid to in case…' She'd trailed off, and winced inwardly when she'd seen Leo's expression darken.

But then he'd put the protection aside and said, 'I will make it up to you Angel. You shouldn't have ever had to endure that torture.'

She'd reached a hand up to his face and jaw. 'You don't owe me anything. It's over now, we're here, he's not. I never thought we'd be together again, like this.'

Leo hadn't said anything, he'd just joined their bodies in one cataclysmic thrust, stealing any more words from Angelica's mouth and any rational thoughts from her head.

Angelica heard the sounds of someone wading out of the water and lifted her head, shading her eyes with her hand. Leo was emerging from the sea and he took her breath away. Dark hair wet and flattened to his skull only drew the attention to the bone structure of his face.

In short swimming trunks that left little to the imagination, he was hewn from rock and steel. Every glorious inch bronzed and rippling. He was a sea god. A maruading pirate. And he was coming for her, it was in every taut line of his face and body.

'You should have come in, it's beautiful.'

'I'm enjoying the view.'

'Are you, now?'

She nodded. He reached down a hand and said, 'Time for a siesta?'

Angelica lifted up her hand and he grabbed it, pulling her up. Her skin was sandy. She felt young and carefree. As she'd felt when she'd first met Leo. Until he'd dumped her. She pushed aside the unwelcome dark shadow. No shadows here. She knew what this was. A diversion. An exorcism. A sexorcism.

'That sounds good.'

A wicked glint came into Leo's eye and before she knew what was happening, he'd ducked down and she was over his shoulder, one hand on her bottom, tapping it, and as he headed back towards the sea he said, 'A siesta is only earned after a little physical exercise.'

Angelica squealed as they hit the water and once they were out deep enough, Leo dunked her. She came up spluttering and laughing. 'You're so dead, Falzone.' She splashed him and he ducked under the water and pulled her under. They kissed, and their bodies intertwined as they rose lazily back to the surface, sucking in gulps of air.

She had her legs wrapped around Leo's hips and her arms around his neck. Mouths hovering mere centimetres apart.

A little breathlessly Leo said, 'I think that's enough exercise for now.'

Angelica rocked her hips against Leo's erection. 'I agree. I'm ready for my siesta.'

They swam back into shore and walked up the small beach, hand in hand, across the lush lawn and into the villa.

Dusk was falling over paradise a few hours later, as Leo looked out over the view. They'd spent the afternoon in bed and he hated to admit it but it hadn't felt like just sex. It had felt somehow deeper. As if they were coming back to each other. As if there'd just been some sort of a hiatus in their relationship, and not a violent schism.

He would never ordinarily choose to come to a place like this with a woman, a lover, because it would send all sorts of wrong signals.

And yet he hadn't hesitated to suggest it to Angelica. *Angel.* But this was no ordinary situation and it never had been with her, not even when they'd first been together. All the usual rules had gone out of the window. She'd been almost more independent than him.

He'd had no hint of her falling for him, which was why he'd got such a shock when she'd blurted it out. She'd said it was an infatuation. Maybe she was right. She'd been young. He had been her first lover. They were both older and bruised and battered after the last three years. If Angelica had been a romantic, she wouldn't be any more.

So, she was the perfect woman to bring to a place like this because they both knew this had no future, not once the chemistry had burnt itself out.

A noise from behind him made him turn around to see the staff completing setting the dinner table on the terrace. There was a buffet set up on a table nearby, groaning under the weight of different foods. Fish, salad, pitta bread, hummus, succulent meat on skewers.

And then Angel appeared looking like a vision. In a strapless long loose kaftan-style dress of a million different colours, her hair caught up in a loose bun. Even from here he could see the golden glow the sun had added to her skin. And he noticed too that she looked less...weary. Jaded. There had been a little frown etched between her eyebrows since they'd met again—*since you kidnapped her,* pointed out a voice. Leo's conscience prickled. He would make sure neither she, nor her family, would ever want for anything again.

What about when she has a family of her own? asked another little voice. Well, then she wouldn't need his protection anymore. Leo's chest tightened at the thought of someone else having that privilege in her life. Angel would make an amazing mother.

He wouldn't be part of that scenario. Even just the thought of risking the same thing happening to Angel that had happened to his mother—gunned down in cold blood—was enough to have a familiar roiling sensation in his gut, and his breath becoming more shallow.

He focused on her now to divert his mind form the horror. She was gracious with the staff, smiling and gesticulating and thanking them for such a beautiful display of food. They beamed at her. He could empathise.

She saw him and walked over. Barefoot. Face free of make-up. No jewellery. Eyes very green. She'd never looked more beautiful. Leo focused on that to stem the rising tide of panic.

She said, 'Did you see the layout of food? It looks

amazing. They've outdone themselves. Come on, I'm starving.' She caught his arm and led him back into the flickering light of candles dotted around the space and he allowed her to soothe the jagged edges inside him.

They filled up their plates and sat down. Angelica said, 'It's been so long since I've been able to just sit like this and eat good food.'

'Still not cooking for yourself?' Leo asked, unwittingly opening up the conversation to a memory of the past.

Angelica wrinkled her nose. 'I'd like to say that I used the three years of purgatory to learn to cook well but I'm afraid I was working so much it was invariably takeout or food at work and if I was with…you know who, he had chefs cooking for us.'

'I did a cooking course in prison.'

Angelica nearly choked on some pitta bread. Her eyes were watering but she took a sip of water before Leo had to go and pat her back. 'You…what?'

Leo nodded. 'Quite a fancy course too. I can chop vegetables like a pro and I can make an assortment of pasta dishes and slow-cooked stews. My boeuf bourguignon got special praise from the teacher.'

'That doesn't sound like it was all so bad…'

Leo made a face. 'To be perfectly honest, while it wasn't a nice environment and I learned to watch my back after I got stabbed, the worst part of it was probably the boredom. And the sense of impotency.'

He looked at her. 'The thought of you, out there with him.'

Angelica's eyes were huge. Bruised. 'I'm sorry.'

'You have nothing to be sorry for. It was all him. I

boxed and did some self-defence too…to feel stronger, to be able to protect myself.'

Angelica's cheeks pinkened. 'I, er…noticed that you were a little more…muscular.'

Leo arched a brow, enjoying her embarrassment. Enjoying this whole unexpected scenario, on a tiny idyllic slice of land in the Caribbean far away from the trials and tribulations of the last few years. 'Did you, now?'

She scowled and threw an olive at him. He caught it with lightning-fast reflexes and popped it in his mouth, smiling. In fact, he felt like laughing. And he hadn't felt like laughing in a long time. Probably not since he was last with this woman.

He said, 'So tell me about this more meaningful work you want to do…'

Angelica was trying not to let her emotions get out of control but if she closed her eyes she could almost imagine that she and Leo had never broken up. It was seductive and dangerous, because they had. And then, as if that hadn't been enough, they'd been rent even further apart.

'I've been feeling for a while that I want to get out of modelling. It's a relentless business and I have no desire to be an influencer or start my own make-up or clothing line. I've been thinking about setting up some sort of charity, an outreach programme to target young people involved in areas controlled by gangs and crime, not just in Italy but all over…'

Leo popped a morsel of meat into his mouth. 'How would it work?'

'By offering a really comprehensive way out…bursaries, scholarships. A whole escape route through education with accommodation. A new life, far from their old lives.'

She went on, blossoming under Leo's intent interest. 'For instance, it was a religious charity that helped my mother to leave with my brother, but they could only afford to stay in Italy, where they would surely have been tracked down. I could afford to send them further afield, which…actually didn't work out too well in the end, because Aldo still managed to find them.'

She sat back, a little dejected. 'I don't know, maybe it's not such a great idea.'

Leo sat forward. 'Aldo had an agenda. He wanted you and so he went after information about you specifically. That's the only reason he found them. It *is* a good idea. It would take a lot of time and planning and coordination and fundraising, but it's possible. If I hadn't been sent to a foster home on the mainland through the same sort of charity that had helped your mother and brother, my life would have been very different. But you're right, at the moment it's disparate groups and the funds aren't there to give them a real, solid chance. If Aldo and I had been sent further afield, maybe to another country, who's to say that he would have stayed entangled with some elements from our home?'

'You didn't stay entangled,' Angelica pointed out.

'No, because after losing my entire family I had no illusions about how toxic that world was. My father wasn't even a big player, he'd just got into debt and couldn't pay the dues. The guy who killed them all was high on drugs, a loose cannon.'

'What a pointless waste of life…and to have witnessed that was horrific.'

Leo took a sip of wine but Angelica noticed that his hand wasn't quite steady. 'I think the only reason they didn't come after me was because I was eight. Too young to be a threat and not important enough to chase to use, even though they were and are using kids those ages to do their dirty work.'

'My father wasn't a big player either,' confided Angelica. They'd always skirted around the specifics of what had happened in their pasts before tonight. 'He owned a shop and he'd been threatened into storing drugs and guns. A rival gang broke in and stole everything one night and he died because of that.'

Leo reached across the table and took Angelica's hand. 'I'm sorry.'

She looked at him, grief heavy in her chest. 'I'm sorry too.'

'We got out and you got your family out…they're free.'

'Yes.' Angelica let the peace of that wash over her and her heart ached for Leo's loss. So much worse than hers. She said, 'I get it, you know…'

'Get what?'

'Why you don't want to have a family. Who would want to risk that kind of trauma again?'

'Precisely.'

Angelica wanted to say more but there was a look in Leo's eye warning her off. He'd made the decision to close himself off to that risk and it wasn't up for discussion and she'd be a fool to think she could persuade him otherwise.

Obeying a rogue urge, Angelica stood up abruptly. Leo looked up at her. 'What are you doing?'

'Going for a swim.'

'It's dark.'

Angelica shrugged. She walked away from the terrace, down the garden and onto the beach. The moon was so bright, it lit up the beach and water. Then she undid the knot holding her dress up and let it drop to the ground.

She looked behind her to see where Leo had followed her to the edge of the beach. 'Coming?' She turned around and ran straight into the water and dived underneath the silky surface, telling herself that she needed to eke out every moment with Leo while they were still together because soon enough it would be over again and— A shape under the water made her squeal even though she knew it was him.

His hands went around her waist and held her. They could stand where they were—the water came up to Angelica's breasts and Leo's lower belly. His hands moved up, cupping the firm flesh, thumbs rubbing across her pebbled nipples. She sucked in a breath, hands going to his arms where his muscles bunched under her fingers.

'No more talk of the past, hm? Let's just enjoy this.'

As if she'd needed him to confirm her own thoughts.

She went close to him and wound her arms around his neck. 'Sounds like a good idea.'

'The car is here.'

Angelica sighed and turned away from the view of the iconic blue/green of the Caribbean Sea. She slipped shades over her eyes so Leo might not read how sad she was to leave this bubble behind.

They'd spent two more days in paradise, in a haze of sensual abandon, eating, drinking, swimming and sleeping. They'd been careful not to stray into the past again, keeping their conversation light and focused on the present.

And now, they were headed back to New York for a couple of days because Leo had meetings, and Angelica had a shoot booked for an iconic jewellery brand. They hadn't discussed exactly how much longer they'd continue this fake marriage but they both seemed to be tacitly agreeing not to question it. For now.

Leo was standing a few feet away in chinos and a light blue short-sleeved polo shirt that enhanced his darker tan and virile power. Muscles bulging under the short sleeves. He had lost the tight, slightly stern look he'd had since she'd seen him again.

It was as if they'd both unwound the shackles of the last three years and let them go.

'OK, I'm ready.' Angelica took a breath and filed away the memories of this idyllic hiatus, and let Leo guide her into the back of the car, his hand on her arm doing little to stop the inevitable physical reaction to his touch.

For a moment she felt panic. What if no other man ever made her feel as he did? What kind of a life would that be—always comparing someone to your first love?

Not love. It's not love, Angelica desperately told herself as they were driven to the tiny island airfield, looking out of the window in a bid to avoid looking at Leo. But, she knew she was lying to herself. Nothing had changed. She was still in love with Leonardo Falzone.

Angelica realised that her linen trouser suit wasn't really appropriate when they arrived in New York and the temperature had dropped precipitously since they'd been here before. Winter was coming.

Leo had spent most of the flight on his phone and laptop, working. Angelica had spoken with her New York agent, who was excited about a potential opportunity for Angelica to become the face of one of the world's most famous beauty lines. Angelica knew that at the age of twenty-four, which some might consider the twilight years of her modelling career, she was incredibly lucky to still be in demand, but she told her agent she'd think about it. Signing up to a deal like that was a commitment that once she would have jumped at but which now felt constrictive.

Leo reached for her hand across the back of the car and she looked at him, forcing a smile.

He frowned. 'Hey, what's up?'

Absurdly, Angelica felt like crying, her emotions far too close to the surface. She shook her head. 'Nothing, just post-holiday blues.' She told him about the conversation with her agent.

Leo said carefully, 'Shouldn't you be looking a lot more excited? That's a massive opportunity. I've even heard of them.'

Angelica smiled for real this time. It had been an ongoing joke since they'd met that Leo hadn't the first clue about the fashion and beauty industry, not even recognising iconic designer names.

'It is, and I'm grateful for it but…it feels like a watershed moment. If I keep taking jobs like this, I'm committing to a life I'm not sure I want any more.'

Leo looked at her for a moment and then said, 'The philanthropic wing of Falzone Global Management is here in New York.' His mouth tightened. 'Needless to say, Aldo didn't have much use for them in the last few years. I could set up a meeting for you, if you like. They'd be great for advising you on how to take the next steps in creating a charity.'

A spurt of excitement filled Angelica's gut. Her eyes widened. 'Could you really? That would be amazing.'

He nodded. 'Of course, I'll do it right away. Do you want to meet them today?'

Angelica shrugged. 'Why not?'

'You can come to the office with me, then.'

'OK.' She grinned.

Leo reached out a hand and fleetingly touched her bottom lip with his thumb. 'That's better.'

Angelica's heart hitched. She brought up her hand and caught Leo's wrist and she nipped at his thumb with her teeth. His eyes flared golden. So much more golden in the last few days than that unreadable black.

He spread his hand to the back of her head and tugged her closer, dropping his mouth to hers. The kiss was slow and thorough. The kiss of a couple who had indulged for the last few days and who had relearned every inch of what they liked. It simultaneously made Angelica's heart soar, and drop. Because she knew the end was nigh. She pulled back. They were entering Manhattan and the tall buildings soared into the sky around them.

Leo said, 'There's an event tomorrow evening at the Met museum.'

Angelica pulled back slightly. 'Do you need refined elegance or distraction from your convenient wife?'

Leo felt a punch to his gut when Angelica said *convenient wife*, even though he knew she hadn't meant it to be a dig in any way. But it just reminded him of how he'd commandeered her down the aisle, bent on revenge, and his conscience pricked.

'You know you don't have to do this, Angel. If you want to call an end to this at any time, you can.'

She tensed and drew back. 'Are you saying you don't want to be married any more?'

Leo felt another punch to his gut, one he didn't want to investigate. 'No, I'm perfectly happy with this arrangement for as long as you are. I'm conscious that you weren't given a choice at the beginning and I don't want you to feel like you still have no choice.'

She relaxed a little. 'I'm happy to be here…for now.'

Leo looked at her. She was remarkable. To have gone through the mental torture that Aldo had put her through for years and then, just when she thought she was free, to find herself being marched down the aisle again. And she'd taken it all on board with an equanimity and stoicism that shamed him. Not to mention a wicked sense of humour—wearing clothes designed to shock and provoke.

He said, 'I'm sorry that I didn't know what you'd been through. I'd never have asked you to do the things you have if I'd known.'

She suddenly looked a little shy. 'It hasn't been *all* bad.'

An image presented itself in Leo's mind, their intertwined bodies on the vast bed in the beautiful villa in the Caribbean. Pleasure coursing through his blood. Sweat cooling on their skin. And then, diving into the sea to cool off…

'No,' he agreed, feeling a little exposed. 'It hasn't been all bad, and I will make it up to you. You and your family won't have to worry about—'

Angelica put a finger to his mouth. 'You don't owe us anything, Leo. I don't regret knowing you. I'm here because I want to be.'

Before he could respond to that she said, 'I think I'll aim for refined elegance tomorrow evening. You don't need anyone to deflect attention any more, you're back.'

For the first time in Leo's life, he felt a sense of kinship, of having someone by his side who cared about what happened. He'd thought he'd had it with Aldo but, in hindsight, Aldo had always gone his own way and Leo should have seen that for what it was much earlier.

The car came to a stop outside the building housing Leo's office. 'We're here.'

Angelica suddenly looked a little concerned. 'Are you sure it's OK to just land me in with your philanthropy team? I'm sure they're busy...'

Leo hid the little jolt he felt at her very natural and genuine concern for others. To think he'd doubted her was another shameful stain on his conscience. And yet selfishly he knew he wasn't going to take the higher road and insist on ending this marriage... If she was happy to stay for now, then he wasn't about to let her out of his sight.

'It'll be fine, they'll be only too happy to help. They've had nothing to do for the last three years and this project is one I'm willing to get behind too.'

Angelica stopped and looked up at him, eyes huge and green. 'Oh, wow, Leo, that's so kind.'

For a second Leo was oblivious to the busy Manhattan sidewalk, all he wanted to do was grab Angelica, bundle her back into the car, go straight to the apartment and recreate the magical sensual dream they'd just experienced for the last few days.

Gruffly, he said, 'It's really not kind at all. It's the least I can do.'

* * *

Angelica was still buzzing later when she got back to the apartment ahead of Leo. He was still in meetings. She'd seen him through the glass window, moving back and forth, gesticulating. She'd seen how some of the women around the boardroom table were mesmerised. And some of the men. She couldn't blame them.

He'd spotted her and had come out for a moment. He'd kissed her, in front of all of those people. An automatic and easy gesture that had almost felled her. She'd floated back down to the lobby, high on the new possibilities that her charity idea could actually work and on that kiss. Imagining for a moment—dangerously—that this could somehow be real. A real marriage. A real relationship. A partnership.

But it wasn't. They were just playacting for a little longer.

Michael, the apartment manager, was there, welcoming her back, only reinforcing that fantasy. He said, 'I'm going to go now. I've left the supplies Mr Falzone asked for in the kitchen.'

'Supplies?'

Michael nodded. 'I believe he's going to cook this evening?'

Angelica held her tongue and then said a little bemusedly, 'OK, thank you.'

When Michael had left, Angelica went into the kitchen and saw vegetables in bowls. There was meat in the fridge. And wine. Angelica groaned softly. Leo was going to cook? Was he deliberately trying to make her fall for him again?

That evening Angelica was doing her best to remain as detached as possible but it was the hardest thing she'd ever done. Leo had returned to the apartment and after disappearing to the gym for an hour or so, he'd returned and was now freshly showered and wearing soft jeans and a loose shirt, sleeves rolled up, and preparing the ingredients for a stew with professional-chef levels of competence.

Angelica was dressed in sweats and a baggy top, hair up.

Leo looked at her. 'Would you have preferred to go out to eat?'

'Not at all, this is far more entertaining.'

He looked a little embarrassed. 'I have to admit I find it relaxing.'

He'd poured her a glass of wine and she took a sip. He glanced at her. 'So tell me about the meeting with the team.'

Angelica couldn't help grinning. 'It was amazing. I mean, it was also a little scary, because, in order to really go for it, it's going to take an incredible amount of work and money...but if we can set it up properly, this could be a real game-changer for young kids and teens locked into criminal gangs, all over the world. A real lasting way out, not just being moved to a different part of the country you live in.'

She went on, 'For really young kids, born into mob families, it would have to involve a parent who might want to leave also, or being put into foster homes...and that'll take an enormous amount of resources. The government in Italy are already involved in a project to remove children from dangerous situations and so there's always a possibility of working with them.'

'Sounds like you made a lot of headway.'

'Well, thank you for letting me use your resources to see if it's a possibility.'

He looked at her. 'They're your resources too, Angel...'

She squirmed a little. 'Yes, but...we won't be married for long so...' She trailed off, not even sure if she wanted to be broaching this.

But Leo was shaking his head. 'Even if we're not married, I'd like to be the first investor of this project so you won't have to look elsewhere for initial funding or support.'

'You really don't have to do this out of a sense of—'

He held up a hand. 'Don't even say it. I'm doing this because it's a cause I believe in. I came from that background too, remember? Of course I'd love to see more kids and teens be offered a chance of another life.'

'I... OK.' Angelica felt inordinately grateful. 'That's very generous of you.'

Leo made a face. 'Aldo didn't exactly do much in the way of philanthropy while he was in charge, so it'll be good to have a worthwhile project to invest in.'

Of course Leo was thinking of the optics too, not just of easing his conscience where Angelica was concerned. That actually made her feel both better and worse at the same time. She shook her head at herself—she was being ridiculous. 'Well, thank you, we'll only go ahead with it if we think we can make it work, without putting people in danger if they leave those situations. That's the last thing we'd want.'

He looked at her. 'I'm sure you can make it work.'

Angelica felt a warm glow in her chest. It had been a long time since she'd shared aspirations and dreams with anyone.

'How are your mother and brother?'

'They're good. I'd like to see them again soon.'

'I have an invitation to a charity ball in Venice in a couple of days—you could come back to Europe with me and go see them then?'

Venice. The place where she'd first fallen for Leo and where he'd broken her heart. She hadn't been back there since. She had a feeling of foreboding that if she said yes, then maybe they'd have come full circle and both realise it was time to move on. She knew she couldn't keep going like this indefinitely. Each day it was getting harder not to drown in her own emotions.

'OK, that sounds good,' she said as lightly as she could.

Leo continued chopping and slicing his ingredients for his stew and, to save herself the mental torture of witnessing this far too appealing domestic side of Leo, Angelica muttered something about video-calling with her mother and brother and left the kitchen.

CHAPTER TEN

THE FOLLOWING EVENING Leo waited in the foyer of the Met museum for Angelica. She was coming directly from her shoot so it had made sense for them to meet here. He was at the top of the steps, having run the gauntlet of paparazzi. They'd all wanted to know where Angelica was.

A car pulled up at the bottom of the steps and, as if he could sense her, Leo went still. She'd said she would choose elegance this evening over shock value but he found he couldn't care less either way. Whatever she wore, she'd be amazing.

The back door of the car opened and one of the museum staff helped her out of the car and when Leo took her in, his legs felt weak. He knew she was a beautiful woman. But right now…she was transcendent. So much so that a hush went over the crowd. People arriving stood back, as if she were royalty. And she looked regal. Like a queen.

She was wearing a white dress. Satin, strapless. A straight sheath of material that skimmed over her curves. Her skin glowed, the after-effects of the Caribbean sun. It made Leo think about the fact that he'd noticed the sun brought out freckles across her nose.

She wore a simple diamond necklace and drop earrings. Her hair was up in an elegant chignon. She oozed sophistication and elegance and for a second Leo was almost felled by the fact that he wouldn't get to see her blossom into an even more beautiful woman as she got older. Become a mother. Work on her charity.

He didn't want that, he assured himself. That was in her future. Not his. And she deserved it. What they had now was enough. He ignored the sharp pang in his chest. In a bid to stop his mind from going down a path of investigating the fact that maybe it was too late to avoid pain, he went down the steps to meet her. And as he did, the crowd went wild. But he hardly heard them, all he could see was her, so luminously beautiful. And it wasn't just because she was physically beautiful, it shone out of her because she was a good person.

She looked at him, a mischievous glint in her eyes. 'Will I do?'

Leo felt a little choked. He nodded and managed to get out, 'You look stunning, Angel.'

Her cheeks flushed. 'Thank you, you don't look so bad yourself.'

He put out his arm and she slid hers through it. They made a striking couple, Leo in his black tuxedo and with Angelica's white dress. Eventually they made it into the event itself.

Angelica let out a breath and said a little shakily, 'I would have expected dressing formally would garner less attention.'

Leo shook his head. 'I don't think it's possible for you to go under the radar, no matter what you do.'

Sounding a little wistful, Angelica said, 'To be perfectly honest, going under the radar sounds lovely.'

Leo's conscience twinged again. As long as they were married she would be in the eye of the storm. She was tugging him forward now and they stood at the top of the stairs leading down into the crowd. He found himself tensing at the thought of being surrounded by so many people but then as if hearing his thought Angelica took her arm out of his and slid her hand into his.

He looked down at her and she said, 'Ready?'

He nodded, suddenly feeling less tense. And he noticed that, all evening, she made sure that they were never too surrounded by people, by staying close to the edges of the crowd, and orienting themselves so they were facing into the crowd rather than the other way around.

That sense of kinship was back. And he had to struggle against leaning into it. Because she was not always going to be with him. At that prospect though, instead of feeling a sense of relief or *rightness* Leo felt winded, as if someone had just punched him in the gut.

But it couldn't be any other way. He could not have this woman in his life and not be crippled with fear that he'd lose her. He had to let her go.

'OK? Do you want to move?'

Leo realised they'd moved more into the centre of the crowd but he was OK with that. *As long as she's by your side.* He looked down at her and all she could see were those huge pools of green. He had a moment of déjà vu to shortly before they'd broken up when he'd felt panicked that she seemed to have such a hold over him. And then she'd told him she loved him.

He sucked in a breath and forced himself to be rational. That was a long time ago. As she'd said herself, she'd been infatuated, and maybe he had too. But that was all.

And now…it was just about chemistry and making the most out of this marriage for both of them.

He shook his head. 'No, I'm fine.'

Angelica squeezed his hand and Leo had the very sick sense that he wasn't fine at all.

Two days later

There was a knot in Angelica's gut as the water-taxi made its way up the iconic Grand Canal of Venice, to where Leo's apartment was situated, in one of the majestic palazzos lining the canal.

They pulled in at the landing jetty and Leo jumped out athletically before turning to give a hand to Angelica. She was wearing wide jeans, silk T-shirt and a light cropped jacket.

Leo led her into the reception area of the palazzo where the concierge greeted Leo with genuine affection, telling him he was so glad that Leo had been exonerated. It made Angelica feel emotional too.

Leo's apartment was on the second floor and took up the entire space. Parquet flooring and ornate original features. Oriental rugs. Soft, comfortable furnishings and coffee tables groaning under books on art and photography. When she'd been with Leo three years ago, he'd used to spend almost as much time here as in Rome.

If Angelica wasn't booked on a job, she'd used to curl up here while Leo was working in his office and flick through the books.

When they walked in she noticed something—empty spaces on the walls. 'Where are your paintings?'

Leo had been building up a small curated collection with an art broker from New York.

'Aldo took them because they were pretty much the only

thing he could lift easily from the apartment. Luckily this was entirely in my name so he couldn't get his hands on it.'

Angelica shook her head. 'Unbelievable. If I'd known I would have tried to stop him, but I never came here with him.' And she was so thankful for that. As painful as some of the memories were here, she didn't need Aldo adding to the pain.

'It's fine. Faye Holt, the art broker, is doing a great job of retrieving them for me.'

'I'm glad.' There had been one she'd loved, by Matisse.

Leo looked at his watch. He was in a three-piece suit and, even after a transatlantic flight, he looked mouth-wateringly vital and gorgeous.

'I have to go to a meeting for the afternoon, but I want to show you something first…if it's here,' Leo said enigmatically.

Angelica followed him out of the living area and into the corridor where the bedrooms were. In the main bedroom, that had a small balcony/terrace overlooking the canal, Leo reached for a clothes bag that was hanging in the wardrobe. He took it out and laid it on the bed and pulled down the zip, revealing shimmering gold and chiffon and lace and silk. A dress. Ethereally beautiful, with delicate capped sleeves and a low bodice.

'What's this for?'

'The event tonight. It's a masked ball.'

Angelica noticed the feathered matching mask, attached to the dress.

He said, 'I know you can dress yourself but I took the liberty of having a stylist organise a dress.'

Angelica reached out and touched the material. 'It's beautiful, of course I'll wear it.'

'What will you do for the afternoon?'

Angelica looked at Leo. 'Actually, I have a Zoom meeting with the philanthropic team to talk about plans for the charity.'

'Great…well, if you need anything just text me.'

'I will.'

Leo looked at her for an unnervingly long time until Angelica felt herself blushing. 'What are you doing?'

Leo shook his head as if he was coming out of a trance. 'You mesmerise me.'

Angelica rolled her eyes, and held up her hand. 'We're married, Leo, you don't have to say those kinds of things to me.' *Especially when we both know that you'll undoubtedly be saying something similar to the next lover you bring here.*

Leo came close and touched Angelica's jaw. 'I've never said anything like that to another woman and I don't intend to.'

Angelica's insides twisted. 'Leo, stop, you really don't have to—'

He cut her off by swooping down and placing his mouth over hers, igniting an immediate fire between them. *Ignite?* Who was she kidding? The fire never seemed to go out.

She was clutching his shirt to stay standing when he finally broke the kiss. Angelica was breathing harshly. 'What was that for?'

Leo said, 'I can't imagine not wanting you, Angel… you're part of my blood.'

She felt shaky. Was Leo finally admitting that perhaps he could feel something more permanent for her? 'Me too.'

He straightened up. 'As much as I'd like to stay here and exorcise this fever, I can't.' He went to the door, and looked back. 'See you later?'

Angelica just nodded, her heart still pounding, skin hot. He disappeared and Angelica sank back onto the bed. Leo had just given her something with one hand and taken it away with the other. *He wanted to exorcise her from his blood.* Not admit that she might mean more to him.

Nothing had changed. If she told him she still loved him, he would surely end it all over again. Exactly as he had before. Full circle. It was nothing that Angelica didn't know and she had to dampen down the flame of hope that she was confusing with desire, or she really would never recover.

Stepping into the ballroom of the palazzo just a bit further down the Grand Canal from Leo's apartment was like stepping back in time. Flaming lanterns and massive candles lit the space in a golden glow.

Leo and Angelica were relatively restrained in their choice of clothes compared to some of the guests in full medieval-style costume with elaborate masks to match.

Leo wore a classic black tuxedo, and the stunning gold dress fitted Angelica like a dream. The matching mask sat over her eyes and she quite liked not being instantly recognisable.

Wait staff moved through the crowd with glasses of sparkling wine and canapés.

'I see someone who I need to speak to, on the other side of the room.' Leo was taking Angelica's hand and leading her through the crowd. She noticed that he seemed far more comfortable in crowds now. And, as they approached the person he wanted to talk to, he let her hand go. He introduced them and Angelica smiled politely but she soon found that Leo was engrossed in his conversation. *He didn't need her any more.*

Whatever advantage she might have brought to him in his initial phase of relaunching his business, it was well and truly expired now. And soon he would realise that and waste no time in casting her off. Albeit, salving his conscience by helping her with her charity project.

Angelica felt a pang. That wasn't fair—she was sure that Leo meant it when he said he was interested in the charity, but suddenly Angelica wasn't so sure if she wanted to have any involvement with his company, potentially having to deal with him, or see him.

But could she now jeopardise work on the charity just to make things easier for herself?

'Sorry, I didn't mean to exclude you.'

Angelica blinked out of her spiralling thoughts to see that Leo's acquaintance had moved on. She shook her head. 'It's fine. I know these things are networking opportunities.'

'Maybe you'll be back here hosting a charity event of your own soon?'

You. Not we. Another death knell. Angelica smiled. 'Maybe.'

'Dance with me.'

Angelica felt like pulling free and leaving, getting into a water-taxi and going straight to the airport. A decisive clean break. But Leo was holding her hand and the surroundings were seductive enough to believe that maybe the world outside wasn't waiting for her to start over again. Just yet. Would one more night be so selfish?

'OK.'

Leo led the way through the crowd to where couples were dancing to a mellow jazz band. He swung Angelica into his arms and she hated the way she fitted so easily. *Like coming home.* No. Coming home would be when she bought a place near to where her mother and brother lived in Madrid. She would set herself up there, and continue to work until the charity became more solid. And then she would worry about fundraising.

'Where are you?' he asked.

Angelica swallowed the emotions threatening to strangle her and forced a smile. 'Nowhere, sorry.'

Leo stopped dancing. 'Do you want to go?'

'But we just got here. Don't you have more people to meet?'

Leo shrugged. 'Not especially. Everyone knows I'm back now.'

'I'm really pleased for you, Leo.' Those damned emotions were rising again.

'Come on, let's go.'

Angelica let him lead her out, grateful for the chance to get herself back under control, and hopefully stay that way for a few more hours. *One more night.*

They were in a water-taxi on the Grand Canal within minutes. The night air was crisp and cool and Angelica huddled into her faux-fur wrap. Leo put his arm around her and pulled her into his side, and guiltily, storing up every little moment, Angelica revelled in it.

Far too soon they were back at the palazzo housing Leo's apartment. They walked up the jetty and Angelica's dress swirled around her legs in the breeze.

When they were back in the apartment, Leo pulled

off his bow tie and opened a top button. 'Would you like a nightcap?'

Angelica never really drank much but for once she fancied something. 'Sure, maybe a little watered-down whiskey?'

Leo raised a brow. 'Going straight for the hard stuff?'

'Why not?' she said lightly, shucking off the faux fur and pulling off the mask, laying them on a nearby chair.

Leo came back with two glasses and handed her one. He'd taken off his mask too. They clinked glasses and Angelica took a sip. She wandered over to the windows that looked out onto the canal and opened them, standing out on the small balcony.

Water taxis caused waves down below and a couple of gondolas meandered in their wake, couples ensconced in the back, snuggled into one another. Just as she and Leo had been. How many of these couples were on the verge of ending? She felt incredibly melancholic for a moment.

From behind her Leo said, 'Angel...'

She turned around and Leo was across the room. He put down his glass and said, 'Come here.'

A spurt of rebelliousness made her say, 'Please.'

His mouth quirked. 'Please.'

It was as if an invisible wire connected them. She was no more capable of disobeying his command than she was of denying herself breath. She lifted one foot at a time and picked off the high-heels sandals and dropped them to the floor.

As she walked towards him she reached behind her and found the zip, pulling it down. The dress loosened around her chest and when she got to within a couple of feet of Leo she pulled the small cap sleeves off her shoulders and down her arms, and then the front of the dress, revealing her breasts.

She watched his eyes widen and flare as she tugged the dress over her hips and down her legs, stepping out of the mound of gold silk and lace. Now she wore only her underpants. She reached up to her hair and pulled out the pin holding it in place so it fell down around her shoulders, almost touching her breasts.

She felt something very primal about coming to stand before him like this. As if she was presenting herself for his final delectation. She hadn't told him that she knew this was the last time they'd ever be together. Her conscience pricked but she pushed it down. They didn't owe each other anything after tonight.

Leo stepped forward and thrust his hands into her hair, tipping her face up to his. 'You are…*everything*,' he breathed.

Angelica smiled tremulously. 'Kiss me, Leo.'

He did, covering her mouth with his and sending her thoughts scattering. *Good.* She didn't want to think any more, she wanted to indulge in this night and savour every second.

Leo picked her up and carried her into the bedroom. Under the shaft of moonlight shining through the window, he stripped off his own clothes until he was naked. Angelica ogled him shamelessly, coming up on one elbow, her gaze travelling over his chest, abdominals, to his narrow waist and to where the thrusting power of him made her mouth water.

'Lie back.'

She did, and he hooked his fingers into her underwear and pulled it down and off. Leo put his hands on her legs and smoothed his way up, to her thighs and higher, pushing her legs apart as he did, exposing her to his dark golden gaze.

He came down on his knees on the floor at the end of the bed and then he proceeded to press his mouth against the inside of her legs as he came closer and closer to the juncture where her legs met.

Angelica's hands were clutching at the sheets, trying to find something to hold onto as Leo's warm breath against her sensitive skin made her skin break into goosebumps.

He pushed her legs even further apart and Angelica's breath came fast and shallow. She felt utterly exposed and yet unconcerned. She could feel the delicious abrasion of Leo's stubble against her inner thigh.

And then his mouth was there. On her. His tongue exploring her with a thoroughness that made her back arch off the bed. He reached up a hand as if to soothe her, passing over her midriff and finding a breast, squeezing the firm flesh and trapping a nipple between two fingers and squeezing, causing a sharp burst of pleasure to arrow all the way down to his wicked tongue.

The man was remorseless, ignoring Angelica's breathless pleas for mercy, until she felt herself tightening all over, hovering on the precipice before hurtling over the edge into wave after wave of pleasure so intense, she tried to put her legs together, but Leo wouldn't let her, keeping his mouth on her until she was spent and silent, breathing as if she'd just done a marathon.

She hadn't even realised her hands were in his hair and she was gripping his head. She took them away. 'I'm sorry...'

He came up over her body, grinning. 'Don't be.'

Angelica's heart spasmed. He looked so much younger and carefree. She scowled at him. 'You're evil.'

'I know, and I fully intend to be a lot more evil.'

Angelica reached for his shoulders and somehow, gathering strength into her jelly limbs, she pushed him so that he fell onto his back on the bed. She pressed him down and said, 'Not so fast.'

Leo was unperturbed. He put his arms behind his head, reminding her of how he'd gained her trust by letting her restrain him. Another heart spasm. She should have known to trust him from the start…but then they wouldn't have had all of this…

She started pressing kisses to his chest, finding the flat disc of a nipple and teasing it with her tongue. She put a hand on his lower belly, feeling the muscles contract, and explored further, circling his erection with one hand as she made her way down and down until he was now rigid with tension.

Taking her time, she let her hand explore his stiff flesh, feeling how the skin slipped up and down over the shaft, and then, when she could see perspiration on his brow, she bent forward and put her mouth around him.

Madre de Dio…he was going to die right here on this bed. And he knew if he did he would die happy. Angelica was a sorceress, taking him to a place he'd never been before, because he usually didn't like lovers performing oral sex on him—until Angelica, that was. He'd always felt too exposed. But the first time she'd done it to him, back when they'd first got together, it had been so innocent and obvious that she hadn't known what she was doing that he'd given into the temptation, and now…he'd created a monster.

She was as merciless as he had just been, pushing him over the edge before he could stop himself, taking all of him, and then sliding back up his body, with those soft curves, and a smile like the Cheshire Cat.

Leo hauled her up all the way. They were glued together. He cupped her bottom and then gave one cheek a playful slap. 'You'll pay for that.'

'Promises, promises.'

She put her head down, into the place where his shoulder met his neck, her breath feathering over his skin. A feeling of intense peace washed over Leo, the kind of peace he'd never thought he'd experience again.

He ran his hand lazily up and down Angelica's back, letting himself recover, and then he heard a gentle snore and smiled, letting that sense of peace lull him into joining her.

CHAPTER ELEVEN

WHEN LEO WOKE the next morning he felt both amazingly relaxed and hungover. But not from drink. A sex hangover. Images filled his head. After he and Angelica had initially fallen asleep, they'd woken again a while later, filled with mutual hunger. A hunger that had bordered on desperation sometimes.

They'd finally fallen asleep again around dawn. And now… Leo cracked open his eyes. The sun was high outside. And the bed was empty beside him. He put out an arm. It was cold.

He came up on one elbow, feeling as if he'd missed his footing even though he was lying down. He threw back the covers and got up, heading straight for the shower. Afterwards he pulled on the first things to hand, jeans and a loose shirt, a niggling sense of unease trickling down his spine.

He went out into the main part of the apartment and for a second didn't notice anything but then he saw her. She was standing at the open windows, looking out onto the canal.

She was dressed in the jeans she'd worn the previous day, sneakers and a sweatshirt. Hair pulled back in a ponytail. She looked ridiculously young. Then he noticed the suitcase beside her and her handbag, across her body.

The unease intensified. Maybe she'd got booked for a job. 'Angel?'

She turned around and Leo noticed that she was pale and her face was set. She also had shadows under her eyes but then that wasn't a surprise. They hadn't had much sleep.

Trying not to let the unease show in his voice, he said, 'Are you going somewhere?'

She nodded. 'I'm afraid I've been lying to you, Leo, and myself a little bit too.'

He frowned. 'What do you mean?' Suddenly he felt cold, thinking that perhaps all this time, when he'd believed in her story, maybe he'd missed an even bigger agenda…

Oblivious to his cynical mind whirring into action again, she said, 'The truth is that I still love you, Leo. I never stopped. I convinced myself I had, or that it hadn't been love, but it was a lie.'

She shrugged minutely and tried to force a smile but Leo could see the emotion in her eyes and, like a coward, he would have preferred in that moment that perhaps she had been lulling him into a false sense of security for some nefarious end. This was far more threatening. He could feel himself closing off, shutting down.

She said, 'Believe me, I get the irony of being back in more or less exactly the same spot having the same conversation, three years later.' She let out a short harsh laugh that didn't sound like her at all. 'You'd think I'd have learnt by now.'

'I didn't give you much choice,' Leo had to concede. 'I dragged you back into my life.'

He said now, 'Angel… I'm sorry I can't say what you

want to hear. It's not something I've ever wanted in my life…a lifetime commitment, family.' So why did the words feel like ash on his tongue?

He noticed her throat working as she swallowed. 'I think the worst of it is that I understand, because I lost someone too. And I grew up surrounded by the threat of violence all the time.'

'But…this is the thing…none of us are guaranteed a life without pain, or loss. Some experience more than most, granted…but do you not see that by choosing to close yourself off to the risk of losing anyone ever again, you're doing a disservice to the memory of your parents? And your brothers?'

A red mist of pain came over Leo's vision. 'It's precisely why I can't have what they never experienced.'

'Just because you survived, it doesn't mean that you have to forgo love and happiness in your own life. I know you don't love me, but some day you might meet someone and you deserve to be happy, Leo, you're a good man and you've created something worth sharing. It can be very lonely closing yourself off. I did it for three years to survive that marriage and it almost killed me.'

Leo couldn't think straight. He felt a multitude of things all at once. Panic. 'What will you do? Where will you go?'

Angelica looked resigned. Sad. He had done that to her. He'd also made her laugh and sigh and moan and—

'I'll go to Madrid. I think I'll buy a place there, to be near Mama and Paolo. Then I'll continue working while getting the charity up and running, and then, hopefully some day soon, retire from modelling and work full time on that.'

'And what about the rest of your life?' Leo wondered

why he was asking her this. He had no right. He should let her go.

She hitched up her chin. 'I want love, Leo. And I want a family. I want to bring up kids in an environment where they won't feel threatened. Of course there's no guarantee of peace and safety anywhere but some places are better than others. I want to be happy. Fulfilled.'

Those sentiments hit Leo hard. He thought of how it had affected him to see happy families—abject fear. 'You will be. You'll be an amazing mother and wife. And philanthropist. You'll change lives. You deserve to be happy, Angel.' Again, the words were like ash, souring his tongue.

'Thank you. I have something for you.'

She came towards him and held out a chain. It took him a second to register what was on it. A Murano glass heart, green, gold and orange, and her engagement ring and wedding ring.

He held out his palm and she dropped them into it. His head was full of the memory of her spotting that little glass heart in the window of a shop three years ago and how he'd immediately wanted to give it to her, so he'd gone in and bought it.

'I can't believe you still have it.'

'I kept it. But it's yours. And the rings are yours too. I donated the one Aldo gave me to charity, maybe you can do the same with these.'

Angelica had gone over to pick up her case and was walking to the door of the apartment before Leo came out of the past. He turned around. He felt as if he were under water, or watching her through glass. He wasn't even sure if she'd hear him if he called her name.

She stopped at the door and then, as if deciding not to say anything, she opened it and then she was gone. She didn't even look back.

Much like the day when she'd walked out that first time, he had an instinct to run after her. But how could he when he couldn't give her what she wanted?

Leo stood there for a long moment, with the necklace and rings in his hand. He looked at them stupidly. The heart seemed to glow, as if to mock him. *You have no heart.* No. It stopped beating the day his family lost their lives.

But he could feel it now, thumping heavily. As heavy as the stone in his gut. And the boulder in his chest. He felt very tired all of a sudden, as if he'd been trying to roll a ball up a hill for ever and it had just rolled down again, flattening him in the process. What was the name of that Greek king? Sisyphus?

Without really thinking, Leo went over to where Angelica had been standing at the window and looked out, and down. There was a water-taxi, and the driver was helping her in. She was wearing sunglasses and facing forward but he knew she was crying.

He'd made her cry. More than once. He'd also unwittingly fed her to Aldo, who had been so jealous of anything Leo loved that he'd wanted her for himself.

Leo's hand closed over the necklace and rings as that word resounded in his head. *Love. Loved. Love.*

Things were falling into place now, like pieces of a jigsaw. How out of it he'd been after Angelica had left— *after you rejected her.* How easy it had been for Aldo to take advantage of Leo's distraction.

Because Aldo had seen what not even Leo had seen. That he'd fallen in love with Angelica.

Of course he had. She'd turned his life upside down and inside out and he hadn't been able to handle it. So he'd rejected her rather than face the fact that he was a coward and too scared to seize love when it was gifted to him.

He looked down again to see the water-taxi pulling away from the landing pier, joining the traffic of the other water-taxis, boats and gondolas on the busy canal.

And suddenly, Leo knew that Angelica was right. About everything. What had she said? *I know you don't love me.* He'd fallen in love with her the moment he'd laid eyes on her.

He stuffed the necklace and rings in his pocket and ran.

Angelica couldn't even hide her sobs. She wondered how many women this water-taxi had ferried up the canal, sobbing noisily in the back, tears streaming under their black shades. The driver was ignoring her anyway, so presumably it wasn't that uncommon.

She was standing in the back of the boat, hanging onto the railing, calling herself all kinds of a fool for letting herself be hurt by the same man twice.

It took Angelica a minute to hear it over her crying and the engine and the general noises on the canal but then she heard, 'Angel! Stop!'

She looked around and had to lift her shades up to see better. In another water-taxi, closing in on them fast, was Leo, jumping up and down and gesticulating. He looked crazed. Angelica's mouth fell open.

The boat came alongside hers and Leo was shouting instructions to the driver to get closer. He stood up on the edge of the boat and Angelica squealed, 'What are you doing? You'll fall in!'

Leo braced himself and then leapt the short distance between the bobbing boats, landing in the back and almost toppling over. Angelica reached for him, catching him. She looked down. 'Your feet are bare!'

He'd run out straight after her? A tiny seed of hope bloomed in her chest. Leo caught her arms and glanced away for a moment to say something to the driver. Angelica didn't even register what, she couldn't look away from him.

He looked at her. She shook her head. 'What are you doing?'

'Am I too late?'

'For what?'

'To come with you.'

'Where?'

'Wherever you go, for ever.'

Angelica put a hand to her mouth to swallow a little sob. The tears kept coming. She shook her head. 'No, you're not too late. But…what are you saying, Leo?'

He smiled and wiped at her tears with his thumbs. 'I never want to be the cause of your tears again. What I'm saying, *amore mio*, is that I love you. I've always loved you but I was too scared to admit it, and we paid an awful price for my cowardice.'

Angelica turned her face into Leo's hand, kissing his palm. She looked up at him. 'It wasn't cowardice, it was self-protection.'

'You're right, by choosing to cut myself off from you,

from love, I'm insulting the memory of my family. They deserve better, *I* deserve better, and you definitely deserve better. But…do you really want me? After all I've put you through?'

'You have to ask me that? I love you, Leo. I never stopped. I want to have a family with you and grow old with you and see our grandchildren turn into adults.'

Leo's eyes shone suspiciously. 'I'll do my best. It might take me a while to get used to the notion. I used to have panic attacks when I saw happy families.'

Angelica interlaced her fingers with his. 'We'll go as slowly as it takes, my love, and before you even realise what's happening, we'll be a family.'

Leo kissed her as they swayed with the motion of the boat. Unbeknownst to them they had become surrounded by sightseers and paparazzi who regularly trawled the canal looking for celebrities.

The pictures of Leo and Angelica kissing passionately went viral. As did the pictures of him placing a Murano heart around her neck, and rings on her finger. Speculation was rife as to what had happened but there was no doubt, as the boat turned and went back to the palazzo, that they were very much in love and happy.

In fact, their obvious passion and love inspired a well-known designer to offer them an extortionate amount of money to appear in an ad campaign together, which Leo only agreed to once all the proceeds went to Angelica's new charity.

EPILOGUE

A MONTH AFTER their viral boat moment, they were back
in Venice to renew their vows with a formal blessing.
With the bride in full agreement this time. Angelica wore
a whimsical white ruffled gown and an antique lace veil,
with a bouquet of assorted seasonal flowers.

Paolo, who'd brought his girlfriend, walked Angelica
down the aisle and her mother was there too, with her
boyfriend. Fully reunited, safe and happy. Angelica was
grateful every day for that fact.

And then, three years later, they were back in Venice
on a holiday break. As they walked down the narrow
streets, something caught Leo's attention out of the corner of his eye and he stopped and faced a window.

In the reflection he could see himself with a two-year-
old boy, his son, Luca, on his shoulders. Angelica was
beside him, eating a gelato, and handing it up to Luca to
take a bite. Strapped to her front in a papoose was their
newest arrival, their baby daughter, Sara.

She'd told him it would happen without him even realising it, and it had. They were a family. And sometimes it
terrified him, but mostly it gave him an immense amount
of pride and love and awe. And hope.

He looked down at her and smiled. She saw their reflection in the window and she smiled too, because she *knew*.

She slipped her hand into his and they carried on their way, just one more family among the many others. Maybe a little more in love, and maybe a little bit happier, because of the journey it had taken for them to come back together again. For ever.

* * * * *

Did you fall in love with Bride of Betrayal?
Then make sure to catch up on
these other dramatic stories
by Abby Green!

"I Do" For Revenge
The Heir Dilemma
On His Bride's Terms
Rush to the Altar
Billion-Dollar Baby Shock

Available now!

ENEMY IN HIS BOARDROOM

EMMY GRAYSON

MILLS & BOON

For Granga

One of the first readers to take a chance on me

1931–2025

CHAPTER ONE

Diana

HE'S WAITING FOR ME.

The winding glass and stone lobby of Iceland's international airport is packed with families, business travelers, an excited-looking group of women sporting massive backpacks and hiking boots, and a harried young man trying to keep his gaggle of high school students together.

Pure chaos. The kind I usually enjoy when I'm traveling as I watch the people around me, spinning stories in my head about where they're from and where they're going. Reassuring myself there are good people in the world as I watch parents comfort overwhelmed children and friends excitedly make plans.

But as I hold Ari Valdasson's gaze, the chaos and stories fade. All I can hear is the thundering of my own heart. He looks just like he did three months ago when I turned and our eyes locked in the Metropolitan Museum of Art. White-blond hair, a chiseled face comprised of sharp angles and punctuated by dark brows. Towering above the other people in his orbit, clad in a tailored black suit molded perfectly to broad shoulders and a lean waist.

Beneath the crisp white shirt and perfectly knotted black tie is a sculpted chest dusted with curling blond hair. A chest I became intimately familiar with when I ripped his shirt open and slid my hands over every inch of heated skin I could find. When he eased me back into the mattress, muscles slick with sweat as he gripped my hips and pushed inside me, filling me until I couldn't tell where I ended and he began.

I swallow hard. I'd left the Baccarat Hotel in the early hours of the morning. I hadn't wanted to leave. I'd wanted to curl up in the circle of his arms, savor the heat of his body, see his smile when he first opened his eyes. Craved the intimacy so much it had scared me into slipping out of bed, grabbing my things, and sneaking out the door.

I'd been walking toward the subway, telling myself I had done the right thing, when Liam had called me. One of my two best friends. The only one still talking to me, and even then he's pulled back, too, ever since Aislinn withdrew from our lives. So when he said he had a favor to ask, I said yes without hesitation. There's nothing I wouldn't do for him.

Including pretending to be engaged.

What, I wonder for the umpteenth time, *are the odds the man I indulged in my* first ever *one-night stand with would turn out to be my best friend's half brother?*

My gaze darts back up. Dark blue eyes bore into mine. More like cold chips of ice set into an angular face marked by cheekbones I could sharpen an ax on. His sculpted, prominent jaw narrowing to pointed chin balances his sheer masculinity with a sense of regal authority.

Authority I'll be submitting to for the next four weeks as I serve as a corporate negotiator between AuraGeothermal and Hellas Global Shipping.

I square my shoulders and walk toward Ari. Each step tightens the muscles in the back of my neck. He watches me with icy detachment. So different than the man I met in the halls of the museum. A man who watched me with fire in his eyes and a confident tilt to his lips as he'd approached me with slow, measured steps.

The desire had been instant. But the warmth behind his smile, the attentiveness as we'd wandered the museum, had reeled me in. I'd never met a man as handsome as Ari, nor one who had put me so at ease even as he'd ignited desires I'd never experienced before. All reasons why I'd done the unthinkable and ended up in his bed that night.

Stupid reasons, stupid decisions, I remind myself as I close the last few steps between us. Decisions that will not be repeated.

"Miss North."

His voice rumbles through me, rich and deep, slow and deliberate. I inhale deeply, try to grasp onto some semblance of control, as I set my suitcase upright and hold out my hand.

"Mr. Valdasson."

He doesn't even glance down at my hand. Just stares at me. My first test.

I keep my hand out, tilt my head to one side. Yes, the man's seen me naked. Well, almost. As naked as I allow myself to get with another human being. But I'm not going to let that intimidate me, distract me from my job.

At last, he reaches out. His hand engulfs mine, his long, tapered fingers sliding over my skin and leaving little fires smoldering in their wake.

Oh, good job, I mentally snap at my hormones. If one handshake is all it takes to remind me of how he trailed his fingers down my neck right before he kissed me in Central Park, the next four weeks are going to be me roasting in a different kind of fire. One of the hell-on-earth variety.

He lets go. I resist the urge to smooth my hand over my pants and give him a polite smile.

"I didn't expect you to meet me."

He arches one condescending eyebrow. "I'm not here for you."

Well, screw you, too.

"I see."

"Georgios Xenakis's plane just landed."

My curiosity piques. Georgios Xenakis is the CEO of Hellas Global Shipping, the Greek shipping and logistics company currently battling out a contract with Ari's geothermal energy company. It'll be my job over the next four weeks to help them settle their differences, iron out a contract, and finalize their business deal.

Or as Liam once described my career, helping grown adults settle their squabbles. He's not wrong. I love what I do, helping businesses and executives overcome disagreements and find common ground so they can move forward. Using the communication and mediation skills I developed through years in foster care and honed in college to make a difference.

But every now and then, it feels like mediating a quarrel between toddlers.

The image of Ari Valdasson, CEO of one of the world's most respected geothermal energy companies, with a net worth exceeding well over a billion dollars, squabbling like a child makes my lips twitch.

"Something amusing, Miss North?"

"Not at all, Mr. Valdasson. I'm looking forward to working with you and Mr. Xenakis."

"Then, you won't mind altering our schedule for the day and meeting at two."

He's testing me. I wrap my professionalism around me like a shield, tilt my chin up, and give him a thin-lipped smile.

"Of course not."

Yes, we have a history together. A brief night we both went into knowing it wouldn't go beyond sunrise. It's been three months since I saw Ari. One month since Liam ended our supposed engagement. I'm very good at my job. I know I can make a difference here if Ari can put the past behind him and focus on business.

Ari turns and walks away. I stare at his back. Is he just this rude with me? If he's like this with everyone, it's no wonder Aura's negotiations with Hellas aren't going well.

He glances over his shoulder at me. "The limo's outside."

I shoulder my bag and follow in his wake. We step outside into a chilly drizzle. I grimace just as Ari looks back at me. His expression doesn't change, but I can feel his disapproval, cold and biting. I steel myself against it, against the faint, hurt pulsing beneath the layers of shield I've built up over the years.

He turns to face me. "Problem?"

Irritation creeps in. Even during the torturous dinner in New York where Liam introduced me to his long-lost half brother, Ari wasn't this abrupt or discourteous. He had been distant, focused primarily on Liam and asking questions about Liam's childhood with his adopted parents, his time in foster care after they passed in a car accident. They'd chatted business, college, careers. He'd asked a bit about my degree and my work. Formal, polite, as if I hadn't just been straddling his naked hips twenty-four hours prior.

None of the disdain or loathing seeping from him now.

"The only problem is if our history together is going to be an issue for you."

He leans down. I breathe in and immediately regret it. A heady scent fills my senses, smooth whiskey and cedar with a touch of earthiness. It sparks memories, memories of me gasping his name as my fingers delve into his hair, of the feel of his body against mine as our limbs tangled together, of his pressing the sweetest kiss to my temple as I drifted off to sleep.

"If an isolated incident from three months ago was going to be a problem, I wouldn't have hired you in the first place."

The warmth evaporates at the frigid ice in his tone. Frustrated by my own weakness, I raise my chin.

"Why did you hire me?"

"Undergraduate degree in business with multiple semesters abroad in Europe and Asia. Internship with a German logistical operations company the summer before your senior year. Graduate degree from Georgetown School of Foreign Service. Three years working for the New York City Economic Development Corporation, and now, just over a year with Lumen International Consultants."

I raise an eyebrow. "Impressive recitation, but also a little creepy."

"You have experience working with Greek companies as well as logistical operations with international transportation. Every reference I contacted spoke highly of you."

"Surprised?"

He cocks his head. "Given that you lied to me, yes, I'm surprised."

Guilt swells in my chest, a pressure pushing on my ribs as I try to take a deep breath. As far as Ari knows, I did lie. We spent hours together that night, from wandering the Met and strolling through Central Park to dining at an upscale French eatery before tumbling into bed. As the elevator doors had closed and the car had whisked up toward his penthouse, he'd pinned me against the wall, wrapping my wrists in one grip as his other hand had brazenly cupped my breast.

"Is there anyone *else*?"

I'd been telling the truth when I said no. But he didn't know that.

Couldn't know it.

"While I appreciate the vote of my confidence in my professional abilities," I say with as much calm as I can muster, "I'm not just referencing your and my personal history. Will your brother's and my breakup be a problem?"

The anger evaporates so quickly I wonder if I imagined it. Ari contemplates me with an almost bored expression.

"Your relationship with Liam, and its recent demise, are none of my concern. Neither does it affect your purpose here."

My heart drops. This is what I was afraid of that morning in his hotel room. Of how much I felt for a man so quickly, a man who made me feel me strong and beautiful, even as he cherished me. Not just with drugging kisses and mind-blowing sex, but with intimate words and devotion that had stripped me bare, left me aching to share more of myself with him.

He'd seduced me long before he'd ever touched me.

Whereas he, I think bitterly, *felt nothing more than old-fashioned lust.* Easily sated by a quick fling, the kind he probably has every time he travels internationally. He didn't feel anything for me that night. The only thing he feels right now is anger because I lied.

He doesn't even know half of the lies I spun. Lies, I remind myself as guilt tries to creep in, necessary to honor Liam's request and protect someone we both loved, even if she wants nothing to do with us.

"You're right, Mr. Valdasson. It is none of your concern." I nod to him. "I'm glad we're on the same page."

He turns and walks to the curb where a sleek black car is waiting. A young man in a black suit is standing next to the passenger door, dark brown hair combed back from a broad face dominated by a strong nose and a deep dimple in one cheek.

He steps forward. "Welcome to Iceland, Miss North. I'm Viktor, one of the chauffeurs for AuraGeothermal."

"Diana, please." I smile at him. "Thank you."

He glances at my backpack and messenger bag. "Do you have more luggage?"

"No, this is it."

Seven. That's how many times I moved between the ages of four and seventeen, bouncing from one foster care home to another. Each time I packed up my belongings—donated clothes, a couple notebooks, a toothbrush, a comb, and a ratty stuffed dog—and moved on. For the first two, everything went into a pillowcase. By the third, I was fortunate enough to get a donated pink backpack. It didn't make the moves any less painful. But it was slightly less humiliating. I learned to pack light in those years. A habit I can't break.

Viktor takes my bags and heads to the trunk. Ari opens the door for me. Suddenly tired—from the flight, from my interaction with him, from my own foolish feelings—I don't even look at him as I get in.

"Thank you, Mr. Valdasson."

"I'll see you at two, Miss North."

He closes the door. I stare ahead, breathing out a sigh of relief when Viktor gets in and pulls away from the airport. I don't turn my head, don't look back to see if Ari is watching. Partly out of pride, but partly because I need to establish that boundary for myself. He's my boss, not my lover.

As we move away from the airport, Viktor rattles off the features of the limo, giving me something else to focus on.

The interior is dimly lit with glowing blue lights, adjustable with a touchscreen. With a tap of my finger, I can turn on the built-in hot-stone massage or adjust the settings of the roof so I can view the sky as if I were standing outside instead of being whisked down a winding highway toward Reykjavik to the headquarters of one of Iceland's most well-regarded geothermal energy companies.

The car is nicer than some of the hotels I've stayed in.

Viktor meets my eyes in the mirror. "Is there any scent you'd like?"

"Scent?" I repeat with a slight laugh. "You're joking."

His grin is infectious, a welcome change from the granite-faced man we left behind.

"No, ma'am. Built-in aromatherapy."

"I'll pass for now, but that's incredible." Wind slams against the door of the car. I wince. "I read Iceland is famous for its windstorms."

"We are. Right now it's ten meters per second, or just over twenty miles an hour. Still safe for us to drive in this vehicle."

"Good to know."

Liam would have been quietly amused by the spa-like touches. Aislinn would have been touching everything and anything. Or at least the Aislinn I knew before this whole mess would have. The old Aislinn was bright, bubbly, able to see the good in everyone. Some might have mistaken her kindness for weakness. But on one of the darkest days of my life, she was there. She never wavered. Never shied away from my tears, my nightmares, the pain that wracked my body.

She was one of two constants in my life.

Until she wasn't.

My chest tightens, bands of tension pulling on my lungs until it hurts to breathe. Ten months. Ten months since Aislinn started to pull away. Nine months since we found out she was dating a man nearly twice her age, eight since the wedding.

And three months since Aislinn's husband, Dexter, accused Liam of being in love with her, threatened to destroy Aislinn's father, Liam, even me, if there was even the slightest hint of an affair.

Enter one fake engagement. It had cooled Dexter's jealousy and directed his attention away from us, giving Liam and I time to dig deeper into how such a selfish, creepy bastard ended up married to our best friend.

Except four weeks ago, Dexter dropped dead of a heart attack. We'd gone to the funeral, hoping his death would be the end of it. Cold, yes, but the man had been a brute. Yet aside from thanking us for coming and congratulating us on our engagement, Aislinn had been frosty, distant.

Nothing had changed. Liam and I quietly ended our so-called engagement. He's still convinced there's something going on. I know he's still digging into Dexter's past, into Aislinn's life the past ten months. But he's withdrawn, too, fixated on either his research or his decision to open his own firm.

My fingers brush the silver heart dangling from my wrist. The one engraved with Lucy's name. Liam had bought an emerald green collar, and Aislinn had purchased the dog tag. I'd seen it for the first time when Liam and Aislinn snuck Lucy into the hospital to see me after the attack. I'd lain there with a dog snuggled against my side, Aislinn's hand in mine and Liam standing guard by my bed. For the first time in years, I'd felt safe. Loved.

My eyes burn as I wrap my fingers around the heart. Most of the time I can grasp on to logic, remind myself this isn't like Aislinn. That Liam's right and something's wrong. But every now and then, doubt slithers in through the cracks and stirs up old fears. Fear that I will never truly be able to trust, to depend on anyone. That somewhere along the line I did something I wasn't supposed to, or didn't do enough, and Aislinn pulled away because of me.

I know that's not it. But God, it's hard to keep those intrusive thoughts at bay. Especially when I've just had a run-in with the man who's been haunting my dreams for the past three months. A man who's just reminded me why it's best to keep people at a distance. I've lost Aislinn. If Liam finds out I slept with his brother, will he feel angry? Betrayed?

Will he leave, too?

Another gust of wind buffets the car. I stare out over the surreal landscape of dark craggy rock and swirling mist, the wind shrieking across the lunarlike terrain. It's strange but beautiful, unlike any other place I've ever been to. If negotiations go smoothly, I'll extend my stay for at least a few days and explore a bit before I return to New York.

A part of me wants to tell Ari everything before I leave. Our night together may not mean anything to him. I want him to know I didn't lie. But he isn't worth risking that answer. No matter how attractive I find him, my feelings will fade with time. Loyalty, commitment, love, the things I have with Liam—and hopefully with Aislinn, too—are far more important.

I settle back in my seat and close my eyes. I have five hours until my meeting with Ari. Five hours to shower, eat, get dressed, and brush up on some research. He caught me off guard at the airport. But when I walk into his office this afternoon, I'll be ready. Ready to tackle the challenge of negotiations between Hellas Global Shipping and AuraGeothermal.

And ready to close the door on my interest in Ari Valdasson once and for all.

CHAPTER TWO

Ari

I STARE OUT over the calm waters of the Old Harbor. Esja's snow-covered, flat top looms in the distance. Boats put in and out of the harbor, ferrying fishermen and optimistic tourists armed with cameras, hoping for a glimpse of a humpback whale.

A sight as familiar to me as my own name. It eases some of the tension in my neck. Tension created by a woman I should have left in my past. A woman who thwarted my one attempt at salvaging any blood family I had left.

A woman whose memory has haunted me ever since I woke up to find her gone, except for the scent of jasmine lingering on her pillow.

Hiring her was best for AuraGeothermal. Not hiring her would have been giving her power, allowing one fleeting night to take precedence over the future of a company my grandfather built from the ground up. When negotiations with Hellas came to a screeching halt, I reached out to my contacts, who all recommended Diana's firm. And the firm recommended Diana. They confirmed everything Liam had bragged about during our dinner from hell three months ago—her graduate degree from Georgetown, the diverse range of companies she'd worked for, and most importantly, she'd worked with a Greek client last year and a shipping firm the year before that.

Her background check had come up clean. So, too, had the investigation I'd ordered for my own edification. Diana North was a well-respected professional with an exemplary work record, no financial issues, and an apartment in New York's SoHo District. Aside from a boyfriend in college, she'd had no serious relationships since college. There'd been no hint of a romance with anyone.

Including my half brother, Liam.

Grief punches through my defenses, tightens my gut a second before I wrestle it back under control. Four years, I'd been searching. Searching for a brother my bastard of a father had told me died with my mom during birth. And when I'd finally found him, I'd allowed myself a cautious flare of hope.

One that was snuffed out when Liam had walked into the restaurant in New York with Diana on his arm and his ring on her finger.

I slip my hands into my pockets. Curl them into fists. My brother spent the second half of his childhood suffering in foster care. He'd had the benefit of loving adoptive parents the first ten years of his life and a peaceful, middle-class life. But that had been yanked from him by a distracted driver blazing through a stop sign, leaving him alone, penniless, shifted from home to home while I lived in luxury, traveled the world, had access to the best education, cars, clothes, and homes money could buy. I earned my place at AuraGeothermal, but money helped get me there. Liam had scrounged and clawed his way to success. He should never have had to fight those battles. We should have been equals.

Instead, I had everything. He had nothing. Yet I sat across from him the night we first met, coveting the woman he proposed to hours after she snuck out of my hotel room. Their engagement may be over, but the guilt lingers. I wanted to tell him. So many times, I picked up the phone to call, text.

I couldn't do it. Couldn't ruin his happiness to assuage my own conscience.

I don't know who disgusts me more: Diana for lying and coming between my brother and me, or myself for still wanting her.

Seeing her in the lobby of the airport had sliced at me, a deep stab I hadn't anticipated. She'd walked down the crowded hall, one hand wrapped around the strap of her bag and the other tucked in her pocket, eyes drinking in everything around her. That glimpse of her amber gaze had catapulted me back to a gallery on a late summer afternoon and my first sight of a stunning woman in front of a painting of ballet dancers. Unlike the other visitors posing for pictures or glancing at the art before moving on to the next, she'd stood just a few feet away, arms crossed over her chest, naked grief written on her face. A grief I'd felt in my bones.

And then she'd turned. Turned and given me a slow, shy smile that had bolted through me like lightning. Not just heat, although there'd been plenty of that. There'd been something else beneath the desire, something deep. A recognition, a connection to someone who had experienced, and survived, loss.

I turn away from the window and stalk to my desk. No more thoughts of that night. Our meeting at the airport had been the first test. If she had tried to flirt, to tease or seduce, I'd have sent her back to New York on the first available flight. But she'd passed with flying colors.

I glance back out over the harbor. This is the best thing for AuraGeothermal. It's good for me, too, a chance to regain control and prove to myself, and Diana, what happened between us was nothing more than basic lust.

Once that's dealt with, I'll reach out to Liam. Explain, apologize, and hopefully build a relationship with the only blood family I have left.

My intercom buzzes.

"Sir, Miss North is here."

My pulse remains steady, my focus fixed on the task at hand.

"Send her in."

I move back to the window, my back to the door. The door swings in on a soft sigh, followed by a quiet click as it closes.

"Hello, Mr. Valdasson."

I steel myself against the sound of her voice, warm and rich, with that faint smokiness that ensnared me the first time we spoke. I slowly turn to face her. She's changed out of the striped T-shirt, leggings, and black jacket she had on at the airport. Now she's sporting cream-colored pants, a mint-colored jacket, and a darker green silk shirt underneath. Her thick, dark hair is pulled into a loose bun at the nape of her neck. Every inch the professional as she walks into my office, a brown leather briefcase in hand and a tan jacket draped over one arm. The only thing she kept on is a small silver bracelet with what looks like a heart dangling from it.

Counting this moment, I've seen Diana in person four times. Yet I know the shape of her face, from the slightly rounded chin I kissed to the defined jaw I grazed with my teeth. I know the cupid's bow in the middle of her full lips, the long column of her neck I teased with my tongue as she arched beneath me.

I know her body in a way I've never known another woman's.

Guð, I hate us both for that.

"I'm meeting with Georgios Xenakis and his team tomorrow morning."

She blinks. "Then, we better get to work." She motions toward a round table on the far side of my office. "May I?"

At my nod, she walks across my office. Confident, collected. She pulls a laptop and a notebook out of her briefcase before taking a seat. She looks up at me, her face schooled into a friendly, polite expression, ready to work.

"Tell me about your project."

I sit across from her.

"AuraGeothermal is already a leading authority in geothermal energy production. We provide a substantial portion of the energy used to produce our country's electricity through four plants in Iceland."

Her lips curve into a slight smile. "Something to be proud of."

Some of my tension eases. If she can see what this company means to our country, what it means to the employees who have given AuraGeothermal years of their lives, then perhaps this can be salvaged.

"It is. But the demand for green energy solutions is growing. We have an opportunity to meet this need and invest in other avenues."

"Potentially a lot of profit."

My fingers tighten on the armrest of my chair. "Along with long-term sustainability for AuraGeothermal, more jobs, and economic benefits for my country."

Diana jots something down in her notebook. "And part of this plan includes generating green hydrogen, converting into ammonia for transportation via Hellas Shipping to the Port of Piraeus in Greece, then changing it back into hydrogen before distributing it across Europe."

"Yes."

She flips back a few pages, studies her notes. "But negotiations have soured. You've invited Xenakis here as a last attempt to salvage the deal, including inviting him to your company's annual conservation gala."

"Yes."

A suggestion made by one of my executives. It wasn't a bad idea. I'd say it was even a good one, if Xenakis was the kind of man to be swayed by how much a company invested in its community. But given that most of our conversations have revolved around profit margins and expenses, I don't think he gives a damn about the impact AuraGeothermal has on the environment.

Her eyes flick up to me. "You think Georgios Xenakis is being unreasonable with his requests."

"No."

Confusion clouds her gaze. "Oh?"

"I know he's being unreasonable."

"Ar..." She pauses. "Mr. Valdasson, I've read over everything you shared with me. While Mr. Xenakis has a different way of communicating, his request to manage the shipping timelines and be involved in setting the price are reasonable requests."

I bite back a scathing retort, one that would have insulted not only Georgios Xenakis and his over-the-top verbosity, but Diana's ability to perform the basic functions of the job I'm paying her a substantial amount of money to do.

But I'm not going to let anger guide my actions. I don't need to give in to emotions. Not when the facts are clear.

"Are you aware of the history of AuraGeothermal?"

She nods. "Founded in 1965 by your grandfather. The role of CEO was handed over to your father, Gunnar Helgisson, in the early nineties. You successfully completed a takeover of the company four years ago."

"*Takeover* is a kind word." I lean back in my chair. "A professional term that doesn't touch on the near loss of something vital to our economy. It would have left hundreds of people stranded without jobs and Iceland at the mercy of international interests."

My tone is casual, but anyone with half a brain could pick up on the disgust underlying my words, the disdain for a man who nearly sank the empire his father built for his own greed. I should have more respect for the dead. But it's hard to summon any nostalgia for the man who treated my mother and me like trophies instead of family.

Diana doesn't flinch as she keeps writing. Her pen flies across the paper. She's calm, composed. No hint of the vulnerable, grieving woman who caught my attention in the museum, the lover who met my desire and demanded more.

This is good. A chance to replace the fantasy with reality. I don't want to use anger, or any emotion, to get her out of my system. My mother taught me a lesson she learned the hard way from my father: to feel something for someone was to give them power.

I will not cede power to Diana again.

"Your father was looking to expand internationally. Global expansion of AuraGeothermal and shifting resources from Iceland to the Continent."

I raise a brow. She's done her research. "Yes."

"That must have been difficult."

"The only difficult thing was realizing how close AuraGeothermal came to being downsized and having its resources split up." I smile coldly when she looks up. "I always knew my father was a bastard. My only surprise was that he had managed to conceal some of the worst details of his plan for so long." I turn my gaze to the harbor. "He had a stunning home on the water near the University of Iceland, vacation homes in the Mediterranean, a string of mistresses. Paintings any museum in the world would pay a small fortune for. And he still wanted more."

"Does Xenakis know about your father?" she asks.

"Anything that's public information, yes."

Diana bites down on her lower lip. I snuff out the flare of lust before it has a chance to grow.

"The experience with your father… It's impacted your ability to trust outsiders."

I stare at her. She stares right back. This is part of what drew me in that night. Her ability to pick up on subtleties and instantly see what I keep private from almost everyone else in my life. Back in New York, it was a novelty, refreshing and even calming to talk with someone I didn't feel the need to keep my guard up around.

Now, however, it's unsettling.

"My abilities are fine. The experience taught me a valuable lesson, one I continue to remind myself of as we navigate negotiations."

"Have you thought about telling Xenakis more about your father's trying to bring in outside—"

"No." My voice whips out. "This is a business negotiation, not storytelling time."

"But if he had more context—"

"This is not up for discussion, Miss North."

Her lips thin into a straight line, but she doesn't pursue it any further.

"I read your summary of what communications have been like between you and Mr. Xenakis so far. Do you have any hard copies, like emails, I could read?"

I don't like the idea of her reading my correspondence. But I know it's because I don't want my former lover getting deeper inside my head. I need to think of her as a negotiator, an employee.

I get up and print off the most recent back-and-forth between Georgios Xenakis and me. Diana accepts them, grabbing the corner of the paper so our hands have no chance of accidentally brushing. With her hair pulled back, I can see the tiny wrinkle between her brows, the narrowing of her eyes, the flickers of emotion as she reads.

Very different from our night together when her hair had fallen like a waterfall over her shoulders as she'd straddled my hips and sank down onto my cock. Hair cascading around her face and grazing my chest as I'd gripped her thighs.

Kristur.

I stand, turning away so she can't see my cock swelling against my pants. I cross back over to my desk and pull up the latest proposal for the ammonia cracking plant just outside the Port of Piraeus. I read it once, twice, noting several concerns as I resist the urge to look over at Diana.

It's lust, I remind myself. Simple lust, nothing more. I responded to her so strongly back in New York because I'd been on the cusp of a life-altering change. A moment I never imagined could be possible for over two decades. I was unsettled. Raw. Allowing myself to experience emotions, to feel hope, for the first time in years.

A chance I lost as soon as I let emotions get the better of me and allowed myself to feel something more for what was supposed to be a simple one-night stand.

"You're very direct in your communication."

I glance over at Diana. She's still sitting at the table, a printout of email in one hand, a pen grasped in the other as she jots something down in her notebook.

"Yes. And?"

She finishes her note and lays her pen down before standing and walking toward me.

"Xenakis's communications are more subtle." She holds up the printout. "Formal."

"A mask for unrealistic demands."

"Have you asked him why he wants more control over shipping and pricing?"

"I have." My lip curls at the memory. "More experienced. Shipping is his business, not mine. Either I trust him to do his part or I don't."

"Do you?"

The short answer is no. Xenakis wants more control over

my company. The last time that happened, AuraGeothermal nearly lost everything. And I almost lost the one thing I had in my life I cared about. I've spent the last four years rebuilding this company back up and serving as the leader my father should have been. I'm not surrendering anything to a dramatic billionaire who wants his own way.

But I also know we can't move forward until Xenakis and I break this stalemate. One of us has to give. I need Diana to do her job and get Xenakis to agree to my terms.

"Trust is not something that comes easily to me."

Darkness creeps into her eyes before she glances down at the paper in her hand. It wasn't a statement to hurt her or remind her of what happened. It's simply a fact.

"Ari—"

My chest clenches. "Mr. Valdasson."

Her head snaps up. Her lips thin into a straight line before she inclines her head.

"My apologies." Her voice is just as icy as mine. "I'd like to go back to the beginning, review everything that's transpired between you and Mr. Xenakis. I'd also like to review the proposals you've made so far, as well as any you've received."

I glance at the clock. "I have a meeting in an hour."

"Then, we'll cram as much as we can into that hour. After that, if I can have a space to work in, I can conduct some of my review by myself."

I can see why she's good at her job. But I don't like how quickly she's taking control.

"Thirty minutes. I have other things to attend to before the meeting."

"Forty-five."

I arch a brow. "This isn't a negotiation."

"It's the future of your company."

Anger flares. "Don't manipulate me."

Her eyes flash, russet fire. "I'm not. I'm stating facts. You want this to be successful? Then, I need to know more about what you want beyond what's on that contract. Details about your company's culture, the logistics. Details only you can provide."

I lean toward her. "I hired you, Miss North. You work for me."

"And I need you to trust me to do my job."

Silence falls. The words hang in the air between us. Her cheeks pale, but she doesn't back down.

"Thirty minutes, Miss North." I close the distance between us until I'm towering over her. "Take it or leave."

She stares at me. I can see the contemplation in her eyes, the desire to fight in the tense set of her jaw.

But then she sighs softly and shakes her head.

"This was a mistake."

"What?"

When she looks at me again, the pain in her eyes has me wanting to cross to her. I thrust my hands into my pockets and lean back, away from temptation. Away from her.

"You don't trust me. You'll never be able to trust me."

"Not personally, no. But this is business."

Her shoulders drop, as if the weight she's been holding up all this time has finally won the battle. "They're not mutually exclusive."

I smother the fire inside me, reach for the ice that has kept me in control all these years.

"You left my bed and walked straight into my brother's arms."

"I didn't lie about there being no one else. Liam told you, we got engaged later that day," she says, trying to hold on to her calm. Judging by the tremor in her voice, just barely.

"Yes, because a few hours makes such a difference." I smile coldly. "Tell me, Diana, had he already told you he cared for you, and sex with me helped clarify your own feelings? Or did you use me to give yourself a confidence boost before throwing yourself at his feet?"

She strides across the room and picks her briefcase up off the table, stuffing her laptop and notebook inside.

"We're done here."

I beat her to the door, slide between it and her. She glares up at me, color high in her cheeks.

"Let me out or I'll scream."

"Leave, and I'll sue you and your firm for breach of contract."

Her fury washes over me, hot and potent. It hits my skin, slips beneath. The air sharpens, not just with anger, but with the one thing I swore I would never let myself feel for this woman again.

Desire.

We stare each other down, wills clashing, breaths mingling. Her lips are parted, her breathing growing more ragged with each passing second. I don't have time to savor the bitter triumph of knowing I'm not the only one affected. Not when my cock hardens in an instant.

Her gaze drops to my mouth as she sucks in a shuddering breath. Just like she did in Central Park right before we surged together and kissed like we'd been starved for touch for too long. Never had a simple kiss rocked me so deeply.

Diana leans forward enough to bring her lips dangerously close to mine. She wants me. And I want her. I want her more than anyone I've ever desired in my entire life. It's a living, pulsing thing inside me, a need to take, to possess.

I should let her walk out. Put as much distance between us as possible and never contact her again. No woman has ever tested my discipline, let alone made me want to throw the rules I live by out the window. She's dangerous.

But letting her walk away would be failing. I need to get my cock under control and my mind back where it belongs.

Diana's effect on me is a concern. But AuraGeothermal needs her expertise.

And I need to do this. Regain command and exert my authority.

It nearly kills me. But I pull back. Just a fraction, but enough space to make it clear I have no intention of kissing her. Her eyes widen, then darken with embarrassment and shock a moment before she jerks back.

"Make your choice, Miss North."

Despite the blush of embarrassment on her cheeks, she tilts her chin up. Damn it if I don't respect her for standing her ground.

"You've already made it for me, Mr. Valdasson."

I ignore the bitterness beneath the rough huskiness of her voice as I step back.

"Then, let's continue." I move away, walk back to my desk and sit so she can't see the bulge in my trousers. I glance at my watch. "We're down to twenty-seven minutes."

It's interesting to watch her, to see her visibly wrestle her emotions back under control. But she does it with surprising ease. In a matter of seconds, the woman teetering on the verge of losing her equanimity is gone, replaced once more with the professional who strode into my office and tried to assert herself in my space.

She walks to my desk and sets her briefcase down, taking her things out once more with cool efficiency. When she finally sits, her face is smooth, her eyes opaque. She asks me questions in a voice bordering on robotic. No hint of passion, no emotion whatsoever.

I've won the first battle. Established my dominance, refused to cede control. Didn't let lust take over.

I've won. So why do I feel as though I just lost something important?

CHAPTER THREE

Diana

I LET MY head drop onto the back of the sofa. It's nine o'clock. The harbor is a dark void outside the window. There's a faint outline of the mountains on the far side of the water, the glimmer of snow on the peaks.

It was strange seeing the sun set just before four in the afternoon. I wonder what it would be like to be here in the peak of winter, when the longest bit of daylight is just over four hours. *Or,* I think with a small smile, *the days of the midnight sun when the sun doesn't fully set.*

But I won't be here for either. God willing I'll be out of Iceland in less than two weeks.

My heart starts to pound. It's been over seven hours since Ari delivered his ultimatum. I was so angry I almost punched him just so I could have the satisfaction of seeing him thrown off balance.

Angry, until my hormones decided to kick into overdrive and I nearly kissed him. I'd seen the desire in his eyes, heard it in the deepening of his breathing, felt it in the heat coming off his body in palpable waves. The moment we'd first kissed in Central Park had come roaring back, how his lips had fused to mine in a powerful, electrifying kiss I can sometimes still feel. It was like being woken from a bland, colorless dream world and yanked into a vivid, colorful existence where I had felt every beat of his heart against my breast, every line of tense muscle beneath my fingers as he'd kissed me like he'd never stop.

But today he'd pulled away, leaving me humiliated and exhausted. Our near kiss had been nothing but a minor occurrence in the grand scheme of his day. And unless I want to risk my career or the reputation of my firm, I am stuck working for the bastard.

My heavy sigh echoes in the room as I let my eyes drift shift. I could write a lengthy list about all the things wrong with my situation with Ari. But the most painful of all is realizing the first man I truly felt a connection with, not just in bed but emotionally, is unfazed by our attraction. Can turn it on and off like a damn faucet.

Another sign I did the right thing by walking away back in New York.

My fingers reach for the heart, my thumb caressing the silver. I've touched it so many times over the years Lucy's name is starting to fade. I should stop wearing it, put it in a jewelry box for safekeeping. But I can't. For so long, it had been a reminder of the moment my life changed for the better. Now, when my world is slowly crumbling around me, the charm is a tether to memories of happier times. Memories helping me keep my head just above the surface.

I open my eyes and sit up, scrubbing my hands over my face in a desperate attempt to wake myself up. After my and Ari's brief discussion, he'd left for his meeting with a terse order to email him a summary of what I did that day. It had taken considerable effort not to lob something at his head as he'd walked out. But regardless of how much I loathed the odious man, I had a job to do.

Thankfully, Ari's secretary, Malla, is much nicer than he is. Like Viktor, she either doesn't know or doesn't care I was engaged to Ari's brother. She offered me a small office on the floor below. A cozy space with ivory walls, a desk, and a whiteboard. I'd worked in there for several hours, reading through corporate policies, proposals, and pages of emails between Ari and Georgios Xenakis, as well as their various staff members. It had been a lot to wade through, but each page had helped me form a plan.

Until the soft shushing of heat blowing in through the vents abruptly stopped. Malla popped her head in a few minutes later to let me know the heating system had malfunctioned on that floor. But, she'd added with a smile, Mr. Valdasson was out for the rest of the night and she was sure he wouldn't mind me using his office.

I smirk. I'm sure he would mind very much, which gives me no small degree of satisfaction.

Slate gray walls threaded with strands of gold. Lights built into the ceiling that can be adjusted to a variety of brightness settings. There's the glass table and tufted black office chairs off to one side. Ari's massive desk in front of the bank of windows that overlook the harbor, a modern behemoth fashioned out of a giant slab of what looks like marble. Potted ferns soften the room, but just a fraction.

I would have preferred my bright, airy office back in New York with my leather chair and soaring bookshelves. But as far as workspaces go, this one's been satisfactory.

Especially when I think of how easily he walked away as I stood by the door, chest heaving and body throbbing as I tried to control both my anger and my desire.

God, I can't stand him.

Irritated with how much time I've spent thinking about him, I rise and drift over toward the windows. It's been cloudy ever since I arrived. I look up, peering at the night sky with the faint hope of seeing a glimmer of the Northern Lights.

"You won't see them tonight."

I bite back a yelp as I spin around. Ari stands in the doorway, feet spread, hands tucked in his pockets. Casual yet powerful.

"What?"

"The lights." He closes the door behind him. A shiver traces its way down my spine, a not completely unpleasant sensation. "I assumed you weren't keeping watch for me out there."

I arch an eyebrow at him. "What are you doing here?"

"I could ask the same of you."

The humiliation from earlier tries to creep back in, but I beat it back as I straighten my shoulders and maintain his gaze. If I have to jump in the harbor to cool my ridiculous lust, so be it, but I will not let him see the effect he has on me again.

"The heat went out on the lower floor. Malla said I could work in here since she didn't expect you back tonight."

He glances at the clock on the wall and frowns. "It's past nine."

"And you can read time. Well done."

I inwardly wince. I'm not usually snarky. My job is to help people overcome their differences, communicate, and solve problems, not poke at the ego of the man who hired me.

Thankfully, he ignores my sass. "Why are you here so late?"

I gesture toward the papers spread out over the glass coffee table. "There's a lot of work to be done. Reviewing what's been done so far, conduct a cross-cultural analysis, start drafting strategy recommendations."

He stares at the pile of papers.

"Did you sacrifice a forest?"

"I've been staring at a screen for hours." I walk over to the couch and sit, inwardly wincing at the three dozen pages arranged in piles. "I prefer paper."

My stomach does a long, slow roll as his gaze snaps back to me. "Why?"

I pick up a sheet outlining AuraGeothermal's proposal for who will manage the logistics of the shipping. "I like the feel of it. Something tangible. Something I can connect to."

I'd spent hours huddled in a corner of that godforsaken yard, curled up with a book from the school library as I hid from my foster father, Dale. Scribbling on faded notebook paper, seeing my thoughts turn into concrete words. When I'd see that sudden flare of drunken fury in Dale's eyes, I'd wonder if that night would be the night he hit me so hard I'd never wake up. In those moments, I comforted myself with the hope that one day someone might find my diaries jammed into the tin can littering the grass along the fence. Would know I existed if I suddenly disappeared.

My head jerks up. Ari is still watching me. Is it just my imagination, or has something in his face softened?

No. Trick of the light. The man can barely stand the sight of me.

"How late are you staying?"

I glance at own watch. Grimace when I see it's closer to nine thirty now. I didn't sleep well on the plane. Altogether I've been up for nearly twenty hours.

"Hopefully another forty-five minutes. But more if I need to. I want to be prepared for the meeting tomorrow."

I pause. I have an idea, a good one. He's not spitting fire at me, so I might as well give it a shot.

"What about starting with the geothermal tour tomorrow?"

Ari frowns. "Why?"

"You two have been battling this out over video conferences and in boardrooms. High-tension business environments. Putting you somewhere new could neutralize some of that tension and give you a chance to show Xenakis what you work on, not just tell him."

He doesn't reply, just stares. The mask is still firmly in

place. The same mask he wore during the dinner with Liam. Detached, imperial, unreachable.

So different from the man I locked eyes with in the Met. The man who had gazed at me with a masculine appreciation I'd felt all the way down to my toes, and an understanding of the sadness I'd been fighting. I'd seen it plenty of times before, but that night the grief had hit hard. Aislinn being so far out of reach, Liam burying himself in work, and a painting that reminded me of a simple childhood rite of passage I'd desperately wanted. Reminded me of the day I found out I wasn't wanted.

I'd turned. The connection between Ari and I had snapped into place as his understanding had soothed my fraying edges. I had known in an instant that the handsome man in the museum recognized what I was battling, saw his own grief and loss reflected in me. And then he did the one thing I hadn't realized I'd so desperately needed.

He'd stayed.

I've never believed in love at first sight. I know better than to believe in fairy tales. But if anyone was capable of making me think happily-ever-after could be a reality, it would be Ari.

Was Ari, I mentally correct myself. And it hadn't been real. It had fallen apart the next day. Even if our connections to Liam hadn't destroyed any possibility of more, Ari had no interest in me beyond casual sex. After my one failed attempt at a relationship in college, I hadn't done much dating. But I'd made a promise to myself that if I did find someone I could let down my guard with, could imagine a future with, it would be someone who could reciprocate, let me in and share himself with me.

Ari isn't that kind of man. I would always be kept in a constant state of guessing whether or not he was going to leave.

"All right."

I blink in surprise. "Oh. Okay." I stand and start to gather my papers. "What time would you like me there?"

"Eight."

Lovely. By the time I make it back to my hotel and shower, I might be able to squeeze in a few hours of sleep before I have to get up and get ready.

"Problem, Miss North?"

I bite down on my tongue so I don't stick it out at him.

"Not at all." I slide the organized stacks into various folders. "Just a little tired."

"I don't require you to work this late."

"I know." I glance up at him as I put the folders into my leather bag. He's watching me, or rather, watching my hands as I pack everything up. "But this is part of the job. Work until it's done."

I finish arranging my tote and head for the door. Ari crosses the room and beats me to it, but this time he opens it for me.

"Nice change of pace," I mutter as I start to walk by.

"Why did you and Liam break up?"

I stop so fast I nearly stumble.

"What?"

Ari leans against the doorframe, his hair nearly silver in the dim light.

"Why did you end your engagement?"

I swallow hard. "It was a mutual decision."

He leans down until his nose nearly touches mine, even closer than this afternoon.

"Why?"

The last time we were this close, we were tangled up in bed together. Which does absolutely nothing for my self-control. I tilt my chin back to better meet his gaze, show him I'm not afraid.

But all it does it bring our mouths closer together.

"We realized we were better off friends."

"And who decided that?"

His breath feathers across my lips. God, I can smell him, that delicious blend of whiskey and cedar, power and wildness. My traitorous body tries to pull me forward, just like before, but I'm prepared this time. I stand straight and tall even as that delicious, curling heat makes my body languid.

"We both did."

"Did you tell him about us?"

Icy guilt douses my lust in one fell swoop.

"No."

"Feeling guilty?"

I cock my head at him. "Guess that makes two of us."

My barb hits its mark. His blue eyes turn as cold as glaciers as I stalk past him.

"Eight o'clock."

As I turn around, he closes the door in my face, leaving me in the atrium outside his office. I force myself to walk at a sedate pace to the elevators, to not look back over my shoulder at his door.

I wanted to kiss him. Again. Even though I resisted, I hate myself for that, especially when he was just using my reaction to solicit information. I let my guard down for two seconds because he accepted my idea for starting tomorrow off at the geothermal plant and because he was asking questions about why I liked paper.

I quicken my pace as I walk out into the dark night. I sneak another glance upward. But all I see is a blanket of low-lying clouds.

If I'm trying to find a positive, at least I was right. The man I started to fall for that night isn't real. Really, Liam saved me with his proposal. Saved me from getting hung up on a man who is the last person in the world I should be having romantic thoughts about. Ari is pretentious. Arrogant. Rude.

My fingers tighten on the strap of my bag. Even though we're completely wrong for each other, and he has no interest in me besides what I can do for his company, it still bugs me that I was so wrong about him. Growing up the way I did made me highly attuned to people and their personalities, their moods and triggers. The Ari I met that first night in New York was powerful and confident, yes. But he was also respectful, charismatic, generous.

I'm not the first woman to be blinded by a man's true nature because I find him attractive, to fall for an act. It's just a blow to my ego, both personally and professionally. If I just keep reminding myself of how truly cold-blooded Ari Valdasson is, this will stop.

It has to.

CHAPTER FOUR

Diana

STEAM RISES FROM the snow-covered landscape. Tall silver towers rise up to the sky, the bases shrouded by mist. Ripples cross the surface of a small lake on the other side of the parking lot even though the temperature is below freezing. The sun hasn't risen yet, although I can see a haze of gold along the peaks of the mountains. A light snow started just before Viktor turned the car into the parking lot of AuraGeothermal's Snjóheiði, the first geothermal plant Ari's grandfather built. Now the snowflakes spin and dance as they fall to the ground, creating a faint dusting of white on the path curving from the parking lot to the main entrance.

I glance down at my watch. Ten 'til eight. I'll start waking up in a couple minutes. But right now, I just want to enjoy the moment of seeing something I've never seen before.

It took me over two hours to fall asleep last night. Every time I closed my eyes, I saw Ari. Felt his weight on top of me as he made love to me, then next to me, as I allowed myself the rarity of sleeping with a lover for the first time in years. My romantic experiences have been few and far between since Brian.

My chest clenches. Brian had been sweet, a biology major with aspirations of becoming a doctor. We'd met in a communications class. He'd been cute, with a boyish smile and an infectious laugh. When he'd invited me to coffee, I'd been flattered. When he'd kissed me, I'd felt the faintest fluttering of butterflies, a whisper of possibility. Maybe I could let down my guard, let someone in.

Six months in, I hadn't let it down enough. Brian had wanted more, had wanted to deepen our relationship much quicker than I was ready for. It hurt him that I wouldn't let him see me naked, wouldn't share the scars from Dale's attack.

So he left. Like my mother. Like the constant rotation of foster parents and case managers.

Like Aislinn.

That's why, I reminded myself at one o'clock in the morning, my experience with Ari packed such a punch. After Brian, I'd dated casually, only allowing a couple to progress to physical intimacy. Like Brian, my previous lovers had wanted more, so I'd ended things before they could. It had been nearly two years since I'd kissed someone, much less gone to bed with them. My hang-ups with Ari were rooted in satisfying sex—really, really satisfying sex—and nothing more.

My brain and my heart argued off and on until I finally succumbed to sheer exhaustion, only to be yanked awake five hours later by my alarm.

At least the view was worth getting up for. Watching the snow glittering in the air, the steam swirling, is a balm I desperately needed. Already the days are slipping by. I hope I'll at least have some time to explore. I've always enjoyed the places I've traveled to. Some have stood out more than the rest. The ivy-covered storefronts and lantern-lit streets of Montmartre in Paris. The meandering lanes between the stone buildings of Heidelberg in Germany. The striped flower fields of Japan's Biei.

But as I think about leaving Iceland, returning to New York, I feel vaguely unsettled.

"Good morning."

The gravelly voice yanks me out of my reverie. I turn to see an older man with a weathered face and thinning salt-and-pepper hair standing a few feet away. His head is tilted to one side, a slight smile lurking about his mouth, even as his deep-set eyes darken with suspicion.

Georgios Xenakis. CEO of Hellas Shipping, worth close to two billion dollars. Father of three, widowed in his midthirties when his wife died four weeks after giving birth to their daughter, never remarried.

I run through the facts in my head as I smile and hold out my hand.

"*Γειά σου*, Mr. Xenakis."

His eyes widen in surprise as he steps closer and takes my hand.

"*Γειά σου*, Miss North. You speak Greek?"

"I've just spoken two of the ten words I know."

"You know more than most. I recognized you from the picture on your firm's website." He releases my hand and gestures to the surreal landscape around us. "What do you think?"

A small burst of energy slips through me. This isn't just a simple question or making polite conversation. It's a test. I can see it in the way he holds my gaze, his own eyes assessing and watching me for any hint of deceit. The way he leans in slightly as he searches for deeper insight versus casual observation.

"AuraGeothermal is an efficient operation." I gesture to the collection of buildings just beyond us. "Their commitment to reducing their environmental footprint has been very successful to date. Reduced water usage, land restoration, supporting local businesses in the nearby towns." I hold his gaze. "The company is dedicated to their causes."

"Dedicated, yes." Xenakis's smile remains in place, but his

eyes harden. "To their causes here. To Iceland. Collaborating with outsiders, however, is another matter."

"There are challenges with communication—"

"Challenges?" Xenakis snorts. "Miss North, I've never met a man so dismissive, arrogant, and blunt as Ari Valdasson."

You and me both.

"I understand. But," I add before Xenakis can retort, "what Mr. Valdasson and AuraGeothermal are trying to do align with your own beliefs about green energy. I wouldn't be here if I didn't think there was a solution to both your concerns."

He rolls his eyes. "The only reason I'm still here, Miss North, is because the shipping time between the Port of Piraeus and Reykjavik is half the time it would take for me to ship from California or Indonesia." His hands come up, spread apart to illustrate the vast distance between said destinations and Greece. "That and Mr. Valdasson's offer to finance the majority of the construction of the ammonia cracking plant was appreciated by my government."

"But you're here. And now so am I."

I hesitate. Ari's hostile takeover of Aura from his father is public knowledge. But the details Ari shared last night, the ruin his father had almost inflicted to ensure the deal went through, can only be found in a smattering of local articles published here in Iceland. The international coverage pitted father against son, progress against isolationism.

"There's a lot of work to be done, and a lot of misunderstandings to get through. But," I add, "I believe a path can be forged."

Xenakis's phone rings. His face tightens as he pulls his phone out of his pocket, then eases as he reads whatever's on screen.

"My apologies."

"Everything all right?"

"Yes. Yes," he repeats, as if to reassure himself. "You were saying?"

"Miss North."

Ari's voice rings out, making Xenakis and I both turn. My breath catches in my chest. He's wearing a navy blue suit that deepens the color of his eyes. With the snow swirling around him, he looks like a Viking prince dropped into the twenty-first century.

Geez. I have been reading one too many historical romances.

"Mr. Xenakis."

I manage to hide my wince at Ari's cold greeting. Xenakis tenses next to me.

"Mr. Valdasson."

Ari's eyes dart to me. "Miss North. I see you and Mr. Xenakis are already acquainted."

"We met five minutes ago." I state the facts, keep the emotion out of my voice. "We were discussing some of the initiatives AuraGeothermal has made in reducing their carbon footprint and investing in local communities."

Ari's gaze flickers between Xenakis and me. "If you'll follow me, we're ready to begin the tour."

Xenakis and I glance at each other as we follow Ari up the path. Xenakis raises his eyebrows in an I-told-you-so gesture. I stay silent. There's nothing I can do in the moment. Yes, we're off to a tense start. But that doesn't mean negotiations can't be saved.

The main entrance of AuraGeothermal is comprised of glass and timber. Amid the backdrop of snow and mountains, it reminds me of a glacier jutting out of the hillside. We walk into a surprisingly warm lobby.

"Low-emissivity glass," Ari comments as he notes me staring out the massive windows. "Triple-glazed for thermal insulation and soundproofing, tempered to withstand the windstorms. Everything we do here is to reduce our own energy consumption even as we generate it. That and ensuring we create a positive environment for our employees."

The pride in his voice is almost imperceptible. But I hear it, feel it resonate deep within my chest as we follow him to a crescent-shaped desk in the middle of the lobby. A young man with a round face and bright blond hair waits.

"Good morning, Atli. How's Sigrún doing?"

Atli's cheeks flush a deep red as a huge, toothy grin spreads across his face. "As well as one can at seven months with twins, *herra*."

Ari's gaze sharpens. "Tell me if you need anything. Either of you." A ghost of a smile crosses his face and makes my chest clench. "Or rather all four of you."

"Twins?" I say out loud.

Ari's head snaps around, eyes narrowed, but Atli's smile grows until his eyes crinkle into slits.

"I couldn't believe it either. A boy and a girl." He slightly shakes his head and reaches beneath the desk, pulling out two dark blue bags emblazoned with AuraGeothermal's logo— wavy bands of pale blue and white to symbolize the Northern Lights, with the company's name written below in bold print. He hands Ari the bags, which he passes to Xenakis and me.

"Hard hats and safety goggles for later in the tour."

Xenakis glances at the young man. "Is he our tour guide?"

Ari smiles thinly. "You'll be with me for the tour."

"You?"

"Yes."

Xenakis is surprised. But beneath his bluster and frustration, I think he's pleased. Pleased and intrigued.

The tour takes over an hour. And it's fascinating. I know of the concept of geothermal energy. But seeing it in person, from the geothermal wells drilled deep down into the earth's crust to the huge steam turbines that convert the thermal energy into power, makes me even more appreciative for the work AuraGeothermal does.

Something else I didn't expect is Ari. It's hard to reconcile the man who professed to care about his employees last night and the arrogant CEO I've been dealing with on a professional level. Yet every time we encounter someone, he knows their name, greets them like he did Atli. A few times he asks questions, remembering details like children's birthdays or someone's recent loss of a parent. He's still reserved, professional. But the personal investment is obvious. Ari doesn't just know AuraGeothermal inside and out. He knows about the people. Cares about them.

Xenakis notices, thank goodness. As we walk, the tension bleeds out of his shoulders. His surly expression gradually disappears, replaced by genuine curiosity.

I don't want to get my hopes up. But maybe, just maybe, this is the start of getting negotiations back on track.

Ari walks us into the lobby at the end of the tour and points to a flat space in the distance.

"The future sight of our green hydrogen-and-ammonia production facilities."

Xenakis tenses next to me. My hope evaporates in an instant.

"Have you considered my offer?" Xenakis's voice vibrates with suppressed anger.

Ari stares at him. "It's still under advisement."

I can practically hear Xenakis's teeth grind.

"If I may ask, Mr. Xenakis," I break in. "What offer?"

"Mr. Xenakis has generously offered to partially finance the new construction of our facilities here in Iceland and the ammonia cracking plant in Greece."

Ari's flat tone tells me he thinks the offer is anything but generous.

"Mr. Valdasson?" Atli motions to Ari. "Sir, you have a call from the Energy Authority."

"If you'll excuse me."

As soon as Ari is out of earshot, Xenakis whirls around.

"This, Miss North, this is why this entire deal is in jeopardy." His face reddens. "I should have known better than to do business with a man who threw his own father out of the company."

"Mr. Xenakis." I keep my voice firm, calm. "I understand you're upset. But Mr. Valdasson's takeover had nothing to do with trying to take control of something that belonged to his father."

"It doesn't matter. He sacrificed family to keep the company isolated. People warned me against working with him." He throws his hands up in disgust. "I should have listened."

"Are you familiar with the details ?"

"Yes. Gunnar Helgisson wanted to expand AuraGeothermal overseas with the help of an American company. Valdasson didn't like that." Xenakis jabs a finger in my direction. "Rather than work with his father and try to find a solution, he influenced the board to vote Helgisson out." He shakes his head in disgust. "The man even gave up his father's name and took another. How can I trust someone willing to be disloyal to his own family? Someone who doesn't believe in legacy?"

The situation is spiraling, and spiraling fast. I mentally ask for forgiveness and take the plunge.

"Did you happen to read any of the articles that that were published here in Iceland?"

Xenakis's sullen glare gives me my answer.

"The company Helgisson was working with was well-known for encouraging successful firms to expand into other markets while downsizing their original locations. A lot of people lost their jobs because of that organization. Entire communities dried up when companies shut their doors and moved to another city or country." I pause, trying to think of how best to phrase my next words without betraying my promise. "I wouldn't be surprised if a similar situation arose with the deal Helgisson was working out to expand Aura-Geothermal."

Some of the red disappears from Xenakis's face. He releases a long, shuddering breath.

"I was not aware of that. Only that Helgisson had a vision that differed from his son's."

"Mr. Xenakis."

I flinch, turn to see Ari standing just behind us. His face is still set in that calm, expressionless mask. But his eyes are furious.

"If you'll excuse me a moment, I'd like to speak with Miss North."

Xenakis inclines his head to Ari before offering his hand to me.

"Thank you, Miss North." His grip is warm, his handshake so enthusiastic that it makes me smile. "For everything," he adds with a gravity that eases some of my tension. Ari might be angry. But maybe, just maybe, Xenakis will take the hint I gave him and make something of it.

"You're welcome."

I follow Ari through the lobby, down a winding corridor lined with canvas prints of the plant in various stages of construction over the years. He leads me into a small conference room and shuts the door. The window overlooks a milky blue geothermal pool.

I turn and face Ari. He's leaning against the door, hands tucked casually into his pockets. But there's nothing casual about the way he's staring at me, fury glinting in his ice-blue eyes.

"What were you and Xenakis talking about?"

Irritated, I arch an eyebrow. "Swapping recipes."

His glare sharpens. "I overhead some of it, Miss North."

"Then, why bother asking?"

"What I shared with you about my father was said in confidence."

"And I didn't say a word about anything you told me that night," I shoot back. "I encouraged Mr. Xenakis to read some of the more detailed Icelandic articles so he could better understand why a son might remove his father from his own company. You know, instead of hoarding information and refusing to even discuss a collaboration."

"I told him his offer was under advisement."

I roll my eyes. "You might as well have given him the middle finger."

"Don't think that because you've been reading up on geothermal energy you know what's going on here, because you don't," Ari snaps back. "I hired you to help Xenakis see reason, not side with him."

"You should have hired me because I've negotiated other deals that hinged on issues like this. You want to dictate how Xenakis runs his business, but you want him to stay out of yours? How is that fair?" I soften my voice. "Family and honor are important to Xenakis. He has three children of his own, numerous siblings and cousins. The disagreement and the takeover are public knowledge. But the details behind it—the downsizing, the outsourcing—aren't talked about outside of Iceland."

"I'm not using my father's betrayal as a sob story to influence business dealings."

"It's not…" I pause, breathe in deeply through my nose as I try to find some balance. "Relevant details aren't an emotional manipulation. They're facts. Your father tried to ruin a company you care about, and the people who have been loyal to it, for money. You're apprehensive about letting someone else in. Trusting them. It's understandable. But instead of presenting the challenges you've overcome, you come across as cold, uncompromising, and overly blunt."

"Stop the psychoanalysis. The *facts*," Ari says as he walks around the table, "are that Georgios Xenakis can come across as charming and persuasive. Qualities that mask his need for dominance."

"Are you seeing Mr. Xenakis for who he really is? Or are you comparing him to your father?"

His eyes harden into sharp chips of blue ice. "Speaking of *blunt*."

"If your history with your father is impacting your negotiations with Mr. Xenakis, it's either something that needs to be addressed, or you need to reevaluate if you can work with him."

"Xenakis may not be my father, but he has qualities that have my guard up. As it should be," he adds when I start to speak. "You're young, Diana. You don't know the kind of pain men like my father can wield."

My last memory of Dale rears its head. The almost feral look on his face as he loomed over Lucy whimpering in the snow. I can taste the sharp bite of fear. Hear the crack of his belt wielded as a whip. Feel the burning pain in my back and Lucy's trembling body in my arms.

"You'd be surprised."

I realize too late I've said the words out loud. Ari's step slows. He tilts his head to one side, his eyes assessing. I give myself a mental shake to pull myself out of the past and quickly steer the conversation back to business.

"If Xenakis is wanting more say in operations simply for profit or power, we'll deal with it. But," I add, "I truly think there's more than that."

"Helvítis."

He rolls his eyes and looks away. Anger flares inside me.

"Disagree with me all you like, but don't disrespect my opinion." I square my shoulders and step forward. "I'm entitled to one after the years I've spent doing what I do, and doing it successfully."

"You are entitled to your opinion. It doesn't make you right."

I stare at him. It's hard to reconcile the man standing in front of me with the one I saw just a few minutes ago, the one who remembered that Drifa in the geology department just had a granddaughter or that Einar the security guard was going on vacation next week.

I've dealt with mean executives before. Boorish finance officers, lying lawyers, and cutthroat revenue officials. But I've never dealt with one whom I have a shared history. As much as I wanted to quit last night, I won't. Not just because of the threat of a lawsuit, but because I need to prove to myself that I can do this. Do the job I love and put Ari in the past.

But I need a break. Distance.

"I'm done talking about this right now."

"We're not finished—"

"We are." I pause. "For now. This conversation isn't going anywhere. You have a guest waiting, one who you at least claim you want to work with, although I'm starting to have serious doubts about that. We have nothing kind to say to each other. We have a meeting scheduled later today. So for now, let's just walk away."

"Yes, you're good at that."

I freeze. Then I laugh, a low, harsh chuckle.

"Your brother may fit the literal definition of *bastard*, but you more than match the figurative one, Mr. Valdasson."

I brush past him and walk out of the conference room. By some miracle I remember my way through down the hall, around the corner, and into the lobby. Xenakis is thankfully nowhere to be seen. I force a smile for Atli and ask him to call Viktor and let him know I'm ready to leave.

I'm nearly at the door when heat flares across the back of my neck. I glance over my shoulder to see Ari standing by the stairs, his gaze fixed on me. I turn around and walk out.

The cold air fills my lungs, brisk but stimulating. The snow is falling faster. I walk through a cloud of swirling flakes and mist towards the parking lot. Viktor pulls the car up to the sidewalk and gets out to open my door.

"How'd you like the tour?"

"It was very enlightening." I muster a smile. "I have a new appreciation for the field."

"Glad you liked it." Viktor closes my door, circles around, and climbs in. "I hope to be working there myself in two years."

"Oh?"

Viktor meets my curious glance in the rearview mirror. "Mr. Valdasson is paying for my degree at Reykjavik University as long as I work for AuraGeothermal for four years." He grins. "Not that I ever plan on going anywhere else with the pay and benefits they offer."

I lean back into the leather seat. Who is Ari Valdasson? The generous, charitable CEO? Or the arrogant, selfish leader who puts on a mask and plays a role?

Worse still, why do I care so much?

I stare out the window and watch the snowy landscape pass by.

CHAPTER FIVE

Ari

I ARRIVE BACK to my office just a few minutes before my meeting with Diana. I hadn't planned on spending all day at the plant. But right after Diana had left, I found Xenakis talking with one of my engineers. He'd been surprisingly cordial—the friendliest he's been since the first time we met nearly a year ago. He didn't bring up my father or the take-over. But he did ask more questions about the hydrogen and ammonia facilities here in Iceland. There were no signs of suspicion or anger. Just genuine curiosity.

Through it all, from my conversation with him to the un-expected visit with our maintenance department and a trip to our plant farther north, I thought of Diana.

I punch the button for the elevator. I was hard on her. I'm angry with her, but I'm also angry with myself. And that anger is seeping into how I deal with her.

Damn it, she's right. Why did I bring her on board if I'm not going to let her do her job? She's made more headway in twenty-four hours than I've made in months. I'm not shar-ing the details of my father's betrayal. But letting down my walls a little—letting Xenakis see the personal side of our company—is something I can do.

The elevator doors open. I tense as Diana raises her head and her gaze meets mine. She's wearing the same navy suit she had on earlier: a sleek blazer and pants that follow the long length of her legs. She has on a thick black coat, her maroon leather messenger bag hanging from her shoulder. Her fingers tighten around the strap.

Cold, icy beauty. None of the warmth I saw in her interactions with Xenakis, the friendly smiles she gave my staff as she listened to everything they had to say.

Disconcerting to see traces of the woman I'd bonded with so quickly and unexpectedly in New York. A woman who had listened, seen parts of me I'd thought long buried. When she'd asked questions, it wasn't out of pretense or design. It had just been her. Her quiet, genuine warmth had drawn me out from behind the wall I'd erected decades ago.

Now she stares at me with chilly professionalism.

"Mr. Valdasson," she says, her voice professional but cool. "I left my report for the day on your desk. If you have any questions, I'll be in at eight tomorrow."

I almost miss the glimmer of pain in her eyes. It's faint, but it cuts me, sharper than any knife. She starts to brush past me. A fist grabs my heart, squeezes.

"Stay."

The look she gives me would be amusing if she weren't so irritated. "I just put in a twelve-hour day. I'm tired. And I'm hungry," she says with a slight sigh. "Malla told me you had to drive up north today, so I know it's been a long day for you, too. I just want to—"

"Let me buy you dinner," I interrupt, not letting her finish.

Her mouth drops open. "What?"

Business, I tell myself. This is just business, reestablishing a working relationship with a woman who just might be able to salvage this deal.

"I had an interesting conversation with Xenakis after you left," I continue. "The conservation gala is in two days. It'll be the first time I have another opportunity to talk with him outside of a traditional business setting, and I'd like your opinion."

She stares at me for so long that I wonder if she's going to say no. Then a slight smile crosses her face—one that eases some of the tension inside me.

"You're already paying for my expenses. Alcohol not included," she adds with a not-so-subtle sassiness.

"I'm assuming you've never tasted Brennivín before."

She bites her bottom lip, thinking. "Why the sudden change of heart?"

Her voice is quiet, her tone curious with the faintest hint of vulnerability that tugs at me.

"I disagree with you on how to best approach this," I say finally. "But whatever you said to Xenakis today worked."

Seconds drag out. Then, finally, she answers.

"All right."

The restaurant is only a couple blocks away, tucked down a winding cobblestone street reserved only for pedestrians. Diana's eyes widen as we walk down a flight of stairs flanked by two ponds with shallow fountains gurgling despite the freezing-cold temperature. Lanterns glow on either side of the doors, which look more like the entrance to a fortress than one of Reykjavik's highest-rated restaurants.

"Wow," she murmurs.

It's hard not to take pleasure in the touch of excitement in her faint smile. As we walk inside, she takes in the drapes of burgundy silk across the ceiling, the dimly lit chandeliers, and the gleaming hardwood floors with wide eyes. One side of the restaurant houses long tables with tufted leather chairs, reserved for large groups and boisterous families. The bar is a work of art, with slightly darker wood than the floors, trimmed with ornate carvings that gleam in the dim light. Behind the bar, glass shelves host bottle upon bottle of blended wines, liquors, beer, and some of the world's finest spirits.

To the right are smaller, more intimate tables, with chairs on one side and booths tucked into small recesses in the wall on the other. The same fabric that drapes across the ceiling falls in panels to the floor, providing pockets of privacy.

Our waiter seats us. I order shots of Brennivín for both of us. When the waiter sets down the glasses, Diana eyes them curiously.

"So, do you just…do it?" she asks.

I smirk at her. "Have you never had a shot?"

"It's an honest question," she responds. "Do you just toss it back? Chase it with anything?"

"Sounds like you might be more of an expert than I am."

She smiles, pure, unabashed pleasure lighting up her face. Even during our time in New York, I never saw that on her face. I don't quite know how to handle it, nor do I know how to handle the tightening in my gut.

"Working as an international corporate negotiator means I've been to a lot of places and experienced a lot of different kinds of food and drinks." She picks up the glass. "People bond over food."

Something in her tone catches me—a hint of the sadness I glimpsed on her face as she stared at the painting of the dancers back in New York. I know from both our dinner with Liam and the background check I'd had run that they'd met in foster care. That she'd been in the system for years. Had she dreamed of taking dance lessons as a little girl? Or maybe she'd taken them once, in another lifetime before everything had changed.

She picks up her shot glass and holds it up. "Toss it back," she says with a smile, then proceeds to do just that. I watch, wide-eyed, as she downs the shot.

"Oh. That's different," she adds, blinking.

"Iceland's national drink." I don't even bother to hide my

slight smile at her unexpected streak of adventurousness. "Nicknamed the Black Death."

Her eyes flick up to mine. "You're not serious?"

"Deadly."

She stares at me for a moment, then throws her head back and laughs. I watch, mesmerized, as her teeth flash white in the dim lighting and her eyes dance.

"I think that's the first joke I've ever heard you utter, Mr. Valdasson."

"I'm more known for my wit than my humor," I reply.

Her lips curl into a smile. "I didn't even realize you had any."

I can't help but return her smile as our waiter approaches. Diana orders a Brennivín cocktail while I order whiskey neat. She nods her head to me when the waiter asks what we want. A small sign of trust, one that warms me far more than it should. I order in Icelandic, enjoying the furrow between her brows and her narrowed eyes, like she's trying to decipher what I'm saying.

"So," she says once the waiter departs, "what do you want to know?"

"As I said before, any details I shared with you the other night remain in confidence," I begin.

"I didn't share anything that wasn't publicly avail—"

I cut her off by holding up a hand. "However, I had another conversation with Xenakis this morning after you left. He was more agreeable today than he's been in months."

"You two certainly have different expectations when it comes to business. I also think there's a big cultural misunderstanding here."

Our waiter interrupts us as he sets plates of rye bread with creamed butter and Icelandic salmon on our table.

"Why don't you want Xenakis to know about your father?"

"One, because I'm a private person. Two, I want this deal to succeed on AuraGeothermal's own merits, not pity."

"But what if it's not pity?" Diana presses. "What if it's context? Right now, Xenakis sees you as the man who shoved his own father out because he didn't want to play nice with others."

"I don't play nice with others," I say bluntly.

Diana's gaze turns sad. "I don't think you let yourself play at all."

I sit back, unnerved by the jolt of truth in my chest. When was the last time I did something for fun?

A memory flickers. The summer before my mother passed. I hadn't realized at the time that she'd been pregnant, but she had been exhausted and sick for nearly two months. One day, she came into my room, eyes bright and face glowing. She took me out to the yard and we kicked the ball back and forth. A simple afternoon, yet it plays out in my head as vividly as I were there.

Grief reaches up and clutches at my throat. It takes a moment to wrestle it back under control. My eyes flick up to hers. The compassion and empathy in her gaze is temptation and warning. I want to accept what she's offering, lean into her ability to see me like no one else has.

But the warning wins out. That and common sense. I brought Diana here for business, to reestablish boundaries while making use of her talents, not break open my chest and let my tumultuous past bleed onto the floor. Not when she has yet to share any of herself. Even during our night together, her answers to my queries were vague. The one detail she divulged was that her mother had left when she was four and she's never known who her father was. At the time, I found her ambiguity intriguing.

Now, as she pushes me to share my life with a man I don't trust, it irritates the hell out of me.

I raise my glass to my lips. "You grew up in foster care?"

Her eyes snap up to mine, instantly wary.

"Yes."

I can tell from the way she utters that one word that it wasn't pleasant. I know plenty about Diana's life after she graduated with honors from a high school in New York. But other than knowing she grew up in foster care, I know nothing about her childhood, including why she ended up there in the first place. When I had the investigation run on her, I told myself the details of before weren't important. A move I now regret. Did she confide in Liam? Tell him about the reason why the Degas painting made her sad?

The sounds of the dining room fade around us. I've been focused all day on Diana as the professional, then Diana as the woman, that I had forgotten Diana's role as the ex-fiancée of my brother. Forgotten—or pushed aside, a small voice taunts—for my own selfish desire.

My phone rings. I pull it out and glance at the screen. It's the event planner for the gala. I nod to Diana.

"Excuse me," I say.

She blinks in surprise. "Of course."

I stand and walk away from the table. Taking Diana out to dinner was the right thing to do, even if she's still pushing me to share more than I'm comfortable with. Her analysis is detailed, knowledgeable. She's good at what she does. If I can focus on her role as a negotiator and push aside the glimmers of warmth I've experienced over the course of our dinner, this can work.

I tap my phone screen. "Valdasson."

CHAPTER SIX

Diana

WHAT AM I DOING?

When I walked out of my small office at AuraGeothermal, I was in a good place. I'd clawed my emotions back under control, spent over ten hours working, sinking into my role as negotiator, and pushing thoughts of Ari out of my head—replacing them with how I was going to approach my boss, Mr. Valdasson. And then the elevator doors opened, and everything went to hell.

It's not chemistry but this connection. Seeing his deep passion for his company, his affinity for his country, the people he literally laid everything on the line for and fought for against his own father, takes those initial feelings from our first night together and sends roots spiraling down so deep I'm not sure I can ever wrench them loose.

I sink back into the booth, staring morosely at my cocktail. *What am I going to do?* I know I can do my job. That's not in question. But the more time I spend with Ari, the more I wonder if I'm going to be able to leave Iceland with my heart intact.

My phone rings. I glance down. My stomach drops, even as the sight of the name brings about a sense of calm, a familiarity.

Liam.

"Hey, Liam."

"Hey, Sweet Pea."

I roll my eyes even as I smile. "You do realize I'm twenty-eight, right? I think I'm due for an upgrade on my nickname."

Liam's deep chuckle is comforting, familiar. "How's my big brother treating you?"

My fingers tighten on the phone. "Okay."

The humor evaporates out of Liam's voice. "Everything all right?"

"Yes." I force a smile, hope Liam can hear it in my tone. "He's just…"

"A tight-ass?"

I grin. "That's a good way to put it."

"Yeah, I was a little surprised when I met him. The few times we'd talked on the phone he seemed excited to meet, but when I actually met him, he was pretty distant."

I bite down on my lower lip as guilt makes my stomach roll. "Maybe he was distracted. Or nervous."

"Or maybe he's just a tight-ass."

"Maybe." I hesitate. "Has anything happened?"

A frustrated sigh meets my ears. "Nothing. Nothing's happened. That's what's so frustrating. Not a single word since the damned funeral." There's another long pause. "This isn't her, Di."

I bite down on my lower lip. As much as I appreciate having a friend like Liam, a part of me also hates how well he knows me. Knows how hard I'm struggling not to think this is somehow my fault, to not let myself imagine the worst-case scenario of never having Aislinn in our lives again. To not add her to the long list of people who haven't stuck around.

I think back to this morning, to the text I sent, as I do without fail once a week.

Hi. I miss you. I love you.

I scrolled through my history this morning. Nearly ten months of sending Aislinn that text, and not one reply. There have been plenty of weeks when I thought about not sending it, but I still do. As hurt as I am, I can't imagine not sending it. If Liam's right and there's something else going on, I don't want Aislinn to be alone.

Alone is safe. But alone is lonely, painful.

"I know. I do. I just…"

"Can't help but wonder," Liam says softly.

"Yeah. What can I do?"

"What you're doing now. Listening. Being there for me, even if I keep canceling on you." Before I can reassure him—even if his constant cancelations have hurt—he continues, "I suspect you already gave up a lot."

My mouth dries. "What?"

"The fake engagement. Just a feeling."

I swallow past the thickness in my throat. Before I can reply, he swears.

"I'm getting a call from a client. I won't push right now, but sooner or later, we'll have to talk, Diana."

"Yes," I force out.

"Love you."

"Love you, too."

He hangs up.

I sit there for a long moment, the phone pressed to my ear. Then, slowly, my hand falls to my lap. Before I can even process the fact that Liam knows something is wrong, I become aware of a presence. I look up and freeze. Ari is standing just beyond the table. There's no humor in his gaze, no playful smirk on his lips. There's just a hard coldness.

Before I can say anything, a waiter passes by.

"Excuse me," Ari says. He reaches into an inner pocket of his suit, pulls out his wallet, and hands the waiter a credit card. "Would you run this, please, and box my food to go?"

"Ari—"

"Was that Liam?"

He's probably not even aware of the slight inflection when he says his brother's name. That flash of pain that makes me small and cowardly.

My lungs are so tight I have to focus on forcing out my next words. "You know it was."

"It's none of my concern."

"Ari, please—"

"It's not any of my concern," he repeats, his voice colder than the freezing temperatures outside. "I actually consider today progress, Ms. North."

"Oh?" Not what I was expecting.

"Yes. It wasn't just us working together. I had an opportunity to see you in action, how you handle professional situations. I can acknowledge your value as a corporate negotiator."

The words themselves are complimentary, but I hear the insult in his emphasis on words like *professional* loud and clear.

The waiter returns with Ari's credit card, a bag, and a plate of noodles covered in a creamy sauce and topped with fried onions. The waiter hands Ari his card and the bag, and sets the plate in front of me before disappearing.

"Skyr cream sauce pasta with crispy onions, toasted walnuts and cilantro." Ari nods to me. "Enjoy your dinner. I'll see you at eight tomorrow."

Then, before I can say anything, he leaves. I watch him walk away, watch him do exactly what I recommended this morning.

I'm failing myself. I'm hurting Ari—not because he cares for me, but because I'm damaging any possibility of a relationship between him and Liam. At this point, I also can't imagine a scenario where I don't hurt Liam on some level. It's not that I slept with his half brother and didn't tell him, but now I haven't told him for months. The longer I've gone, the deeper a hole I've dug for myself, until I can't see a way out where Liam and I stay friends.

Stop!

I wrap my fingers around my bracelet, around Lucy's dog tag, as I mentally throw the brakes on my runaway panic. I take a deep breath, release it. I'm imagining the absolute worst-case scenario, not just because of my situation but because of Aislinn. That kind of thinking isn't going to help me stay focused.

Somewhat calm, I manage to eat a couple bites. But my appetite is gone. I pick up my cocktail, take a long, satisfying drink before setting the glass down, grabbing my coat and bag, and making my way out the door. There's no sign of Ari as I drift along the quiet streets of Reykjavik on a winter's night.

Can I do my job? I question myself as I walk through the cold. *Can I stay emotionally objective and do the best thing for AuraGeothermal?*

I thought seeing Ari yesterday would wipe away the magic of that night. He brought down my walls—walls I spent years building—and that, I acknowledge with some reluctance, is why I walked away the next morning. Not because it was the right thing to do, but because I was scared. I didn't want to get too close. Didn't want to fall deeper, and then be abandoned.

Didn't want to get abandoned? a nasty voice whispers in my ear. *Or didn't want him to not like what he saw and leave? Like my mother. Like the numerous foster parents who declined to adopt me. Like Brian.*

For a moment, my world shrinks, narrows down to the fear that has ruled me ever since my mother told my first foster family she wanted nothing more to do with me and walked out of my life forever.

I stop and suck in a long breath of Arctic air. It cleanses

me, wipes away the fear. I had enough in my life before Ari. I just need to focus on doing my job, doing the best thing for my client.

And then I can finally make things right.

I'll tell Liam, I decide. Before I leave Iceland. He can do with the information what he wishes. I hope that doesn't include cutting me out of his life. But that's not my choice to make.

And whether or not I like it, it's the price I'll have to pay for my night with Ari Valdasson.

CHAPTER SEVEN

Ari

WAITERS DRESSED IN white dress shirts and black vests, with ties, move in and out of the guests. The silver trays they balance host dishes like Icelandic lobster tucked into small shells and topped with crème fraîche and puff pastries filled with a mix of skyr, smoked trout, and chives. The buffet tables along the outer rim of the room offer heartier fare like grilled Arctic char with a skyr cream sauce, pan-seared Icelandic lamb with wild mushrooms, and sea scallops with beetroot purée. The bar includes mead, birch wine, and vodka, along with numerous other high-end wines and liqueurs from around the world.

I examine one of the frosted crystal vases filled with poppies, bluebells, and wild ferns on top of tables draped in white. Everywhere guests look, they see Iceland, from the locally sourced food and the musicians playing lilting tunes on the dais to the unique centerpieces designed by a florist in Bogarnes.

Perfect.

Every recommendation from Diana has been spot-on. Yet instead of thinking of the gala we've hosted for the past four years, of the client I'm trying to secure a very important contract with, I'm thinking of her.

I've been aware of her from the moment she walked in—

wearing a stunning dress the color of mulled wine, the fabric clinging to the curves of her breasts, the nip of her waist, the flare of her hips, with an intimacy I envy. A cape drifts from the sleeves and back of the dress as she moves through the room with quiet grace. Her hair is partially pulled back from her face, leaving the elegant slashes of her cheekbones and the strong line of her jaw bare to anyone's gaze, as loose curls tumble down her back. Tiny diamond studs glint at her ears, the only other jewelry she wears besides the silver bracelet with the tiny heart she's never without.

It's been two days. Two days since every twisted, ugly emotion that first rose up inside me in that damn restaurant New York reappeared as I overheard Diana tell my brother she loved him.

Fury. Outrage. Jealousy. Beneath those lurked confusion, pessimism. Liam had confirmed that he and Diana had broken off their engagement the last time we spoke. Yet the way she spoke, the familiarity and affection in her words, sounded more like a current lover than an ex-fiancée.

I want to hate her for the effect she has on me. For the need that nearly made me go back to the restaurant and demand answers. For that split second of pain, like someone had just clawed out the inside of my chest.

But hate is the reflection of love. Another investment of emotion. So instead I concentrated on work—not just contract negotiations, but on the everyday tasks that keep Aura-Geothermal running. I arrived at seven in the morning and left at eight at night, responding to any emails she sent with brisk efficiency and conducting meetings with a degree of coolness to reinforce the professional boundaries between us. The punishing pace kept me focused, kept my thoughts off her and Liam and whatever relationship they still had.

My hands tighten into fists. I've only met him once, but I've imagined him for the past four years. Dreamed about who he could have been in the years before that, when I thought he died with my mother.

But now, every time I hear his name, all I can feel is anger. Resentment. Even the few conversations we attempted on the phone were brief, colored by the emotions seething in my chest whenever I thought of him with her.

I let my guard down the other night. And in less than two hours, I was given a stark reminder as to why Diana and I can never cross that line again. A woman I desire and despise in equal measure.

Love you, too.

I've never been in love. It works for some. I've never been interested. I loved my mother, and when she died, so did my capacity to allow that emotion into my life again. There are times I almost hate that she loved me so much, and I her, because the few times I allow myself to remember just how deeply she did, it fucking hurts.

Malla appears beside me.

"Everything seems to be going smoothly," she says.

"It does." I smile down at her. "Thank you. The event team did most of the work."

She glances off to the side. "And Diana."

My pulse kicks up a notch. "Diana?"

"She's been a huge help. She drove up here early and helped us set up. Laid down tablecloths, put up centerpieces..." Malla grins up at me. "I'm really glad you brought her on. She's nice."

"She is." My voice is flat.

"Is it hard?"

"What?"

"Just...working with your brother's ex-fiancée."

I arch one brow. "I didn't realize that was public knowledge."

She scoffs. "Everyone knows. But when you hired her, we figured it meant everything was okay."

"It is," I lie. "Whatever happened between Miss North and my brother does not impact her ability to serve as a negotiator and help finalize the contract with Hellas Shipping."

"I'm glad. I really like her."

I do, too.

I bite back the words.

Just then, a woman approaches. Vanessa, I remember. Vanessa Renfield. An American lawyer based in Paris, specializing in international finance. Smart, determined, confident. She'd suggested a fling when we'd met in Spain a few years back, but I'd already been in the middle of a casual affair. I have no interest in marriage or love, but I have a firm rule about monogamy. My father's casual affairs drove my mother into the arms of another man. I won't repeat his mistakes or cause the same pain he did.

"Miss Renfield," I greet.

Her smile is dazzling. "You remembered."

"Of course. The conference in Madrid."

"Thank you for inviting me." She gestures with a jewel-bedecked hand to the grand ballroom, the floor-to-ceiling windows offering unparalleled views of Iceland's wildlands at night. "This is incredible."

"I'm glad you could make it."

She lowers her chin, gazes up at me from beneath thick lashes. A practiced move, one I would have noticed and followed up on three months ago with an invitation to dinner, then a room at one of Reykjavik's luxurious hotels.

But now, all I can see are brown eyes, not green. Thick brown hair, not styled red curls.

Vanessa takes a bold step forward. "May I have this dance?"

Out of the corner of my eye, I see Malla grimace. I shoot

my secretary a warning look before turning back to Vanessa. I have no intention of inviting her anywhere. I would never ask another woman out in the presence of a former lover. Even if Diana weren't here, other than a casual appreciation for Vanessa's physical beauty, there's no spark of attraction.

But that doesn't mean I can't dance with a beautiful woman. Can't welcome a few moments of distraction.

I incline my head and extend a hand to Vanessa. "Shall we?"

Diana

I glance, for what feels like the dozenth time, at the dance floor where Ari holds a stunning redhead in his arms. Her black gown follows the line of every sensual curve before flaring out at her knees into a fall of silk. She laughs up at Ari, confident in her body and her ability to attract, to seduce.

Judging by the way Ari is smiling down at her, the feeling is mutual. I turn my head away.

There's nothing tying us together—nothing but one night, three months ago. I have no reason to be jealous. No reason to be hurt, especially when Ari thinks I betrayed both him and his brother. Yet, as I steal one more glance out of the corner of my eye, I can't deny the pain that seeps through me like poison.

"Diana?"

I turn, forcing a smile when I realize it's Malla. "Sorry. Busy night."

She's looking at me as if she suspects something, her gaze shifting between me and the couple on the dance floor. "Are you all right?"

"Of course." I lay a hand on her shoulder. "A lot of work in a short time. Thank you, by the way, for making sure Mr. Valdasson practiced his speech."

Malla's expression brightens. "Of course. I think it went over amazingly."

"It did."

Ari had taken every single one of my suggestions, which I'd left in the typewritten report on his desk the night we had dinner, and turned them into a speech. He thanked Xenakis and Hellas Shipping for all their contributions so far, highlighted how much he was looking forward to their continued partnership, and touched on AuraGeothermal's commitment to the family they'd built within their company, to their community, and to their homeland. I'd watched Xenakis and his team out of the corner of my eye, seen every point hit home.

Tonight was a giant leap forward.

So why, I thought with no small amount of self-loathing, couldn't I just be happy with our accomplishments? Why did I have to be jealous of the smile Ari gave the redhead? Why did I have to feel sick to my stomach as her hand moved up his arm to his shoulder, the intimate way her fingers glided up the sleeve of his tuxedo?

"Diana?"

I looked down at Malla.

"Yes?"

"If there's ever anything you need to talk about, I'm really good at listening."

I almost say something. Almost take her up on her offer to be a listening ear, a supportive shoulder. I like her. Truly like her. But will she still like me if I tell her the truth? If I tell her everything that's transpired over the past three months?

I think not.

"Thank you." I give her a small smile. "I'm going up to the top deck. I could use some air."

I don't miss the hurt in her eyes. I hate myself even more when she returns my smile with one of her own.

"Of course. Take all the time you need."

Before I can reply, Viktor approaches and asks her for a dance. Judging by the shy yet very bright smile Malla gives him, she won't remember my refusal for long.

I slip out of the ballroom. A woven basket offers thick blankets and shawls. I grab one and wrap it around my shoulders. The deck just off the ballroom is crowded with people in tuxedos and elegant gowns. Waiters drift in and out, holding trays of champagne and appetizers. Fire pits and outdoor heaters battle back the cold.

I move past the crowd, heading for the stairs. Each step takes me farther away from the crowd and deeper into the cold.

The upper deck is simply designed, a slate gray stone floor with a glass railing and a couple of black chairs and benches for those who want to linger and take in the view. The posts in between the glass have circular lights built into the base. The dim lighting lets my eyes adjust to take in what little I can see of the borders of Þingvellir National Park. From what little I can see, it's stunning. Craggy rocks, shaped by generations of volcanic activity. Deeper in the park are waterfalls, fissures, and even a lake with an underwater gorge running between tectonic plates.

Another place I want to come back to. If there's time.

That sense of oddness, almost like an ache, returns at the thought of leaving Iceland. It'll go away. My emotions are off. I'm reaching out, grasping on to the familiarity of nature to steady me as I grapple with a situation I never imagined possible.

With a man I never should have looked twice at.

I came out to the gala early, needing something to focus on besides my tumultuous evening with Ari. It's been two days since he walked out. Two days of briefings in the morning, followed by detailed reports at the end of the day. Each meeting with him has been quick and frosty—a recitation of what

I did that day as I reviewed contracts, met with members of the Hellas Shipping team, the AuraGeothermal board of directors. Business. What I do every day in my job.

Except each time I saw Ari, each time I talked with him, I saw the way he looked in the restaurant—the flash of pain before his emotions vanished behind a wall of ice.

I reach the top deck of the hotel. I look up, as has become my habit over the past few days. But once again, I'm thwarted by the clouds scuttling across the sky.

"Only forty percent of Icelandic tourists see the Northern Lights."

My body tenses even as the warm huskiness of his voice flows over me.

"Maybe I was just looking at the clouds."

There's silence behind me, then a slight, barely audible chuckle.

"Iceland has plenty to offer."

My heart twists. I missed that, the casual camaraderie we had started to develop. The easy way I can just…talk to him. Not watch everything I say. Similar to the ease of my relationship with Liam and Aislinn.

I've never felt that way about anyone else. Not even Brian. The harder he pushed, the more I resisted. Not once did I feel the instant ease I experienced with Ari, that snap of connection.

And look what happened.

I turn. Ari is standing at the top of the stairs, looking impossibly handsome in his black tuxedo. The material molds perfectly to his broad shoulders, trim waist, and muscular thighs. I can think of a dozen men who would look ridiculous in a bow tie, but Ari commands it, every inch the leader he is.

"It was a good speech," I say, trying to keep my tone neutral.

He tucks his hands into his pockets and wanders toward

me. "I'm glad my negotiator approved. Xenakis seemed to approve, too. And given that he's had at least two shots of Brennivin, I'm not surprised."

I bite back a smile. "I wouldn't look a gift horse in the mouth on this one."

He walks toward me, slow, measured steps that make my heart race.

"You left."

My breath hitches in my throat. "I just needed some fresh air."

"Did you?"

He's staring at me, demanding answers when I have none to give.

I hesitate. I want nothing more than to go to him, to reach out and touch him. But it would be the stupidest thing I could do. Not just for my professional career, not for the goals he set for his company, but for us. We're both damaged people, hurting, burdened by guilt for the one thing we have in common: Liam.

"Go back to the party, Mr. Valdasson."

"What about you?"

I tilt my head to one side. "What about me?"

"It's freezing."

"Are you always this observant?"

He swears. "Why did you leave the ballroom?"

I think of the redhead. Try not to let my jealousy show. "I told you, I needed some air. It's been a long day."

"Really?" He walks toward me, slowly, eyes glittering in the dim lighting. "Because I saw the way you looked at Vanessa and me."

"It's none of my concern."

I repeat his words from the other night. Tell myself they're true even as I ache inside.

"Dance with me."

My mouth drops open. "What?"

He holds out a hand. "Dance with me."

Stupid. I stare at his hand, try to stifle the want that surges inside me. It would be so stupid to dance with him.

My heart takes hold of my body before my brain can catch up. I place my hand in his. His fingers close over mine and he pulls me closer. My breath catches as one arm wraps around my waist, his hand splaying across my back. We move across the terrace with slow, lazy movements. A gentle wind makes the gauzy cape of my dress dance behind me. Ari stares down at me, eyes searching, probing.

Heat suffuses my body. I pause, drape the shawl over a chair as we spin past. Cold air kisses my bare shoulders, but I barely register it.

"Vanessa is a lawyer."

My mind blanks for a moment. "Vanessa?"

"The redhead."

I look down, hope he doesn't see my petty jealousy. "She's beautiful."

"She's not a lover."

I hate the flicker of relief in my chest. "It's not—"

"No, it's not any of your concern. I thought about not saying anything when I saw you leave the ballroom." His fingers tighten on mine. "But then I decided to give you the answers I've wanted for the past three months."

I press my lips together, look away.

"Ari—"

Imagine," he continues as he draws me closer, hard muscle beneath the silk of his tuxedo, "how I've felt, Diana. Three months. Three months of trying to distance myself from the thought of you, the feel of you, because every thought is a betrayal to my brother. The one I searched for four years after thinking him dead for most of my life."

My eyes widen. "Dead?"

He cocks his head to one side. "Liam didn't tell you?"

"No. No, we… A friend of ours was going through a rough patch at the time. He told me a couple days before you and I met that you had contacted him. That you were going to have dinner."

"Our mother had an affair. Given that my father had half a dozen in the years prior to when she fell pregnant, I'd say she was justified." The fury in his tone evaporates as a shadow passes over his face. "She died giving birth to Liam. My father told me Liam died with my mother."

Oh God.

"How did you even find out he existed?"

"I came across documents about Liam's birth during the takeover. Papers with my father's signature approving Liam being sent to America to be adopted. He could have cared less if she had her own affairs. But he took her getting pregnant with someone else's baby as an insult." He glances over my shoulder, out into the darkness. "Even then, there was barely anything to go on. No adoption agency, no record of what name he was given."

"And then he registered for the ancestry website," I murmur.

Ten months ago. The last night I remember Liam, Aislinn, and I together before Aislinn started to slip away. Aislinn had suggested doing the DNA kit. Liam and I had gone along with it because it had been important to her. We gathered at my apartment, completed the swabs, and mailed in our samples. We went out afterward and got a round of drinks to celebrate.

One step forward. Aislinn had laughed as she'd raised her glass of champagne in a toast.

We'd been so happy that night. None of us could have imagined the falls awaiting us.

"I'm sorry, Ari."

His gaze snaps back to me. "Sorry?"

I raise my chin. "Yes."

"Tilgangslaust."

My jaw clenches. "I don't know Icelandic, but I gather that wasn't complimentary."

"Meaningless." The word slices through me. "My brother lost his birth family, then his adoptive family, and spent years in foster care when he should have had the stability and luxury I grew up in."

Beneath the anger vibrating in his voice, I hear the guilt. The ache.

"And then, just when I have the chance to make things right, you walk in the door holding his hand. Less than a day," he adds cuttingly, "after leaving my bed. I have never once swayed from doing what needed to be done. But you, Diana, put me in a position where I had to choose between telling my brother that his fiancée had been naked beneath me the night before or letting him enjoy his happiness."

My heart breaks. I should have told Liam. But I took the coward's way out, let fear make my choices for me.

"I'm not—"

"And then I overhear you say 'I love you' to him. You told me things were over." His hand tightens around mine. "Are you toying with him?"

"No!" I pause, glance around to make sure we're still alone. "I told you, Liam and I have been friends for years. We've said 'I love you' since…"

My voice trails off. A hospital. Machines beeping. The pain thankfully faint under the power of medication. Aislinn sitting in a chair on one side of the bed. Liam on the other. Both holding my hands.

We love you, Diana. We're not going anywhere.

I believed them. And now, for whatever reason, Aislinn is gone. What if Liam disappears when I tell him the truth?

My gaze flickers to Ari. I know he won't be around. He despises me. But for one moment, I let myself feel the ache that rooted itself inside my heart the morning I woke up wrapped in his arms. The first time I ever truly longed for something more with a man.

"Since when?" Ari demands.

I blink, refocus "Years. Well before our engagement, and we'll probably keep saying it until we're dead. I love him. But I'm not in love with him."

I never was, I want to scream.

"Yet you were at one point." Ari presses forward, relentless and determined. "You said yes to his proposal. You wore his ring."

"I did." My reply is weary, my entire body exhausted.

Ari's eyes narrow. "You said yes and you wore the ring. But you were never in love with him, were you?"

Damn it. I walked straight into that. If Ari detects any inconsistencies, I have no doubt he'll investigate until every secret is laid bare.

I start to pull away. Ari's hand comes up, past the edge of fabric and onto my bare back. His fingers graze the tops of my scars.

I freeze. Shock tethers me to the ground as my breath hitches in my throat. A prickling sensation creeps up my back. A prickling that flares into fire. I can feel it, feel the belt.

"Diana?"

His voice sounds far away, like he's talking underwater. I pull back and this time he lets me. I reach out, grab the railing. A shudder passes through me as I fight back against the memories, tell myself the pain isn't real. But my own words are drowned out by the phantoms of my past. Lucy's frantic barking. Dale's angry shouts. Adrenaline pumping through me, propelling me across the yard. I tense, readying for it. The first snap of the leather right before the pain. I flinch once. Twice. Three times.

"Diana!"

Ari's voice breaks through. My breathing is fast, hard. Slowly, I manage to get it back under control, to push away the nightmares and ground myself in the present.

I force myself to look at Ari. He's staring at me, hands curled at his sides, his jaw tight. There's shock in his eyes. Shock and anger.

He knows. Through my receding panic, I can see him connect the dots. That, more than the memories, strips me bare. Leaves me raw and vulnerable.

I did this. I let him get close. Opened the door that night in New York when I let my guard down and shared parts of myself I've never shared with anyone. Not Liam and Aislinn, not former lovers.

And now we've slid even deeper. It doesn't matter if Ari never asks, if I never tell him. He knows the scars are there.

I'll be furious with myself later. Use this to maintain the distance I should have been maintaining all this time. But for now, I wrap numbness around me like a shield.

"I'm fine." I force myself to walk calmly to the chair where I left the shawl. Wrap it around my shoulders. "It just…" I clear my throat. "An old injury."

He's still angry. But his eyes soften a fraction. It's enough to have me wanting to lean into him, to share even more.

And therein lies the danger. The more I share, the more I fall. The deeper I fall, the harder it will be to pull myself out of the darkness when he leaves.

Sooner or later, they all leave.

"Diana—"

"I'm going back inside."

He doesn't follow me as I walk away.

CHAPTER EIGHT

Ari

I STALK OUT of the conference room. The silence behind me is short, ended by raised voices spouting off in English and Greek as I walk away. Anger pulses through me, molten lava burning me from the inside out.

After the gala last night, I was fool enough to think the deal with Hellas Shipping might go through. Xenakis saw AuraGeothermal as a profit-focused organization, not a company committed to green energy and providing for both its employees and its country. Our tour of the geothermal facility and last night's reception had been steps forward. Small steps, but after the monumental backsliding of the past year, it was still a victory.

Until this morning. Until the bastard showed up thirty minutes late to the review of the new proposal with a scowl on his face and reddened eyes. I didn't see him drink a lot last night. But then again, I had been away for a good thirty minutes chasing after—

Nei. Right now I need to focus, to think about what's going to happen next. To examine and plan for the very real possibility that this deal just suffered a catastrophic blow it may never recover from.

Xenakis had settled in. Diana had cordially passed him a copy of the proposal, but he'd barely glanced at her. I highlighted the recent changes, kept my tone polite despite my irritation. Xenakis had said nothing until the end when he'd leaned back in his chair, rubbed at the bridge of his nose, and said he needed time to think.

My hands curl into fists as I stride past a wide-eyed Malla and into my office, slamming the door behind me. I'd asked Xenakis how long. I'd caught Diana's warning look, but I'd ignored it. I don't tolerate disrespect from anyone, including guests. My team worked damn hard on that proposal, and they deserved an answer. So when Xenakis had snapped he'd get back to me on his own time, I'd coolly pointed out that not only had my team expedited their work to accommodate his visit to Iceland, but that AuraGeothermal had capitulated on several points.

And then Xenakis had sat up, looked me straight in the eye, and nearly spat out the words that set a match to my simmering anger.

Your so-called concessions are worthless to me.

Everyone had frozen. Even Xenakis's own eyes had widened, as if he'd realized he'd gone too far. He'd started to speak, but I'd stood and leaned across the table, palms flat on the surface to keep myself grounded.

We're done here.

And then I'd left.

I need to get out. Get away from my office, the building, the city. I punch a button on my desk phone.

"Malla, put me down as unavailable the rest of the afternoon. Reschedule any meetings. Only contact me in case of emergencies."

"Yes, sir."

"Have my car brought around front."

"Yes, sir."

I turn and look out the window at the harbor, at the snow-capped peak of Mount Esja. There are other companies I can review, other ports that can still provide the services and land we need to expand. This is a roadblock, not a death sentence.

Just business. Nothing more.

This, I think irritably as I press the button for the lobby, is what comes from allowing personal feelings to enter into a business deal. To let Xenakis see not just the professional but the intimate aspects of what we do.

The doors are halfway shut when an arm stabs between them. The doors open back up. Diana slips inside.

Case in point.

Her subtle scent of jasmine wraps around me, teases me. Has my anger shifting to a new target: me. I've never been tempted to this extreme by any woman before. Now, when my mind should be anywhere but sex, anywhere but on my brother's ex-fiancée, she dominates my thoughts.

She's wearing a velvet green dress with long sleeves and a slim-fitting skirt down to her knees, an ivory coat draped over one arm. With the tie around her waist and the little bow just above her hip, she looks like a Christmas present. One I want to unwrap slowly and savor every inch of skin I unveil as she murmurs my name.

Until her eyes meet mine and I'm yanked back to last night on the terrace of the hotel. To that moment when my fingers slid over thin raised lines. Scars, I'd realized a split-second before Diana had gone rigid in my arms and stepped back.

The scars could be from anything. Falling out of a tree. A bike crash. But it hadn't been hard to figure out from the way her fingers had gripped the railing like it was a lifeline, the way her eyes had gone wide and unseeing, her breath coming in shallow pants as she'd flinched, to know the scars had been inflicted by someone else.

My jaw tightens. Someone who had better be dead or in prison. Those are the only two ways I won't kill them myself.

Diana waits a beat. I say nothing, simply return her stare.

She steps inside, keeping several feet of space between us as the doors close and the car descends.

I glance down at her out of the corner of my eye. She's staring straight ahead, her face smooth, her dark cloud of hair caught back in a clip that shows off the elegant curves and angles of her face. No hint of the fear or pain I glimpsed last night.

It had been a few minutes after she'd gone back downstairs when the realization had hit me—why she kept the camisole on when we'd had sex in my hotel. She'd told me she was keeping it on with such casual confidence that I hadn't paid much attention. Would I have liked to see her naked? Hell, yes. But I'd been so intoxicated with the feel of her body, the taste of her skin, that I hadn't asked why. I'd just assumed she felt more comfortable and left it at that, especially when she'd pulled down the bodice and I'd filled my hands with her bare breasts.

Knowing the secret she was protecting, that even as we made love she was hiding something so painful, makes me want to pull her to me and shield her from the world.

Except, I think with the faintest hint of a smile, *Diana doesn't need protecting.*

"Here to critique me?"

She shakes her head. "Not right now."

Her voice is quiet. Soft, soothing.

"Taking the afternoon off?"

"I saw your eyes—"

I glance down at her with an arched brow. "And?"

"—when Xenakis said the concessions were worthless."

The back of my neck tightens. Like someone's reaching beneath my skin and twisting the muscles into tight knots.

"And?"

She looks up at me then, rich brown eyes as soft as her

voice. Glowing with compassion. The stiffness inches down from my neck into my spine. I don't want her pity.

"You looked like you could use company."

We ride the rest of the way in silence. I've never let a deal get under my skin. Not even when I challenged my father for ownership. All I saw then was a battle to be won.

But, as I glance at Diana out of the corner of my eye, I know at least part of the reason. Her existence strains my usual reserve, pulls emotions I usually don't feel to the surface. She's pushing me to share, be vulnerable once more.

Before last night, just thinking about how she's been encouraging me to share would have made me furious. But now, as I think back to the brush of her scars beneath my fingers, remember the frantic gasps of her breath creating puffs of white in the cold evening air, I accept that she has deeper secrets than me.

The doors slide open. I step out. My SUV is parked outside the doors, a combination of luxury and strength that can handle Iceland's roughest highland roads. A vehicle that lets me escape the city when I need to drive, to get away.

Except now as I look over the gleaming exterior and polished windows, I can't picture driving away without Diana in the passenger seat.

I don't look back as I start forward.

"Coming?"

A moment later her flats tap against the marble floor behind me. We walk outside. The wind tears at my coat, my hair. I walk around to the passenger door and open it for her. Catch another whiff of jasmine tangled with the ice-cold crispness of Arctic air.

Neither of us speak as I navigate the city. It's not until the towers of Reykjavik are behind us and snow-covered hills before us that I speak.

"When people think of the company, they think of my father or me. No one thinks of my mother." I see a flash of blue eyes, a brilliant white smile, a soft laugh that wraps around me like a comforting embrace. "She was the one who kept my father leashed in the first few years after my grandfather's death. She's the one who encouraged him to lead the company the way my grandfather would have wanted."

"I didn't know she was involved."

My smile is quick, bitter. "Most don't. She grew up in Ísafjörður, over five hours north of Reykjavik. She finished her degree in northern Iceland and moved here. She interviewed with my grandfather and got a job with AuraGeothermal. My father was the chief operating officer at the time. They met on the job."

It should have been a fairy tale. A love story. Handsome executive meets beautiful environmental specialist when she stands up to him over an alteration to one of the geothermal fields. Instead, it turned into a loveless marriage that turned my mother into a shadow of herself.

"My mother came from a fishing village of just under three thousand people. She understood the value of investing in the people, in the country. She was the one who pushed my father to pursue initiatives that bolstered Iceland, local economies. Scholarships, small businesses, research."

"Losing her must have been hard on both of you."

"No. My father was a bastard before her death. He was just smarter then. Before he got greedy." I remember my mother navigating her car down this very road, the echo of one of her and my father's arguments ringing in my ears. "From what little she said, the man before the vows was completely different than the man who appeared after their honeymoon."

"Why did she stay?"

I wait a beat, swallow decades of anger, remorse.

"Me."

The guilt is always there. Most days, I can exist without

thinking of it. But now it surges up. The guilt of knowing my mother stayed, put up with my father's affairs, condescension, and misogynistic manipulations, because of me. When I think of her, the sheer brilliance and kindness of her existence, the only reason I don't regret being born is because she loved being a mother.

"She wanted to stay at home until I started primary school. My grandfather passed away when I was about a year old and my father took over as CEO. He 'encouraged' her not to return to work after I started the first grade. Fulfill her duties as a 'wife' and 'mother.'"

"But she wasn't happy."

"No. When we were together, yes. When she got to be a mom without my father looking over her shoulder and criticizing her for being too soft on me."

Diana lets out a soft scoff. "I…"

Her voice trails off. I glance over, my chest tightening when I see the sadness etched onto her face. The same sadness I saw as she stared at the painting of the ballerinas.

"What?"

She shakes her head. "I'm glad you had that."

She didn't. I know it. Feel the longing, the ache. Silently curse the woman who hurt her daughter.

"I was fortunate." I nod to the passing landscape. "My father refusing to hire her back didn't sway her loyalty to my grandfather or the company. She's the one who taught me about allegiance. Commitment. She told me that, if I chose to take the role, she hoped I would lead as my grandfather had."

"A big responsibility to task a child with."

I smile slightly. "She didn't phrase it like that. It was an honor." My lips thin. "My father never saw it that way. He saw his position as a status symbol. He always wanted more— more recognition, more money, more things."

"The international expansion would have given him all of that," Diana murmurs.

"Even though he and I didn't see eye-to-eye, I was initially intrigued by expanding to other countries. It wasn't until we were almost too deep that I realized what that expansion would cost us here at home.

"There are things I could have done better with Xenakis," I admit. "I want this deal. It's good for AuraGeothermal. Good for our economy, and for expanding green energy to other countries. But I will torpedo it in an instant if I think there's any risk to my employees."

Silence reigns in the car. I look over, then blink in surprise. Diana is watching me, eyes luminous with an emotion I can't decipher. An emotion that disappears so quickly I wonder if I imagined it.

"Xenakis didn't give you much reason to trust today."

Her validation matters more than it should.

"If the deal fails, will it affect your employment?"

"No. I haven't failed to mediate a deal yet. But I see my job like a marriage counselor."

I grimace. "I would prefer not to think of Xenakis in a wedding dress."

"I was thinking of you as the blushing bride." She chuckles when I frown at her. "Most of the time, a solution can be found. I think that's true for this, too, but I don't know for sure. Not after this morning. Sometimes the best thing for everyone is to walk away."

My shoulders tense. She'd said something similar after the tour of the geothermal plant when she tried to defuse our argument. I'd responded cruelly. Thought her ability to walk away proved her a fickle woman with no true loyalties.

Except now, with my hands on the wheel, I can feel the raised, ridged skin beneath my fingertips. Connect the sorrow on her face with what I suspect was her mother's abandonment. Did her mother leave those scars? A foster parent?

We both fall silent, absorbed in our own thoughts. Ten minutes later, she's fallen asleep. The gray wintry light sneaking through the clouds magnifies the dark half-moon circles beneath her eyes. Malla told me the security log showed Diana didn't leave until well after midnight last night, reviewing and tweaking the proposal long after everyone else had gone.

Who is this woman who is fighting for my company? A woman who nearly admitted last night that she may have said yes to Liam's proposal, but she was never in love with him.

For the first time, I contemplate another possibility. Could there be something else? An ulterior motive I'm missing?

I shove that thought away. I'm reaching, trying to make sense, when the truth is right in front of me. It has been all along. Things may have happened exactly as Diana said and she and Liam had had no romantic entanglements before our night together.

But it doesn't change the fact that what happened between us derailed my reunion with the only blood family I have left.

One more look at her sleeping face, lips slightly parted, lashes dark against her skin. One more indulgence of memory, of the way her eyes glowed when she saw me in the museum, how her lips curved into that unabashed smile that snapped something into place I haven't been able to get rid of.

One more look. And then I focus on the road in front of me.

CHAPTER NINE

Diana

I WAKE WITH a start as the engine cuts off. I blink, staring out over the snowy landscape as my mind catches up. Embarrassment creeps up my neck as I slowly raise my head and glance over at Ari. He's staring out his window, his face angled just enough for me to see the cut of his jaw, the slash of cheekbone visible beneath strands of ice-blond hair.

Regal. Commanding. Yet when he spoke of protecting his employees, of loyalty and commitment, I heard something else beneath the cool voice. Something fierce and primal that had made my skin grow hot and my heart drum a slow, steady beat against my ribs.

I start to speak. To tell him thank you for confiding in me.

And then I glimpse what Ari's staring at. My mouth drops open.

"Wow."

Black sand glimmers under the pale light of the setting sun. It stretches west for what seems like endless miles. The beach is narrow at high tide, a thin strip of midnight standing between the crashing waves of the Atlantic and the dramatic basalt columns creating random steps up the soaring hillside. Pillars of dark stone jut out of the dark blue to the east, large stepping stones for some mythical Nordic creature, or a perch for a siren.

This is the kind of place where magic exists.

"Ari," I breathe, "is this Black Sand Beach?"

He turns, but I continue to stare past him. Try to soak up everything: the distant hum of the waves crashing onto the shore, the wind whistling outside, the glittering water.

"Reynisfjara."

His voice shivers through me, leaving my throat dry and my tongue tied up in knots as I look at him. His eyes are fixed on me, the same dark blue as the ocean behind him.

"It's beautiful."

"It is." He glances back at the beach. "My mother and I would spend hours driving the Ring Road on weekends my father was home. We always stopped here and walked along the beach."

Another layer I didn't expect in Ari Valdasson. The love he has for his mom and her memory draw me in. I can't stop my admiration for a man who respected his mother, who not only listened but took her lessons on being a good leader and turned himself into who he is today. Took charge when his father failed and led his company back from the brink.

I encouraged him to share. I just hadn't anticipated how much his answers would make me like him. Make me want to know more.

He gets out and circles around to open my door for me. One brow arches up at my flats.

"Will those be okay for walking on the beach?"

"Better than heels." I step out, pulling my coat tighter around me as an icy, biting wind whips through the nearly empty parking lot. "And if you think I'm missing out on walking the beach just because of my shoes, you're wrong."

One corner of his full lips quirks up before he looks away. We walk past a dark, low-lying building with huge windows overlooking the beach. A few people sit at booths inside, hands wrapped around mugs as they watch the crashing waves. Tall, steeply sloped hills rise behind, shearing off at the tops into dramatic cliffs draped in snow.

"What's it like in the spring?"

"Green."

One word, yet I can picture it from the depth of emotion in his voice. Vibrant green, a lush carpet of it that follows those steep hills up to the craggy tops.

Two signs stand guard by the entrance to the beach, the left one topped with red, yellow, and green lights. The red light is flashing.

Ari points to the other sign with a map outlining the beach. "We won't go far."

I glance at several people walking close to the water's edge. "Aren't they—"

"Yes." His answer is grim, abrupt. More like the Ari I've been around the last few days. "Iceland is beautiful. But many don't respect that beauty. They take it for granted. Reynisfjara is renowned for its volcanic sand and basalt columns. But it's also known for sneaker waves." He gestures to the water, the swirling waves just offshore. Frowns at a man tugging a woman toward the water's edge. "Even on a calm day, the waves come out of nowhere and race up the beach."

I grasp the lapels of my coat at my neck as another shiver traces down my spine. Ari's eyes narrow.

"Does that change your perception?"

"No." I look around, soak in the scent of the sea sharpened by the cold, the towering cliffs, the shimmering shore. "Nature has always been a refuge for me. Iceland…" I glance farther down the shore to where the land rises toward the sky before turning into a plateau. Part of the rise stabs out into the sea, a natural arch in the rock giving me a glimpse of the water beyond. "It's raw. Untamed. But it's still…soothing. Peaceful."

I probably sound crazy. But it's true. Iceland speaks to both the wounded girl I once was and a streak of wildness that's been pulsing inside me for months. The same wildness that drove me to go for a stroll with a random stranger in a museum and follow him to his bed.

With a soft sigh, I turn back to Ari. My breath freezes in my chest as he stares at me, his gaze intense yet surprisingly warm. Appreciative.

"Ótaminn." His slight smile sends my pulse skyrocketing. "I'm glad you can appreciate its wildness. Shall we?"

I shove my hands into the pockets of my coat as Ari and I walk onto the beach. The sand gives gently beneath our feet. When I woke up this morning, I never in a thousand years would have imagined the day going like this. My professional side is smarting, irritated that I couldn't keep Ari and Xenakis on track. They're both so entrenched in their dislike of each other they can't see anything else. *If,* I think with a frustrated glance at Ari besides me, *they would just talk, they would see how much their goals and interests align.*

But, I also reluctantly admit, if Xenakis had talked to me the way he had talked to Ari this morning, I would have been displeased, at the very least.

"What are you thinking?"

His voice is low, curious.

"That I wish I could have kept things on track this morning." I blow out a frustrated breath. "But I've made it through worse."

I can feel Ari's eyes on me as we walk along the upper part of the beach. He's given me so much today. Far more than I expected. And it suddenly feels grossly unfair.

"My mother forfeited her parental rights when I was five."

He doesn't say anything. Simply listens as I allow myself to slip back into the past. To the spring day when I thought my mother was coming over to take me to my first dance lesson, only to overhear her tell my foster mother she was done. She didn't want to be a mom. She didn't want me.

To this day, I regret running after her. Crying out for my mom, begging for her to come back as she got in a car and drove away without a backward glance.

The last time I ever asked someone to stay.

"I bounced around a few foster homes. Some were okay. Some weren't."

He tenses beside me but stays silent. He's thinking of my scars. When he doesn't say anything, I let out a soft sigh of relief. I'm not ready to talk about them. Not yet, possibly not ever. Just these few words are hard enough.

But I owe him. Not because he expects me to share, but because he gave me those pieces of himself with no expectations. For a man like Ari, that means something.

It shouldn't, I remind myself. But it does.

"No matter what, though," I say, trying to inject some levity into my voice, "I could always go outside. Read. Walk. Dream."

I walk a few steps before I realize Ari is no longer at my side. I stop and turn. My breath catches in my chest. He's standing with his feet planted in the sand, as though he rose from the ground itself. The wind tears at his hair, draws strands across his sculpted face. He stands firm, hands tucked in the pockets of his charcoal-gray coat, eyes pinned on me.

"What did you dream about, Diana?"

My throat tightens. In that moment, I can't remember my childhood dreams. I can't remember anything except what I dreamed about the last three months.

Him.

My tongue darts out, slides along my lower lip. His gaze fixes on my mouth, his eyes turning to fire.

And then his head whips to the side. The moment breaks as foreboding whispers across my neck a second before I follow his gaze and see it. A wave racing up the beach like a speeding train.

Straight toward the couple with their backs to the sea.

Ari

Fjandinn. Fokk.

The curses run through my head as the wave knocks the tourists off their feet. The man's shouts and the woman's terrified screams rise above the roar of the sea. White froth churns up the beach, swallowing them in a torrent of frigid water.

I sprint across the black sand, my feet sinking into the wet. The icy water sends a shock through my system as I dash in. The wave starts to recede, sucking them back toward the sea. I reach the man first, brace myself against the pull of the wave as I grab on to his arm and yank him to his feet.

"Where's Kacey?" he gasps as he clings to my arm. "Where's my wife? Kacey!"

I shove him toward the shore and turn. My heart catapults into my throat as my mind registers the flashes of white and green just feet away from me.

"Diana!"

She has a hand wrapped around Kacey's, is struggling to stay upright and pull the panicking woman to her feet as the water angrily pulls at her legs. I'm at her side in a few strides, reach down and grab Kacey's other arm. Kacey's saturated clothes and shock have turned her into lead weight as she alternates between heaving sobs and shrieks.

Diana and I pull, stumbling backward until the wave finally lets go. The man is waiting for us, repeating Kacey's name over and over as he rushes forward and starts to gather her in his arms. I step between them.

"Hey, get out—"

I plant my hands on his chest and shove. He stumbles back. "You almost got both of you killed."

The man starts to shake, his teeth chattering. "I didn't think—"

"Obviously," I snarl. "None of you do. You just ignore

the warnings and then act as if you have no idea why it happened." I point toward Kacey. "I saw her. She didn't want to go that far. You were pulling her toward the water."

"I just wanted a picture, I thought she was being—"

"The next time she tells you something, you better fucking listen. You don't deserve to be her husband."

The man's mouth is open, eyes wide as he stares at me. I jerk my head in Kacey's direction.

"Go."

He stumbles around me. I turn just as Diana steps back and the man pulls Kacey into his arms. Kacey clings to him, sobbing as he tells her over and over how sorry he is. I stare at them, slowly regain control of myself.

Until I turn to Diana. She's shivering, arms wrapped around her waist in her now drenched white coat. Her hair hangs in wet strands about her face. I glance down, grit my teeth when I realize she's barefoot.

I stalk forward.

"You."

She frowns. "What?"

I'm furious. Livid. Fool. *Fifl*. The anger is easier to latch on to. Better than the fear throbbing in my throat.

"What the hell were you thinking?"

Her mouth drops open. "Me?"

"You could have been killed!"

"So could you!" she retorts.

Her shivering intensifies. I close the distance between us, wrap my arms around her waist, and haul her over my shoulder.

"Ari!" She wriggles against me. "Put me down!"

"You lost your shoes," I snap back.

"I can still walk!"

"No."

"I'm not a sack of potatoes—"

I shift her suddenly so she doesn't have time to fight me. One quick shrug and she slides into my arms, one wrapped under legs and the other around the curve of her back. Her arms fly around my neck, her icy palms pressing against my skin.

"Ari…"

Her voice trails off as I look down. Our mouths are a breath apart. Adrenaline pumps through me, hot and fierce.

"Better?"

She presses her lips together and falls silent. The wind pierces my coat, tiny little knives slicing through the wool straight to my skin. Diana weathers it all with a stoic strength I can't help but admire. But her shivering intensifies as I move quickly up the path to the parking lot.

I tighten my grip when we reach the car and she tries to slip out of my grasp.

"Open the door."

She rolls her eyes as she does so. I set her in the seat and close the door, barely resisting the urge to slam it shut. My gaze cuts to Kacey and her idiot husband as they walk across the parking lot. Kacey is shivering, her eyes trained on the ground. Her husband shoots me a furtive glance before quickening his pace.

"You staying close?"

He looks back over his shoulder. "Yeah, in Vík—"

"Get out of those wet clothes as quickly as you can." I open my door. "And stay off the damn beach."

I climb in, turn the car on, and blast the heat as I crank the seat warmers up as high as they'll go. I grab my phone and type in a quick search.

"Excellent."

"What?"

"There's a hotel nearby."

Diana's shivering has already intensified. It doesn't stop

her from shooting me a look bordering on horrified. If the situation weren't so dire, I would smile.

"Hotel?"

"We have to get out of these wet clothes."

"But—"

I reach over and flip down the visor. "Look at yourself, Diana." Slowly, she raises her eyes to the mirror. My own fear ratchets up a notch as I note the pallor of her skin, the faintest tinge of blue on her lips. "We have to get warm."

"The restaurant—"

"Doesn't have a shower and most likely wouldn't have anything to change into. A hotel will at least have a blanket to wrap up in, if not a bathrobe, and it's closer than Vík."

I can see the moment she accepts our fate. She nods as she settles into the embrace of the seat, trying and failing to keep her teeth from chattering.

I slam my foot down on the gas and drive.

CHAPTER TEN

Diana

NUMBNESS SETS INTO my fingertips and toes as Ari pulls into the parking lot of the hotel. I register a tall, dark building, the front comprised almost entirely of glass. But it's hard to focus on anything but the cold sluicing through my veins.

"Stay put."

I want to argue. Should put up a fight. But I simply sit there, slowly morphing into an icicle, as Ari gets out and circles around to my side.

"Why aren't you affected?" I asked as he unbuckles my seatbelt and pulls me into his arms once more.

"I only got wet up to my waist. You got drenched trying to help Kacey up." He glares down at my coat. "And you're wearing fleece. My coat's wool."

"Lesson learned," I murmur. "Never buy fleece before running into the ocean in winter."

His chuckle vibrates against me, invites me to lay my head on his shoulder and breathe in. His warm scent soothes me. I close my eyes as my trembling lessens.

"I'm not shivering as hard."

"I noticed."

His voice is grim as he walks into the hotel. Someone greets him in Icelandic, although I can tell by their tone they're concerned. I keep my eyes closed as Ari carries me a short distance. The swish of elevator doors opening and closing is followed by a short ride up. I open my eyes as he walks down a hallway, realizing he's following a young man. The man stops in front of a door at the end of the hall and opens it. He looks at me, eyes wide, before turning to Ari and saying something else. Ari replies tersely before nodding and walking in, kicking the door shut behind him.

Larger than the average European hotel room. Open and airy with a huge window dominating one wall and dark furniture. The details rush by as Ari crosses the room in just a few strides and walks into the bathroom.

"Can you stand?"

I nod. He sets me on my feet, keeping one hand at my waist and the other at my shoulder.

"You need to get out of your wet clothes and into a shower." He slowly releases me, then moves over to the marble-and-glass shower to turn the water on. "Start lukewarm. Do not turn it to hot. You need to warm up slowly."

"Yes, sir."

"I'm serious, Diana."

The underlying worry in his voice has me biting back my retort. I nod again and reach back for my zipper. My fingers grasp the metal, then lose it. I try several times, my heart thudding harder against my ribs every time I miss.

My hand shoots out, my fingers splaying across the countertop. I know what I have to do. But God, I don't want to.

"Ari."

He knows. He's been standing next to the shower, waiting for me to reach the conclusion he'd probably reached a while ago.

"I'm sorry, Diana."

The compassion in his voice makes it worse. It would be so much easier if he was cold, disdainful.

"It's okay."

It's not. But what other choice do I have? The dress feels like wet cement. My limbs are stiff, my movements sluggish. I can't do this alone.

I feel the first tug. A moment later warm air touches my bare skin. He stops halfway down, tries to give me the gift of some anonymity.

"I need it all the way, Ari." I clench my eyes shut so I can't see his face in the mirror when he sees them for the first time. "I can't...please."

The dress parts down to my waist. His hands settle on my shoulders, warm and strong, as he pulls the wet fabric down my arms. I know what he's seeing: three scars on my left side. Two stretch from just below my shoulder blade to my waist, the third shorter than the rest.

Maybe the cold has numbed my heart. Maybe my mind recognizes how dire the situation is and has accepted the inevitable. Or maybe I've just receded so deeply within myself I can't feel anything. Just...numbness.

I exhale once my arms are free, a sharp, harsh sound partially muffled by the shower.

"I can get it from here."

Ari's hands fall away. I nearly sway back, feel a tendril of loss. I grit my teeth and shove it away.

"I'll have the door cracked. There's a robe on the hook behind it. Call if you need me."

I wait a few moments before I open my eyes. The room is empty.

I manage to tug my bra over my head and shove my dress and underwear off. I step under the spray, sucking in a breath as the warm water hits my skin. Gradually, it sinks in, penetrates to the deepest layers of my body. I focus on that, the physical sensations, keeping the emotions trying to break through at bay.

Survival, I remind myself as I lather my hair with shampoo that smells like a pine forest. I did what I had to for survival. Nothing more.

Finally, I get out of the shower and grab the robe by the door. It's white and fluffy, enveloping me in cloudy comfort as I step out of the bathroom.

The room is modern, with sleek black furniture and pale gray walls offset by accents like the teal pillows on the couch and crisp white sheets folded down on the massive bed. A kitchenette runs one length of the room, including a glass dining room table trimmed in black.

My jaw drops when I see the food laid out on top.

"How…?"

Ari is standing by the window. He's wearing a robe just like mine, except his stops just below his knees, revealing strong, muscled calves.

"Mussel stew, rúgbrauð with butter and pickled herring, cod with root vegetables, and skyr with wild berries and honey." He nods to a bottle in the middle of the table. "And Brennivín. Just a small amount," he adds as he stalks past me toward the bathroom, "but it can help you relax."

I stare at the table, barely register the door closing behind him as I take in the food.

The last time someone took care of me was eleven years ago. Eleven years ago this month, I realize as I cross to the table and pick up a thick slice of rye bread. It's warm, like it just came out of the oven. I slather on butter and add a tiny slice of herring. One bite has me adding more, savoring the contrasting flavors as I wander over to the window.

He's just being kind, I tell myself as I stare out over the darkening sea. He may loathe me on a personal level, but he doesn't want me dead.

I repeat that, over and over, as I think back to that moment when the waves raced up the beach. When I realized the woman was falling. When I heard the fear in her scream. The same fear that churned through me as I ran into the water. I wouldn't have been able to live with myself if I hadn't tried and the worst had happened.

But God I was scared.

The shivering returns, slamming into me with such force I stumble back from the window and sink into a chair. The same sensation when I heard Lucy's terrified barks that winter day when my world changed. When I rushed out and saw Dale standing over her in the backyard, belt in hand.

I drop my head, suck in deep breaths. I need to get a grip before Ari gets out of the shower. He's already seen enough of me today, both literally and metaphorically. Part of that is my fault. I'm the one who opened up to him on the beach before everything went to hell.

And for what? To expose myself to further pain when my job is over and I fly back to New York? Even if I could somehow reconcile the whole sleeping-with-Liam's-half brother, and even if Ari were the kind of man who would commit to a relationship, I won't risk letting someone else into my life.

And that's okay, I tell myself as I finally get my breathing under control.

"It's okay," I whisper out loud to the empty room.

Ari

I walk out of the bathroom, relieved to see Diana sitting at the table, ladling stew into two bowls. She glances at me, her face smooth, her hair hanging in wet ringlets over her shoulders.

"Better?"

"Yes."

I approach her cautiously. Showing me her scars must have cost her. When I unzipped her dress, saw the three lashes down her back, it took every ounce of self-control not to demand the name of the bastard who had done this to her.

"What's the name of the bread again?"

"Rúgbrauð."

I sit and grab a slice for myself.

"It's delicious. Everything is." She gives me a small smile, a fake one that sends a spurt of anger through me. "Thank you."

"You're welcome."

I wait until she places the bowl of stew in front of me before I speak.

"You shouldn't have gone in."

Her hand stills midair. Slowly, she sets her spoon back in her bowl and leans forward.

"You may be my temporary boss, Mr. Valdasson, but you will not tell me what to do in my personal life."

I grit my teeth. "After everything that just happened, we're back to Mr. Valdasson?"

"I made the right choice. Just as you did. And," she adds with an icy brittleness that rivals the tone I wielded this morning in our meeting, "if you say one word about being stronger than me, I will dump this stew in your lap."

Anger melds with relief. I want her righteous indignation, her outrage. Anything is better than that coldness driving a wedge between us. The coldness I'd been striving for all week, but now doesn't matter. Not after almost losing her.

"It's not that—"

"You saw my scars."

I still. "Yes."

"I'm here today because two people stepped in to stop what happened to me eleven years ago. They could have cowered or run away, but they didn't."

Realization hits. "Liam and Aislinn."

Her eyes glint. She stops, looks down at the table for a moment. I can see her visibly tying the strained threads of her control back together, stitching them with careful precision before she speaks again.

"There have been times I didn't do what I should have."
She looks at me then, her jaw tight, eyes flashing russet fire.
"I vowed the day I got these scars I would never run again.
When I was younger…sometimes a foster parent would be
drunk or just in a bad mood and take it out on the nearest
kid. Sometimes…" Her eyes dart to mine, then away. "Sometimes I hid."

"How old were you? When you hid?"

She swallows. "The last time I remember was when I was
twelve."

I set my own spoon down carefully. "So, a child?"

"It doesn't matter—"

"You were a child, Diana. You don't have to risk your life
to do penance for your past."

She pushes back from the table. "Don't act like you know
me."

My own temper snaps as I watch her walk to the window,
stare out over the darkening landscape as she turns her back
to me.

"How can I?" I demand as I stand. "You keep yourself
locked up so tight I only see the tiny bits you share because
you feel like you have to."

"I've shared more with you than anyone else in a very
long time."

"Including my brother?"

She whirls around, color high in her cheeks. "It doesn't
matter."

"The hell it doesn't." Months of suppressed fury roar to
life. "Do you have any idea what it's like to know you were in
my brother's bed after mine? To wonder what you've shared
with him, what he knows that I don't?"

Her hands ball into fists at her sides. "You didn't even care
that night! You acted like I was barely there."

"What else was I supposed to do? No, tell me," I order as

she looks away. "Tell Liam how we spent the evening before he proposed? How would that have gone over?"

Her sigh is heavy. "I don't know."

I pause. If I had been in Liam's shoes and had found out Diana had slept with someone the night before I'd proposed, I would have wanted to tear down the world.

"You don't know?"

Her head jerks up. "He would have been upset, of course. I just... It's not like we were together before that. So I'd like to think he'd understand, but..."

Her voice trails off as she runs a hand through her hair. Last night, she didn't answer if she had ever been in love with Liam. And now she's not even sure if Liam would have been upset by his fiancée being in another man's bed the night before he proposed.

What the hell happened between the two of them?

"He's still one of my best friends. I don't want to lose that." She scrubs a hand over her face. "I don't want to talk about this anymore. I don't even know why we're fighting. I'm not comparing what I've shared with you to what I've shared with others in my life. If you think what I've shared with you is worthless, you can—"

I close the distance between us and grab her shoulders. "Not worthless. Never worthless."

She freezes. The fight leaves her eyes as she blinks at me as if she can't process what I just said.

"I..."

She tilts her head up. The air between us thickens. Desire sets her eyes on fire as I give into my own and let my fingers trail up the column of her neck, the smoothness of her jaw, then slip into the damp silkiness of her hair.

I could have lost her today. Not just to another man, but permanently. My heart slams into my ribs at the thought.

"Diana."

Her lips part. An invitation I take advantage of as my mouth comes down on hers. Demanding, starving for another taste of her. I should be gentle, seductive. But I can't stop drinking her in, especially when she groans my name, her fingers clamping down on my arms with the same possessive ferocity burning me from the inside out.

I push her back against the glass. Pull back long enough to stare down at her. Eyes glazed, a flush in her cheeks the color of a rose. Beautiful, glorious color that could have easily been snuffed out today. I run my thumb along one cheekbone as the possibility shudders through me.

Her eyes soften. "Ari…" One hand comes up, rests on my face. "I'm all right."

I kiss her again. My fingers tighten in her hair as I growl against her lips. She presses her hips against the hardness of my cock with a boldness that rocks my control. I wrench my lips away, only to swiftly lower my head and blaze a trail down the side of her neck.

I pull her tightly against me. One hand rests on her back. I still. She freezes in my arms, then plants both hands on my chest and shoves, backing up until she's flush with the window.

I know what she's thinking, can see it in the tortured desire in her eyes. When we made love in New York, all she told me was that she liked to keep her top on. It wasn't my place to ask why, so I'd accepted it and what she had offered me.

But now, knowing what lies beneath the fabric, things between us have changed yet again.

"Concierge should be up in an hour with our clothes."

She blinks at my change of subject. "Oh."

"I also ordered pajamas from a local shop in Vík. The hotel will bring them up with our clothes."

Her eyes widen in alarm. "Pajamas?"

"By the time our clothes are ready, it'll be dark. Strong

winds are forecast tonight. Not to mention," I add as I walk back to the table, "we're both exhausted. Rest would be best."

Her gaze darts around. "Both of us? In here?"

"Yes. The rest of the hotel is booked." I nod to the bed, try not to think about what the two of us could do with so much space. "You take the bed. I'll take the couch."

"I can—"

"No."

A frown crosses her face. "I've slept worse places than on a couch."

"And tonight you don't have to," I reply calmly, even though the hint of what she endured in foster care is enough to reignite my anger. "You suffered more than I did out there. Take the bed, Diana."

I look away, focus on the food in front of me. I need fuel, energy to keep me going for what I'm sure is going to be a very long night.

Because there's no way in hell I'm going to sleep knowing Diana is just a few feet away.

CHAPTER ELEVEN

Diana

I WAKE UP in the night, heart pounding, my breath coming in short gasps. A sharp whine echoes in my ears, followed by a snap and a desperate bark. I can smell the stench of that backyard—fetid garbage piled in heaps made more pungent by the crisp sharpness of winter.

And I can still feel it. Lucy's tiny, cold body shivering in my arms. My heart pitching into my throat as I close my eyes. Brace for the next sudden stinging lash, the burning pain that follows and sinks so deep into my skin I'll never fully be rid of it.

The bed dips. I scramble back, away. It's dark, too dark. I can't see. I know Dale's in jail, he's not here, but I can't see—

"Diana."

Ari whispers my name. This time my whimper is one of relief. A moment later his arms come around me, strong yet gentle as he pulls me onto his lap. I curl into a ball, my hands sneaking around his neck as I bury my face in his chest.

He doesn't say anything, just rocks me back and forth. Gradually the tension bleeds out of my body. I should feel embarrassed, humiliated. But I don't. I feel safe. Protected.

I start talking, knowing if I don't say it now, I may never get back to this point of being raw enough to tell him what happened.

"Her name was Lucy. A chocolate Labrador I found in my foster father Dale's backyard. It wasn't a bad home at first. But his wife ran off a couple months after I got there, and he became angry. He drank a lot."

It had been so lonely in that house. So fearful.

"Lucy's fur was all matted and her ribs stood out against her skin. She was so tiny." I smile. "But she came right up to me, tail wagging, tongue lolling out. She had so much to be sad about and she was so happy. Dale only went out on the porch to toss garbage into the yard, so I set her up with this old trashcan and piled trash on the sides. Stuffed a blanket inside and snuck her food and water every day. I took out the trash every morning so Dale wouldn't have an excuse to go back there."

A tremble passes through me. Ari strokes a soothing hand down my hair.

"We made it two weeks. I'd known Liam and Aislinn for a couple months by then. Our high school counselor put us all in the same theater class because we were all foster kids." I smile slightly. "At first we hated it, felt like she was calling us out. But looking back, it was the best possible thing that could have happened to us.

"We started meeting up in the alley behind the house and took Lucy for walks to the park." I hold up my wrist. The silver heart catches the light of the moon, glints off the four letters etched onto the surface. "It was the happiest I'd been since I was put in care. Maybe even in my entire life."

I stop. Need a moment to catch my breath before I continue. Ari doesn't push. He just gently sways back and forth as he continues to hold me.

"And then one day, Lucy barked. I was inside the kitchen making Dale's lunch. He heard her and was sober enough to figure out it was coming from the backyard. He stalked out with his belt. He hated dogs. I ran after him." My voice catches. "He'd already found her. Cornered her. She was whimpering and then he brought the belt down and he..."

Tears start coursing down my cheeks. "I heard her cry. I ran across the yard and tried to pull him away. He pushed me. I tried jumping on his back, but he flung me off like I was nothing."

I still remember that feeling, the sheer anger at being so helpless against someone with more power. Of feeling like once more I was failing someone in need.

"I darted around him and grabbed Lucy. I tried to run, but Dale tripped me. I fell. I saw him bring the belt up, so I curled around Lucy and I... I held her."

Ari's arms tighten around me. I can't see his face. I don't want to. Not yet.

"Liam and Aislinn came through the back gate. Liam shoved Dale mid-lash. That's why the third scar is shorter. Dale was strong. But so was Liam. And he was furious."

I can still hear the crack of Dale's nose breaking. Fists against flesh. Of Aislinn on her knees next to me telling me I was safe, that she and Liam were here, before she yelled at Liam to stop before he killed Dale.

"A neighbor had seen what happened and called the police. Dale tried to say Liam had been attacking me and I got in the way when he was trying to chase Liam off. But the neighbor confirmed my version of what happened."

I suck in a shuddering breath. And then I look up at him. He's staring down at me, his face solemn, his eyes glittering with an icy rage.

"*Friendship* is a pale word for what I have with Liam and Aislinn. They both went to court with me. Liam took the stand and told the jury everything. I have no doubt his testimony is what helped get Dale locked away for so long. And Aislinn..." Just saying her name makes my chest ache. "Aislinn stayed with me in the hospital. Rubbed the medicated lotion the doctors gave me onto my back every night for weeks."

"And Lucy?"

"My new caseworker got Aislinn and I into a group home. Liam was eighteen and found an apartment nearby. He kept her until I aged out of the group home. She passed away three years ago." More tears roll down my face. "Liam and Aislinn were there, too. She was…she was…"

Years of grief threaten to break through. I put a hand on Ari's chest, push back. His arms tighten for a moment.

But then he yields. I stand up and walk to the balcony doors. The clouds are gone. The moon shines down, making the beach glitter and the sea sparkle.

"The only two people I've trusted in this world since my mom left are Liam and Aislinn."

The bed creaks. I can feel the heat of his body as he stops behind me, resist the urge to lean back into him. I've given him enough tonight. It's time to stand on my own two feet.

"Why are you telling me this?"

I turn, start to reply, when something catches my eye. I turn back to the window. There's a hint of green just above the sea.

"Is that…?"

The color shifts. Brightens.

"Yes."

Ari's voice is right next to my ear, deep and husky. I lean back toward him, hesitate when I feel his bare chest against my back.

A ribbon of emerald and purple winds its way across the sky, a slow, curling dance as the hues deepen.

"Oh my God."

More threads of color weave their way across the stars, shifting, glimmering for miles on end. My smile is so big it makes my face hurt.

We stand there, bound together by the incredible display of nature taking place above us and the truths we've shared. For one moment, I allow myself to simply feel, to enjoy.

Gradually, the colors start to fade. The ribbons shrink, still beautiful but dimmer.

"You're lucky."

Ari's breath is warm against my ear. I shiver.

"How so?"

"Many tourists come to Iceland to see the Lights. Many leave without seeing them. Or," he adds as I turn to face him, "they see a sedated version of what you just saw. Most don't realize the pictures and videos show different levels of light than what you can usually see with the naked eye."

"Then, I'll count myself lucky."

His face sobers. "Lucy was lucky to have you, too."

I stare at him. Tears burn at the backs of my eyes. "Why do you say things like that?"

He frowns. "What are you talking about?"

"Things like that," I say as I drop a finger in his direction. "Things like what you said in New York."

"What I said in New York?" he repeats.

"It's so much easier when you're cold. When I think you hate me."

"I don't hate you, Diana."

"See? Things like that."

One side of his mouth quirks up. "So what am I allowed to say?"

I run a hand through my hair. "I don't know. I just know when you say things like that, I feel like you see me and…" My voice trails off.

Ari steps toward me. I step back, coming up against the cool glass of the balcony doors. "Would it be so bad if I saw you?"

"Yes."

The word is wrenched from the depths of my soul, buried under years of hurt and rejection.

"Why did you tell me?"

"I don't know."

He leans down. "I think you do know. You wanted to tell me. Wanted me to know. I think you are far more lonely, Diana North, than you even realize."

His words hit home. I've been telling myself for years that my friendships with Liam and Aislinn were enough. That I would never be ready for a relationship—a love that would require baring my body and my soul. I told myself I couldn't give enough of myself to another person. But the truth is far more cowardly.

I'm scared. I'm scared of showing someone the deepest depths of my trauma, of them seeing it and doing what almost everyone else in my life has done: walk away. Liam and Aislinn are my miracles. Miracles don't happen twice in one lifetime.

As we stand there, I become aware of his state of dress, or lack thereof. He's wearing nothing but boxers molded to his thick, muscular thighs. My sharp inhale echoes in the room. He's hard, a swell of black fabric that makes my thighs clench.

His body jerks. My head snaps up. The tendons in his neck are taut, shoulders tense.

"Ari—"

His hand drops away. He steps back.

"Go to bed, Diana."

Confused, I stare at him. "Ari—"

"Go. To. Bed."

I walk past him, my eyes downcast. I crawl back into bed, pull the sheets and blankets over me, and roll away from him. I hear him wrestling, moving about the room. There's the faint squeak of the couch as he settles back down.

I close my eyes, breathe in. Breathe out. Fight the now-familiar sting of humiliation.

If he wouldn't have pulled away, I would have offered myself to him. For the first time in my adult life, I had wanted someone to see my scars. Wanted to show him that part of me willingly, not because I was forced to. But my wounds have become a barrier between us, my confessions rebuilding the walls I just tried to tear down and driving him away.

It's for the best, my mind whispers. I don't need anything more with Ari. He's my boss. I still haven't figured out how to tell Liam what happened. And above all, every time I confess something to Ari, every time we touch, I slip closer and closer to that edge he brought me to in New York. The edge between keeping myself safe and falling back into the familiar pattern of abandonment.

The more I learn about Ari, the more I realize he wouldn't leave out of cruelty. But he would leave. Ari's not the kind of man to fall in love. And even if he were, I don't think I'd be able to accept it. Wouldn't be able to live without fear hovering over me.

It doesn't matter, I tell myself as my eyes flutter closed. It doesn't matter.

Ari

She's beautiful in sleep. Spread out on her stomach across the bed, her face turned toward me. Her lashes lay dark against her skin, although the rest of her face is pale compared to the bruised half-moons beneath her eyes. She tossed and turned most of the night.

I turn away and move quietly into the kitchen to make a pot of coffee. Between our adventure yesterday and the rough night, we're both going to need it.

Her whimpers woke me, the soft, frightened cry of a broken child. When I went to her, when she heard my voice and turned to me, she rocked me to my core.

I've never once let a woman get that close. Losing my mother the way I did, sinking deeper into apathy and using it as a shield against my father, left me with the notion that I would never be capable of loving someone again. It was easier that way, the concept furthered when I discovered the depths of my father's mistakes. Instead of hurting, it made me angry. Anger is empowering. Grief weakens, brings you to your knees.

I've told myself so many times over the past three months that I responded to Diana the way I did in New York because I had started to crack the seal I'd kept over my heart for so many years. And perhaps it did make me more susceptible to the jolt of emotion I felt when I looked at her. But I know now, as I watch her sleep, her body rising and falling with soft, even breaths, that not just any other woman would have caused that reaction. It's her. Diana.

And after what she shared last night, that feeling is stronger. My admiration for Diana, the fortitude she showed at seventeen when she chose protecting an innocent over her own life, has deepened. I will do everything in my power to make sure the monster that marked her never sees the light outside prison again.

Her revelation heightened my envy of my brother, too. Envy, though, not jealousy. I always thought of one being the same as the other. But last night, for the first time since Liam and Diana walked into that restaurant, I wasn't jealous of their relationship. I was grateful for it. Liam had saved Diana's life. Saved Lucy. The bond that was created between Liam, Diana, and their friend, Aislinn, is something I don't fully understand, but I recognize it's real.

But one glaring fact continues to needle me. Not once did Diana say anything that indicated any romantic feelings for

Liam. That, coupled with her dodging my questions at the gala, reinforced what she'd been saying from the beginning: she and Liam had not been romantically involved until he proposed. Was Liam the one in love with her? Did she say yes out of obligation, because he saved her life all those years ago?

More questions. Always more questions.

Her eyes flutter open. She sees me. The slight smile that curves across her face, warm and sleepy, has me curling my hands into fists at my sides so I don't do something stupid like reach out and touch her.

She blinks. Realization hits her. She sits upright, one arm holding the sheet to her chest. A blush creeps up her throat and over the line of her jaw. I know she's embarrassed—that I made her feel that way last night.

I want to tell her how bad I wanted her, how all I could think about was touching her, tasting her, claiming her. But I couldn't do that. Not when she was in such a state of heightened emotion. When we come together again, it won't be because we're driven by grief and memories of the past. It will be because she wants me.

"We should be safe to drive back to Reykjavik," I say.

"Okay," she replies.

"Xenakis texted me this morning."

The apprehension disappears from her face, replaced by curiosity.

"Oh?"

"He wants to meet as soon as we're back. Alone, just the two of us."

"And you're okay with that?"

She's looking at me with a mixture of cool professionalism and quiet understanding. Letting me know with one glance that she'll support my decision to walk away.

"Yes. Either it'll get us back on track or I'll leave knowing I need to look elsewhere."

She throws back the sheet and gets to her feet. Even in gray fleece pants and black shirt, she's stunning. I watch her carefully, relieved when I don't see any sluggishness or stiffness to her movements.

"I want you, Malla, and the rest of our team to meet with Xenakis's. He's approved it. Find out what feedback they've received, if any. Start addressing those concerns. I'll text or call you as I get more details from Xenakis."

She nods as she moves over to the bag the concierge brought up last night with our freshly laundered clothes.

"The box underneath is for you, too."

She stills, frowning at me before setting the bag on the floor and opening the lid of the box. She stares down at the simple black flats nestled in tissue paper.

"You bought me shoes."

"You lost yours."

Her throat bobs as she swallows hard. One hand comes up, her fingers tracing over the smooth leather.

"Thank you."

Her voice is quiet. But the gratitude in those two simple words, the underlying shock, punches straight through me.

I turned away last night when I saw the invitation in her eyes. I wasn't going to take her in the aftermath of a nightmare, of reliving the most horrible moment of her life. But things have changed. Since the beach, since her confession.

I walk toward her. She straightens quickly, squares her shoulders as she turns to face me. Strong. *Stubborn,* I think as her chin comes up. Fear in her eyes, but she stands her ground.

"We have to deal with Xenakis first."

Confusion clouds her gaze. "Yes."

"And then," I add softly as I stop a foot away, "we'll deal with us."

She blanches. "There is no *us.*"

"There was."

And there could be again.

She's not ready to hear that part yet. There's still plenty for both of us to consider before taking that step. Plenty to deal with, like Liam and just what the dynamic is between him and Diana.

But I'm done pretending.

"I thought we could push past what happened between us." I lean down, just an inch, but enough to inhale the scent of her. "But we both know that's impossible."

The fear flares. If that were the only emotion in her eyes, I would walk away. I'm not my father.

But I see the longing. The desire. The small shudder that races through her body, the goose bumps on her flesh despite the warmth of the room.

"Soon, Diana."

I don't give her a chance to reply as I turn away. I want to push more, kiss her until she's breathless and soft against me.

Just a little longer, I tell myself as I open the door.

"I'll get the car warmed up."

And then I close the door on temptation.

CHAPTER TWELVE

Diana

I'M SO EXHAUSTED my eyeballs feel like lead weights in my skull. I blink, try to refocus on the words I was just reading. But the text shifts, blurs, no matter how hard I squint.

I give up and lean back in my chair. My eyelids give up the fight and I close my eyes.

Two days. Two days of nonstop working to come up with the new draft of the proposal. A draft I started on my phone on the ride back from Reykjavik. Not only did I have a lot of work to do, but it gave me something else to focus on besides Ari. Ari and his promise that we were going to talk about us.

The muscles in my shoulders clench, the tightness traveling up my neck to my head.

...we both know that's impossible.

He didn't say another word on the drive back, other than to answer any work-related questions I had. He dropped me off at the hotel to change so I didn't walk in wearing the same dress as yesterday. That would have started a flurry of rumors I had no interest in dealing with. Once I arrived at AuraGeothermal, I went straight to the conference room to meet with the teams. Ari had already shown up and disappeared into his office.

I didn't see him for nearly twenty-four hours. Someone told me he and Xenakis had gone out for site visits to some of the other geothermal fields. When he walked into the conference room yesterday afternoon, I only felt the tiniest spark of heat.

Okay. Maybe a small flame. But I still kept things calm, cool. He did, too, as he told us about a successful meeting with Xenakis before Hellas Shipping's team had done another review and added their own corrections, after which the proposal had come back to Ari's team and me.

The team left two hours ago. I should have, too. But I stayed, reading and rereading it, tweaking the occasional word and cross-referencing the final draft with all of the feedback we received.

"You look exhausted."

I bite back a shriek as I sit bolt-upright in my chair.

He's standing in the doorway, legs spread, hands tucked into the pockets of his suit. Black, like always. His shoulders are thrown back, his handsome face smooth. The same powerful stance, the same focus I've seen for over a week.

"I sent the proposal to Xenakis ten minutes ago."

My mouth drops open. "What?"

"Jon told me that the team had completed the final draft this evening. I reviewed it myself and sent it. Xenakis returned to Greece this afternoon."

I frown. "Why?"

"His daughter is pregnant with her first child. A month early, but they had reason to believe she was very close to going into labor."

Some of the pieces click into place. "That's why he's been short-tempered and unfocused."

Ari nods. "He's promised to give me an answer by the end of the week. I've given everyone who's been working on this the next two days off."

My lips curve up. "That's generous."

"There's somewhere I'd like to take you tomorrow. Þingvellir National Park."

The invitation throws me for a loop. I should say no. But Þingvellir is one of the places on my wish list to visit. I said something to that effect to Malla yesterday during one of our breaks.

"You're not playing fair."

The smirk disappears. His eyes darken, grow heated.

"No. I'm not."

The logical part of me is shouting to say no, to step back. A twisted, self-deprecating part of me wants to spend just a little more time with him before we talk about what happened between us at Reynisfjara. Before I make it clear we can't repeat that again.

"All right."

Triumph flares in his eyes. "Two o'clock tomorrow. Sleep well."

And then he's gone, leaving me with the sinking sensation that I have just said yes to the devil.

I decide the next day that, devil or not, the deal was more than worth it.

I'm standing on the stone deck of Fontana hot springs. We drove through the snowy moors of the park, occasionally catching a glimpse here and there through the shifting mist and snow. Ari refused to tell me where we were headed until he pulled into the parking lot of the springs, a small complex that sits on the shores of the lake. Behind me is a low-lying building that houses the lobby, café, and locker rooms. The deck hosts several pools, all with varying temperatures and setups. One is shallow, with random balls of stone to lean against and bubbling springs creating bubbles on the surface. Another is fashioned out of rock, a giant hot tub perched on the edge of the lake. There are several showers, a wooden building that houses a couple of saunas, and farther out, a dock that stretches out onto the lake. Aside from a couple people in the locker room who were packing up leave, there's no one else there.

It should be bleak. So much gray, the visibility limited by the mist. But it's not. It's soothing, calm. Standing there with light snow falling, wrapped in a robe, I'm content. I can't remember the last time I felt this way.

"Beautiful, isn't it?"

I breathe in that delicious scent of cedar and something darker.

"It is."

I turn and inhale sharply. With the snow lightly dusting his hair and a slight smile lurking about his lips, all I can think is that he looks like a Norse god brought to life.

"Which one should we get in first?"

He holds up a finger, then walks over to a small glass door built into the massive window that stretches across the face of the building. A young man walks up and opens the hatch. Ari orders in Icelandic, and a moment later, he's handing me a tall plastic flute filled with sparkling, golden liquid.

"Now you can decide which pool you want to get in."

I shouldn't like this. Shouldn't enjoy these luxuries—luxuries made even more special because they're coming from him. I make a good salary, but not enough to feel comfortable indulging in extravagances like this on a regular basis. There's always that sense of what-if. What if the worst should happen and I lose my job? I always live in a state of alert, of preparation.

Something, I realize, I've never fully acknowledged. Even when I told myself I had a good life, I've always lived each moment not with embracing but with reservation. Always holding myself back and waiting for the other shoe to drop.

"Diana?"

I jolt myself out of my reverie and look up at Ari.

"The rock one."

He stares at me for a moment longer, but doesn't say anything, just gestures for me to lead the way. When we get there, he holds out a hand for my champagne. Suddenly shy, my hand stills on the belt of my robe.

He wasn't kidding when he said he'd take care of everything. When he picked me up from the hotel this morning, there had been a black bag with gold lettering waiting for me: hiking boots, a wool coat, a thick scarf, and mittens. Three swimsuits in varying jewel shades, all one-piece and all with high backs that covered my scars. The women getting dressed in the locker room probably thought I was crazy, tearing up as I pulled each suit out. Liam, Aislinn, and I always bought presents for each other on our birthdays and at Christmas, would fight over the check whenever we all went out to eat.

But I can't remember the last time someone spontaneously bought me a gift. Not just a gift—clearly, they said how well he knew me.

I keep my gaze focused on the lake as I finally pull the belt and shrug out of the robe, draping it over the railing. The cold air brushes over my skin and sends a not-unpleasant shiver through my body. I face Ari. His eyes glow hot as he takes in the classic red swimsuit with the scooped neck.

"Good choice."

"Thank you." I hold out my hands, take both his glass and mine, and say, "And thank you. You didn't have to."

"No. But I wanted to."

My reply dies on my lips as he takes off his robe, revealing the carved muscles of his chest. I don't even realize I'm staring until he quietly clears his throat. Mortified, I hand him back his champagne.

"Thank you."

I narrow my eyes at the smug humor in his voice before stepping into the water. The sudden shock of the heat against the cold air on my skin makes me suck in a breath. I pause, waiting for my body to acclimate.

"Take it slow."

"Yeah," I gasp out. "Definitely taking it slow."

"We've got all the time in the world."

I hear it, the promise in his voice. I shiver, then step deeper into the water. It takes a couple of minutes, but finally, I sit down, letting out a satisfied sigh as the water closes over my shoulders.

"What?"

I glance over at Ari. He's standing a couple of feet away, giving me the space he knows I need, even though I didn't ask for it out loud.

"More than worth it."

I take a sip of my champagne, enjoying the bubbles dancing on my tongue.

"Why are you doing this?"

"What?"

I roll my eyes. "You know what. You didn't have to do this for me."

He holds his own glass up, studies the bubbles sparkling within.

"My father bought me a Mercedes for my seventeenth birthday."

I blink. "A Mercedes?"

"Yes. And to celebrate my graduation from primary school, he paid for myself and several school friends to go on a tour of Paris, Rome, and London."

"Wow."

"He didn't do it to be kind. It was all a matter of prestige. Of showing everyone exactly how much money he had by illustrating what he could buy with it. But I still took what he offered. Enjoyed it even."

He takes a sip of champagne, then suddenly turns and looks right at me.

"I never looked at any of the gifts he gave me with the same gratitude as you looked at a simple pair of shoes."

My hands tighten on my glass. "It just surprised me, that's all."

"You have worked night and day to help my company. You helped us make more progress in just over a week than we've made in over a year. I took Xenakis to the field where my parents met. I told him about my grandfather and my mother."

Pride tightens my throat. "Wow."

"It wasn't easy. But you were right. He understood my reasoning for taking the company over." One corner of his mouth quirks up. "Understands why I gave up my father's last name and took my mother's."

It takes a moment for the implication of that to sink in. But when it does, emotion roots me to the spot.

"Your mother's name was Valda."

His face is somber, his eyes glinting with memory as he nods. "Icelandic last names usually refer to 'son of' or 'daughter of.' Once I learned the depths of what my father did, I changed my name. My mother taught me far more about honor and commitment than he ever did. He loved profit. She loved her country and its people." His gaze grows distant as he stares out over the water. "I didn't think Xenakis would understand that. But he did." He nods toward the lake. "I brought you here because I knew you would enjoy it. It was a small way to say thank you, and," he adds with another small smile, "to see the look on your face."

It takes a moment for me to find the simple words I need to say. "Thank you."

We sit there for a few minutes, enjoying the water, the mist, our drinks. Once I have my emotions under control, I gesture toward the wooden structure near the edge of the lake.

"So sauna after the pool?"

"Not quite."

Ari stands. Drops of water slide down his chest and over the carved muscles of his stomach. My mouth dries.

"Follow me."

I down the rest of my champagne and hand my glass to Ari, who hands them to a passing attendant. It takes me a moment to realize he's bypassing the pools and the saunas and heading for the dock.

"Are you insane?"

He shoots me a small, cocky grin. "You said you wanted the full experience."

I cross my arms over my chest as the cold starts to settle back in. "Yeah, the warm, relaxing experience."

I eye the dark surface of the water, not reliving one of the most terrifying moments of my trip here. He stops and turns to me, his face suddenly serious.

"I won't make you. I will never make you do anything you don't want to. But," he adds in a low, seductive voice that reminds me once more of a devil in disguise, "you'll regret it if you don't at least try it."

He's right. He's right, and he knows it.

Gritting my teeth, I glare at him. "Fine."

"Don't sound so excited, Miss North."

He walks out onto the dock, his black suit clinging to his firmly rounded buttocks, water droplets clinging to the rippling muscles of his back. He gets to the end and waits for me to join him.

"How deep is it?"

"Here? Three and a half, four feet."

I suck in a shuddering breath. "Okay. So only freeze to death, not drown."

He holds out his hand. "I won't let anything happen to you."

I stare down at his outstretched hand, wanting, desiring. I don't know if I can.

"Don't look ahead. Just focus on now. On this moment."

Slowly, I slide my hand into his. His fingers close over mine, a delicious pressure that warms my hand even as winter wraps us in a cold embrace of wet mist and swirling snow.

"Three, two, one."

I step off the dock. Barely have time to gasp as my body pierces the water.

CHAPTER THIRTEEN

Diana

COLD. SO COLD I can't think for a moment, can only suck in a shuddering breath as my feet hit the bottom and my knees buckle. An arm of steel bands around my waist and hauls me up, keeping my head above water.

"You did it."

Shivering, teeth chattering, I look up at Ari and manage to smile.

"I… I did it. Now what?"

"If you can manage, stay in for a minute or two."

"You m-must be j-joking," I stammer.

"No. But only if you're comfortable."

As he talks, he sinks down until his shoulders are fully submerged.

I gape at him. "Aren't you freezing?"

"Cold, yes. But I've been doing this for years."

I force myself to stand there, shivering, the water lapping gently at my skin. After what feels like the longest minute of my life, Ari stands.

"Ready?"

I frantically nod. His chuckle is deep, rolling through me a second before he leans down and scoops me into his arms. I should protest but I'll take any warmth I can get. That and enjoying the feeling of being in his arms, even if it's only for a moment.

I cling to him as he walks out of the water. The breeze stings as the cold air hits my wet skin. He carries me back up to the deck and over to several freestanding showers. I start to get down, but his grip on me tightens.

"Pull that one."

I reach over and pull a chain, gasping in relief as warm water rains down on us.

"Oh, thank God."

He chuckles again.

He shifts. Liquid fire floods my body as I slide down his, inch by torturous inch. He waits until my feet touch the deck, then steps back, the small smile on his lips.

"Now it's time for the sauna."

I narrow my eyes at his retreating back, but I'm still too cold to not follow. As we round the corner, I glance around, realizing we're still alone.

"Is it always this empty in the winter?"

"No." He grabs the handle of one door and pulls it open. "I paid for us to have the last few hours to ourselves."

My mouth drops open.

"What?"

"I wasn't sure if you would feel comfortable being in a swimsuit around others."

"So you just rented out the entire hot springs? What about the people who had reservations?"

"They were contacted yesterday. Offered a variety of options, including paying their original fees as well as the fees to go to any of the other hot springs in Iceland, with transportation included."

"But…" I try, and fail, to mentally tally the magnitude of what he's done. "That must have cost a small fortune."

"And?"

A gust of wind whips around the edge of the building. I shiver. Ari opens the door.

"Get inside."

I walk in, arms wrapped tightly around my middle, trying and failing to process what he's just told me. I don't know which is beating louder inside my heart: my desire or my fear.

Inside, the sauna is hot, wet. A circular window curves out toward the lake. I sit on one of the wooden steps, my breath hissing out as the steaming hot wood hits my bare legs. He closes the door behind him and sits down a couple of feet away.

"What are you doing?"

He tilts his head to one side. "What do you mean?"

"You know exactly what I mean." My hands fly up, gesturing to the room around us. "Taking me on an excursion, buying me swimsuits, paying to shut down the hot springs for just the two of us? We're not... We can't be..."

When he simply stares at me, I glare at him.

"Say something. If you're trying to seduce me—"

"Stop."

The temperature in the room drops by ten degrees with the sheer force of ice in his tone.

"This has nothing to do with seduction."

"Doesn't it?" My voice is desperate. I need to believe this is just about sex, because if it's something more, anything more, I don't know if my heart can take it.

"Am I enjoying the sight of you in that swimsuit? Yes. Did I take advantage of the situation in the lake to hold you? Yes." He leans forward, his eyes blazing. "But I brought you up here today not to seduce you, but because I wanted to see you happy."

My brain scatters in a thousand different directions.

"Happy," I repeat.

"Do you have any idea how much I tortured myself with

the knowledge that Liam was raised in foster care? Imagining scenarios of what I've heard life is like in some of those homes?" My scars start to itch. "I was grateful to find out he wasn't abused, just neglected.

"Grateful," he repeats. "I saw you risk your life for someone you didn't even know. Learned how you turned one of the darkest moments in your life into something that propels you forward, even when you're afraid. How you looked at a damn pair of shoes like I had just bought you a diamond necklace.

"So yes," he repeats, "I wanted to do this because I wanted to see you happy."

I've hurt him. Again. Why? Why can I not just accept the good things in my life? Why do I always have to look at them through the lens of suspicion and pain?

I turn to face him, forcing myself to push away all the negativity, all of the hurt, loss, and abandonment. I strip it all away, leaving myself raw, open, vulnerable.

Slowly, I reach up and place my hand against his cheek. He stills, his body frozen, even as the heat swirls around us, inside of us.

"I feel like I'm always saying sorry to you." My thumb traces the sharp line of his cheek. "I'm sorry. I'm not used to gifts being given like this from people I barely know."

I start to pull back, but his hand comes up and covers mine. I stare at his fingers over mine. "How do you know me so well?"

"I could ask the same."

I blink, surprised. "What do you mean?"

"Do you realize you saw more in me in a matter of days than most have seen in my lifetime? You knew exactly what drove me, what's making me fight for my company." His gaze starts down to my lips, then back up to my eyes. "So I ask you, Diana North, how do you know me so well?"

I don't know who moves first. Only that when we come

together, the fire that's been burning between us explodes. There is no seduction. No finesse. Just raw, pulsing need.

Ari drags me onto his lap and growls against my mouth before his tongue plunges inside. I cry out, arch against him as one hand clamps down on my hip, the other pressing at the small of my back, urging me closer as I grind against him. I murmur his name, half a dozen times, if not more, before he wrenches his mouth away and trails drugging kisses down my throat.

My head falls back as his lips tease the sensitive skin just above my breasts. My eyes fly open as his fingers slide along the neckline of my swimsuit. I look at him, see the silent question in his eyes. I should stop. Need to stop.

But God help me, I can't.

I lean back, see the answering inferno in his eyes a moment before he yanks down my suit and bares my breasts. The heat of the sauna kisses my skin a moment before his mouth latches onto me. My hands grab his shoulders as I writhe, begging him for release as he licks, sucks, nibbles on me as pleasure winds me into a tight, pulsing knot of need.

I jolt as he slides one finger over the material covering my most sensitive skin. I thrust my hips toward him, a moan escaping as he pulls the fabric aside and teases me with long, slow strokes up and down my folds.

"Ari!"

When he slides one finger in, I detonate, my body clamping down around him as I thrash, writhe, cry out as pleasure spirals through me. I collapse against him, my breath coming and fast, heaving gasps.

Maybe a minute passes. Maybe ten. Dimly, I realize that Ari is stroking small circles over my back just below my neck. Soothing strokes that, combined with the aftermath of my pleasure and the heat of the sauna, leave me feeling languid.

"Are you all right?"

His question snaps me back to reality. I want to scramble off his lap, hide in a corner. Instead, I force myself to stay where I am as I raise my head to meet his gaze.

"Yes."

My gaze starts moving down to the hardness pressed against my thighs.

"Although feeling a little guilty."

His chuckle is low, sultry in the heat of the room. "You don't owe me anything."

"I know, but—"

"I didn't mean for that to happen."

Mortified, I start to scoot off his lap, but he anchors me in place with one muscular arm.

"I didn't mean for that to happen, because we have a significant amount of unfinished business between us." The heat disappears, replaced by a cold that penetrates deeper than the waters of the lake could ever reach. He smooths a strand of hair out of my face.

"You don't have any idea what you do to me, do you?"

Before I can answer, he stands.

"We've been in here longer than the recommended amount of time, I'm sure."

His slight smirk eases some of the tension inside of me.

"What about—"

"Later." He surprises me by leaning down and pressing a soft kiss to my forehead. "I don't regret what happened in here. But I never want you to feel like you owe me anything."

"I don't."

"Good." He squeezes my hand. "Let's enjoy the rest of our afternoon. We can talk later."

I ignore that last statement as we walk out of the sauna and back into the cold. We spend another two hours in the various pools, sipping wine and champagne. We don't repeat our earlier interlude, but the intimacy our time together cre-

ated lingers. Brushes of our hands. Long glances. A relaxed
atmosphere that reminds me of New York.

Night has encroached on the lake by the time we disappear
into our respective locker rooms. I take my time with a long,
leisurely shower before bundling myself into fleece-lined leggings and my favorite sweater. I walk out of the locker room,
happy, relaxed—only for every single one of those sensations
to disappear when I see Ari standing out in the hallway, his
face set back into that cold mask he wore when I got off the
plane last week.

I still, my fingers clenching around the strap of the bag
he gave me.

"What is it?"

"Malla called. Liam's here."

CHAPTER FOURTEEN

Ari

THREE MONTHS AGO, I wandered into the Metropolitan Museum of Art the night before I was going to meet my long-lost half brother. We'd only been chatting for a few weeks at that point, finally connected thanks to an ancestry website. The next few weeks had been pleasant, getting to know each other through messaging, then email, and finally the phone call that led to me flying to New York to meet him in person.

I can still remember the restless energy that moved through me as I wandered New York, the grief, guilt, and anger all bound up into a pulsing knot inside my chest. I went to the museum because I needed a distraction. I wandered, seeing everything and nothing, as I relived the last thirty-eight years of my life, wondering what they would have been like if I had had a brother beside me.

Now, as the elevator doors to my penthouse slide open, there's no anticipation, no faint flicker of hope. There's only anger. Anger and a possessive jealousy for the woman at my side, who just two hours ago, was nearly naked in my arms as her body shattered around me.

A woman I suspect my brother is still in love with, even if she doesn't feel the same way.

Liam stands there, one hand casually tucked into his pants pocket, the other wrapped around a glass of what appears to be the whiskey from my library. He shoots me a brash grin from a face so similar to my own it's like looking in a mirror.

"Hello, brother."

His gaze shifts from me to the woman next to me. I keep my hands at my sides, even as I want to wrap them around his neck.

"Di!"

He surges forward, wrapping her in a hug. She returns it, even as she shoots me a glance. I look away. The sight of my brother holding her in his arms, even in a gesture of friendship, makes my blood boil.

Liam releases Diana and turns to me, offering me his hand.

"Sorry to drop in on you like this. One of my clients invited me to join him on a European tour, which included a stopover in Iceland, and I thought, why not? See my brother, see my best friend."

My gaze starts to bounce back and forth between Liam and Diana.

"Best friend," I repeat.

Liam blinks.

"Yes. Just because our engagement didn't work out doesn't mean we can't be friends." He grins at Diana. "Right?"

"Right," she says weakly.

"Well," I say with a tight smile, "we're happy to have you. Your *friend* has been instrumental in helping move our deal forward."

"She's the best."

The familiarity in Liam's voice, the pride, makes my jaw harden. Fortunately, we're interrupted by the ring of the doorbell.

"I asked my secretary, Malla, to have dinner delivered." Liam looks surprised. "You didn't have to do that."

"It's a long trip from New York. It's the least I could do."

Dinner passes at the same pace as a snail making its way

across a highway, dodging traffic. Smoked salmon with dill-infused crème fraîche and pickled red onions, crispy Arctic char tartare, and grilled scallops with seaweed butter taste like ash. I force small talk with my brother over appetizers. It's a macabre repeat of our dinner in New York, with Liam and I chatting as Diana sits quietly. Every now and then, she responds to a question of Liam's, putting on a smile before he looks away.

But, I realize halfway through the pan-seared Icelandic cod with mashed root vegetables, Liam isn't a fool. He continues to talk, laugh. But he's aware of Diana's mood, his eyes darting to her face with an increasing frequency that makes me grit my teeth through the end of our meal.

"Malla ordered chocolate lava cake topped with berries and Icelandic honey for dessert."

Liam's eyes widen appreciatively. "I don't think I've eaten this well in…ever."

Guilt cuts through my anger at the reminder of the stark difference between how Liam and I were raised.

"I'm glad you're enjoying it." I stand. "I'll bring dessert into the library."

I leave before either of them can say anything. I need a moment to get myself back under control, to analyze and figure out the best way to proceed with the evening.

One way or another, this needs to be settled. Tonight.

Diana

I watch the flames in the hearth. Better that than looking at Liam and giving him even the tiniest hint of what his brother and I were doing just before he arrived in Reykjavik.

How, I wonder as I watch an errant spark shoot out toward the edge of the hearth, *was I partially unclothed in a sauna on the shores of an Icelandic lake two hours ago?* And now

I'm in the penthouse of my client and former lover while his brother, my best friend, stares at me with such scrutiny it makes me feel like spiders are crawling over my skin.

"It's nice having you here," I finally say.

"Is it?"

Surprised at Liam's dark tone, I look over "What?"

"I know you've been keeping something from me, Di." He pushes away from the table and walks toward me, anger written across his face. Anger and, I realize with a sinking heart, hurt. "Ever since the day I asked you to pretend to be my fiancée."

"Liam…"

God, I don't want to have this conversation. Not now, not ever. But as he scoffs and walks back to the fireplace, I know I have to. I thought keeping my night with Ari to myself would protect our friendship, not harm it.

Liam speaks before I can.

"You didn't have to say yes, you know."

I frown. "Of course I did."

He whirls around then, hands clenched into fists at his sides. "No, you damn well didn't. Do you think you have to keep paying a price to be my friend?"

The words act as a lance and stab straight into the heart of my deepest fear.

"No." I shake my head. "No."

"Don't lie to me." His voice drops down, so low I can barely hear it over the crackling logs. "Please."

I slowly walk over to him. Square my shoulders as I suck in a shuddering breath. As I confront the harsh truth of what he's saying.

"I don't think I have to. But," I add as he raises his head, "sometimes it's almost a…compulsion. A little voice whispering to do something just to make sure. It's hard to realize how much that fear has been driving me." I reach out and lay a tentative hand on his arm. "But I know without a doubt that I said yes back in New York because I wanted to. There's nothing I wouldn't do for you and Aislinn."

"I know." His inhale is sharp, sudden. "I don't want to lose you, too, Diana."

The words comes out harsh, guttural. My heart breaks at the pain in his voice, the ache for someone who may be lost to us both. I hug him, fighting to keep my tears at bay. A moment later he hugs me back, crushing me to him as if he's holding on for dear life.

A log falls in the fireplace and sends up a shoot of sparks. A creak sounds behind me, but I ignore it, focusing on my friend.

"I shouldn't have doubted you," Liam says quietly.

Guilt curls in my stomach. I start to speak, to confess my own sins, but someone else speaks first.

"Am I interrupting a reunion?"

My stomach drops to my knees. I pull away from Liam and turn my head to see Ari framed in the door.

"No." I look between Liam and Ari, my friend and my lover. "No, we just—"

"Don't deny it." Ari's voice is as hard as the rocks stabbing out of the black sands of Reynisfjara. "Allow me to congratulate the happy couple. Again."

Liam frowns. "We're not engaged, Ari."

Ari's eyes flick to his brother. "Then, what did I just overhear?"

The arrogant tone makes my very thin thread of patience snaps. "It's none of your business."

His gaze shifts back to me. Fury makes his eyes burn. His body is coiled tight, as if he's ready to spring forward and attack. The connection between us disappears, replaced by suspicion and jealousy, pain and betrayal.

It'll never work.

My breath freezes in my chest. I don't know what's worse—realizing Ari and I will never work, or finally accepting that I hoped for something more all this time.

"Really?" His voice is silky, deceptive softness layered over ice. "I would say given the events of the past three months, and especially the last twenty-four hours, it is very much my business."

Liam head swings back and forth between the two of us. "What are you talking about?"

The world presses down on my shoulders. It's heavy, too heavy for me to keep up any longer. Maybe Liam will hate me. Maybe he won't. I should have told him months ago.

"He's talking about how we slept together the night before you proposed in New York."

Ari's eyes widen slightly, as if he didn't believe I actually said it. Liam's mouth drops open.

"What?"

"Yep." I walk over to the couch, grab my coat, and shove my arms into the sleeves. Frantic energy pumps through my veins, keeps me moving. "Now it's out in the open. I'm going back to my hotel."

"You can't just leave after—"

I hold up my hand as Liam starts toward me. "I can and I will. I've shared my secret. Now I need some time alone."

I don't even bother looking at Ari as I walk out. I can feel his eyes burning twin holes in my back, but I keep my gaze forward as I leave his penthouse and let the door close behind me.

One long elevator ride later and I am out in the winter's night. The wind is frigid, tearing at my coat as I move down the sidewalk. I hunch my shoulders, register the cold. But inside I'm numb. So exhausted it feels like even my bones are tired.

I may have just lost my one remaining friend. And if Ari

didn't hate me before, he did in those moments before I unveiled our secret. I don't know if I preferred his indifference and occasional loathing or the raw, pulsing anger when he thought Liam and I were getting back together.

It doesn't matter. I'd like to think Liam will be understanding and our friendship will survive this. I'll find out soon enough. And as to Ari, I had feelings for him once. I survived.

Survive.

My life's motto. Always surviving. For the last eleven years, I had something more with Liam and Aislinn.

Do you think you have to keep paying a price to be my friend?

Liam was right. There's always been a fear lurking beneath the surface, a fear that one day people will see the real me. The me that drove my mother away, that sent me from one foster home to another, that motivated Dale to bring that belt down across my back.

My eyes grow hot. I don't like this fear. Don't like confronting just how much it's been ruling my life. I'll have to deal with it. Have some hard conversations with myself, with Liam. God willing, one with Aislinn, too.

And Ari—

No. That door is shut.

My steps are heavy, my feet slapping against the sidewalk. The wind stings my cheeks. I don't even bother glancing at the sky as I slowly make my way back to the hotel.

CHAPTER FIFTEEN

Ari

I DON'T GO after her. A display of significant will as I want nothing more than to grab her by her arm and drag her back in here.

I stare at the empty door Diana just walked through. Slowly gather my anger and shove it down as deep as I can before I turn to my brother. The brother who is innocent in all of this. The brother whose face I wanted to pummel when I walked in and saw him holding her. Telling her he hoped it wasn't too late.

Liam is glaring at me.

"What did you do to her?"

"You heard her." I walk over to the cart and pick up the whiskey decanter. "We slept together."

"How…? When did you two even meet?"

"The Metropolitan Museum of Art, the day before you and I had dinner." Whiskey splashes into the glass. I focus on it, the play of light through a fall of amber. "A chance encounter. We talked, we had dinner, we had sex."

I turn back just in time to see Liam make a face.

"Okay, can you stop saying that?"

Guilt creeps in. I take a long drink, savor the burn down my throat.

"Had I known anything about her, Liam, including that

you two were close enough to get engaged the following day,
I never would have—"

"Wait." Liam holds up a hand. "Did she not tell you?"

My fingers tighten on the glass. Of course Diana has more
secrets.

"I can only imagine what else she's kept from me."

"Bet you can't," Liam muttered as he runs a hand through
his hair.

"Then, enlighten me."

He looks at me then, our mother's eyes staring out of a
face so similar it's disconcerting.

"The engagement was fake."

For a moment, there's nothing. Slowly, I become aware of
a dull roaring in my ears, a pounding in my chest as I stare
at my brother.

"What?"

"My engagement to Diana was fake."

I take another sip of whiskey. Puzzle pieces that never
quite fit suddenly fall into place. Beneath the logic is a tangle of emotions: relief, shock, anger. I'm not sure which one
to unravel first.

"Hmm."

Liam explodes. "That's all you have to say?" He stalks toward me, jaw tense, blue eyes livid. My baby brother has a
temper. "You sleep with the woman who's like a little sister
to me and all you have to say is 'hmm'?"

I'm trying to pay attention to Liam while I process the
magnitude of what he's just divulged.

"Yes."

He pushes me. I hold up my drink, barely keep the whiskey from sloshing over the rim.

"Damn you." He's fired up, his chest rising and falling, his
eyes slits. "Do you have any idea what she's been through?"

Anger takes over. I raise myself up to my full height. Even

though he's only an inch or two shorter than me, I stare down at him.

"Don't you dare suggest I'd do anything to hurt her."

Haven't you? a nasty voice whispers in my head as I think back to those first few days when I raked her over the coals.

"You don't know what she survived in foster care—"

"If you even think of comparing me to Dale Cliffton, I will break your nose."

Liam stares at me. "She told you?"

"She did."

"And Lucy?"

I think of Diana, nearly a woman but still a child, huddled over a shivering dog, whimpering in pain and fear, even as she uses her own body as a shield. Think of the silver heart hanging from her wrist with the etched name that's starting to blur.

"Yes." The word comes out like it's been scraped over rocks.

"Wow. Just…" Liam takes a couple aimless steps to the side before stopping and running his hands through his hair. "Wow."

"Once you've recovered your ability to do more than repeat a couple words, enlighten me as to what the hell has been going on for the past three months."

Liam turns back to me.

"She really didn't tell you?"

"No," I bark.

So he tells me. He tells me about Aislinn and how she slowly slipped away until she cut Liam and Diana out of her life completely. There's pain in his voice when he talks about Aislinn's husband threatening to destroy all three of them if there was any hint of an affair between Liam and Aislinn. How Liam lied about an engagement to protect them from Dexter's wrath and buy himself some time to look deeper into the man's background. And how even after Dexter's sudden death, Aislinn still refused to speak to them. Knowing Diana's history, I can only imagine how deeply her friend's sudden and unexplained withdrawal hurt her.

I listen. I absorb every detail. His story deepens my understanding, along with my respect for Diana. I had accused her of switching loyalties in the blink of an eye, of not being able to honor a commitment.

I couldn't have been more wrong.

As I listen, a primal part of me is surging to life. One I've been denying for so long. One that makes my blood race and my body hard even as my chest starts to ache, an ache that spreads until my whole body is throbbing with the need to touch her.

"God, I'm an idiot," Liam mutters more to himself than to me as he paces in front of the fire. "I knew something was wrong. I knew it and I didn't push because I was so focused on keeping Dexter at bay and finding out what was wrong with Aislinn that I just ignored Diana."

"Diana is not one to share her feelings."

"No," Liam agreed. "She's not."

He suddenly grimaces.

"What?"

"Sorry. It's just…" He waves a hand in my direction. "She's like a little sister to me. The thought of you and her…" He shudders. "I know she's not… I know she's had…" He holds up both hands. "I'm just not going to think about it."

"That would be wise."

Liam sits on one of the tufted chairs, leans forward and props his arms on his knees.

"I've been watching out for Diana, and Aislinn, for years. Those girls…" His voice trails off. He clears his throat. "I loved the people I knew as my mom and dad. They never hid my adoption from me, but they loved me like I was their own."

I remember the picture he messaged me when we first started talking. Robert and Norrine Whitlock, a sweet-faced older couple with their arms wrapped around a grinning baby Liam.

"I'm glad you had that," I say quietly.

I mean it. Liam received far more love with Robert and Norrine than he ever would have growing up in our house.

"But when they died…" He stares into the fire. "The first year was the hardest. Going from having a home of your own to being shuffled around while the state tried to track down family to take me in. When they didn't, I got used to it. But then I met Aislinn and Diana." His smile is lightning fast and just as bright. "They brought me back to life. Diana went through so much, and yet she was always sneaking me little gifts, things I needed like pencils or notebooks at school. She baked a cake for my birthday. First one I'd had in eight years."

I take in every detail, hunger for more. Relish the insight into this woman who's been haunting me for the past three months, into the brother who rallied against the odds.

"She's very loyal."

A trait I both respect and loathe right now. How much anger could have been spared if one of them had simply told me the truth?

Liam sits up. "I want to know you more. Your history with Diana doesn't change that for me."

His words wipe away my frustration. The massive chain that's been wrapped around my chest for months loosens.

"I'd like that."

"Your relationship with Diana is none of my business. But she's incredible, Ari." He looks at me then with a cold anger that reveals the cutthroat lawyer I read about. "If you hurt her, I will find ways to bleed your personal finances dry before I cut you out of my life without a backward glance."

"Noted." I toss back the rest of my whiskey and stand. "Now, if you're done playing overly protective big brother, there's someone I have to see."

Diana

I'm steps away from my bed when the knock sounds at my door. My head lolls back as I let out a groan. There are only two people who would be knocking on my door this late. I don't have any interest in seeing either one of them.

I trudge over to the door, peek through the hole. Ari's handsome face fills my vision.

I lean back, heart pounding. I hadn't really believed he would seek me out. Not tonight, perhaps not ever, with how angry he'd been right before I dropped my bombshell.

"I know you're awake."

I close my eyes and lean my forehead against the door.

"Liam told me everything."

I freeze.

"The fake engagement. Aislinn. Everything."

My stomach sinks. "Is Liam mad?"

"He's mad you didn't tell him about us."

"There is no *us*." I clear my throat. "This doesn't change anything."

"Don't lie, Diana. Not to yourself and not to me."

Pain stabs deep. "Haven't you heard? I'm really good at it."

Silence. For a moment, I wonder if he's left.

"I didn't take you for a coward."

Irritation makes me stand up straight. "What?"

"A coward," Ari repeats. "Afraid you won't be able to keep your hands off me?"

I wrench open the door, hoping he's leaning against it and he'll fall flat on his rear. Unfortunately, he's standing straight and tall in the hall, dominating the space with his massive shoulders and looking stupidly handsome as I hover there in a bathrobe with my hair falling in a wild cloud around my face.

I hold up my hands, wiggle my fingers.

"No trouble at all."

He arches one brow before he just walks right into my hotel room. Before I can tell him to get out, another door opens down the hall. I quickly close mine.

"Afraid to be seen with me?"

I whir around, furious to see a mocking smile hovering about his lips.

"What if someone recognizes you? Snaps a photo of you outside my room, or starts to ask questions about us?"

"None of their business."

Frustrated, I step back, circle behind the couch. A physical barrier between us.

"Do you have any idea what would happen if even a whiff of scandal got back to my boss?"

"Us nearly having sex in a sauna in a national park wasn't scandalous enough?"

My cheeks, and a significant portion of my body, flush with heat.

"This isn't a joke, Ari. This is my career. My life."

"You're right." The amusement vanishes, replaced by a sudden intensity that roots me in place. "It's not a joke. Why didn't you tell me the engagement was fake when you arrived in Iceland?"

I raise my chin. "Because Liam asked me to tell no one."

His eyes burn into mine. "Are you in love with Liam?"

"No."

"Have you ever been in love with him?"

"No."

"Is there anyone else?"

"No!" I shout. "I told you that night, there was no one but

you. There was no one for over a year before I met you, and there's been no one but you since that night."

As soon as I say the words, I flinch. Why did I say that out loud? Worse, why did it have to sound so pitiful? Desperate?

"You've been a part of me ever since that night, too, Diana." He stalks toward me. Slow, predatory movements that send twin thrills of apprehension and lust spiraling through my heated veins. "No one else. Just you. Every time I smell anything even remotely resembling jasmine or rose petals, I see you in my mind, spread out on my bed." I step back, but he follows me, step for step until the wall's at my back and I can go no farther.

Trapped.

And there's nowhere else I'd rather be.

"Every time I get in an elevator, I remember how it felt to touch your skin for the first time."

His hand drops down, his fingers tracing over the back of my hand, my wrist. My eyes flutter shut as his touch dances over my skin, so light it's almost maddening.

I feel the warmth of his breath on my neck just before he speaks.

"I've had the taste of you on my tongue for three months."

Oh. My. God. Heat pools between my thighs. Wild, reckless heat that demands to be satisfied. A need I've been denying I even had.

My eyes fly open as he grabs my chin in a gentle but firm hold.

"For the first time since that night, there are no barriers. No guilt holding us back. Nothing but ourselves."

The future opens up before me, a frightening void where I can't see what comes next. I can plan for myself, control my own actions and feelings. But Ari is a wild card I never saw coming, a man who can seduce me with a single look, make me crave an emotional connection I never thought I would want.

I should push him away. I should tell him our relationship is nothing more than business, will never be more than business. That I don't want him the way he wants me.

Instead, I wrap my arms around his neck and kiss him.

My lips barely touch Ari's when his arms wrap around my waist like a steel vise, and he crushes my body to his. He slants his mouth across mine, ravages as he makes a sound in the back of his throat like a hungry growl.

The sound has me arching my hips against him, frantically rubbing my thighs against his thick hardness.

"ég þarfnast þín."

His words vibrate against my mouth. I part my lips to ask him what he just said. His tongue slides in, dominant and intimate. I gasp, open wide. Arch against him as my hands race up his chest, delve into his hair.

One last glimmer of sanity tries to rise to the surface, a frantic whisper that this is too fast, that we need to slow down.

And then I think of the last three months, of waking up with a throbbing between my legs and an ache in my heart I told myself over and over again didn't matter, couldn't matter. Of pushing away memories of being cradled in the dead of the night in a warm embrace. Feeling safe and protected. Wanted.

I silently tell my sanity to go to hell and surrender myself to Ari.

He senses my yielding, takes us both deeper. I moan into his mouth as his hands find the belt of my robe. One swift yank and the robe parts. His hands come up, shove the material off my shoulders and leave me in nothing but a tank top and panties.

His hands roam, greedy. His tongue teases, demanding.

I give him everything and demand more as I kiss him back with an abandon I've never allowed myself.

His fingers latch on to the hem of my shirt. He starts to pull up. I tense, but before I can react, say anything, he lets go. One hand settles on my waist. The other comes up to cup the back of my head, cradling as he kisses me.

Heat stings my eyes. I plant my hands on his chest, push him back. He lifts his head, his breathing labored, eyes burning blue.

"I forgot—"

I lean up, give him one hard kiss.

"You stopped."

"Yes."

I lay one hand on his cheek. The beginnings of stubble are rough against my palm.

"Ari…"

The kiss he places on my forehead has my eyes drifting shut, the only defense I have against the tears building behind my eyes.

"I'm sorry, Diana. It won't happen ag—"

"No."

I shake my head as I open my eyes, stare up into the blue gaze I've dreamed about for so many nights. I grab one of his hands in mine, guide it down. His eyes blaze hotter, his entire body tensing as I place his hand over the hem of my shirt.

"Diana."

I look up at him. Even though my heart is pounding, I nod.

"Please."

His fingers wrap around the hem. Slowly, ever so slowly, he inches the shirt up, his knuckles grazing my stomach. Cool air kisses my breasts as he pulls it higher, higher still.

Then the shirt is gone and I'm in nothing but my underwear. My hair cascades down my back, covering my scars, but I'm still nervous.

No. I'm scared.

Ari lowers his head, rests his forehead against mine.

"Tell me what you need."

I suck in a shuddering breath. "I need to show you. Before this goes any further, I need to show you."

He shifts, presses his lips to my brow.

"I'm here."

The tears nearly escape at the total acceptance in his voice. The strength even as I hear the shudder in his voice, know he's holding himself back.

For me.

Slowly, I turn. Every movement is punctuated by the thud of my heart against my ribs, so hard I wonder if I'm going to pass out. I grab my hair, pull it to one side.

Leave my back bare to his gaze.

Time stretches. I stand there, mostly naked, shoulders thrown back even as I quake inside.

Then a hand cups my shoulders. Ari turns me back around. Fury shimmers around him, a shroud of emotion so visceral I can almost reach out and touch it.

"If he ever comes near you again, I'll kill him."

Fear spurts through me. Dale won't have another parole hearing for ten years. But the thought of Ari confronting him has me fisting my hands in his shirt.

"I swear to God, Ari, if you do anything stupid to get yourself hurt, I'll…" My voice trails off as a low chuckle rumbles in his chest. "What?"

"You care."

"Of course I care, I…"

I break off, mortified. I start to step back, but he reaches out and grabs me around the waist once more. Takes care to place his arm well below my scars.

"I care, too."

He cradles my head in his hands, kisses me as he nudges

me back toward the bed until my knees hit the edge and I sit. He strips off his jacket and tie. My mouth waters he unbuttons each button with quick, deft movements. The rest of his clothes follow a moment later.

And then he's gloriously naked, his cock jutting out from his hard, muscular body.

"Condom?" he nearly growls.

"I'm still on the pill. I haven't…" I blush. "There's been no one in a long time."

"There's been no one since you, Diana."

I reach for him, but he captures my wrists in his hands, almost the same way he did in the elevator in New York.

"Not this time." He steps between my legs. "I need you, Diana. Now."

He leans down and kisses me, tumbles me back onto the bed as he covers my body with his own. I wrap my arms around his neck, kiss him back as his hardness presses against me. When he slips inside, I close my eyes on a moan.

I missed him. Missed this, the connection, not just the physical pleasure as he thrusts inside my body, but that familiarity, a recognition I feel in my soul.

We climb together, thrusting, arching, hands roaming, mouths seeking. Pleasure spirals, builds, molten hot. I cry out his name as I peak. He follows a moment later, his body shuddering as he buries his face in my hair and groans my name.

CHAPTER SIXTEEN

Ari

I WAKE WITH a warm body curled in my arms and the sound of my phone ringing. Irritated, I roll over and grab it as Diana murmurs.

"Yes?" I bark.

"Good morning to you, too."

I slowly disentangle myself from Diana and move to the far side of her hotel room.

"Hello, Xenakis." I pause, the sound of his voice registering. "You sound happy."

"I am." I can hear the man's smile from several thousand miles away. "I have a granddaughter. A beautiful granddaughter."

I smile slightly. "Congratulations."

"Thank you." His sigh is deep, relieved. "My daughter made it through, too."

I still. "Were there concerns?"

There's a pause on the other end of the line. And then, quietly, "Yes. She was diagnosed with a condition a month or so ago that made this last stage of pregnancy challenging. The same condition my wife passed from a few weeks after our daughter was born."

I pinch the bridge of my nose. Xenakis's behavior suddenly makes sense. Had I allowed my past experiences and prejudices to guide my decisions the past few weeks, the outcome of my deal with Hellas Shipping would have looked very different.

I glance back at the still-sleeping form curled under the sheets. Diana is truly a wonder at her job. But will she be able to take her own advice when it comes to her personal life? Let down her barriers and trust that I'll accept her?

"I'm glad she's all right."

"As am I." His voice lightens. "I was too excited last night to sleep, so I reviewed the contract. Are you free to fly to Athens today or tomorrow?"

I pause, tamp down the surge of satisfaction before I reply. "I am."

"I'd like for Hellas and Aura to sign the contract."

Pride floods my veins. "I'd like that, too."

I hang up, move to the window and gaze out over the harbor. Think about what this will mean for the company, for expanding what we do.

For honoring my mother and the grandfather I never knew. The legacy he created and she fought for.

"Ari?"

Diana's soft voice flows over me. I turn, my heart stilling as she smiles at me, her face soft and glowing from sleep and a night of lovemaking.

"Was that what I think it was?"

I cross over to her, kneel on the bed, and kiss her. "It was. Come with me."

Her eyes widen. "What about your team—"

"They'll come, too. But I want you there. This wouldn't have happened without you."

She meets my eyes. Hope fills me as she slowly nods. "All right."

Hours later, Diana and I walk into the soaring hall of a seaside villa just outside Athens. One of several vacation homes Xenakis maintains for international visitors, set on the far end of a resort with stunning views of a jewel-toned sea and white beaches. The other members of my team, including my chief financial officer, public relations head, and lead legal counsel, are flying in later this afternoon. A strategic move that gives Diana and me a little more privacy, a little more time to figure things out between us after the dust settles on the contract.

I follow her through the villa, watch her as she explores each room, fingers lingering on the azure-colored furniture or stroking the marble banister that leads up to the second floor.

She saves the main bedroom for last, eyes roaming over the Grecian columns, the arched windows overlooking the sea, and the massive bed dominating one wall on a raised dais.

"Cozy."

She smiles at me, but her face is strained.

"Everything all right?" I ask as I move to her side.

"Yes." She clears her throat. "Yes, of course."

"You told me to talk to Xenakis. Let him in." I reach out, tuck a stray strand of hair behind her ear. "Why can't you do the same to me?"

She leans into my touch, just for a fraction of a second, before standing and walking toward the window. I clench my fingers into a fist, force myself to stay seated.

"Do you know why I left your hotel that morning?"

I think back to the moment I woke up, reaching for her, only to find cool sheets. Surprise, then shock, then anger.

And beneath it all, pain.

"No."

"Because I didn't want to leave."

I give up fighting. I stand and cross to her, stopping just a couple feet behind her. Close enough to feel the warmth of her body. Far enough away not to crowd.

"Do you like to deny yourself what you want?"

"When it comes to relationships, yes." She crosses her arms over her middle, a physical shield against whatever she's confronting. "Liam and Aislinn are the only two people I've been able to trust, ever since I was a child. That trust came out of something traumatic and ugly."

I've never been a violent person. But every time I've thought of Dale Cliffton, it's been closely followed by vivid images of what I would do if I ever saw that man face-to-face. He should be grateful he's in prison.

"And there's no room for anyone else."

She rubs her hands up and down her arms even though the evening is warm. I take a step closer, inhale her scent.

"It's not that." Her voice is so soft I have to strain to hear it. "I'm afraid."

"Afraid of me?"

"No!" She whirls about, her eyes flashing with russet fire. "I've never been afraid of you, Ari." She reaches out and grabs my hand. "Not once."

I swallow past the tightness in my throat. Even when she's hurting, she's thinking of others. Thinking of me.

"I'm glad."

She drops my hand, steps back. The fear returns. The fear and a shimmer of frustration.

"Then what?"

"I told you about my mother."

"You did."

She curls in on herself, shoulders hunching, chin dropping to her chest. The strong, confident woman I know disappears. When she looks at me through the waterfall of her hair, I see the abandoned child, the broken teenager.

I gather her in my arms. For a moment she's stiff, unyielding. I do what she did for me the day I stalked out of Aura-Geothermal to drive south; I wait.

Slowly, her body relaxes. Her arms come up, tentatively at

first, and then she wraps them around my waist with a fierce need that rocks me to my core.

"I thought we were going to be a family again." The words are muffled, murmured against my shirt as she buries her face in my chest. "I'd been in care for a year. She came to visit. She was supposed to take me to my first dance lesson that day. My foster family bought me a ballet dress. My mom told me I looked like a princess."

Her voice catches, trembles. I hold on, stroke a hand over her hair.

"She asked me to wait in the other room while she talked to my foster mom. I knew something was wrong." She leans back and my heart cracks at the tears glinting in her eyes. "I knew. So I snuck into the kitchen. I heard my mom tell my foster mother she was terminating her rights as a parent. She didn't want to do this anymore." She closes her eyes, scrunches them tight. Tears escape, tracing their way down her cheeks. "My foster mom asked if she had any idea what this would do to me. My mom said…"

She shudders. Her voice trails off. I keep one arm banded around her waist, cup her face with my other hand and kiss her on the forehead.

"…she didn't want me anymore."

She breaks. Deep, heart wrenching sobs as she cries into my shirt. I hold her through it all, cursing myself for not being able to fix it, aching for the girl who never knew a mother's love.

Her cries subside a minute later. She leans back and swipes a hand across her cheek.

"I'm always afraid there's something about me, something wrong with me, and when others finally get to know the real me, they'll leave. My mom did. I never got adopted. The guy I dated in college wanted to move so fast, and when I wouldn't match his pace, he broke things off. Dale beat me. And now

Aislinn…" Her chin drops. "I've texted her every week since she left. Not once has she replied. The invitations to the wedding and the funeral came from her adoptive parents."

A deep, shuddering sigh escapes before her voice quiets to the point I have to strain to hear her next words.

"What if it's me, Ari?"

I slide a finger under her chin, slowly tilt her face up until she meets my eyes.

"You told me at Reynisfjara my father didn't define me. Your mother doesn't define you."

"I know. I know that," she repeats, but I still hear the note of desperation, the fear. "But what if…"

She shakes her head. Then she looks up at me. Her hands slide up my chest, around my neck. Blood stirs. Desire kindles.

"I want you."

I lay my hands over her wrists, try to grasp on to some semblance of control.

"Diana…"

She leans up and grazes her lips across mine.

"Please."

I surrender. One quick movement and she's in my arms, her head tucked in the crook of my neck, one hand on the back of hers, and the other resting over my heart. I walk to the bed, lay her down. She watches as I unbutton and shrug out of my shirt, her eyes fixing on my chest and then lower as I take off my pants. My cock's already hard for her, my body aching. It's been twenty-four hours, but it feels like it's been years.

She shifts, gets to her knees.

"Touch yourself."

The softly uttered command sets fire to my blood. I wrap my hand around my cock, stroke. Every muscle in my body hardens as she unzips her dress. With one shrug, the straps fall down her arms, the bodice to her waist.

No bra. Just her incredible breasts, her nipples hard, her skin glowing in the dim lighting of the cabin.

"Don't stop."

I clench my teeth and keep moving my hand. How was I ever satisfied with something so mundane as touching myself? After having Diana, after being inside her wet heat and experiencing not just the physical satisfaction but the pleasure of being with someone I care about, I know I'll never find anything like it again.

Don't want to find anything else.

She slithers out of her dress. My brain nearly short-circuits at the sight of a thin band of black lace barely covering the skin between her thighs, tiny straps looped over her thighs.

"Diana."

One corner of her mouth curves up. I see her confidence in the lustful glint in her eye, the upward tilt of her chin, the proud set of her shoulders that make her breasts jut out toward me.

She holds out a hand.

"Make love to me, Ari."

I'm on the bed before the words are out of her mouth. I ease her back onto the silk sheets, slant my lips over hers and claim her with a kiss that has us both groaning into each other's mouths. My hands are sliding up her sides, my fingers grazing her breasts, my cock straining against the tiny scrap of fabric. Her fingers slide into my hair, anchoring my head as she kisses me with an uninhibited passion I greedily take.

I finally tear my mouth from hers. Her huff of protest turns into a long, drawn-out moan as I trace my tongue down her neck, place an open-mouthed kiss to the sensitive dip at the base of her throat. I trail farther down still to her breasts. One graze of my lips on the swell of her breast. A gentle nip on one hardened tip. A long, slow lick of the fullness beneath.

"Ari."

I suck her into my mouth, feel like a god when she arches up against me. I alternate between gentle and demanding, drink in her cries as our thighs press together, our hips undulating in rhythm.

I do the same to her other breasts before kissing my way down her belly. Her breathing quickens as I reach her hips. I trace one finger over the material and nearly embarrass myself when I feel the wet heat, inhale the scent of how much she wants me.

"God, Diana." I clamp my hands down on her hips, trapping her in a vise as I capture her eyes with mine. "Do you know what you do to me?"

Her throat bobs. Doubt intrudes.

And then she lets out a shuddering breath.

"The same you do to me."

Humbled, burning, I lower my head. Breathe her in. Then, slowly, I run my tongue over the fabric, taste her through wet silk. Her hips bow off the bed as she cries out.

"Ari!"

I turn my head, lick the skin just beyond where the fabric ends. I continue to taunt her, tease her, until all I can smell is her and I'm so goddamned hungry for a taste I can't take it anymore.

I hook my fingers in the fabric, pull it aside, and feast. Her scream of pleasure fills me, spurs me as I lick, suck, nibble, kiss every inch of her. Her hips pump faster. Her breathing is coming in rapid gasps. Her hands grasp the sheets, move to my hair, pull at my shoulders.

When she comes apart, I drink her in, savor every drop until she's limp and trembling. I start to move up her body when she raises her head off the pillow.

"My turn."

My harsh exhale has her grinning. She rises up, her breasts grazing my chest before she plants a hand just above my stomach and pushes. I lie back, grabbing a pillow and tucking it under my head as I watch her.

God, she's beautiful. It's not just the stunning slash of her cheekbones or the elegant shape of her face. It's the fire in her eyes, the sweetness in her smile even as she shoots me a look that's anything but innocent.

It's her. Diana. And I'm in love with her.

Before I can even begin to recover from that realization, she wraps a hand around my cock and gently squeezes. I suck in a deep, harsh breath.

"I don't think we got around to this last night."

Her husky voice wraps around me, slides over my burning skin as her fingers caress, glide, stroke.

"We got a little distracted.'

"Just a little."

She leans down, her hair falling over her shoulders and around her face.

"Wait." I reach out, grasp her hair in one hand and gather it to one side. "I want to see you."

Roses bloom in her cheeks, but her smile is pure feminine power. She trails teasing kisses down my hard length, one hand wrapped around me and the other braced on my thigh. The more she taunts with quick flicks of her tongue and slight grazes of teeth, the harder it becomes to not simply tumble her back onto the bed and slide inside her.

Her lips part. She takes me into her mouth and I nearly come right then and there.

"Diana."

Her name is a groan, a prayer. Every touch brings me closer to the edge.

"Now."

I sit up, ready to push her back and take her. But she stops me, puts a hand to my chest.

"Ari."

Did I think stopping myself from following her out of the living room took effort? Because holding myself back now is pure torture.

And then she does the last thing I ever thought she would do.

She turns her back to me.

I see them through her hair. Four scars. Thick, raised, discolored. Evidence of one man's derangement. Evidence of a young woman's bravery and giving heart.

Slowly, I reach out. Lay one finger on the top of the first scar. She sucks in a breath and I snatch my hand away.

"Diana—"

"Don't stop."

Her voice is thin but determined. I reach out again, trace my fingers up and down. One scar, two, three. Then down the fourth, shorter than the rest. The one interrupted by the two people who saved Diana's life.

"It's a mystery to me," I say quietly, "how you think you're not enough." I lower my head, kiss the back of her neck. "Thank you."

She looks back over her shoulder at me. The fear lingers. But so does the desire. She leans forward, plants her hands into the mattress. Need slams into me as she arches her back and pushes her hips back against mine.

I clamp my hands down on her, the heat of her skin searing my palms. One thrust and I'm inside her. Her body tightens around me, pulls me deeper as I struggle to draw the pleasure out. Hard to do when she's pushing back against me, back arched and skin gleaming in the moonlight.

"More."

Her command rips away the last of my control. I reach around and press a hand to her stomach, urge her to arch up until her back is flush against my chest. My hand drifts up, cups the weight of her breast as she turns her head and

I capture her mouth with mine. Each thrust drives us both higher. She moans into my mouth, pushes back against me as she takes me deeper.

Then she's coming apart, her body demanding more even as she spirals up and over. I follow moments later, groaning her name against her lips as I keep her body pinned against mine.

It takes a few moments to regather my strength. To remember to ease her down onto the mattress and collapse on the sheet next to her. I reach out and wrap an arm around her waist, pull her back against my chest. I've never been a touchy lover after sex. Once it's over, it's done.

But making love with the woman I love… Even though I'm temporarily spent, I can't stop touching her.

"That was…"

"Incredible," I finish for her as I press a kiss to her neck.

"Yeah," she murmurs sleepily. "That."

Thirty seconds later and she's out, her soft breathing punctured by the occasional snore that makes me grin.

A grin that quickly disappears when I remember what precipitated our lovemaking.

I brush another strand of hair from her face, stare down at the woman who has quickly become more important to me than anything else in my life. The dark contrast of eyelashes against fair skin. The lips parted in sleep.

I draw her closer still, needing to feel her in my arms as I pull a sheet up over both of us. She didn't just show me her scars; she trusted me with them. A massive step for us.

But I also remember the pain, the fear just before she asked me to make love to her. I know the kind of power those emotions can wield. How they can drive even the most logical person to make mistakes they never thought they would.

I stare at her for as long as I can before sleep finally pulls my eyes shut.

CHAPTER SEVENTEEN

Diana

I WAKE TO bright sunlight and a comforting warmth at my back. It takes a moment for me to remember I'm in Greece, not Iceland, and the naked man behind me is Ari.

I press back into his embrace for one fleeting moment before I inch my way out from under the heavy arm over my waist. A glance at the clock makes me grimace. Nearly seven o'clock. We're supposed to be at Hellas Shipping's offices at eight thirty. With showering, getting dressed, eating breakfast, and driving to the office, I don't have much time.

Xenakis had arranged a dinner for the entire AuraGeothermal team at an exclusive restaurant with stunning views of the Acropolis. Thankfully Ari's chief financial officer, public relations specialist, and legal counselor hadn't commented on us taking a separate, earlier flight, or asked questions about which villa I was staying at on the resort. Xenakis was late meeting us, but he arrived with dark circles under his eyes and a huge grin, proudly showing off photos of his new granddaughter.

My breath catches as I glance back at Ari. He looks just like he did back in New York: blond strands falling over his chiseled face. The muscles of his back bared to my gaze, a silk sheet draped over his hips and legs.

I want nothing more than to climb back into bed with him.

To wake him up with a kiss or straddling his waist and taking him inside me.

But in the light of day, my bravado from the evening before evaporates. Yes, Ari and I have incredible sex. We like each other, even respect each other, after finally clearing the air over Liam's and my deception.

Except liking someone isn't enough. Plenty of foster parents liked me. But none of them liked me enough.

I shove away my intrusive thoughts and sneak into the bathroom. Twenty minutes later, I'm showered, dressed, and ready to face the final event in the AuraGeothermal–Hellas Shipping negotiation. Navy blue business jacket and skirt. Hair pulled back into a low bun. Professional, confident, strong.

Nothing like the woman who straddled her boss's naked hips and asked him to take her from behind last night.

My cheeks turn pink. Last night was…incredible. Earth-shattering. How is it that every time we make love, it only gets better?

I stare at myself in the mirror. When I turned my back to Ari last night, it was a massive step for me. Ari didn't just understand the magnitude of what I was sharing with him—he honored it, cherished me even as he took me to new heights of pleasure.

I brace my palms against the marble countertop and suck in a deep, steadying breath. Ari obviously cares for me. And I care for him. I…

No. Today is not the day for examining my feelings. Today is the day to get contracts signed and finalize the deal between AuraGeothermal and Hellas.

I turn and bite back a screech at the sight of Ari in the doorway, wearing nothing but a smug grin.

"Good morning."

"Good morning." My eyes drift down from his handsome face to his muscled chest, lower still to his—

Focus.

"Our meeting's in ninety minutes. The map estimates a forty-minute drive with traffic, so—"

Ari cuts me off with a fierce kiss, one that makes my toes curl.

"I'll get dressed." He trails one hand down my neck, his fingers deftly tugging at the top button of my blazer. "Maybe I could help you, too."

My breath hitches in my throat as the blazer falls open and Ari starts working on the buttons of my shirt. "I'm already dressed. Or at least," I say faintly as my blouse parts, "I was."

Ari plants an open-mouthed kiss to my breast swelling above my bra. My thighs clench as my head drops back on a moan.

"I can't get enough of you, Diana."

His words fill me. But not enough to completely erase the doubt. Even as his hands slide under the hem of my skirt, pull it up around my hips and slide my panties down around my knees, the fear lingers, dulling some of my pleasure as he slides inside me.

He stares at me in the mirror, his blue eyes twin flames of desire. I meet his gaze, meet him thrust for thrust as he fills me. I'm tender from last night, but his movements this morning are gentle, long and slow, teasing even as he satisfies us both.

My peak this morning is a long, slow roll, one that builds with exquisite pleasure and leaves me gasping in its wake. Ari finds his almost immediately after me, filling me with his heat.

"I would apologize."

His withdrawal leaves me with an ache, not just physical but deeper. An ache that thrills as much as it frightens. I pull down my skirt and start to rebutton my blouse, but he wraps his arms around my waist and pulls me back against him just like he did last night in bed.

"But?"

"But I'm not the least bit sorry."

He lowers his head to my neck, kisses the juncture of my throat and shoulder. My eyes flutter shut.

Is it possible? Could we truly have something more than just sex? Can I trust Ari enough to be happy?

"Me neither."

His eyes narrow as his face darkens. My heart pitches down to somewhere in the vicinity of my feet.

"About last night—"

An alarm goes off. Swearing, he walks back into the bedroom. He's only gone for twenty seconds or so, but it's enough. Enough for the reservations to rush back in, for the doubts to take over. Was he about to say last night was just like New York? That our affair is enjoyable but short-lived?

Even if he was going to say something else, the fact that I immediately jump to worst-case scenario tells me everything I need to know about my ability to be in a true relationship right now. I'm not ready. I just realized a couple nights ago I've been holding on to a fear that the two people I trust most in this world would abandon me if I wasn't the perfect friend. How can I possibly get into a romantic relationship?

"Confirmation call." Ari walks back in. "They're expecting us at eight thirty."

I smooth my hand over my skirt. "Then, you'd better get ready."

His eyes narrow. "Diana—"

"Later." I force a smile onto my face. "After the contract?"

He leans back, his gaze hardening a fraction.

"Don't do this."

"What?"

He swears softly, his curse harsh yet melodic. "Pull back."

"I'm not."

He advances. I waiver, lean back before I stand my ground. But Ari sees enough. A shutter drops over his face.

"I'm getting dressed."

I want to go to him, circle my arms around his waist, lay my head against the warmth of his back. Breathe him in. Ask him to stay.

He yanks on his shirt. He starts to glance over his shoulder. I take a step forward.

And then he turns away.

My heart starts to pound. I have never once let a lover touch my scars. The last person to touch them besides me was Aislinn when she helped care for the fresh wounds. At times, I've managed to see them as a reminder of my own strength, an odd sign of the friendship that binds Liam, Aislinn, and I together. Other times, they've burned with the memory that I was only in Dale's house because I wasn't wanted anywhere else.

But last night, when I looked up and met Ari's gaze, saw the passion burning in his eyes, I knew. I knew I wanted him to be the first, not just to see the scars in the context of a lover, but to touch the most vulnerable part of me. And yes, it frightens me that I want him to be the last. To give him that kind of trust, to hope that he won't leave, that we won't fail.

My jaw tightens as I suck in a deep breath. I gave him so much last night. Yes, I'm nervous today. Apprehensive. I'm not pulling away from him. I just need time to think, to process.

I close my eyes. Breathe in. Breath out. Wait for my heartbeat to slow. When my emotions are quiet, when I'm back in control, I open my eyes and walk out into the hotel room. Ari's nearly dressed, his customary black suit and tie. He doesn't even look at me as I grab my purse off the table.

"I'm going to walk to the café. Would you like anything?"

"No. Thank you."

"Velkomin."

The word rolls off my tongue as if I've been saying it for years. Ari's hands still on his tie. He looks at me then, his face blank. His lips part. I pause, my hand on the doorknob.

Then he shakes his head and turns away.

Time, I tell myself as I walk out into the hall and close the door behind me. We both just need a little time.

I only wish I believed it was as simple as that.

Ari

I sign the last paper before I turn to Xenakis and accept the offered hand, force a smile.

I'm not going to let my personal life interrupt finally achieving this milestone. No matter how acutely aware I am of Diana in the corner of the room. No matter how many times my eyes sweep over her high-waisted green skirt that follows every curve of hip and leg, the white shirt I enjoyed unbuttoning this morning, and think how incredible she looks.

"I'm glad we made it."

I blink, focus on Xenakis's grinning face.

"I am, too."

I'm pleasantly surprised to find I mean it, too. After spending those two days with Xenakis and learning more about his personal circumstances, I'm looking forward to partnering with him.

We chat about our upcoming board meetings that will finalize the deal. People mill about—accountants, lawyers, public relations professionals already drafting up press releases in anticipation of everything going through.

Diana waits in the background. A tall, broad-faced man leans down and whispers something to her that makes her smile. I clench my teeth, try not to look like I'm growling at the camera.

Finally, we're done. Xenakis shakes my hand again and then turns to speak to someone else as I make my way over to Diana. The man is still talking to her.

"...dinner tonight."

Diana turns and glances over her shoulder at me. Her instant smile loosens the fist that's been wrapped around my heart since this morning.

"I can't." She looks back at the man and gives him a polite nod. "But thank you for the offer."

The man opens his mouth as if to press his case. One look at my face sends him scurrying away.

"Careful," she says softly, her tone amused. "You might start rumors about the two of us."

"Something we'll have to deal with sooner or later."

The teasing light in her eyes dims. "Ari—"

"There you are, Diana."

Diana turns to Xenakis and smiles, her professional mask in place. They make small talk before Xenakis turns to me.

"If you have the time, I'd like for you to stay a few days. Tour the port and the site of where the cracking plant will go."

I can tell by the look Diana giving me she thinks it's important for me to say yes.

"Yes." I frown. "Although I need to contact our board president and vice president. I told them I would be flying back today and available tomorrow to discuss the deal with them ahead of the board meeting next week."

Xenakis waves his hand. "No need to alter your plans."

I turn to Diana. "Would you do it?"

Her eyes widen. "What? Present to the president?"

"Yes. You know this contract inside and out, probably better than me. Any questions you're not comfortable answering, just defer them to contact me privately."

It's incredible to think that just under two weeks ago, I barely trusted her to be in my office alone. But I've seen firsthand why she has the reputation she does. In the short time I've worked with her, she's fought for AuraGeothermal. She has the knowledge to answer far more questions about the recent developments than anyone else at the company.

"Yes." She nods. "Yes, I can do that."

Xenakis's big smile lets me know I made the right call. "Wonderful. I'll make the arrangements."

Diana waits until he's out of earshot before she turns to me. "You're really okay with this?"

"Yes." I lean down, lower my voice. "I wouldn't have offered if I didn't trust you."

Instead of looking pleased or happy, my words have the opposite effect. Her face falls a moment before she catches herself and glances down.

"What?"

"Ari…you don't have to do this."

I frown. "What?"

"I… I just need time. You don't have to put me in charge just to show me—"

"Careful." The warning comes out like a bullet as I try to control my sudden anger. "I asked you to represent me because I trust you, Diana. I'm not manipulating you."

She glances around, but most of the people have moved out of the conference room and down the hall to a larger space where refreshments are being served. She waits until the last person drifts out before walking over and closing the door. When she turns, she looks more like a prisoner about to walk to the gallows than the woman I made love to last night.

"I didn't say you were manipulating me, Ari."

"Didn't you?"

One hand comes up, her fingers pinching the bridge of her nose. "I just don't want you to think you have to—"

"What? Do what you do?"

Her hand drops to her side as her head snaps up. The bleakness is gone from her eyes, replaced by furious fire.

"What?" she snaps.

"Say and do things you don't want to because you think you have to earn other people's love instead of just being enough?"

"That is not what I think you're doing!"

"Isn't it?" I fire back. "Or could it be that you're more than comfortable encouraging me to confront my fears and overcome my trust issues while you use yours as a shield?"

"That's unfair." Color sweeps into her cheeks. Anger crackles around her like a lightning storm about to unleash. "You had others depending on you. I asked you only to share what was relevant. And I only asked you to trust me professionally. I never once pushed you to trust me personally."

"No," I reply quietly. "You didn't."

I don't know if she ever will. It's becoming all too easy to picture her by my side, in my bed, yet always just out of reach. Her face falls. I wait, torn between hope and hopelessness. I have my answer seconds later when she does what I've seen her do several times since she arrived in Iceland. I can almost see her mentally gathering her emotions, pulling them close, closer, until she can lock them away inside and present Diana North, corporate negotiator, to the world.

Leaving the real Diana hidden so deeply I don't know if I'll ever be able to reach her.

"I should head back to the villa and pack."

The door closing behind her is a loud, harsh click.

And then there's nothing but silence.

CHAPTER EIGHTEEN

Ari

I STARE OUT over the Port of Piraeus. Tankers and cruise ships dominate the docks. A few ferries move in and out with ease, carrying tourists to islands like Santorini and Rhodes. In three to four years, Hellas Shipping will deploy its new fleet of ammonia tankers, bringing the ammonia we create into Piraeus. Tanker trucks will then take it to the ammonia cracking facility in Eleusis eighteen kilometers away.

A dream I've been working toward for over a year. Signing the contract is just the beginning. We'll break ground for the cracking plant in two months. Our main plant in Iceland will begin adding on in late spring when the cold eases and the days are longer. But we're moving forward.

My hands tighten on the railing. The sun is warm on my skin, the temperature a balmy twenty-one degrees Celsius. Yet inside I'm cold. Empty. There is no satisfaction, no sense of accomplishment, not even a flicker of happiness.

There's nothing.

I keep seeing Diana as she looked back at me, framed in the doorway of the conference room. For a moment, I thought she would stay.

But then she walked out on me.

I hang my head and let out a harsh breath. I'm torn between wondering if I asked too much, pushed too far, and feeling rejected. When I think of how she pushed me the past few weeks to trust Xenakis, open up, I'm angry.

No, I mentally correct as I turn away from the port and stalk back into my hotel room, I'm furious. How dare she demand so much? Ask, ask, ask, yet keep her own heart hidden so deep no one can reach it, including the man who loves her.

I stop, scrub a hand over my face. I love Diana. I don't believe in fairy tales. But I know I fell a little bit in love with her the moment I laid eyes on her in the museum, when she turned and whispered that husky hello that sank into my skin and wrapped itself around my heart.

A love that's only deepened the past few weeks. Witnessed her dedication firsthand, admired her compassion, appreciated her strength and intelligence. Been humbled by her resilience, awed by her loyalty.

I woke up yesterday knowing I wanted to tell her. It is fast, very fast, given that we only reconciled days before. But I know how I feel. I never want her to question me, question us, the way she has other relationships in her life. Want to offer her that security, that guarantee that as long as she wants me, I will never leave.

Then I walked into the bathroom. Saw her with that expression on her face, the one she'd worn when she walked into the restaurant with Liam in New York. So I stepped back, gave her space. I needed it, too, needed a moment to regroup after the sting of rejection. I assumed we would talk later.

And then she uttered those words at Hellas. Confronted me with the very real possibility she wouldn't be able to overcome her past.

I want to understand. I want to give her the time she needs. But it hurts. It really fucking hurts. Even when I realized my father had no interest in me as a child, his rejection was dull, an ache for what could have been but never would be. I'd had my mother, had a good life to lean into.

Diana's rejection ripped me in two.

I stalk back into the penthouse suite of my hotel. After Diana left, I had no interest in staying in the villa. Not when I could still smell her on the sheets. Could still see her on her hands and knees, see the raw vulnerability on her face as she shared the deepest parts of herself with me.

What happened between sunset and sunrise? Does she regret sharing herself with me? After everything I've done to overcome my own trust issues, can she not see that I'm not going anywhere?

My phone rings.

"Valdasson."

"Góðan daginn." I wince as Xenakis chuckles. "How's my pronunciation?"

I start to reply, then pause. "It was a good attempt."

"How diplomatic," Xenakis says, amusement in his tone. "My daughter's in-laws have invaded the hospital and I need an excuse to leave. I'd like to move our tour up by an hour."

"I can make that work."

Xenakis is waiting for me fifteen minutes later in a stretch limo. Three weeks ago, the sight of the gleaming white behemoth would have made me roll my eyes. Now it makes one corner of my mouth curve up as a chauffeur opens the door for me. The interior is done in gray leather with rounded lights built into the ceiling. Xenakis is sitting in the rear seat, a pop-up table covering his knees as he types away on a laptop. He greets me as I sit on the longer seat that runs the length of the limo.

"Coffee?"

"Yes, please."

Xenakis puts away the table and computer as he reaches over to the bar and pulls out a small coffee cup and saucer.

"Greek coffee," he says as he pours from a silver thermos. "Made with a small pot called a *briki*."

"Usually served with foam on top?"

Surprised, Xenakis smiles. "Yes, *kaimaki*." He reaches under the bar and pulls out a small box. "My personal favorite addition to a good cup of coffee—baklava." He hands me the cup and saucer, then another small plate with the layered pastry. "You enjoy Greek cuisine?"

"I learned a great deal the past couple weeks." I nod to my plate. "What I've had so far, I've enjoyed very much."

"Your research included food?"

I inhale the rich, nutty fragrance of the coffee before I take a drink. "Miss North."

One of Xenakis's eyebrows arches up. "So we're back to the more formal Miss North?"

My first instinct is to tell him it's none of his damn business. But I bite back the nasty retort. Remind myself that Xenakis is more social than I am, more open to sharing aspects of his personal life in the course of doing business together.

"Yes."

"That's unfortunate."

I pause, my cup raised halfway to my lips. "Why?"

"I hoped you and Miss North would finally admit how you felt." This time his smile is slight, contemplative. "Find the happiness I had with my wife, even though I had her in my life for too short of a time."

The thought of losing Diana grips me with a panic I haven't felt since the ambulance whisked my mother to the hospital.

"Diana is an incredible woman," I finally say.

"She is that." Xenakis shakes his head. "She reminds me of my daughter. Fierce, strong, loyal, but beneath it all a caring heart that I sometimes worry carries too much." He looks out the window. "She caught on pretty quickly as a child that her mother had died after giving birth to her. I tried my best to let her know how loved she was, how neither her mother nor I would change a single thing if it meant not having Zoe here. But she still lived with that guilt for so long before I finally caught on."

I'm not used to heartfelt conversations, especially with men I don't know beyond a business setting. But the raw grief in Xenakis's voice, the parallels between his daughter and Diana, prompt me to speak.

"Diana's childhood made it hard for her to trust." I glance out the window, at the buildings speeding by. "How did you help your daughter?"

"It wasn't easy. There were times," Xenakis says quietly, "when I was too impatient. I wanted her to be better. But I wanted it on my timeline, not hers. I wanted to help my daughter, yes, but I wanted her to get better for me, too." He scoffs. "Selfish."

I sit there, my body frozen as the car speeds down the road. He might as well be describing me. I want Diana to trust me so she can finally let go of the pain and fear she holds on to so tightly. But I wanted it for me, too. I wanted to know she wouldn't choose fear over me. And in doing so, I pushed her away.

"I love her."

"I know." Xenakis chuckles. "You know, these past few months I've thought you were cold, rude, and dismissive. An immature young man who didn't want to share."

"Given that I thought you were overly dramatic and con-trolling," I say with a slight smile, "I'd say we're even."

"But I've seen another side of you, too, Valdasson. A young man who stepped up and took responsibility. Who protected his people and his country. Those are the kind of qualities I see in my son-in-law, and I consider him to be one of my own. The kind of qualities that will make you a good part-ner. I care for Diana," he adds, his deep-set eyes intense. "I do not make these remarks lightly."

My throat tightens. *"Ευχαριστώ."*

"Much better than my butchering of your language this morning." Xenakis inclines his head. "You're welcome."

"I'll have to learn more before my next trip." I glance at my watch. "Speaking of, I have to cut this trip short."

Xenakis laughs. "I was hoping you'd say that."

CHAPTER NINETEEN

Diana

A FISHING BOAT putters out of the harbor toward the open sea. A ginormous cruise ship drifts across the water toward the port. Overhead, I hear the distant call of a wild bird.

I stand on the balcony just outside Ari's office. The ocean is calm today, the only movement marked by the waves that, at this height, look like ripples. In less than twenty-four hours, I'll leave it all behind. The island, the stark beauty of a wild land, people like Malla and Viktor.

Ari.

I glance around his office. The first two times I was here, I saw the grandeur, the power. But now I see the touches that make it him: the pictures of the geothermal fields, the mountains and the wetlands. A lava rock. Books written by Icelandic authors. A framed letter from a school child who toured one of his plants. A man who takes more pride in his work, his legacy, than any other man I've met.

My heart has sustained many cracks over the years. I never thought any could be bigger than the one my mother inflicted when she walked out on me. But as I walked out of the conference room yesterday, my heart didn't just crack.

It broke. Shattered.

And it's my own fault. Yes, Ari pushed me. But he was right. I had enforced a double standard on him, constantly pushing for him to share something that was deeply painful. I justified it because it was for the job, for the company and people he said were more important than anything, while keeping myself locked up tight.

I presented to the president and vice president yesterday. Never have I been more nervous doing my job than I was during my speech. I've cared about every project I've ever worked on, but this one was personal. Not just because of Ari, but because I had become personally invested in AuraGeothermal, too, in the people and the work they did.

But in the end, the board leaders had been pleased. It had taken me nearly ten minutes to compose a text to Ari letting him know the good news, to find the right words. He'd replied with a simple thank you.

When it was my turn to step up, to grow as Ari has these past few weeks, I faltered. Now I've lost him.

No, I mentally correct as I cross my arms over my chest and lean my head against the cool glass, failed. For the first time in my life, I was greedy. I took everything Ari offered. I made progress. I won't deny myself those achievements.

But when the man I was falling in love with needed me to tell him I cared, I retreated. When he placed his trust in me, freely and without any strings attached, I responded with accusations instead of acceptance.

I turn away from the window. My flight is scheduled for tomorrow morning. I'll fly straight back to New York. My firm notified me they already have another job lined up. Something that would have excited me in the past.

Right now I just want to curl up in a ball and sleep.

I walk past Ari's desk, glance down at the typewritten report I left him. I pick it up, read it through again as I have half a dozen times, checking for errors. There are none. I know this. But it gives me a reason to linger, to spend just a little more time in this space that's wholly his.

I reach the end of the letter, the one I always include in my final reports.

"Thank you for giving me the opportunity to support your company."

The paper crinkles in my grasp. It's cold. Dismissive. Everything I accused Ari of being. Yet when push came to shove, he stepped up, confronted his past, reluctantly revealed his deepest pain to a man he previously thought an enemy.

While I hoarded my own hurts and used them as a buffer between us.

I read the last line again. If I was being completely honest with both Ari and myself, I would tell him how he was the first lover I ever trusted with my deepest secrets. The first man I truly shared myself with, body and soul. I would tell him how much I admired his loyalty, his commitment to being the leader his father hadn't been, his dedication to finding the brother he never had the chance to know. How easy it was to be myself, to laugh and joke, talk and just be.

I would tell him I love him. That I'm terrified one day we'll wake up and it won't work out.

But, I realize with chilling clarity, I'm suddenly, horribly afraid of not taking that risk. For the first time in my life, the possibility of trying and living without is not nearly as frightening as the possibility of living with a what-if hanging over my head. And if Ari still cares for me after everything that's happened.

Tears spill over. One slides down my cheek and falls onto the letter. It may be too late.

But it may not be.

I crinkle the paper into a ball and pitch it into a trashcan on my way to the door. I stick my head out.

"Malla?"

Malla looks up and smiles, although her face is sad. "Yes?"

"Any chance you could see if my flight could get changed to Athens for this afternoon?"

She brightens, like I just told her magic was real. "On it."

I shoot her a smile and close the door, rushing around the office and gathering up my things. I'll need to run back to my hotel and get my passport, a couple overnight things. Do I text Ari now? Call him? Or do I surprise him?

The door opens behind me.

"Wow, that was fast. Were there any flights…?"

My voice trails off as I turn around and see Ari standing in the door. He looks just like he did that first night when he found me standing at his window, searching the skies for the Northern Lights. Handsome as sin, dominant in his realm. His face is smooth, his expression calm.

But there's one key difference. His eyes are blazing with a swirl of emotions I can't fully decipher, fiery blue as he steps in and closes the door behind him.

Ari

"Leaving so soon?"

Diana stares at me, eyes wide and lips parted. I scrape together enough willpower to not go to her and yank her into my arms.

I tell myself that if I give her love and she wants nothing to do with it, I'll accept it. I have to. But I'm not letting her walk away. Not yet.

"Actually, I was getting ready to get on a plane."

I step forward.

"Don't go."

She smiles at me. "Ari—"

"I love you."

She stops. Her eyes widen. "What?"

I take another step forward. Then another.

"I love you. I finally accepted it a couple of days ago, and I should have told you the moment I knew. I was afraid it would make you run. I didn't know if you were ready. But then, in Greece..." I pause and hold up my hand as she starts to speak. "Wait. Please, just let me finish. I accused you of not trusting me. But you've given me so much these past few days. I told you that you had unfair standards, that you were constantly pushing me. I'd be lying if I said there wasn't a sliver of resentment attached to that. But I also understand you were pushing me to be a better leader, to work toward what I wanted for my company, my country, and myself. Whereas I..." I think about her scars. "I can't believe I even begin to compare my pain to yours."

"Stop." She shakes her head. "My pain is not more important than yours. It doesn't mean I get more leeway in this relationship to hold back, especially after I've been encouraging you to move forward." Her eyes glimmer. "And you've grown so much."

I close the distance between us and take her hands in mine. "You said 'relationship.'" She nods, her smile tremulous. "But you were leaving?"

There's a knock on the door.

"Come in."

Diana starts to pull away, but I tighten my grasp.

Malla walks in, a huge grin lighting up her face when she catches Diana's in my joined hands. "You slipped by me, Mr. Valdasson."

She holds up a piece of paper. "I got you on a two o'clock flight to Athens, Diana, but I'm guessing you won't be needing it."

"No," Diana says quietly. "I won't."

I wait until the door closes behind my secretary before I pull Diana into my arms and kiss her. With desire, relief, and love.

"You were coming back to me."

She leans back slightly. "I'm still scared, Ari. But I don't want to live like that anymore. I told myself that Liam and Aislinn were enough. And they're still my friends. The brother and sister I never had. But I made my life so narrow. And then I turned my head and you were there. And you were handsome and so sexy," she says with a small laugh, "but you also just saw me. Right from the start. And even when I was being sassy or snarky or disagreeing with you, you still…" Her voice trails off as she cups my face. "You still love me."

"More than anyone."

"There's no expiration date, no timeline—"

"I love you, too."

I stand there for a moment, rocked by the trust and love she's given me.

"I can't promise there won't be days when I doubt. Days where I may struggle or pull away."

She grazes her fingers along my cheek, tucks stray hair behind my ear.

"I won't ask for you to put up with my moods. If you could just wait for me, I'll always come back to you."

I shift, pulling her closer to me. "That's where you're wrong."

She frowns. "What?"

"You didn't just put up with me the last couple of weeks when I was rude and arrogant, when I pushed you away. You didn't just wait for me, you fought for me. Encouraged me. And yes, there were times when you gave me the space that I needed. But you didn't just put up with me. And I'm not just going to put up with you. We're in this together, flaws, broken pasts, all of it."

She buries her face in the crook of my neck. "I thought I'd lost you. Pushed you too far away."

"The next time you try to walk away, I might have to go caveman on you again and toss you over my shoulder."

She chuckles. "Wouldn't you be more of a Viking?"

I kiss the tip of her nose. Her brow. Her lips.

"Speaking of, I know this is just the beginning, but I want you to be with me. I don't want to leave Iceland, but if we need to talk alternatives—"

"I don't want to leave Iceland either."

I stare at her. "You don't?"

"No. I fell in love with you and your country and your people. This is the first place that's ever felt like home. I'm still going to work," she adds quickly. "I love my job. And I'll go back to see Liam and, hopefully, Aislinn. But I want to build a life here with you." She hesitates, sucks in a deep breath. "I want to stay, Ari. And I want you to stay." Fear leaps into her eyes, but so does determination, the sight of it so raw and powerful it rocks me to my core. "Stay with me, Ari."

I told myself I would wait, give her time to get used to the idea of my feelings for her. But knowing what I do now, sharing this with her, I know I don't want to wait one more second. I drop to one knee.

Her eyes go wide.

"Ari—"

"Diana North, you're strong. Resilient. Kind, with a surprisingly snarky streak." She laughs, even as tears start to fall down her face. "Please be my wife."

"Yes."

She nods as I surge up and gather her in my arms.

"Yes."

I grasp her left hand, bring it to my lips, and place a kiss on her finger where the ring will go.

"You made me believe in second chances and forgiveness."

"And you," she says, "helped me learn to trust. To love."

I hold her in my arms as we stare out over the harbor.

"Welcome home, Diana."

EPILOGUE

Diana
Seven Years Later

I STAND ON a ledge, staring up at the water flowing off the cliff
into the pool below. Cool water droplets kiss my face. I've
seen it dozens of times over the years. But it never gets old.

"Mama!"

I turn and smile as Ásta walks toward me in her bright
yellow raincoat, one hand firmly clasped in Ari's.

"Hi, baby."

I crouch down and hold out my arms, close my eyes and
smile as my daughter steps into my arms and wraps her
chubby arms around my neck.

"Boo-tee-ful waterfall."

She stares up at the water. She has my hair, thick and dark.
But she has her father's eyes, bright blue and inquisitive.

"It is." I kiss her cheek before I look back at Ari. "Have
fun?"

"We climbed the staircase no less than four times."

I laugh as I tilt my head up for a kiss. He brushes his lips
over mine, a quick kiss with the hint of something more as
his tongue darts out and teases my lips.

"Ari!" I swat at his shoulder with my free hand. "You're
a tease."

He grins at me as he rakes my body with a brazen gaze. "Not a tease, *Ástin mín*. A promise."

I shake my head even as desire kindles and flickers to life inside me. Seven years later, including six of marriage, and I still want him as badly as I did the first time I laid eyes on him. Some things don't change.

But, I reflect with a smile as I bounce Ásta on my hip, some things do. Ásta will be three next month. Old enough to travel with Ari and me to Greece to tour the ammonia cracking facility just outside Athens and celebrate two years of being operational. She'll also have a chance to see her godfather, Georgios.

My smile grows. It's hard to believe that seven years ago Ari and Georgios nearly hated each other on sight, and now they're closer than ever, both personally and professionally. Their collaborative investment in the cracking plant gained worldwide recognition. The plant opened a few months late, but it's been running steadily ever since. Georgios and Ari never waste a chance to pick on each other. But their working relationship is strong, steady.

When I found out I was pregnant, Ari asked me about asking Georgios to serve as godfather. Given that neither of us had a father figure in our lives and Georgios had done so much for us, it was an easy choice.

My phone buzzes. I pull it out of my pocket and glance at the screen.

"Switzerland next week?"

Ari pulls out his own phone and opens the calendar.

"I'm free."

I rattle off the dates to him. I wasn't sure how Silverstone would feel about me permanently relocating to Iceland. But my boss had been surprisingly supportive, even giving me the option of working from Reykjavik and coming in every few months for a one-on-one meeting. I'd eased back on my

workload since having Ásta, but still took projects that interested me and aligned with Ari's and my schedule.

"Good. I'll have Viktor to drive us to the airport."

I click my tongue. "Remember, he and Malla are on their
honeymoon."

Ari rolls his eyes. "Right."

I playfully tap his shoulder. "I think it's great they're finally tied the knot and are getting a vacation."

"Except I'll be down two employees for nearly a month.
Three, if you count Atli." He grimaces. "Another set of twins.
I don't know how he does it."

I nudge his shoulder. "Don't be a grouch."

"Don't be a grouch," Ásta echoes.

Ari's smile, so full of love and affection for our daughter,
melts my heart.

"How could I be," he says before he kisses Ásta on the
nose, "when I have my two best girls by my side?"

I grab his hand, gently navigate it to my stomach.

"What about three girls? Or," I add with a teasing smile as
his eyes go wide, "perhaps we can add a best boy."

"Diana…"

My smile deepens as he leans in and kisses me with a
passion I once thought fleeting, but now know will be mine
forever.

* * * * *

MILLS & BOON®

Coming next month

GREEK BOSS TO HATE
Michelle Smart

Footsteps approached.

Draco dragged a breath in through his nose, inhaling the soft scent of her perfume, and braced himself before turning to face her.

'You've tidied up,' Athena said brightly, as if nothing had happened, as if she hadn't just cruelly insulted his mother and he hadn't cruelly rammed some home truths down her throat.

'Someone had to.'

She shrugged. 'Not much point in keeping it tidy or unpacking. I'll be out of here soon.'

His mind unwittingly zipped to her bedroom. If he'd had to imagine it, he'd have pictured it like a witch's coven, not the soft, feminine, spotlessly clean room that it was. 'Not for another two months.'

'You'll have sacked me by then.'

'No.' He drilled his stare into her. 'That is not going to happen. You are going to spend the next two months tied to my side. By the time you're released from the contract, you'll be as sick of me as I am of you. Now,

drink your coffee. We need to get going—we've got a
long day of work to do.'

Continue reading

GREEK BOSS TO HATE
Michelle Smart

Available next month
millsandboon.co.uk

COMING SOON!

We really hope you enjoyed reading this book.
If you're looking for more romance
be sure to head to the shops when
new books are available on

Thursday 18th December

MILLS & BOON

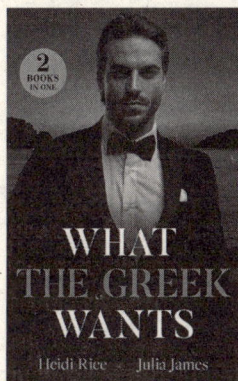

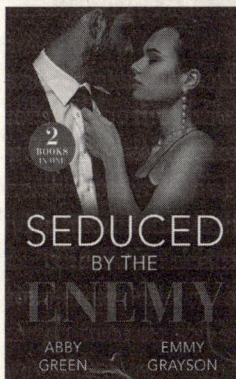

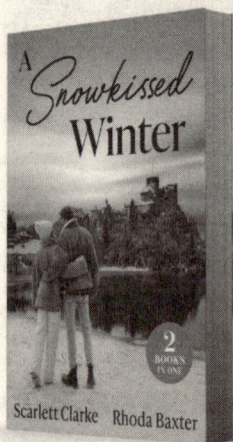

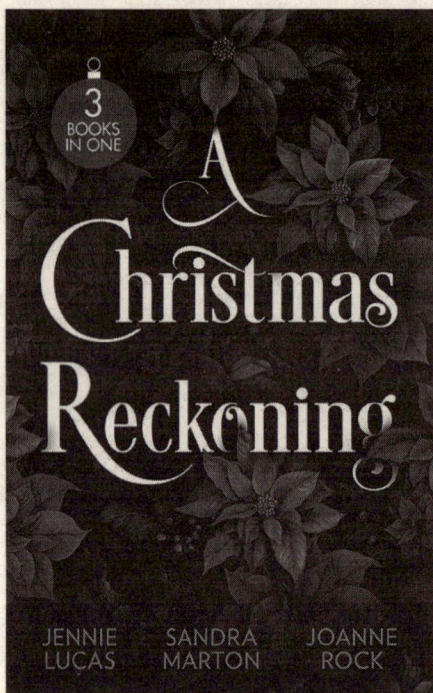

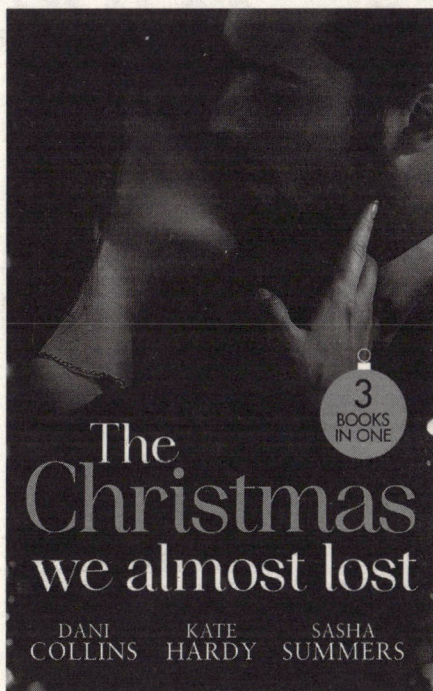

LET'S TALK

Romance

For exclusive extracts, competitions and special offers, find us online:

- MillsandBoon
- @MillsandBoon
- @MillsandBoonUK
- @MillsandBoonUK

Get in touch on 01413 063 232